Wonderful Adversity:

Into Africa

An adventure of personal survival, learning and taking, if not making, positives out of life's many challenges...

Jonathan & Patricia
Porter

Wonderful Adversity: Into Africa

Copyright © 2016 J.T. Porter & P.M. Porter
All rights reserved

ISBN: 1530652812
ISBN-13: 978-1530652815

Jonathan & Patricia Porter

The purpose of this story is to inspire, encourage and support. It is meant as a positive reflection on a challenge filled life. Everything is based on personal experiences, from a personal perspective, thus it is a very personal story. However, for readability, clarity and protection of all concerned, certain events have been combined, adjusted, compressed, re-ordered and potentially altered. Although Wonderful Adversity: Into Africa is pretty close to the actual life story of Jonathan, it is presented here as a 'based on a true life story', not a biography. Many of the incidents in life, if written as they happened, in full Technicolor, would be taken as fiction. Some are omitted, some are adjusted for believability - and if you don't believe what is written here, then the truth would blow your mind! Everything is *based* on fact, as are all the characters, albeit often composites, herein. If you associate with one of the characters, remember that many are combined and taken from diverse time-lines, so you may indeed be a part of it. We hope that every reader will find an association with the better characters herein, even if we have never met! If you feel associated with a 'less attractive (composite) character', we hold no responsibility for that, and since we have generally not named names and adjusted most stories and events, you may prefer not to own up to it, after all, it may not even be you!

    To the many people who have been involved during this birthing process, giving words of encouragement and support, listening, proof-reading, commenting and helping in more ways than we can list. To each of you we say 'Thank you', and hope that you have each gained something from the trauma!

    Enjoy, be inspired, hopefully find some motivation, and remember that all adversity, if treated in the right way, truly can become Wonderful Adversity.

Wonderful Adversity: Into Africa

The Wonderful Adversity series is dedicated to our wonderful daughter Gwenevere, who has been incredibly patient with us during the endless edits, readings and re-readings of this script. Never before has a baby been so patient with its parents!

Jonathan & Patricia Porter

EXPELLED FROM SCHOOL

My parents had lost their small-holding. It was a little farm in Kent, in the South of England, with thousands of chickens, loads of goats, greenhouses and two lovely horses in the field next door. My father had been in a very bad accident, spending months in hospital, and with one thing and another, it was time for them to 'downsize', sell up and move to Sussex.

They purchased a small house at the edge of a government housing scheme called a 'council estate'. The bungalow was small, with a tiny garden. My mother brought a couple of goats with her... much to the neighbours' surprise. For me it was exciting since the new two-bedroom bungalow was right next door to a large primary school.

I was eight years old and I loved school, I mean REALLY loved school. I was an avid reader, and according to the 'government assessment' already had the reading age of a sixteen-year-old. Well, I was the last of five kids, and my next oldest brother was five years older than me. I had to survive. I found great solace in books and read everything I could find. Reading gave me knowledge, giving me the ability to communicate with my older siblings, and adults, most of the time. Most of all reading gave me a place to be. Whether in a factual book learning about dinosaurs or a story book, such as reading Isaac Asimov and discovering the Robot stories. Reading was where I found my personal space.

The ability to 'get out of bed and into school in less than ten minutes' was a novelty compared to the long trek across muddy farm fields in Kent. It meant that I was always early to school, and full of energy to learn. Sadly, I had not fully embraced the fact that the community was far less rural, and those personalities and the teachers' approaches would be different. I was only eight, after all.

My new teacher was not keen on me. He did not like the fact that I 'apparently' argued a lot in class. I considered it only helpful to assist the teacher when he got something wrong, or needed to clarify what he was saying. It was only for the betterment of a good education for me and my classmates. On reflection, I was a bit precocious, but at the time I saw it as being supportive.

"So we have coal power stations and nuclear power stations..." he started the lesson.

My hand shot up "Would that be nuclear fission or nuclear fusion, Sir?". He had no idea what I was asking.

Reddening in his face he said, "It doesn't matter."

I objected. I wanted my friends to know more. "I think that the class needs to know the difference, Sir."

That was enough for him. I had only been in his class a few weeks, but that was enough. "Porter. Go to the Headmaster." So I did.

Wonderful Adversity: Into Africa

As I walked down the student art-work lined halls to the headmaster's office, I rehearsed in my head what I was going to say... "I think that teachers should know the difference between fission and fusion." Yes, that was a good thing to express to the headmaster!

However, when I knocked on the headmaster's door, I had not prepared myself for the sight before me.

The leader of the educational establishment sat there, balding in a non-glamorous manner, overweight, sagged behind a desk piled with papers, a bottle of whiskey clearly visible. His speech was slurred by the numbing activity of alcohol upon his brain. "Whaaat have yoooouu done boooyyyyyyyy?"

I decided that my situation was not as bad as his and, ignoring his question completely, stated "Sir, I think that you drink too much. You would be a better headmaster if you didn't drink like that."

For some unknown reason, that was enough to enrage him. I was unable to fathom out why. It was the truth after all. His face turned redder than a beetroot, his head flashed like a warning light and he yelled at me "GET OUT OF MY OFFICE." That was the first time that I heard that phrase... but I complied, silently. He added some slurred and mumbled verbiage about waiting outside the office. So, being a compliant child, I sat on the bench and waited.

Within minutes my parents were called from the 'house next to the school', only to be told that "Your son should be moved to another school." Rather embarrassing for my parents, and they made it clear to me that it was a bit of a problem.

Was this adversity? HOW WONDERFUL! Getting expelled was about to give me a massive boost.

The next week, I started at a school on the other side of town. My new teacher was ex-military. He started almost every lesson with a story. They all began "When I was in the army..." His tales enthralled me, because they were true life adventures and interesting, with loads of new facts! When I asked a question, he would either answer it or tell me to research it. He always demonstrated that 'not knowing the answer was an opportunity to learn' - both for me and for him. He was strict, oh boy, was he strict, but I loved every moment of his classes. I never saw being expelled from the last school as a problem, it simply opened a new door of opportunity in my life. That was my first wonderful adversity moment!

THE MARKET

"You have to sell all of those goods before you can be collected to come home," my father told me, leaving me under the grey skies of an open market one Saturday in October. The land next to the railway line was used for a weekend market, and my job was to sell toys for the family business.

I would lay out my stand early in the morning, and spend the day touting for business.

"C'mon luv, you know you wanna buy some of these great fings for ya kids, don't ya!?"

"Any two items for fifty pee!"

"Awww, c'mon missus, you wanna buy sommat...."

I found the 'little London accent' helped to gain attention, but most of all I was learning at the age of ten, yes, ten years old, how to manage a market stall, make and manage money, draw a crowd and close a deal!

Today some would say "Oh, my goodness, that is just so awful. How can a father drop his son in a market place to sell items before he will collect him and take him home!"

Let me tell you straight up, it was one of the best things my father ever did for me. I didn't see it as a punishment, for it was not meant as such. No, this was a learning opportunity. I learned to catch the attention of a crowd, draw them in and to manage on my own. I took responsibility for money. If I was hungry and had not sold anything, I would barter goods with the hot dog stand. I learned fast, and the market folks liked me.

Of course, this was the 1970's, and a lot has changed since then, but not all for the good. I had no mobile phone, and had to go to the phone box when I had sold everything. I would call to let my mother or father know that I had earned the right to be picked-up. They ran other stalls at other markets, so it was a fair deal.

This mixing with adults on a trading basis, built my confidence up, and I found it easy to communicate with all sorts of different people.

My confidence was to be short lived. At the age of eleven I had to leave my "When I was in the army" teacher and move on to secondary school. Within weeks I was in hospital.

Wonderful Adversity: Into Africa

BEATEN UP

Apparently, it annoyed certain other students when I sat at the front of the class and asked lots of questions in science lessons. They wanted a different approach; more larking around than sound learning. So, three of them decided to teach me a special lesson.

As I left the school dining hall, two boys held me and a third punched me straight in the jaw. My top, front right incisor left my mouth and blood started to pour out. For the next fifteen minutes I was hit, punched and kicked around the school playground. My 'extracted' tooth continued to provide football practice for the rest of the day.

With blood all over me, my face bruised beyond recognition, I waited for my mother to take me home. I was shaking. I was bleeding. I was broken. The dentist made it clear that I would need a false tooth, but that it would take months before they could work in my mouth since the swelling had first to go down, and braces be used to return the displaced teeth into a reasonable position.

As I walked, painfully, with my mother along the street my legs started to fail. My left arm was not responding as it should and I was soon on the way to the hospital.

I could not walk properly, and my left arm did not respond to my mental requests to move. That beating had done something more than just knocked my tooth out.

I was admitted to the children's ward, and put in a bed next to a freshly diagnosed diabetic lad. How wonderful. Not that he had diabetes, but that he had to learn to do injections! That meant that I had the opportunity to learn too! Together, we injected oranges until they exploded! I learned to give injections through this amazing opportunity! Giving injections may not seem like a terribly useful skill, but what I learned there helped me save the life of one very dear to me, as we will share later on.

The deputy head from the school came the next day, and gave me a book on 'learning to write'. I laughed. I had been able to write since before I started school! But, this wise lady had another plan. "Learn to write using your left hand, as a therapy," she advised. So I tried.

Working through the book, making those repeated writing exercise scribbles of the same letter, time after time, again and again. The idea of re-educating my left arm through learning to write was giving me new skills, boosting my creativity. It is a skill I retain today. I then added to the challenges and taught myself to read upside down. Next, to write upside down. This being in hospital for a long time was a fantastic opportunity to extend my learning! Those lads did me a favour! They really did!

The doctors didn't really grasp what was wrong with my legs. They simply didn't respond as they should. Perhaps it was trauma? Perhaps it was neurological? Perhaps it was simply psychological? They ran their tests. As a young person you do not care too much what the cause of something is, you simply focus on the effect it has on your life. You choose whether that is a positive effect, or a negative one! Of course, there were days when I wanted to cry, shout and be angry. There were times when I wept and had vengeful thoughts towards those who had physically harmed me. But, overall, it was a magnificent change of course, with added value!

For me, I was spending lots of time in a hospital, and had the opportunity to learn different things. I asked the nurses and doctors questions. I passed time listening to those who came in for a variety of medical reasons. Appendicitis, broken limbs, various illnesses, etc. - this was better than a book, this was real life. However, I was not getting better myself.

I would be allowed home, for short periods, for 'recovery'; released from the hospital into the care of my parents, with a wheel chair. Time went by, and I did not appear to gain enough control of my limbs to return to a normal life.

One afternoon, my father was driving his sales van down a country lane when he came across a school bus that had broken down. This was in the days when people helped each other, without fear of recrimination; long before the internet and instant accusations of 'child molester' to anybody wanting to help a child. He asked if any of the kids needed a ride home in his van, helping with the logistics of transporting some of them to their respective homes. The last child he dropped off was a young Chinese girl. He took her to the door of her home, making sure that she was home safely. He wanted to simply explain why this plump, bobble hat wearing sales-fellow was dropping their daughter off, instead of the school bus!

There on the wall was a brass plaque in English and Chinese. It read 'Traditional Chinese Acupuncturist'. As the door opened an elderly, wrinkled and hunched over gentleman, the girl's grandfather, greeted his granddaughter in their home language. Granddad listened to the stream of Mandarin, as the girl explained how she had come home with this strange man. He then asked the girl to thank my father for bringing home his precious cargo, since he did not speak English. He further asked, through translation, if he could do anything in return. Thinking on his feet, my old man thought of me and my challenges, and asked if he could bring his son to their surgery for an assessment. It was agreed. Serendipity is made of these things, it really is!

The next time I was allowed out of hospital, my parents took me to the old man's needle parlour. Granddad lay me on the couch, examined me at length and then placed an initial needle in the back of my neck. Although I was petrified, I found the process fascinating. That first needle appeared to leave me in a dream state. I felt as if I no longer had any control over even the slightest movement in my body. I probably wouldn't have dared to even try to move, as my heart was pumping faster than the pistons on a Formula

Wonderful Adversity: Into Africa

One racing car engine! I had no choice but to go through with this, since my 'needle master' could not understand a word I could say to him. He then set about inserting several dozen needles, setting light to some of them. They did not hurt, but I felt each of them enter my skin. Then he set a timer and left the room. I think I fell asleep, for the next thing I remember is leaving the building.

It had been a useless exercise. Nothing was improved. I felt very disappointed that all those needles, even the ones with little flames on, had no effect on my condition. It is easy to get despondent when challenges come at you like clouds of starlings in the autumn.

My parents told me that the translator had explained "It is as if his muscles, nerves and bones are fighting each other; that's where his problem is." Well, that would explain the pain I had experienced over several months, and the fact that movements were not as they should be. We drove along the winding country roads in silence. The trees looked on, waving their branches in the wind, almost mocking of my situation. I cried.

Then, I started to feel little hot spots all over my body. I remember describing it "like lots of little hot water bottles". When we got home, my parents called the acupuncturist's translator, telling him of my 'hot water bottle experience'. He replied "That is good," so, we went back for more treatments.

In a couple of months, I was pretty much back to normal movements. Whether because of the acupuncture, the hospital or just because 'I got better', we will never know. But I know that the acupuncture made my nerves and muscles respond in ways that they had failed to for months, and so I give that needle point course my biggest apportionment of credit for my recovery. I still had areas on my legs and sides that had no sensation, and still do today. I still had the occasional 'refusal to work' of my left leg, but generally when tired, or after a long journey - but what a small price to pay for having learned so much in an unorthodox manner! I relearned to walk, run and return to normal teenager activities.

I had missed a lot of schooling, but had not missed out on learning, for life experience is a valuable asset, over and above that which can be acquired in front of any blackboard. For some strange, and to this day unbelievable reason, I did not want to go back to the school where this had all started. Would you?

One Saturday morning, I was reading the local newspaper, cover-to-cover, including the adverts section. Something caught my eye. It was not a large advert, but it had the word 'Scholarship' in the heading. That drew me in further. A new school was about to open and they were offering scholarships to local youngsters. I told my parents that I wanted to try the entry exam for the school. They explained, at great length, that they could not afford such a school. However, after much persuasion, and in all honesty I do not think they thought I stood a chance; they took me to the interview and assessment day.

Despite having missed so much schooling, I scored very well on the tests, and the Headmaster, dressed in flowing black gowns, with a red, Windsor knotted tie, navy blue polyester trousers, and shining black shoes, invited me into his office. The walls were hidden by bookshelves, filled beyond their natural capacity with books. I had never seen so many books in an office. He smiled at me, asking me question after question. The ashtray on his desk smelt musty, the carpet on the floor was plush, and I was feeling way out of my league. I adjusted my posture in the squeaking red leather chair, finished in solid oak. Each movement made it sound like I was passing noisy wind. I was not comfortable in this place. This was not where I belonged, this was a posh place. I did not come from posh. Not at all.

THREATENED

The Headmaster proposed a scholarship, for two years, towards my 'O' level qualifications. My parents would be asked to make a small contribution, but the vast majority would be covered by the scholarship. Despite feeling socially uncomfortable, this was an opportunity to learn in a place where I stood less chance of losing the rest of my teeth. My parents agreed, but there was a catch. It was three years of study for me to reach my 'O' levels, and the scholarship was just for two years. So, we agreed that I would do the course in two years instead of three. Nothing like a bit of pressure!

I started at the school in the September, shaking and very unsure of what was ahead of me. For the first time, I was working and learning alongside international students. I had not schooled with people of such varying skin colour, cultural and religious backgrounds before. We were less than fifty in the school, and class sizes averaged fifteen. It was learning heaven! We wore grey herringbone jackets and purple ties with Griffins on them. Furthermore, we ate lunch with the staff where the food was presented in serving dishes. Wow! This was a posh school. My classmates were from Iran, Argentina, Bangladesh, Botswana, Uganda, America, Uruguay etc - places I had not even thought about before. At times, we would talk about our parents. My mother looked after the family business shop, selling toys, and my father was a travelling salesman - and, rather embarrassingly, a lay-preacher. Theirs were a bit fancier; airline pilots, diplomats, bankers, lawyers, big business people – all from a world that I knew nothing of before.

One special classmate was from Iran, yet he always said he was from Persia, and we would compete heartily in every subject. We both sought 100% in everything we did. He was more naturally academic than me, but I was prepared to work harder. It was a great chase, and one that made me work more diligently than ever on my studies. There was a second lad from Iran, and when there was some political trouble, the 1980 siege of the Iranian embassy in London, we all watched it on the television news. Being teenagers, we all cheered for the SAS as they abseiled down the building. At least I thought we all did. I did not understand the issues, but I clearly said something wrong, to this day I do not know what I said, or whether I just was the 'selected target'.

The next day, I found myself held from behind with a beautiful, I would guess ceremonial, knife to my throat with questions about my feelings regarding Islam, Iran, the SAS, politics and other things that I had never even thought about, being poured out at me with venom and passion.

It was my first wonderful opportunity to learn tact, negotiation and not to move my neck suddenly! I had to learn in the next few seconds that religious feelings can quickly overcome rational actions. It was a moment that would be recalled vividly in my future, and perhaps save me from a similar fate... or worse.

It took about twenty minutes before 'reason' returned, but I learned so much from that experience. Principally that we should all be careful what we say about other people's cultures, and religions - for even a seemingly innocent comment, smile or laugh can cause great offence. He had grown up in an environment where 'dramatic actions' such as taking out a knife 'was acceptable', and once it was over, it was over. I had to learn that - and to learn it fast. Later, we both sat down and talked, sharing both of our perspectives, becoming good friends. Even if I kept a little caution in the friendship, considering that I would not forget the fear of a knife to my neck for a long time. His knife was taken away from him, but he stayed in the school. We all learned something bigger than politics and religion from the incident.

The teachers in the school were all amazing, without exception. One, an ex-SAS officer, taught us to shoot (the school had an old rifle range, and some wonderful .22 rifles). I learned to handle and respect weapons, understanding what they can do, a skill that has served me admirably across the world. This particular master was well over six feet six tall, and he spoke in the same manner as the stereotypical 'British Officer' from any of the black and white war movies. If I managed to walk alongside him, rather I would be trotting since his strides were so massive, I could get him to tell me stories about his life, further adding to my knowledge. Once again, an ex-military man, with strict order and vast stories of travel and adventure was providing a role model to me.

I would never have sought the opportunity to go to such a school, if I had not been beaten up at my previous school, and yet this school was exposing me to so many amazing new experiences and opportunities - as well as learning. Perhaps being beaten up, going to hospital and struggling through those experiences was the best adversity of my life. Without doubt, I can trace so many of my skills back to my time in the 'posh' school. However, it all nearly came undone...

WORKING A PASSAGE

My parents' business was really not doing well. They were heading into a bankruptcy situation. They could not afford to keep paying my partial fees, and the school wanted to increase them.

I was called to the headmaster's office. I am sure that those navy blue polyester slacks were glued to the man's legs. He looked at me from in front of the fireplace, his receding hairline with light greying around the edges adding to my respect of his position of authority. "You are a rough diamond. You look dirty and scratchy on the outside, but with work you can be cut to shine," he told me. That was his pre-amble to "I have to tell you that the school fees are going up and you parents will need to contribute more."

Shaking inside, not wanting to leave this island of relative safety, I explained my parents' deteriorating financial situation. Boldly, with the skills of running a market stall, I offered a solution, "But, I can work before school, after school, at the weekends and in the school holidays, and that could count towards my fees." I held my breath, for what seemed like an eternity. He looked at me, head cocked to one side, his smile lopsided. He reached for cigarette, and paused, replacing the packet in its predetermined position on his ordered desk. I do not think that he was used to a student speaking this way, especially since most of the students came from wealthy families.

I stood, my heart beating ever more loudly in my ears, waiting for him to speak, "OK. You can wash up dishes in the kitchen, supervise the junior students' studies, do laboratory preparation and in the holidays you can clean and paint the buildings. In short, you can 'work your passage'."

I looked at him, realising that I had struck a deal. Inhaling the first oxygen for several minutes into my tiring lungs, I exhaled "Yes SIR!" and it was agreed. Each morning I would leave my home, make it to school before 7am, ready to set up the physics and chemistry labs. After each meal I would

Wonderful Adversity: Into Africa

help in the kitchens. In the evenings I would supervise and help with boarding students' studies. I would get home by 10pm, tired but satisfied.

Each holiday I would help move beds, clean, paint, wash windows and weed gardens. I would do practically anything necessary to make sure that I paid my education. I loved that school, its location in a small woodland, the teachers and the amazing library. It was my safe place, and I had to protect it, securing my place within it.

Finally, I passed my 'O' level exams, and got top marks. All because of adversity, wonderful adversity - and a heap of serendipity, people who believed in giving me a chance, and my being ready to take that chance. I was back on track, confident, well-educated, full of new experiences and able to communicate with people of all backgrounds!

I was not quite sixteen, but with my 'O' levels in hand, I was heading to Sixth Form College for 'A' Levels, back into the state education sector. I would take a train to the college, amongst the 'normal population'. I do not deny that I found it hard to be there. The classes had over thirty mixed ability students in each of them. Not all the students wanted to learn. In fact those who did were very much in the minority. There were no foreign students. The place lacked diversity. The teachers spent much of their time 'controlling' rather than 'teaching'. The canteen was more like a factory farm feeding line. There were regular fights on the way to, from and in the educational establishment.

One particular maths teacher had a stammer. He was a great teacher, but we lost half of each lesson to silly giggles as students asked the maths master questions they knew would tie his tongue. I remember wanting desperately to answer a question about the shape of a graph on the board before he did... It was a parabola... just ask any person with a speech impediment to say 'parabola'! Nothing like this would have happened at my previous school.

All the same, I was learning and working towards my goal of going to University to study Agricultural Botany. That was my dream. I was good at science, excellent at biology and outstanding in Botany. I had gained a world appreciation, wanting to work in the science of improving rice yields for the developing nations. Nothing too ambitious!

My parents' business was 'going... going... gone down the pan' in the economic avalanche of the 1980s. There was talk of bailiffs coming to the house, and with all of my siblings having left the nest to start their own independent lives, I took a lot of pressure on myself. I started to crack. The emotional pressure of watching your family lose everything is enormous. You watch your mother and father, day-in and day-out struggle to make the finances work. There were occasional, overheard, threats of suicide. We were eating out-of-date foods, collected from the waste bins at the local supermarket, to make ends meet. It was too much for any family. It was certainly too much for me. I cried myself to sleep most nights. The others I did not sleep.

The economics were dire, and so many companies were failing in the 1980s, it was as if 'going bankrupt' was all the rage. I learned the meaning of 'bank foreclosure', a term no young person should ever encounter. Then, one day at college, it became too much for me. I cracked. I could no longer face going home. I simply walked off the campus and went house-to-house looking for lodgings, and tried frantically to find a job. I needed to be out of the situation at home. I had not have been sixteen very long, and I could not cope with the pressures.

I knocked on the door of a large house, where I had heard that they took occasional lodgers. The retired nurse who opened the door to me made me welcome, but also I could see that warning bells were ringing in her head. Her husband, a medical doctor, was also in. We talked about why I wanted to leave home at such a young age, and how I would pay rent. They were a lovely couple, and although they understood, they felt that others should be involved. They sent me to the Baptist pastor's house, just behind theirs.

The pastor's home was simple. I was invited to sit in a tired winged chair, and handed a glass of water. The pastor came in, and sat in the chair next to me. This man spoke each week about how wonderful God is, something I could not really relate to at that time. Whilst I was there the phone rang, it was the police. I had been reported as a 'missing person'. Shit was about to hit the fan big time.

I was taken back to my family home, by social services. My mother cried. My father cried. We hugged. We fought. Threats of a corporal nature were issued between all parties. It got uglier and uglier. My parents were ready to crack. They were under too much pressure. I was under too much pressure. It was the most unpleasant situation anybody could find themselves in.

I was assigned a social worker since I was now considered 'at risk'. Those were some of the darkest days I lived through. Some of the things said and done... well, let's just say that the wounds heal, but scar tissues cannot truly be erased.

All parties agreed that it was best that I moved to independent lodgings. Thankfully, the nurse and doctor provided me a room and a very convivial solution to my needs. It was clear that my parents' house would be taken by the bank, and they would eventually move to another part of the country. I was used to working, and took a job in Waitrose, the supermarket, on the twilight shift.

Up early. Day at college. Evening at Waitrose filling shelves. Late evening to my digs. Homework. Sleep. Repeat until exhausted. Exhausted I was, but I was still holding my grades at college. Each evening I would enter the pantry, and there on the shelf would be a chocolate cake. It was my chocolate cake. As soon as I finished one, another would be baked. Those chocolate cakes kept me going on the worst of days. Never underestimate the power of a freshly baked chocolate cake! My landlady baked the most wonderful chocolate cake, seemingly just for me.

With just a few months to my final exams I offered to help my parents empty what was left of their home into a van. With the business gone, and the house repossessed, my father had been offered a full-time pastorate in a Baptist church in the wilds of Cambridgeshire. It provided a house and a small stipend. It was, literally, a God-send for my parents.

BROKEN

It was in February, and I was now a strong young man. Just a few more months and I would complete my college, turn eighteen and head to university. The world was my oyster.

I arrived at the family home, well what was left of it, and helped to load the van. My father was excited at becoming a full-time clergyman, and was putting the challenges of the past years behind him. He wanted to sell Jesus instead of toys and sweets. My mother, the animal nut of the millennium, still had two goats left to take with her - and the church had agreed that she could have them in the garden of the manse, where they were moving to. When I was younger I had taken part in agricultural shows with these goats and knew them as if they were my siblings. They would walk with me on a lead as obedient as any dog. However, climb into the back of a van... well, that was a new trick. They refused. They did not want to go. So, I scooped the first goat into my arms and lifted her up into the van, where she was tied to the side. She bleated her heart out, but she was safe. The second, larger goat, had already decided that this was not her preferred activity, not by any means. I bent down and talked to her, looking into black slit goat eyes that look back at you, and through your soul. Thinking that she was calm enough, I lifted her 50Kg (110lbs) mass in my arms and raised her towards the tailgate. She was heavier than I had estimated, but I was used to lifting weights, proceeding with the task.

She kicked violently. Her whole body writhing with a force that took me by surprise. My back was snapped left then right and left again as I refused to drop her. Finally, with a lot of struggle she entered the van. She was unhurt. The same could not be said for me.

My back felt as though it had been slammed by a wrecking ball. Holding the pain in whilst I climbed into the van, I winced at every move. I had agreed to travel to the new house to help unload.

I did not feel good. Pains were streaming down my legs like knives, whilst the ball of pain across my back left me wondering if a hand-grenade had exploded inside my belt.

By the time we reached the destination, I could not walk. When I moved my legs they were too painful to take my weight. I was helped into the new house and left in a corner whilst others unloaded the van. The goats simply jumped out, as easy as that! The local doctor came and prescribed pain killers and a few days bed rest. It helped, but it did not fix the problem.

I needed to get back to college, my exams, university and my future. I finally dosed myself up on large, probably excessive, quantities of pain killers and took a train back to my digs.

Getting off the train was a challenge - each step hurt, and the jarring of dropping out of the draughty carriage was excruciating. I struggled, resting every few yards, each step taking me further into the hell of agony. Finally, I knocked firmly on the door of my digs. That lovely chocolate cake baking nurse opened the door, looked at my face and, before allowing me into the house, grabbed her coat and took me to the doctors' surgery.

I was immediately admitted to the hospital, unable to walk without distress, with a suspected slipped disk.

The cottage hospital appeared to be straight out of the Crimean war. Twenty-four beds, twelve on each side. Those closest to death by the nurses' station at the door; those with the least need for observation at the far end. The large Georgian windows gave a great view of the trees outside. All it needed was some background war noises, and I would have started looking for Florence Nightingale. In fact, they referred to the ward style as 'a Florence Nightingale Ward'.

I was put on traction for a number of weeks. Held flat on my back, no pillow, lots of meds, and lots of pain. This was impacting on my studies. The college asked if I would return to my studies, but I was not sure. I was not earning, and I was either in too much pain to study - or way too drugged up with painkillers to study anything other than the pink fairies floating around me! To be honest, the British Health Service was absolutely amazing, providing three meals a day, medication and all other care for free. Just as well, otherwise I would have been really messed up!

I did have a daily challenge; one with which I took great delight. A particular nurse appeared to have come from the school of 'cold stone'. She was pale, rigid, unsmiling, unwelcoming - some may even say unpleasant. To me she was a great nurse. Strict, precise, operating like a clockwork machine, and always terribly professional. But she never, never smiled. I made it my daily challenge to try to make her smile. I never truly managed it, but I am sure that one edge of her tight, almost unperceivable lip twitched one evening when I cracked another schoolboy joke. Learning about never giving up counts in the smallest of tasks!

Whilst I was on traction I experienced one of the most beautiful moments of any life, the moment of death. Death is inevitable, and yet it is something that so many fail to accept, embrace or try to understand. I was at the 'unlikely to die' end of the ward, and so, in practical terms, several metres away from 'deaths door'. The old chap opposite me was in for something minor, and we would exchange pleasantries across the ward as the days ticked by. I had known him before coming into the hospital, and he was a pleasant chappy, full of stories and warmth.

Each evening the ward staff would come around taking orders for the next day's food; breakfast, lunch and supper. There was always a good choice, even if the food didn't always taste as nice as it sounded! This particular evening, I watched my friend and ward-mate, in the bed opposite me, giving his order to the young lady who held the meal cards.

"Breakfast: Cornflakes or an egg?" she asked.

He responded "Cornflakes please, my love."

Smiling, she enquired, "Lunch: Chicken or Beef?"

He paused, looked her straight in the eyes and stated "I won't be here for lunch."

She hesitated, smiled back and ticked chicken, since he usually took chicken, and there was no way he was going home tomorrow!

"Supper: Soup or a sandwich?" she tempted him. He simply smiled, looked down and away, shaking his head. She shifted her weight uneasily from one leg to another, waited for a long second, and then made a choice for him.

The next morning, we had a great breakfast. I chatted across the room with my grey haired co-conspirator. We slept. We woke. We spoke. It was a normal day on the ward. Then around 11am, I looked across at him. A sweet smell came across the room; a smell I had not known before. He smiled, closed his eyes and smiled wider. His chest stopped moving. I called the nurse. A second later the curtains were pulled, and he was taken to another place in the hospital, where he certainly would not receive any lunch.

I had always been afraid of death. Seeing it. Hearing it. Feeling it. Smelling it. Experiencing death, first hand with a friend, was magnificent. It changed my position on death itself. It is just a step along a path, where you step out of sight of the others. Death is nothing to fear. It is the natural punctuation mark at the end of a life. Some lives are longer; some are incredibly short. Whatever way we look at it, birth will be followed by death, and it is a part in the circle of life that we are all signed onto. Embrace it. Do not fear it.

UNIVERSITY?

After about a month they took the traction off and I started physiotherapy. If I could get back on my feet I might just make it to my exams and stand a chance of going to university. I had applied for a grant, and already held a great university offer. Perhaps, just perhaps I could pull off another 'hospital to education' trick.

The physio came along and eased me to the side of the bed. I felt good. I felt like I could make this work. Surely, the traction had solved the issue of my back and legs.

She helped me to my feet, I stood for less than five seconds before the ripping pain shot down my legs. I crumpled, the physio trying to prevent me falling too far and too fast. Tears streamed down my cheeks as my back exploded. That hand grenade exploding in back of the belt feeling was back with a vengeance. My big toes felt as if they were on fire. It was not something that I could describe. It was not something I would want others to experience.

The nursing team came around, picked me up and lay me back on the bed. The physio felt awful, as if it was her fault, but it wasn't. I blamed nobody. I may have shouted "stupid goat!" but it was not at the staff, it was at the animal a few hundred miles away, that had writhed at the wrong time and broken me!

The next morning a medical team stood around my bed. I was pale, exhausted and still squirming. They decided to send me to bigger hospital in Brighton.

The ambulance came and collected me on a stretcher. Each bump in the road resulted in my screaming in agony. Soon, I was on gas and air (Entonox). It barely touched the pain in my legs and lower back. It did make me feel as if I was floating. I would use it again if I needed to!

The specialist at the major teaching hospital decided that he would operate, and I was sent to the ultra-modern, for the time, orthopaedic ward upstairs to await a slot in the surgery schedule. That would be a couple of weeks.

The date was finally set for my surgery. It would be the same day as I would have sat my first exam for my 'A' Levels. My education was about to slip away in a storm of tears and pain.

The new ward was very different. This was an adult orthopaedic ward with just four young men, of which I was the youngest. The conversations were far worldlier than I was used to. I learned about things that I had never planned on learning! I decided that it was best that I just kept quiet and listened.

This was a training hospital, and the nurses were much busier than at the cottage hospital with its twenty-four-bed Nightingale ward. One nurse decided that I was faking it. She clearly wondered about the genuineness of my bad back. To make her point she was very rough with the bed pan, and that was a pain-filled experience. When she was on duty, I would do everything to 'hold it in'.

The day before the scheduled surgery, I wrote to my parents, a short note, including the line 'By the time you read this I will have completed surgery on my back'. I didn't want them to worry before hand, and they had enough on their plate getting over losing everything. Also, they would feel some culpability since it was their goat that kicked and ripped my spine. I asked a nurse to drop the letter in the post box, and went to sleep, or at least tried to.

Early the next morning a Pethidine pre-med was administered. The prick of the needle was a welcome distraction from the pain in my back. Within minutes, I felt as myself floating above the bed, looking back down at my body. I remember whispering "How did it all come to this?" I cannot remember being taken to the theatre, or coming back to the ward. In fact, several days went missing from my memory.

I felt a toothbrush being shoved into my mouth. It was 'the doubting nurse', also known as 'don't ask that one for a bed-pan'. I felt rough, more than rough. Her face, of all the nurses faces, I got her face to wake up to. She looked at me and smiled, gently apologising with a soft "Sorry."

Wait, what was this, had I been abducted by a 'bed pan nurse look-alike'? She went on, "I went to the theatre, to observe your surgery. I wanted to see what had happened to you. It was worse than any of us thought. You must have been in a great deal of pain."

"Well hello," I thought, "HELLLOOOOOO, yes I was in a great deal of pain!" But I could not voice my thoughts, a) because she was still brushing my teeth, and b) because I was really not coming round from the surgery very well. My eyelids fell as if weighed down by lead weights. I didn't care where she put that toothbrush. I felt rough.

Later, as I came around for a second time, Bed Pan Nurse was still there, sitting by my side. I was in a side room, a single room. The surgery had a complication. Much as the pain in my legs had subsided, the pain in my back had changed. It was as if a five kilowatt electric cooker had been turned on in the small of my back. The heat hurt.

Apparently, there was a massive blood clot back there now. The nurses took it in turns to sit by my bed and watch me. I remember just glimpses of a few moments of coming too and going away again.

Apparently, they took me back to surgery another four times. I have the world's worst hatchet mark on my back to prove it. Something had gone wrong, and they fixed it. But it took time. Most of the time I remained unconscious, and could not care what they did.

Once, I awoke to the most awful smell. It was me. I had somehow managed to empty masses of foul smelling faeces into the bed sheets. Bed

Pan Nurse came running, probably to discover the source of the odour. She looked. She sniffed. She clearly wanted to vomit, but she still smiled and saying "It will be OK," I really liked Bed Pan Nurse now. I wondered how to look somebody in the eye who has washed your own faeces off of your body and bed multiple times, brushed your teeth for you and the like. I was embarrassed. Going back into the land of unconsciousness was a pleasant relief.

I started to have more lucid moments. My Bed Pan Nurse who took pleasure in brushing my teeth (hopefully after washing her hands from the bed pan) seemed to be assigned, or volunteered, to my side more than the others. She explained to me that I had slipped two discs and had a piece of floating broken bone around the injured site. So they trimmed back the discs and removed the chunk of bone. So, that explained the pain!

My wounds would be dressed regularly. Being a teaching hospital, and with me as a co-operative patient, I also helped with 'training practice'. Being in a side room, the nurses could practice techniques on me or read books whilst watching me. I became an expert in 'aseptic procedures'. I would catch them out as they worked my dressings - and they loved it. I would quiz them on their exam topics and even obtained an old copy of Grey's Anatomy (the medical book, not the TV Series) to boost my own learning! I was back to learning from my predicament and making the most out of my adversity!

AMONGST THE WOUNDED

I had entered hospital in the February, the first surgery was on the second of June, and now July was more than half gone. With all but the operation site to heal, it was time to start learning to walk again.

A tall, slim young woman, looking barely any older than myself, walked into my room, she had with her an aluminium walking frame. Her white jacket had a blue trim around the short sleeves, not the markings of a nurse, but that of a physiotherapist. She smiled warmly, parked the frame by the side of my bed, crossed her hands in front of her, and said "Would you like to learn to walk again?" What a dumb question, but it was like music to my ears at that point. My heart leapt out of my chest and I said with conviction "YES!"

She leaned back against the window frame, and looked at me lying in the bed, flat as a pancake. I had all of my tubes removed, and apart from the daily packing of the sizeable hole in my back, a few injections here and there and loads of pills, I was as right as rain!

She started to tell me about the issues of having been in bed so long, and not to get my hopes up, etc, la-di-dah, etc, la-di-dah, plus some more stuff. I really wasn't listening. She had me hung up on the idea of walking again - and that was all that I wanted.

Finally, when she had run out of words of warnings, she leaned over me, helping me to sit on the edge of the bed. The world spun as if I was sitting on the world's fastest carousel. I wanted to vomit, but I would not let that be known. I breathed deeply, shaking, as my legs flopped over the side of the bed towards to the floor.

She stood in front of me, her pretty face barely a foot from mine, her eyes locked to mine, her warm hands-on my scantily covered shoulders. She smiled, offering me a human warmth and contact that I had not experienced in a long time - and she hadn't cleaned up my poop! Had it been a different place and different time I may have had other thoughts, but all I wanted was to walk. Her smile was special. She was a truly caring person and magnificently professional physiotherapist. She explained again that I would feel weak when I stood up. I could wait no longer. It was time to do this.

With her needed help, I pushed myself from the edge of the bed, my bare feet touching the cold floor, refreshing my brain about what 'floor' felt like.

She pulled my body into the upright position and I was standing! Yes, I was standing. There were no sharp pains in my legs, no electric shocks running to my toes. It was a miracle. A miracle of modern science.

I started to fall down. The planet was calling me earthwards! She half caught me on the way, and called for help. Two nurses burst in and together they all put me back into bed.

I was so happy. I stood up for all of one point five seconds! WOW! I was recovering.

It may sound silly, but one point five seconds of stomach turning standing without back and leg pain was worth more than passing my long abandoned 'A' levels.

Day after day, Miss Physio would come by, and I would joke about the concept that, one day I would be able to climb a ladder. She cut me a deal. "If you can climb a ladder before you leave the hospital, I will elope with you!" It gave me hope. Of course, it was not serious, possible, nor professional, but she and the other nurses all joked about it with me. Something that would not be acceptable today, but then, at that moment in my life, for me, it was a purpose. I needed something to aim for. We all need something to aim for, always.

I was moved back to a four-bed ward. But now I had a new role. I was on the mend and could boost the morale of others. In the corner of the room there was a tramp. He had collided with a double-decker bus and broken his legs. He was the least compliant patient on the planet. He would intentionally wet the bed, soil the bed, refuse to speak, beg for alcohol, swear and throw things! The nurses hated dealing with him. I made it my mission to speak to him. Little by little, he spoke back. Over time, he stopped doing his toilet where he shouldn't, accepting that compliance with the nursing staff was the first step towards getting back on the streets, where the vodka bottle, begging and sleeping rough awaited him. Yes, he wanted that life back. He made it clear. Begging, for him, was better than my life. I learned another new thing; some people like to wallow in their situation, complain, be angry and have no desire to leave or change it.

Between my physio sessions I was able to move around in a wheelchair. I liked the wheel chair, it helped to build my upper body strength and allowed me to move to the patients' common room as often as I liked. It was in the common room that I got the best opportunities to work on the morale of others.

One lady had lost her leg in a car crash. She was behaving as if she had lost her will to live. I was privileged to chat to her, practically every day. The nurses would wheel us both in there to chat. I remember telling her that her amputation would open up new opportunities. It was 'just a leg', I reassured her. There was no point in wallowing in the situation, you cannot change the past, but you can always shape the future! Before long, and with the input of many, she started to look forward to her prosthesis, planning to play practical jokes on her friends with it as well! The day she left, she hugged me strongly, thanking me for my support, as did her husband.

Then there was the chap with a broken neck. He had bolts installed into his skull and was on traction, for many weeks. I was able to relate to his challenges, because of my own. We would chat about my time on traction, and I would tell him what was going on around him - a much needed input for somebody in his position. I was realising that my experiences, although painful, had enabled me to appreciate the pain of others in a new and special way, and to do something about it. Life is full of training. We just have to realise that we are being trained, and then use that training when we are given the opportunity.

However, it was not all good things. One chap had a broken leg, which refused to heal. We were both 'long-term inmates'. We chatted one day about having a day out, just to get some fresh air. Now, that was strictly against the rules of the ward. Who would know?

So, we planned our escape to the finest detail. Prisoners of war would have been proud of us! We reckoned that when the nurses had their afternoon briefing they would never notice a wheelchair, being pushed by a chap with full leg plaster, going into the lift. We decided to test the theory. We were right.

We made it downstairs, out through the automatic doors and into the fresh seaside air! We were not dressed to go outside and the brisk weather was a pleasant shock to us both! Wow, we made it. The pair of us smiled as my plastered friend hopped and pushed me along. We should have gone straight back up to the ward. But we didn't. We discussed going further, perhaps to the beach. Well, it seemed like a good idea at the time. But it was not. Neither of us had taken into account the fact that the hospital was at the top of a hill. Nor had we considered the gradient, momentum, potential energy, risk or the tireless work of gravity. Perhaps we should have remembered our medical conditions too.

It started out well, he held onto the back of the wheel chair and I worked on providing resistance to the wheels with my hands. He hopped whilst I allowed the chair to advance a bit. Stop. Repeat. Then, as we got tired, or impatient, we tried to do two hops, then three, then... well, we got faster and faster and could not stop as we careered down the hill. I put the brakes on, but the smooth wheels just kept on skidding down the slope. How nobody spotted this as 'unusual' is beyond me to this very day!

Laughing, crying, bruising my hands, and certainly not helping his broken leg, we must have looked like something out of a Charlie Chaplin movie running at double speed. We finally stopped, breathless at the bottom of the hill. Fortunately, neither of us appeared too physically damaged from the experience. We did both receive a massive dose of adrenaline, and endorphins! Our facial muscles were tired from smiling and laughing, and it took a few minutes to stop our giggling at each other too! However, we now needed to climb the hill and get back into the ward, unnoticed. It took time, and planning, a lot of energy and some tears of pain and anguish, but we managed. We could have been escape artists and burglars combined!

When interrogated by the ward sister with "Where have you two been?" we explained that we went to the main door to wait for visitors, but that we would not do so again. Thank goodness surveillance cameras were not in vogue at that time! I quickly found a different wheelchair and we covered up the escape plan to all but our closest friends on the ward. It brought many smiles, for many days!

One day, one magnificent day, I was taken to the stairwell by my pretty physio, the one who promised to elope with me. She worked with me on the stairs. One step, two steps, three steps... Several days later I could make steps unaided. It was time to abandon the wheelchair. With my back only oozing small amounts of blood and pus, the day of no more dressings was coming fast, and with it release was in sight.

Knowing that I had to leave hospital and get straight into work, I started applying for jobs from my hospital bed. It made sense to me, but not to potential employers. I really couldn't understand why. Nonetheless, one research unit at the local University was interested in offering me a research job. I just needed to be released and go for it.

Towards the end of August, I met with the surgeon to discuss my parole, I mean release, from the hospital. He carried out a thorough physical and told me words that bit to my very core, "You may have the mind of a teenager, but you must remember that you have the body of an eighty-year-old. You must accept that you may never lift more than one or two kilos at a time, and consider that lifting a tea tray may be too much. Oh, and be careful with the walking too."

Talk about knocking the floor out from under me. This big surgeon, the man who had put me back together, was telling me that I was already an old man and should live my life as such.

I took my discharge papers. Left my many friends - staff and patients, and went back to my digs with the Doctor and nurse.

LIVING BEYOND MY MEANS

I couldn't move fast. Walking up hills was still a challenge, but I could get around quite well. I never realised how hard tying shoe laces could be. It is certainly not something to embark upon before warming up the body in the morning. Feet are a long way away from the top of your body, and you must take time and make a plan to reach those far away items. Perhaps my body really was eighty years old. Nonetheless, I insisted on laces on my shoes.

The start day for my first full-time job was in September, in the Agricultural Research Unit at the local University. I took the train to the University, then reported to the labs, for my tasks to given to me. I was to help, at the very bottom of the pile, in the research of Chagas disease.

The pay was barely £25 ($35) per week. Almost as much as the train fare from my digs. All the same, I was not going to turn down working at a University. It was second best to studying at University, at least for me, in my mind, at that time. In order to survive financially I would have to move closer to work, and soon did.

Early each morning I would drag myself to the University campus, enter the sports facilities changing rooms, take a shower and use the toilet there. That way I did not consume water, heat water or use up any toilet rolls out of my little salary. I had to become frugal. Very frugal. My main diet was 'Jacob's [dry] crackers', peanut butter and Marmite (yeast extract). I supplemented this luxurious eating habit by attending parties and eating whatever was available there.

Once inside the lab, I would put on my white coat, go to the animal room and collect one hundred Rhodnius Prolixus. Disgusting little insects, gorged with rabbit blood to make them easier to work with. Taking them, one-by-one, carefully, using a binocular microscope along with my hand-made glass dissection tools, I would remove their central nervous system (CNS). The CNS is the closest thing to a brain such a creature has. Subsequently, I would lay out their Malpighian tubules - or insect kidneys to you and me - in a special solution for experiments. It was like unravelling a ball of microscopic fibres, and you could not damage a single one. Then, one end would be tied to a metal post - well a pin - but under the microscope it looked like a post, and the other laid gracefully in a solution of 'synthetic diuretic hormone' for testing purposes.

Chagas disease, also known as American Trypanosomiasis, is a potentially fatal sleeping sickness, principally found in South America. It is spread by the Rhodnius Prolixus bug, rather like malaria is spread by female Anopheles mosquitoes. The research was to find the chemical composition of the diuretic hormone of the little critters, and then find a specific insecticide to make the population 'piss themselves to death'. A great plan, which would require a lot of CNS concentrate, a lot Malpighian tubules and thus a lot of dissection!

I enjoyed the work itself, for it was very interesting. I learned about many new techniques such as high pressure liquid chromatography and mass spectrometry, things I had read about - but never come into first-hand contact with. I enjoyed working with the lab-techs, but I quickly realised that University was not all that it was made out to be. I realise that I was 'an employee', but I saw the behaviour of students, and faculty members. Much as I enjoyed the technical side of my job, I did not enjoy the working environment, or the mentality of University life.

I had moved to a small, very small, bed-sit close to the University, and got my costs and income almost balanced, but I really needed to find a solution to my earnings, and to be in a different working environment. Perhaps my inability to become a university student through missing my exams did not help me to accept the working style at the University, but whatever the reasons, I really wanted 'out'.

My health was improving, slowly, but I still struggled with walking long distances. After a while the pain would build up in my back, and then my left leg would delay in responding to mental commands sent to it. Consequently, I learned that 'swinging' my left leg could get me through those times, with the least noticeable factors for those around me.

I set out from my bed-sit, determined to find a new job. I went step-by-step, door-to-door, asking every company I came to, as I paraded my services over several miles of roadways. The pain was building with each new visit, but I would not let that show. My left leg was 'swinging' more and more, but it just looked like a mild limp to any passerby.

"Good morning, I am looking for work" I would begin.

Normally, the receptionist would cut me off with "No vacancies" or "You have to be joking, we are laying people off!"

I had always thought about becoming a pilot, and, on the off-chance entered the recruitment centre for the Royal Air Force. A young, beautifully presented in a crisp uniform, military careers adviser stood up and welcomed me in. "What would it take for me to join the RAF?" I asked, chancing my luck.

"Do you have any medical conditions?" he questioned, probably having noticed my left leg was not quite working as it should.

"I am asthmatic, and am recovering from back surgery, but that is all," I replied in all honesty. I pulled my Ventolin inhaler out of my pocket, adding evidence to my truthfulness.

"The application forms are over there," he offered with a gesture, adding, "But I would not waste the ink filling one out. The Air Force will never consider you - in fact no armed force will ever consider you." He turned, almost annoyed at the audacity of an invalid entering the recruitment centre, returning to his desk.

"Thank you!" I called cheerily as I pushed open the heavy door, the only heavier thing at that point being my heart. I was 'damaged goods'. My spirits sunk rapidly to the depths of despair, fortunately, they fell so fast and so hard that when they hit rock bottom they quickly bounced back to operational mode. I would not give up looking for a better job.

I knocked on more doors, and got even more "thank you, but no thank you" responses. Then, as I was about ready to quit the dance, I knocked on the door of a large engineering company.

It was not the most modern company, by a long way. I stood at the reception glass in waiting area watching a dolls eye telephone exchange, with the receptionist operating it. I had read about these things, but thought that they were all withdrawn from service. The receptionist was manipulating, almost massaging, the exchange and patching calls from one place to another with a plethora of cables and jacks in front of a board with holes in it, each one a patch point for a telephone or an external line! It was fascinating. I forgot about why I had entered the building and asked her about the switchboard. Smiling, the diminutive, bespectacled, receptionist explained and showed me how it all worked. I was fascinated. Then, after about ten minutes, she asked "Is that why you came?"

Realising that I had been distracted, I explained "Sorry, no. I am looking for a job."

"Hang on a mo," she smiled, and proceeded to drag a jack and cable from one location to another, repeatedly stating the same thing to each person she communicated with; "I have a young man here looking for work..."

A few minutes later, with a smile and a waving gesture of her hand, I was sent up the old wooden staircase, which smelt as if oil, diesel and a thousand years of dust had been soaked into it, eventually finding my way to the buyer's office.

"Sit down. What do you want?" the gruff question from the portly chap called 'the Buyer' reached my ears crisply.

"I need a job. I want to work," I stated, the pain in my back throbbing away to distract me. I arched my spine in the chair, trying to minimise the growing agony.

"Are you any good at mathematics and can you read drawings?" he shot at me.

"I love maths and I can read drawings," I responded, knowing that the first part was true, but that I had no idea if I would be able to read whatever he sent my way. I needed the job more than anything, and I could learn fast, so, the answer was yes, whatever the question!

"Start on January second," he barked, sending me to Human Resources for some paperwork.

And that was that. Full of joy, I hobbled back to my bed-sit, tired, in-pain, but happy that I had a way forward - with double the money each week! Meanwhile, I had to work my notice period at the University, and, that was not easy.

Nonetheless, I knew that I had made a commitment, and even though the unit was not happy with my resignation, they were pleasant and wished me luck.

During this time, I had decided to attend a local church, just up the road from my little bed-sit. There I had met a young lady, a few years older than I, but we got on really well. We discussed many things, and she helped me a great deal. We both had challenges and we both shared common ideas. We got on. This was my first 'girlfriend'.

On the first of January, I awoke to find myself covered in spots. I had the chicken pox. I had left one job, and was due to start the new one the next day. This was unbelievable. Adversity appeared to be hanging on every lamp post I passed by!

I slept on the couch of my girlfriends flat, and she was marvellous at taking care of me. Calamine lotion is the worlds' most soothing cream when all you want to do is scratch the skin off of your body! The next morning, my supposed first day in a new job, I rang my new employer. The phone was answered by the 'dolls eye receptionist'. She remembered me. I made a mental note to always be nice to the receptionists I come across, for they are the front line of any operation!

She patched me through to Human Resources, and I explained my health challenge. "As soon as you are able, report to work," came the response. Well, that was simple!

Two weeks later, I set off to work, on foot, still scarred from the chicken pox!

BIGOTRY

It was a long walk to and from work, perhaps not for most people, but for my 'eighty-year-old body', it was a challenge. Nonetheless, I was on time every morning, often with a little pain. Pain had become my friend. I had got used to pain. Working with an old body covering a young mind meant that there was no point in complaining, just embracing. So, I accepted pain as a part of my life.

Within minutes of my first day beginning, I was given a pile of drawings to work on. A0 sheets of blue prints - some still wet from the printing process. The soft paper with covered with symbols and lines, all meaning nothing to me. I could not let on that I had never worked with such drawings before.

"Work out the bill of materials for each drawing, then collate the results and let me have them by the end of the day," Buyer snapped. He was more off hand than a prison warden suffering from diarrhoea and toothache at the same time.

I sat at a wonky old wooden desk with a mucky green leather inlay. Opposite me, an older lady, who smoked incessantly, watched me... waiting for me to falter. To my left a girl who had left school early, of Italian descent. She carried some excess weight well, and smiled whatever the situation. The three desks all looked into a common centre. The buyer really didn't like Italian girl. He made it clear. Snide comments, rude comments, unpleasant and unnecessary comments. But, that was his way, and I had to learn to work with such people sooner or later. Italian girl was pleasant, full of life and energy. She would type up the lists that I and my older colleague would create from reading the drawings.

I stood looking at the paper version of an engineering Rosetta stone-like mass on my desk. There were no computers, just pencil and paper. My older colleague opposite whispered to me "If you don't understand it, go to the drawing office and ask."

"Thank you," I mouthed back and took the first of the many blueprints under my arm. It turned out that she could have helped me, but she was, unbeknown to her, doing me a massive favour!

In the drawing office I saw rows of older men hunched over massive drawing boards, scientific calculators under their hands and Rotring pens, of the finest calibre, in slots at the top of their working space. Nobody noticed me coming in. I scanned the room, working as if I were in the market place, hunting a potential buyer for my questions. I found one. A chap in a cardigan, clearly not fitting in with the masses. I approached him.

As I tapped him on the shoulder he jumped, almost entering orbit. He looked at me, startled, amazed "What are you doing in here?" he asked.

"I have some questions," I quietly stated, trying not to rouse the huddled men over their tracing paper.

"Nobody comes in here," he whispered. "What is the matter?"

I explained that I was working in the buying office and had been asked to quantity survey the drawings. He looked at the half-unravelled blueprint in my hands. "Ahhh, the aircraft hydraulic and pneumatic systems for the new military installations," he expressed warmly, clearly personally invested in the hieroglyphics inscribed on my blueprint.

We moved over to a vacant drawing reading area. He pointed out the different symbols, explaining the use of oils, hydraulic and pneumatic systems for special installations. I was learning. As I asked questions about the pumps, valves and flanges he paused, looked at me and responded "We don't know about those things. You need to go to stores and speak to the store-keeper."

I was sent down the creaky metal stairs at the back of the building. I hoped not to be missed from my desk. Finding a battered wooded door marked Goods Inwards, I took a deep breath and entered. The store-keeper was another person who could not believe his eyes at this young man, with a blue-print under his arm, entering his domain. "What the f*&% do you want?" he snapped.

"I have some questions about hydraulic pumps..." It was time to use every bit of tact I had learned, and to work the personality of the man in front of me. I spotted a barn owl in the corner. Before he could throw me out, I went towards the owl, cooing and asked "Wow, is that your owl?"

That was it, we were friends. We talked owls. Lots about owls. He loved his owl - it was his friend in the lonely bowels of the company stores. I am sure that it collected the odd mouse as a bonus whilst at work.

Then, store-keeper pulled my blue-print from me, asking with a glint in his eye, "What do you want to know?"

I asked questions, he did not answer. Instead he pulled inventory from stock for me to see. I got to touch, to smell, to feel and to make function many of the items that were new to me. I learned more in the next hour than could normally be learned in a month. He may not have been a well-educated chap, but he was a very well informed, helpful and encouraging one.

I then asked "So, how does this all go together?"

Before I could say 'how's ya father', I was whisked onto the shop floor. It was in the wake of the Falklands war, and lots of special equipment was still being manufactured. I was standing in the midst of a primitive, but effective workshop.

Without option, I was taken to each station and introduced to the task being undertaken. This was my new family, offering me adoption by force, absorbing me into the family of engineering.

I saw for the first time in my life a CNC (Computer Numerical Control) machine - a basic robot. After a long time had passed, I glanced up at the wooden, Roman numeral adorned, wall clock. Surprised at how much time had passed, I excused myself and ran back to my desk.

There was Buyer, standing guard by my working place. "Where the f$%@ b@$"%@ f@@@@&& have you been?" he fumed, making my own father's interrogations, from when I had been naughty as a child, look like a pleasant day at nursery school. I was learning that engineering is a tough game, and you have to think fast, accept some rough and tough talking, and be ready to account for anything and everything.

"I was clarifying the drawings," I stated, holding my own on the creaky wooden floor.

"Whaddya mean?" he snapped, slightly taken aback.

"You see, here and here on this drawing, we have referenced different pumps, but they could both be the same," I ventured my newly gained knowledge.

He listened, went to his office, looked up some spec sheets, and came back, asking with an accusing tone "How did you work that out?"

I smiled, as I responded, "That is where I have been, Sir."

He turned, closed the half glazed door to his office and sat, glaring at me through the barrier. I decided to keep my head down, and to remain at my desk for the rest of the day. Italian girl reached out her hand, touching me on the arm, saying "Don't worry, he is like that all the time." The older lady smiled a wry smile, which was an achievement with her ash laden cigarette hanging out of her mouth!

Each set of plans got easier, and my interactions in the drawing office became almost welcomed. The storekeeper and machine operators were happy to help me assist in making their lives easier. I was discovering that you have to talk to people at all levels, and that the worst people in any organisation to deal with are those at the top - those who think that they know it all.

I could hack this job, and do it better, quicker and cleaner than it had been done before. Pride comes before a fall... and my fall was coming fast.

DISMISSAL?

Buyer learned to tolerate my wandering, intelligence gathering missions around the factory. After all, I gave results. I was gleaning knowledge and saving the operation money. I would visit Storekeeper almost every day, even if only to see what had been delivered. Every brown box contained a new learning opportunity - and I was learning thick and fast.

To complicate matters, I was scheduled to get married. I was young, not even nineteen years old. But I was mature for my age, and ready to take on responsibilities beyond my years.

Italian girl was also getting married, so we would share ideas and halve our worries. I found working with the women in the company easier than the men, mainly because I did not enter into the crass jokes or pin-up girl ogling mentality. I was never into bum smacking or copping a grope, as others would. Today such behaviour is considered sexual harassment, but then it appeared to be normal-man-behaviour. I wanted nothing to do with it. My mother was a tough lady, and I had already learned to respect women - or get a well deserved clip around the ear!

Dolls Eye Receptionist was, perhaps, my best working ally. If I needed to make an outside call, she always put my call on the top of the list. If a call came in for me, and I was away from my desk, she would transfer it to Storekeeper's phone. That first meeting had made such a difference to her, locked away in the dark reception corner, behind a piece of glass, with an antique! Just by being interested in her job, and treating her with the respect she deserved as a human being had been a massive, positive investment in both of our lives.

My job entailed working out what to order, how many, and then to know the best price. My boss was more creative, and so, he made sure that I never knew what went on behind the closed door of his office. I would watch through the glass in his door as Buyer met with sales reps, leaning forward across the desk, exchanging in hushed tones the deal of the day. I knew something was not quite right, but could not put a name to it.

I suddenly realised that he played a lot more golf, and was taking more and more exotic holidays. Perhaps there was a connection to the hushed tones over the desk moments.

I had been brought up to tell the truth, and to try to ensure that the right thing was being done. When I approached Buyer to discuss my observations, in a similar manner to my ill-fated encounter with the headmaster when I was eight years old, I placed a land-mine firmly under my feet.

"GET OUT OF MY OFFICE," the same phrase from ten years beforehand echoed around his small office, ricocheting off each wall in turn. It seemed to me that confronting people with truth was the best way to generate that phrase!

He set about putting me on probation. He made some phone calls, all put through by Dolls Eye. She was a smart girl, and I am not saying that she did, but she may well have listened into the conversations from her place of crossed lines! Either way, she alerted the Works Council to my predicament, and soon a meeting was called with me, the council and human resources. I was in deep, hot and very dangerous water. I was advised to start looking for another job, but my current job would be kept on, provided I learned to look the other way on certain activities.

I waited until after my wedding, for that made the most sense. Already my pending in-laws found it hard that I was 'not Catholic', 'younger than their daughter', 'physically challenged' and 'not a lawyer or a doctor'. What would 'unemployed' have added to the hot coals on my head.

Back from honeymoon, I started applying for jobs. I had to get out before I found myself dismissed, or had something pinned on me that was not true. I had no intention of becoming a fall-guy.

I read the local paper, and found an advert that promised good salary for a simple sales job. All I had to do was to turn up to a presentation and interview. Taking a day off work, I attended, full of hope and aspiration.

The three men on the interview panel took to me instantly, and after some banter, sales skills demos and my 'Saturday Market Routine', the job was mine, or so I thought.

It was a technical sales job. The topic was new to me, but the promised salary was more than double what I was earning - and they provided a company car. I had gone through the whole interview without them asking my age, which was just a bit below that which they asked for in the advert. I was only nineteen, but the job advert asked for twenty-five years and above.

I received a phone call later that evening telling me I could start in two-weeks' time. I was thrilled. I looked forward to the new challenge, better money and a company car.

Handing in my notice to Buyer, I got to see him laugh with glee. My other colleagues wished me well, and I got a special hug from Dolls Eye girl... I believe she even shed a tear.

I turned up to my new office, excited, exhilarated and ready to make a new career as a salesman. After all, my father sold toys, sweets - and Jesus! So, it was in the blood.

I sat in front of the young lady who would issue me my company car. I was all jittery, but in a positive way. I didn't care what the car was, this was an amazing opportunity! She asked for my driver's licence, which was clean and relatively new. Then, she stopped smiling.

Excusing herself, she entered the Marketing Manager's office. Barely sixty seconds passed before he erupted from the room.

"NINETEEN... NINETEEN... NINETEEN - GET OUT OF MY OFFICE," he did not sound amused.

I had heard these words before, but never so quickly in a relationship. I was confused. I asked "WHY?" Ok, I yelled it.

"You need to be 25 or older to drive a company car. And, who is going to buy anything from a NINETEEN-YEAR-OLD," he retorted. He had a point. I seemed to have overlooked that possibility in my enthusiasm.

I knocked on doors looking for work, once again. As the working day closed, I headed home, feeling a rather despondent.

My day was about to get even more interesting. "I'm home," I called out as I entered the door.

"Who's home?" came the standard reply.

"OUR home!" I retorted, with the ceremonial chant of the return of the hunter-gather, who had not gathered this particular day.

My wife was beaming. She added some news to my day, which was not planned, "I have missed my period!"

"How wonderful!" I exclaimed, hiding the fact that I had left one job and not completed a day in my new job without being fired, and had not actually secured another job before getting home that night. This was not the sort of thing a hunter-gatherer, or a good husband, should expose to his wife.

Fortunately, talk of pregnancy and a baby distracted completely from my having to discuss my employment situation. We went to bed. She slept. I did not. I thought a lot, making a plan.

The next morning, I called the Marketing Manager and told him that "I will work on commission only and provide my own car." He put the phone down on me. Hard to believe, but he did.

I spent time looking for work. It was tough, I was ready to embark on any and every task, but I still felt that I could do the sales job best.

Each morning, for a week, I called the Marketing Manager and told him, repeatedly, "I will work on commission only and provide my own car." Finally, exhausted, he invited me back to his office.

"You are a persistent pain in the arse," he told me straight to my face.

"Tell me something new, Sir," I retorted, adding "But *that* is the basis of being a great salesman!"

We agreed a commission package, a work area and I was off to make sales. Marketing Manager shook his head, a lot, every time he looked at me.

My products were technical telecoms products. This was the modern age - and telex machines were being upgraded to have a small green screen where you could edit a message before printing it out on paper tape and transmitting it to the other side of the world. Then there was another innovation called the Facsimile Machine, also known as the Fax.

Finally, I had a wonderful product called a Key Tel System. Basically, the Key Tel would allow a business to use telephones, make and receive calls, without an operator, without a person patching phone calls through or connecting the company employees to the outside lines. Today, this sort of thing is common place, but then it was magic, cost effective and efficient! Of course, I would never want my old engineering company to hear of such a system, for it would be the end of the 'dolls eye exchange' and my friendly, bespectacled Dolls Eye!

These new-fangled, fandabbywabbydoozie machines were to be my bedfellows, passengers, table guests, and frankly my friends. I loaded my demonstration equipment buddies into my old, unreliable, car and travelled thousands of miles, making demonstrations, and with them sales. Just for good measure, my car would break down from time to time.

Within three months I was the top salesman, and had earned enough commission to purchase my own new car. A small, more reliable, car.

Each month I won prizes for reaching sales targets. My clients loved my approach, it was very unconventional, but it worked.

First of all, I would make telephone appointments. I had learned quite quickly that 11am was the most popular time for appointments in the morning, and 3pm in the afternoon. Thus, I generally offered my potential clients those two times in a tea or coffee close. It is just like offering a drink. If you say "Would you like drink?" the answer options are 'yes' or 'no'. But if you offer "Tea or coffee?' the answer is either 'tea' - or - 'coffee', you have not enabled an option to decline the offer! Therefore, my standard invitation for an appointment would be "So, would you like to meet at 11am or 3pm on Tuesday?" This resulted in a greater acceptance of an appointment being fixed.

Each day, I knew I needed to make six appointments. Not every meeting would result in a full demo, but roughly one in three would. Selling is a simple numbers game. Get the numbers right and the sales happen. The average time for a meeting/presentation was about forty-five minutes. Therefore, I would make three appointments for 11am and three appointments for 3pm each day. I had to make sure that their geographic locations were suitably clustered.

The first appointment, I would turn up to at 9:30/10am. Entering the office, I would speak to the receptionist, just being pleasant, asking a few questions, especially about exactly what the company did, and passing a few compliments to the receptionist on her pleasant manner, knowledge of the business and professionalism. Then, embarrassedly, I would explain that my earlier appointment had cancelled, and I was running early, would it be possible to speak to the boss?

Almost without fail, it worked. Now, in front of the M.A.N. (Money, Authority and Need), I had to present the product. I would adapt each and every presentation to the company sector. Trying to use terms that related specifically to whatever their sector was, my demo was 'a performance, just for them'. All of those days in the market really were paying off, as were the days in hospital, a factory and a laboratory. In fact, I was using EVERYTHING I had learned, and adding to my learning each day.

Watching the clock, I made sure to be out to the next appointment by 11am. No need to apologise, I was on time. The one of a kind song and dance routine repeated itself. Maintaining an eye on the time, I would head to my third 11am appointment - trying to be there as close to midday as possible.

Rushing in, apologising for being late, I would offer to take the boss out to lunch. They rarely accepted, but generally welcomed the offer and allowed a demonstration of the new fangled electronics that the out of breath salesman who understood their industry, but who was a little late, had to offer.

The same procedure repeated itself in the afternoons. Not only did I make great sales, but I got loads of referrals. Some clients were more interesting than others - and some a greater challenge. Perhaps my greatest challenge, and a personal favourite, was to make a sale to an undertaker.

Mr Undertaker, operated a small parlour in a seaside town, a place where it was known people went to live out their days. This call was going to test my skills in communications more than any other.

He was an actual 11am appointment, which seemed appropriate. You do not want to be early to the undertakers, now do you? Perhaps, in hindsight, I should have been late!

I entered the 'shop', and saw the display items. A very sobering experience, but one that brought back my Nightingale Ward memories. The Undertaker came through the door and greeted me. Well, I think it was a greeting. He was so reserved, quiet and respectful, I was not really sure what was going on.

We moved back, past the solid oak coffins, into his office. There, in his monochrome world, I sat in the solid wood chair with leather trimmings. I dared not move, remembering the Headmaster's office and for fear of making bodily noises. Nervously, and without thinking, I asked him "How is business?"

All I wanted to happen at that point was for the world to open up a hole and swallow me. How could I ask an UNDERTAKER of all people, "How is business..."

He looked me in the eye and said quietly and very slowly "Dead actually."

We both looked at each other, our eyes locked if we were microwave transceivers, aligned and tuned. A few seconds of awkward silence hung in the air, like an unpleasant smell. To my relief, we both laughed out loud simultaneously.

I had so many questions coming into my head. After all, how often do you get a one-to-one with such a man - and an opportunity to unravel what happens in such a secretive business sector. "So, how *do* you get business?" I enquired.

It was as if nobody had ever asked him questions about his work, and he started to pour out his vocation in minute detail. I learned so much. Learning most off all respect those who care for the dearly departed, managing the most challenging, yet inevitable, moment of life. I realised my own mortality, and remembered the impending birth of my first child. I made the sale, and I made another friend.

As my revenues increased, so did the demands on them. We decided to purchase a house, and moved with a very pregnant wife to our first house. I was still not twenty years old.

I was working in London, about two hours drive from the house. It was my third 11am appointment of the day. After closing the sale, I asked to use the clients phone to call home to check on my near-term wife. She informed me that she was not feeling well and was about to make her way to the hospital, there was some bleeding where there should not be.

Without a thought for my three 3pm appointments, I transitioned from sitting in my client's office to sitting in my car, and from salesman to racing driver. I am sure that I could have competed for the land speed record. I broke red lights, speed limits and almost every rule of the road. Even considering going around the roundabouts the wrong way, at one point.

I was not stopped once by the police as I left London, speeding down the dual carriageways to the South Coast. Then, as the roads clogged up, I had no choice but to slow down. I was sitting in crawling traffic, with less than two miles to the hospital. Passing a car on the inside lane, something so very minor in comparison to my past hour and half's roller coaster ride, I heard the "whhooooop whooooooop" of a siren, and saw a blue flash in my rear view mirror. Stopping abruptly and evacuating my vehicle simultaneously, I soon arrived at the side of the jam sandwich police car behind me, long before the officer could fully open his door. "You can't stop me. My wife is pregnant and has been taken to that hospital," my right hand was waving at the hospital, barely visible, down the road.

"Then get back in your car and follow us," came the unexpected reply. Wow, honesty was paying off today!

I somersaulted back into the driving seat as the police car, in full twos-and-blues mode, pulled in front of my car, clearing a path for me drive at speed to reach the side of my wife. They simply waved to me as I pulled into the car park.

It turned out to be nothing too serious, and we both headed home, bump intact.

NEW LIFE & ECONOMICS

It was early morning. The road noise was just beginning, and I was ready to leave the warmth of bed. Then, just as I was about to make a cautious step into the early autumn freshness, I felt wetness seeping in large quantities across the mattress.

"It's go time!" I shouted, leaping out of bed, realising that the all essential waters had broken! Go-bag in hand, we drove to the hospital ready for the

Wonderful Adversity: Into Africa

emergence of a new citizen of planet earth.

Watching a child being born is an amazing thing, watching your own child being born is the most amazing thing. It seems impossible to fit the head of baby through such a small hole - but it works! Nature is truly amazing! Matt, who would change much in my life, had entered the world in the traditional messy manner and was growing faster than bamboo in the monsoon season. I was glad that he was healthy, and even happier that I had a good job, or so I thought.

A few weeks after his birth, I was called into the office by the Marketing Manager. I had been doing well, received a proper company car and was being treated outstandingly by all in the company.

"You have done so well, we are going to change your working area" I was told. I would not have minded, but it was going to make more travel, and it was taking me away my most lucrative zones and established contacts. Clearly, being good at what you do can lead to some tough assignments. However, I was not ready to be away even more from my newborn. I felt it might be time to consider a different career.

I looked through newspapers and magazines, looking for a job that would keep me close to home. Spotting a 'CNC Part-programmer trainee wanted' ad, in a free paper that came through the door, I imagined a new job and skill building opportunity. My mind jumped back to the early CNC machine tools from my engineering experience, and the wonderful Dolls Eye Receptionist. I thought about working in a factory again, and having more stable working times, as well as less travel. It was a good thought. So, I applied, and was offered the job on the spot.

This new opportunity meant a cut in salary. It also meant moving to a much cheaper part of the country, so it balanced out. With a young child, we moved to an industrial town in the Midlands. We had to downsize, but that was worthwhile to be home each evening with my little boy. We didn't need a car, for the house was close to the factory.

The street was composed of two lines of terraced houses, each one a two-up, two-down arrangement, with Victorian fireplaces, wooden floors and cold almost-outhouse toilets on the ground floor. They were lovely homes, basic, but lovely homes.

My first day in the new factory was a tough one. I really knew nothing about programming robots, nor did I understand the first thing about sheet metal work. But I was, as always, ready and willing to learn.

My line manager, a senior member of the team, had written all the programmes the company used on their various CNC' machine tools. He looked down on me, treating me with total, unabashed disdain. I did not mind, I had experienced worse, much worse. I focused on learning all that I could from him, but he did not like to share, teach nor encourage.

There was only one way for me to learn to do my job well. Remembering the challenges of learning in my first engineering related job, I went out to the shop floor and watched machines working. I spent hours, many of them in my own time, reading the production programme on a small green screen, whilst concurrently watching the machines move, cut, punch, whirr and buzz. As I had learned before, reception staff and those on the shop floor are the most important, and therefore, I spent a lot of time learning from them. Interestingly, they were thrilled to be seen as a source of information and inspiration. The girl on reception helped me with access to tools catalogues, and could tell me from which supplier each tool came from, along with the principle materials suppliers.

The shop foreman was a massive source of information. But working with him was like learning to swim with a great white shark as an instructor. He was a short man, with a foul mouth, using a particular swear word at least three times in every sentence. Hence, I mentally called him Mr F.

Mr F would come up to me, waddling like an egg-bound penguin, red, round, aggressive and with two perpetual cigarettes. One in his mouth and one behind his ear.

"What the F are you F'ing doing at that F'ing machine?" he asked, in an aggressive but offhand tone. Since Mr F only had one tone, I may have interpreted that wrongly, but it seemed to fit.

"I am watching the programme, and wonder why we do the machining in this particular manner?" I responded.

He was shocked. Normally, people just walked away when he spoke to them. He stood beside me, as I explained line-by-line the programme running, and slowed the machine down for him to see my concern. It was as if a light came on in his head, a moment of enlightenment and understanding. "Well for F's sake go and F'ing fix it and be F'ing fast about it you F'er," he spewed his words onto me, swiftly moving on to see what was going down at the welding bay.

I returned to the office and my unhelpful mentor. Explaining the situation in his existing programme was a total waste of my breath. I could have got a better reaction, and more help, out of a budgerigar than him. He showed no interest, and simply stating "But it works," shrugging his shoulders and returning to his umpteenth coffee of the day.

I changed that programme, and many others. Those modifications, and reading the many thousands of lines of code designed to move a machine, taught me well to start writing new programmes from scratch. The owner of the company would come in and drop a pile of drawings on my desk, with a terse "Programme these for tomorrow's production." The pile was high, but the work was easy. Just read a drawing, a skill well learned from before, and then turn it into a set of machine commands. It was all done in the head, and typed into an old CP/M computer, before transferring to punched tape to send to the machines on the shop floor.

After two months, I noticed budgerigar man was absent more than he was present in the office. He did not like the fact that I had re-programmed

Wonderful Adversity: Into Africa

much of his handy-work, nor that I could programme several times faster than him. Within a few months he disappeared. He went on holiday and never came back. I guess he flew the nest. From then on, I ran the department.

I loved programming. Looking at a drawing of a desired part, and just seeing in my mind's eye the machining movements, speeds and operations - and turning them into a mathematical model - typing the commands and then seeing the parts made on the machine was absolute magnificent. I was happy. G codes, the codes used to direct the machine movement type and contained canned cycles or routines became new words in my vocabulary. Selection of tools using T codes, turning on machine related options using M codes, and always remembering to give accurate X, Y, Z axis data to suit the production requirements became my waking dream. At night it seemed as if CNC code streamed through my head. I loved the precision, the lack of forgiveness and the perfect final product that programming machines brought to my life.

Without a car, and living in a terraced property close to work, our expenses were low, and I enjoyed the walk to and from work each day. It was wonderful. It was just a couple of miles there and back, enabling more family time. I even got to work shifts which gave me more time with my son. However, he did not respond properly when we spoke to him on his right hand side. The doctor thought we were exaggerating, but, after a lot of persuasion, referred him to a specialist. Indeed, he was deaf in his right ear. He was born that way. Simple. Nothing that could be done about it. We were warned that it might affect his balance and ability to do certain things. So, that made me want him to do those very things that might be difficult for him!

As he grew, he did really well, being my pride and joy. One day whilst at work, the owner called me into his office with a yell, it ripped through the whole factory. Mr F was in there too. The office had received a phone call from my wife.

"You must go home NOW, your son has stopped breathing and the ambulance is on the way. Get out of my office now - go home," I spun on my feet, yanked open the door, but could not move. Mr F had grabbed my arm. He dug deep into his pockets and pulled out a set of car keys. "Take my F'ing car and get F'ing going!" he yelled. For the first time I had been ordered out of an office, for a good reason, and been offered a car to meet my immediate, most pressing need.

Mr F had a brand new sports car with an automatic gearbox. I had never driven a sports car, nor been in an automatic car, even as a passenger. I jumped in and thought to myself, in Mr F's tone "you had better not F up this car!"

Arriving at the house before the ambulance, Matt was barely visible on the floor, a neighbour obscuring his body, giving him CPR.

I don't remember reaching the hospital, nor getting home again. But I must have. I read the medical report over and over again, trying to make sense of what had exactly happened to my little boy. The report spoke of febrile convulsions, the need for more medical tests and a lot of other things. I had more learning to do, and fast.

I drove Mr F's sports car back to work the next morning, double checking everything was as it should be. I thanked Mr F as I handed him his keys, but he ignored me, snatching the keys and walking back to the shop floor. I think he smiled, but it didn't matter, it was his way of being nice.

I sat in my office, listening to a forty tonne CNC punch press banging out a tune in the distance, all the time contemplating my son, my future and how much I disliked visiting hospitals. Smack, smack.... bang, bang. Smack... smack... then.... nothing... I paused, looked at the production schedule - it was full. I wondered if I should go and check on the machine. Before I could leave my office I heard the familiar call of "WHAT THE F!"

A key machine in the company production line-up had hydraulic problems. This was going to hit out-put hard. It could result in closure of the firm, but we all hoped not. We could patch it, but the machine was terminally ill.

The owner called me into his office. "I have ordered this new CNC punch press, and it will be here in two weeks," he reassured me, showing the brochure for the latest technology on the market. My shoulders dropped and I inhaled deeply, releasing a long sigh of relief. He had ordered the best possible machine. It was amazing. I was excited at getting to grips with a new programming system along with all that this leap in technology offered.

"However, I cannot afford the programming system," he added in a matter of fact tone, revealing how little he understood its importance.

The new machine was more complex, faster and needed a much more refined programming system to make it work. Such systems ran on mini-computers and cost upwards of twenty five thousand pounds sterling (thirty five thousand US dollars). A lot of money back then. My mouth dropped open. In shock, I stared incredulously at the man.

Immediately exasperated, I huffed "You are bringing in a one hundred and twenty five thousand pound sterling machine, WITHOUT a programming system? Do you know what that means?" I shifted around the room, shaking my head, grabbing both ears from time to time, shivering at the thought of how this was going to turn out. I could work hard, but programme that particular machine, and transfer the required size of programme - on punched paper tape? No, no, no. The owner had lost his marbles. He must have seen my rare speechless moment, and offered some explanation.

"We won a grant for the machine, but there is no money for a programming system," his gaze passing straight through my troubled form.

I ventured "Do you have ANY budget for a programming system?"

The owner looked down, as if praying. He was silent, as was I. The pause was long enough for me to risk asphyxiation from holding my breath. He

Wonderful Adversity: Into Africa

looked up, sheepishly proposing "You can fix it with five thousand pound?"

Remembering my approach from earlier in my career of; *the answer is yes, now what is the question?* I simply, and very quietly, responded, "Yes," turned around, walked back to my office and sat in the corner of the room. Sitting on the floor, my head firmly in my hands, my mind was busy chasing butterflies, but never catching them. This was a big challenge. Could I *really* fix this one? But, life is a big challenge, and if you do not try, you will never know. Most importantly, you will only have failed if you give up trying. The game was on. Getting up from the floor, I stood with my arms by my side, slightly bent, as if ready to draw pistols in a duel for my future.

I had seen the big, mini-computer, programming system that the owner SHOULD have purchased, bulky and impressive. Most importantly, it allowed you to see a graphical representation of the part you had programmed *before* going to production, called a 'back plotter'. The mini-computer system allowed you to thoroughly check the CNC part-programme before screwing up something on the real-life robot, and holding up production on the shop floor. You could even inspect the part on screen!

This was 1985, and the Personal Computer was just becoming a new business tool. IBM PCs were expensive, but there were some new clones on the market. One particular one had been featured in an engineering magazine that I had read. I moved rapidly, scattering some drawings on my very messy desk, hunting the magazine. Scanning the pages looking for the picture stored in my mind. "Right hand page, lower right of the page," I mumbled recalling the location from my visual memory. I had to find the right page. I knew it was there.

'Solve your CNC communication problems with an Olivetti M24 and EPSON PX4,' the company add looked pretty cool (by advertising standards of the day). Without hesitation, I called, asking for a demonstration. Of course, I set the appointment time for 11am.

The salesman arrived in his sporty white car, with racing skirts and a spoiler. He carried the bulky equipment into my office. It was VERY basic. "You write your code on the PC, save it to floppy disk and then, using a cable, transfer the programme to the Epson handheld computer," his smooth talking presentation flowed beautifully. "After that, you can just walk to the machine shop and transfer the programme directly into the controller of your machine - via another cable! No more paper tape, no more magnetic tape. You will be in the world of electronic data transmission!" This salesman was good, very good. It should be noted that 'handheld' then was, by today's standards, more like a large, fat, heavy laptop! It boasted a small LCD screen, just 40 characters wide with a maximum of 8 lines of text display. Quite amazing for its time!

"But what about graphics?" I asked, knowing that we needed good back-plotting, to reduce the massive amount of wasted time and damage on the machine during trial-runs, especially with the additional axis that our new machine would be offering. Through programme control, the new punch press enabled the selection of any one of 44 tools, in less than two seconds tool-change time. Furthermore, for two of the tooling stations, we could even change the orientation of the tool between operations. Hundreds of times per minute we could change the angle of a punch and die, between hits. We *needed* a back-plotter in addition to a tape-less data transfer solution.

The salesman looked at me. He had not expected that question. He was offering 'no more tape', definitely *not* 'no more trial-runs'. He thought for a moment, with his finger parked on his chin, and then said "The Olivetti M24 has a monochrome display adapter with a choice of green or amber screen," he paused for longer than normal in his presentation flow. "My demo unit has a Hercules mono-chrome graphics adapter and, if you like, I will sell you this one." That was not the solution, but he was trying. My face must have shown a lack of total conviction in his idea. He went on, "And we are also able to provide a 20mb hard drive, as a special offer, for today only."

I was in the 'I have to make this work' zone, and had to admit that his product was solid, modern and it would be amazing to no longer work with tape. If we took the hard-drive option, I would not even need to use floppy disks to boot the machine, for the first time ever.

"Is there a programming language provided with the computer?" I asked, wondering whether I might be able to write my own back-plotter.

Salesman came alive, both hands lifting up as if to thank the heavens above, "Oh, yes and every system is delivered with the latest programming language package called GW BASIC."

I knew of BASIC, Beginners All Purpose Symbolic Instruction Code, and had read about it, even dabbling with a few lines on a school Commodore PET 8 Kb computer, but not very seriously. "What does GW stand for?" I asked, feeling a little dumb.

"GEE WHIZ," came the proud reply, followed a second later by "I am sure you could write your own software to back-plot your programmes. These PCs are amazing and with a little effort you will surely be able to make it all work." He was good at selling. I was in need of a glimmer of hope.

Statistically, the salesman's promise reduces logarithmically in value for every step he takes away from a sale. I knew that. But, here was a potential solution, within the budget on the table. Sitting between a large rock and a very hard place, with a ticking clock, a decision, good or bad, had to be made.

We moved next door to the owner's desk, a cheque was written and the demo equipment stayed with me. There were three manuals. One large one called 'MS DOS 2.11', another equally large one called 'GW-BASIC' and the third skinny one with a dozen badly duplicated sheets called 'Writing and Transferring your part-programmes using the Epson PX4'. We were just within budget, but still without what we really needed; a back plotter. The salesman agreed to bring the 20mb hard-drive in a few weeks. No problem, I

Wonderful Adversity: Into Africa

could work with a twin floppy machine until then. It was already many times better than what I had been working with and I would just have to make it work.

The new CNC part-programme editor was better than the old one, but still very simple. For those who know 'notepad' in modern operating systems, then you already have something many times more powerful than I had then.

Line numbers, complicated keyboard commands, the need for three hands - or at least two hands and an agile nose, were often the demands of the day! It worked, and we all felt thoroughly modern!

I wrote a couple of lines of CNC code on the new PC, transferred them by cable to the hand-held Epson, and went out to the shop floor, feeding the code back and forth to a machine tool without any tape involved. It actually worked. I felt twenty feet tall. I had discovered the beauty of RS232 data transfer! It made paper tape look so archaic. We were at the cutting edge of technology! Even Mr F said something close to complimentary.

The owner got all excited, exclaiming, "So, we have solved ALL of our problems! Within budget!" Before I could explain that there was more to it than that, he was already moving, happy as Larry on a sunny Sunday afternoon, and halfway out the door to his Jaguar motor car, off to his restaurant lunch.

I took the GW-BASIC manual home and read it, cover-to-cover, twice. Once I had committed the key words and syntax to memory, I was ready to type some lines of GW-BASIC programming code. I had barely a week left before the new machine would be commissioned, and nobody knew how badly off we would be unless I could make this solution work.

Feeling the weight of around forty people's jobs sitting on my shoulders, I sat in front of the glow of the monitor. The Italian made keyboard was a little sticky and tacky, perhaps spaghetti tainted. If I typed too fast it would freeze, so I typed as if pretending to be a metronome. If I got ahead of myself, I would lose all my work. I learned fast, and swore a lot. Every now and then I had to pause, and wait for the typed characters to catch up.

Having watched machine tools interpret CNC code and numbers to intricate machine movements, I was sure that it would be possible to simulate some graphical representation using this Gee Whiz BASIC thingy! Hercules graphics programming was not something that came naturally. Graphical output was relatively new, and making things look right was tough. Getting a circle to look like a circle instead of a badly laid egg took some doing.

For the next five or six days I did not go home, eating chocolate bars and drinking soft drinks to keep me operational. I sat in front of the machine, sleeping snatches of thirty minutes here and there, on the floor. All the months of sleeping flat on my back on a hard mattress whilst in hospital had me well conditioned to sleep on any factory floor!

The code worked... then failed... got tweaked... worked... added to... failed... tweaked...worked... failed... worked... seemingly ad infinitum. I learned that computer systems tease you with a statement that they love; 'Syntax Error'. It actually means 'you did not write the code exactly as it was needed to be written to be understood by the computer'. To me it meant 'DUMB ASS - TRY AGAIN'. That computer called me a dumb ass more times than I want to remember. Each new 'DUMB ASS' moment motivated me to modify the programme structure. Bit by bit, word by word, instruction by instruction, the machine became more and more polite, and my software more robust.

Finally, just as the installation team commenced unloading the new CNC machine tool using a crane, outside my office window, I achieved my first useable working back-plot for the new robot. It was not perfect, but it would work. I almost jumped for joy, but could not let the owner know how close to cutting the hair holding Damocles' sword above his head I actually was.

I had not slept much over the past few days, but excitement kept me from wanting to sleep anyway. I watched as the beautiful Hammerite blue painted machine was positioned on the shop floor. Then, and only then, did feel permitted to go home, and to sleep.

The next day the machine was commissioned. When the installation engineer asked for a 'test programme', I came out and fed one in by cable. The owner, Mr F and I felt taller than the building. The installation engineer was amazed at the modern equipment and programme transfer - without tape and without a mini-computer. His astonishment was complete when, with probably unjustified confidence, I declared "Just run the programme, I have already proven it on the screen."

If I was wrong, we would scrap the production material and potentially damage the machine. I remembered one story, written in a magazine, of a similar situation which resulted in tens of thousands of pounds of damage and a machine being off-line for weeks. But it was too late now, we had committed, all on my word.

He pressed the start button, the machine came to life, motors whirred, hydraulics hummed and the machine moved a one hundred kilo (two hundred and twenty pound) piece of material effortlessly across the bed. The tool selector spun its massive carrousel around, indexing pins slammed with a clunk into place. The ram smacked down on a punch, leaving a hole in just the right place. The programme continued to run, with hundreds of hits taking place, even with tool rotation between hits. It was something totally new to me, but I had proven the programme in my home-grown back-plotter, knowing what should happen. The part was perfect, first time. I was relieved. I was not alone in that deep feeling. The owner, and even Mr F, were happy and, perhaps most importantly, forty men and women were secured in their jobs for the time being!

Each day I added to the abilities of my software, making it more and more capable. Then, the salesman, who had sold me the equipment, came by with the long overdue 20mb hard-drive. We installed it together. Afterwards, I showed him my progress with the back-plotter. He was impressed, practically admitting that he really did not think that somebody without programming experience would be able to do what I had set out to do, let alone accomplish a functional, high standard product.

As he left, he told me "If you ever want to earn more money, and travel around the country, we have a job for you."

I laughed, explaining "I gave up earning more money to work closer to home, to be near my family, and frankly, I enjoy working in engineering!" Little did I realise how much I would appreciate his proposal in the coming months.

SECOND CHILD

It was New Year's Eve, and I was enjoying time at home with the family. My son was walking, potty trained and had only had one more seizure. I had learned all about seizures and how to deal with them, we even kept emergency medical supplies on hand. Just another skill to keep in my back pocket, just in case I needed it again. He was old enough, and fit enough, to go to the local nursery school for morning sessions, and thus my wife could take a part-time job to support the finances. Much as I enjoyed working in the factory, and being home each evening, the money was tight - and getting tighter with a growing young man in the house. How many new sets of clothes per year can a kid really get through?

We signed him up to for play school, and the missus started looking for a part-time job. The day after she was offered a job, she missed her period. Number two was wonderfully on the way! But, no part-time job, since she did not feel very well, very early on.

Looking at the finances it would be tight, but it could be done. I could work some overtime, and it would be OK. My wife was not carrying well. She had a lot of morning sickness, and so I took on taking our lad to and from his daily social and learning activities, on top of my workload. It was fun, but it did add a good bit of time to the morning starts.

By six months, my wife was in a very bad way, and I had started to crack under the strain. The finances and workload were becoming too much. Dropping the lad into nursery one morning I simply burst into tears. The lady in charge took me into a side room and let me sob my heart out. A big hug and a smile later, she recommended that I call in sick for the day, and go straight to the doctors.

The doctor was a good friend, even if he did not like me teasing him by calling him 'Quack'.

"Morning Quack," I half smiled through my reddened eyes at the professional across from me. I didn't need to say anything more, since he was seeing my wife each week with her complications. He knew the score.

"You need to change jobs," he told me straight. I knew it, but being told it was tough. I did not want to change jobs. I liked my job and my colleagues. I loved my machines, it would be like treachery to leave now.

"I need to tell you that your next child is in danger if you cannot help your wife to overcome some of the challenges she is going through. She is worried by the current situation. Only you can change it," he brutally and honestly lay out the facts.

I called the programming systems salesman. Within an hour I had a job offer with double salary, plus commission and a brand new company car. Sadly, it would mean lots of travelling, again. My new job would entail travelling around the country troubleshooting and solving problems for CNC production. It was a good job, a very good job.

Worried about leaving my team and especially that pretty blue machine, I approached the owner with my resignation, he seemed relieved. "It is probably not a bad thing," he offered, "we have just lost a major contract, and will be downsizing. Maybe even worse. But, that is between us. Not for sharing," he confided.

I agreed to help out by popping-in from time-to-time to check on my replacement, a school leaver, working on an absolute pittance. He had a good sharp mind, but no experience.

My first day in the new job was exciting. No more money worries, a nice car and a great deal of positives to look forward to. I had to make the most out of the way things had played out. My wife was visibly relieved at the change in fortune, we could afford more time in nursery for the lad and purchase all the things we now needed for baby number two, who was getting ready to enter the world.

I drove thousands of miles, having the opportunity to work on the most amazing projects. My ability to read drawings, write CNC programmes, configure and wire RS232 connections, run cables, fix and manage computers, write software to overcome challenges in the factory situation, etc. all came in handy as I encountered new clients every day.

One client was making anti-tank bullet tips. They were machined out of a special manganese alloy that had a nasty habit of 'melting the machine tool', if machined too hard and fast. I walked in and, whilst chatting to the machinist about the problems in production, picked up a shiny, just completed, work-piece to inspect. It was beautiful. Shining, reflective as

Wonderful Adversity: Into Africa

polished silver, finished to the same quality standards as a Rolex watch, it smiled at me! I looked up from my discourse, wondering why everything had gone so quiet around me. All the workers were moving away from me, watching, as if I had some dreaded disease.

"Put it down slowly and carefully," an operator called to me from a few metres away.

I thought they were all joking. But they weren't! It was not just an expensive piece of workmanship, but one that did not like hard impacts without reacting with a sudden violent outcome! These were parts of anti-tank bullets, after all!

A week later, I found myself inside a steel mill, watching armoured plate coming out of the furnace and, after rolling, being sent to a massive CNC Plasma machine, complete with a floodable water bed. It was about the size of a swimming pool, capable of cutting armoured plate at speeds exceeding one metre per minute. The computer to operate it was so old school, it still took up a complete room!

I got to work on solving problems for products to both make and to destroy armoured tanks! How ironic. How interesting. Using all the communication skills from my past, I learned more and more from each site I went to. Every CNC controller was a bit different, every programming system had its quirk. It felt like I was mastering them, one by one.

Everything was not always good. Travelling all of those long miles, I became fond of driving fast. Not a good habit, and one that gave me a scare.

It was a Friday afternoon, and I had travelled the length and breadth of the country during the week. On my way back towards home, speeding at just 120miles per hour (192kph), I felt invincible. The road was almost empty, and I was one of about six cars, in a row, all holding a safe distance from each other. I felt safe, being the last car in the row, even if we were driving 50 miles per hour over the speed limit.

Then I looked in my rear view mirror, to see another car coming in behind me, but not respecting a safe distance. It took me a second, but then I realised that the car behind me was a police car. I started to slow before he flashed lights and allowed his sirens to make a nasty body-noise-like sound for a second.

Slowing down, I pulled in. He parked in front of me. This was not like my police encounter on the way to the hospital. This was serious. I was shaking. My legs were jelly, and my hands wobbled. I could not get out of the car. The adrenalin rush from driving fast was dissipating rapidly. In exhaustion, after the long week, my head fell forward onto the steering wheel.

I heard the knocking of the policeman's fist on my window. Turning my head, rather than wind down the window, I just opened the door. He crouched down next to me. I think that he realised that I was shaking both on the outside and the inside.

"Are you alright, Sir?" he asked politely. You have to love the British Police. They must be the most polite on the planet!

"No, I am sorry for speeding. I know I was doing 120 miles per hour in a 70 zone," my honesty side threw me willingly at the mercy of the law.

"Well, Sir, that is funny," he laughed, "we only clocked you at 104miles per hour!"

He placed his large glove covered hand on my shaking arm, saying, "Don't worry, we will only book you for the 104." He paused, watching, perhaps hoping that some colour would return to my ashen face. It didn't.

"What will happen?" I asked, thinking I would get a fine.

"Well, you will certainly lose your licence," his words, said so kindly, plunging deep into my heart.

"But I need to drive, it is part of my job, and I have a wife and two children to look after," I pleaded.

"I am sorry, Sir, but you will need to explain that to the judge. I suggest that you get a good lawyer," he explained. Taking my details and handing me my 'offence slip', he added "You will be sent your court date in the post." Returning to his car, he drove off.

I sat in silence for at least another ten minutes, and then drove home, at exactly the speed limit.

On the Monday morning I called a fiend, I mean friend, who was a lawyer. He laughed at my story. "You will lose your licence for one year, and be fined at least one thousand pounds. Simple. But I will defend you in court, and try to get a reduction for you. They should take into account that it is your first offence." he informed me.

"How much?" I asked, hoping that it would not be much.

"Well, you know it will be in a court near where the incident happened, so with travelling and paperwork you should budget four thousand pounds for my services," he bargained.

I think that I forgot to breathe for a while, and it is possible that my heart stopped beating once or twice, and then I responded "Can't I defend myself?"

He laughed heartily. Between chuckles, he proposed "You can try... but it will be more costly in the long run!"

The decision took me less than a second. I decided to defend myself.

The court date came in the post, and I took a day off of work to attend. My wife drove with me to the court, in case I lost my licence on the spot and needed to be driven home.

Walking from the car park to the Court entrance was really scary. There were hundreds of policemen, and vans being unloaded with packs of unruly women. There was shouting at the police by the antagonistic hoard exiting each van. Amazingly, the police remained calm and collected.

I had been given a court date that coincided with the Greenham Common peace protesters court date. Lots of women who were campaigning against

Wonderful Adversity: Into Africa

nuclear weapons, who had chained themselves to fences, and committed other acts to get their point of view taken into account, were being arraigned. I had never seen so many policemen, and it made me even more uneasy about the task ahead of me.

Mine was the first case of the day in the Magistrates Court. That means that the case is heard by three Magistrates, no jury, just three Justices of the Peace also known as JP's.

Called to the witness box, I was sworn in. I must have been shaking so badly. It was such a black room, full of police, legal folks and... me.

"Where is your legal representation?" the gown and wig clad JP asked me.

"I... I.... I," the words were in my head, but they couldn't reach my mouth. Another first.

I hadn't breathed in a while and words were clearly not able to come out without a fight. Taking a deep inhalation of stale court air, squeezing as much oxygen to my brain as possible, I launched a bid to liberate the word hostages from my mind. It worked. The words were released and a I stated "I represent myself."

They all smiled, clearly thinking to themselves "This is going to be a good one!"

"Tell us what happened," came the demand from the Magistrate in the middle.

Remembering that telling the truth may not get the best result, but that telling a lie may get a worse one, I decided to go with the full truth. I took another deep breath, making a concentrated effort to release my statement.

"Well, I was driving as the last of six cars, going at over 100 miles per hour on the motorway. After a long week and wanting to get home, I failed to respect the speed limit," I had started, but still had to finish. "Then I saw a police car behind me. At that point I said to myself 'oops you've been caught' and pulled over. That is when the policeman gave me a ticket."

The entire court rippled with a giggle. I felt more at ease. I had said it as it had happened. It was the truth. From the bench in front of the Magistrates, a young woman stood up. She was the police prosecutor. She was the one who was 'taking me down' for my 'crime'. I looked at her, shaking. She looked at me, smiled, turned to the JP and spoke.

"My Lords, I would like to add that this gentleman has a clean licence, is a good citizen and has no record with the police. It is his first offence," she then sat down and looked at her papers.

I just stood in the dock, amazed. The police were now defending me, for free! They were pointing out this was my first offence in the hope of reducing my sentence. The three gowned men walked out the room, leaving me standing in the dock.

A few moments later they returned. The one in the middle looked at me, and to my total surprise stated "We have discussed your situation. I am afraid that we will have to take your driving licence away."

I wanted to die on the spot. At least he almost apologised for taking my licence. "However," he continued "based on your honesty, and the statement from the police prosecutor, we are going to give you the minimum penalty we can." He paused, piercing my soul with his eyes adding "Two weeks driving ban, starting today, and one hundred pounds fine. There will be NO penalty points on your licence." He adjusted his depth of gaze from my soul back to my eyes, adding "Will that be OK?"

I nodded, my life force started to return to my body and then I opened my stupid mouth again. "Thank you," I offered, but let my confidence getting the better of me, adding "Can I have instalments on the fine, please?" Basically, I didn't have one hundred pounds with me, and didn't know how to say it.

The court rippled, once again, with amusement. The JP himself jiggled in his seat. "OK, you can pay it over three months," his gavel smacked the wood in front of him as he declared "Case closed."

It was over. I called the office and explained the situation, and they understood. It happened all the time to folks who drive a lot in technical and sales roles. The fact that I was only 'home-office-bound' for two weeks was a surprise, but a good one.

Had I actually been banned for a year, I would probably have lost my job. Visiting my lawyer friend with the news, he was amazed. He told me "Honesty, the way you put it, is rarely the way to win a case!" His past advice had not been good, I decided to immediately discard his opinion.

My driving habits changed, and I have remained since 'a generally speed abiding citizen'. When I worked out that driving fast had saved me minutes. My lost time from one incident became WEEKS of lost time. The math made it clear that speeding only offered short term gains. All speeding does is get you between traffic jams quicker - and risks a nasty experience with the law!

I did have one other car accident. When I fell asleep at the wheel, but nobody was hurt, unless you count the caravan I drove through. That incident made me take 'driving whilst tired' more seriously.

In life we all start with two bags. One is labelled 'LUCK' and it is full. The other is labelled 'EXPERIENCE' and it is empty. The aim of the game is to fill the experience bag before you empty the luck bag. With all of my adventures I had a pretty full experience bag, and I did not want to test the contents of the luck bag.

Each week I made new sales, solved new problems, made new things, met new people. In fact, my job was amazing, the money fantastic, and nobody could want any more. However, my home-life suffered, with the travelling and long hours. The money meant that the tribe were looked after, but I missed the children, for now I had a daughter too. I loved buying her pretty clothes and would spend far too much on some dress or outfit whenever I could. But that did not make up for not being there.

Then, Wonderful Adversity, once again took a hand in my destiny.

HOSPITAL AND A FIRE

"Your son is very sick, he has a kidney problem and we need to operate," Quack was straight forward, keeping just enough eye contact for me to realise that he was really worried. "I have the results from the specialist. It is not good."

His little kidney was blocked and would need reconstructing - or perhaps he would lose it - or worse. He went from being an active little soul to passive, sleeping extensively, off-colour and weak. I was at work, driving around the country, unable to be there. I could not even make a small percentage of the hospital appointments.

I went into work one Monday morning, for a meeting with my newly appointed sales manager. He had only just been taken on to the company, and I felt sorry for what I was about to ask, but was certain that he would understand.

"My son is sick and waiting to go into hospital. I need to work close to home for the next couple of months to be available for doctors and hospital visits." I pleaded, expecting a simple acceptance, but that was not to be the case.

"With the money we pay you, we own you. Don't you realise we own your arse? You will go where we need you to go, when we need you to go there. That is what being employed on your package means," he almost spat the words out at me, but did not raise his head to look at me. My logic circuits blew, and my rash actions circuits went into overdrive.

Reaching into my pocket, I grabbed my company car keys and threw them across the desk. They slid over into his lap. He sat up straight, head jerked back and his mouth hung open, words trying to form, but not making a sound. He was both shocked and upset, but not as upset as I was.

"In that case, you can stuff your job up a place where the sun does not shine. My son is worth more than this job," it was too late; I had said it. I had just laid explosives around the bridge to my finances, and pressed the plunger of the detonator. BOOM. I felt like I was in a cartoon, and just like that coyote, trying to catch the road runner, had failed to think through the potential impact of my badly, frankly not even, thought out plan.

I was already half way across the expansive office towards the door when he called sheepishly "Perhaps we can discuss this?"

I spun on my heel, still in *impulse drive mode*, "No. No. No! If five minutes ago the life of my son meant nothing to you, then this job means nothing to me," I explained, spinning back on-course, exiting in a rage. I closed the door on the man and that chapter of my life definitively. At least he had not told me to 'GET OUT OF MY OFFICE'. That was an achievement!

I breathed so heavily that my chest hurt, and the breath coming out of my mouth made my head oscillate in reaction to the volume being exhaled. I walked straight out of the company car park and stormed up the road, with my heart beating incredibly hard and fast. At first, I stomped along. Eventually, I calmed down to a walk, and came to realise a few simple facts.

1. I no longer had a job
2. I needed one
3. I was about fifty miles from home
4. I had no transport

Well, things could have been worse! The most important thing is that I would be available for my son and his operation. As I walked more calmly, I started to think about how to get home. It was only a few miles to the nearest train station. I could walk it in less than an hour. The walk would help clear my head.

Then I saw one of those wonderfully British, rural, red telephone boxes at the side of the road. I entered the phone box and looked in the yellow pages for the phone number of my old CNC company.

"Hi, how is business?" I asked over the phone.

"We have just closed down," came the reply. "Things were so bad, I laid off the staff and now am just selling machines and supplies as I can. You made the right choice to take that new job," he concluded with unknown irony.

That was not what I wanted to hear. "Oh, OK. Best of luck, and if I can help, just let me know," I tried to sound supportive, but did not feel very supportive - nor supported!

I stood inside the phone box. Rain starting to tap lightly on the glass. A large truck flashed past me, loaded with sheet steel. I missed factory life.

As I looked into the distance I saw a rainbow in the sky. There as bold as brass, smiling at me, reassuring me that it would all be OK. I took heart, a big breath and tried some logical thinking. Something that had not happened much in the past hour.

I looked again in the yellow pages finding the name of another company I knew of. The owner smoked cigars - big cigars. He drove one of the few cars I knew of adorned with a personalised number plate. He ran a big engineering company.

I dialled the number and asked to be put through to Mr Cigar. "What do you want?" he said, and I just knew that he was leaning back in his chair, puffing on a rolled up collection of tobacco leaves.

Wonderful Adversity: Into Africa

I blurted out "I need a job," and went on, probably incoherently, to explain what had happened.

There was silence. Simply he offered "Report for work on Monday, we will work it out." The phone line went dead. He had hung up.

Was it that simple? Apparently, it was.

On the Monday morning I entered Mr Cigar's office, it was a long office. I walked past the solid oak board room table, and a line of leather upholstered chairs - the sort that make body noises if you move wrong on them. Reaching his cigar box populated desk, I paused, without saying a word. Still laying back in his chair, he opened the conversation with "Tell me more."

I explained, he asked questions. He then asked more questions about my son. "He is on the waiting list for kidney surgery, and I just need to be nearby. I need work, and I need to support my son," it was the truth, the driving force of my actions, and nothing more could be added.

Without a word to me, he leaned forwards tipping the phone off the hook and grabbing it as it fell towards the floor. "Get me the hospital," he ordered his P.A..

In the next fifteen minutes he had a date for surgery for my lad. Matt would be operated on in just over a month. That was the support I needed.

Then, he put me in charge of computer systems and CNC programming for the company. We agreed a suitable, albeit much lower than I had previously enjoyed, salary. We shook hands, his cigar hanging out of his mouth, plumes of grey-white smoke wafting above him. I walked the gauntlet out of his office, into my new job.

I carried out a systems audit, and shocked at my discoveries, asked to see Mr Cigar again. "Yup?" he puffed, along with a cloud of cigar smoke, as I entered the long office.

I started talking as I walked down the line of leather chairs. "At your current rate of operations, you have less than four weeks before your current computer system will fail. You will run out of records," it was a bold statement, but I was confident of my findings.

Laughing, he balanced his cigar away from his body and giggled "Bullshit. Not possible. I paid good money to the best programmers for engineering companies I know, in the country."

I asked him to call in his computer experts immediately. Reluctantly, after some negotiation, he complied.

Equally reluctantly the IT providers sent in a team to explain to me how stupid I was. I sat there as they entered their admin password to the system. They called up report after report showing me clearly that I was wrong. I listened. They sat back smugly, smirking. Mr Cigar stood at the door, wondering what he had done allowing me into his company.

Then, reaching over to the keyboard I pulled up a variables list, accessing their files directly from the operating system. I then hacked into their data files and showed them some reference keys. They looked at each other, back and forth, frowning.

I had encountered the same issue when writing my programmes. When the number of records exceeded 32,767, in old computer systems, you could get a problem - it is to do with managing record indexes and the use of positive only, short integer counters. It was easy to solve, but it had to be coded into their programmes. It was not something I had access to. The easiest option was to use positive *and* negative short integers, counting from -32,768 to +32,767, allowing just over 65,000 records. Alternatively, they could change the data type for record indexing to long integer, but that would change the position of data in the file management system of 'random access files'. However, if they had, moving from two bytes for short integer to four bytes for long integer would have increased the potential number range to +/- 2,000,000,000.

The team tried to argue "You do not have a problem, just archive the older data and keep your active records below the 32k limit," they proposed.

"Indeed," I responded as Mr Cigar was moving closer in, realising that there really was an issue here. "But that would mean that access to the production records more than just a few months old would be complicated - and the company is growing - they need more flexibility, and the ability to have more active records," I hoped that my counter move would result in check-mate.

"Yes, but that is how our system works. It is not a bug, just a limitation," flew the irritated response.

Mr Cigar was not happy. "That is not what you sold me. Fix it," he ordered, knocking their metaphorical king over and declaring me the winner. Off he strode, dropping cigar ash as he did so.

I looked at the team and started "Sorry, but..." I didn't need to complete my sentence.

"You are right," they confided, "we must fix it. Well done for spotting it. Oh, and if you ever want a job..." and off they went off to fix the software problem.

Mr Cigar was excellent at letting me have time for the family, and he tolerated my demands for bizarre working hours. He always got his full measure, packed down and topped up to overflowing, but not always at the normal working hours. Fortunately, the factory ran 24/7 and so, it was easy to make up time or to adjust my working to meet hospital appointments.

During this short time, I convinced the board of the need for new computers. They had money, authority and a real need! So, we ordered a new-fangled computer network. We also ordered a modern 80386 PC server and about twenty 80286 PC based workstations, plus eight new printers. Mr Cigar had suddenly got total confidence in my abilities. I did not want to let him know that I had never installed a computer network before, but that was a minor detail.

The system was all up and running just a couple of days before my lad's

Wonderful Adversity: Into Africa

surgery. So, with the updated software installed, new computers and a shiny new network doing everything it was supposed to do, I took a week off to be present for the surgery on my little Matt.

He looked so very weak, lying on the bed waiting to go to surgery. He looked at me, with his big, round, sweet blue eyes and started asking questions.

"Daddy, where does strawberry jam come from?"

"They take strawberries and crush them up with sugar to make strawberry jam," I replied, but the story was not over yet.

"Daddy, where does raspberry jam come from?" he asked, clearly having seen all the different jams in little packets at the hospital.

"They take raspberries and crush them with sugar, my love," I patiently responded.

"Daddy..."

"Yeeeeeeees," I sighed, trying not to sound even the teeniest bit exasperated.

"Where does honey come from?" he asked, tilting his head to one side. The enquiring mind of a child is insatiable!

"Well, honey is made by bees," I responded, looking around for the anaesthetist so that the necessary reconstruction of his kidney could take place, allowing me to prepare for the next round of twenty questions.

"Do they crush the bees and then add sugar to them?" came the logical next question.

"Uh, no... Let's talk about this after the surgery!" I wearily responded.

Matt and his bed disappeared down the sterile corridor, whilst my wide and I waited for the next two hours. The surgery was successful.

I opted to sleep in the hospital that night, just to be by his bedside.

At 2am I was woken up by the night nurse. "Get up quick, there is an emergency," she whispered.

I was still fully dressed, just lying on the floor, by the side of my little boy's bed. Jumping to my feet, I looked at him, drip in, drain in, he looked fine. The nurse was pulling me towards the door, where Mr Cigar was standing.

What could be the matter? Had I screwed up something on the new computer network? It was only 2am. I was dazed, and nothing made any sense under the poor illumination of hospital night lights.

As I got closer I could see black smudges on Mr Cigar's clothes and face. "The factory is on fire, come quickly," he barely finished the sentence before pulling me away from the nurse. Calling back in hushed tones "look after my boy," I was abducted and taken to the scene of a factory fire.

The word fire has an incredible ability to focus the mind, sharpen the senses and create a worst case scenario in your head all at the same time. I was now wide awake and fully alert.

Something had been left in the wrong bin in the spraying department, and an exothermic chemical reaction took place, leading to a complete wing of the building being subjected to fire and smoke damage.

The fire engines were still there, their red colour dulled by the yellow street lights, the blue flashes from their lights burning long lasting flashes into my retinas. Acrid smoke was still gripping the air, refusing to be blown away by the light night breeze, mocking the people watching. Fire is a powerful friend and yet such an evil enemy.

Finally, the fire brigade allowed company staff back into the building. I rushed up to the server room, which was also my office. I had so many papers in there, and so much new equipment. My mind had conjured up a worst case scenario. I hoped for the best, and planned for the worst. The smoke painted shadows on the walls in depths of grey, and the smell of burnt rubber grew stronger as I climbed each step. All the equipment had been powered down during the fire, and now the electrical supply was being restored sector by sector.

I quickly made sure that nothing could come back on before I had a chance to inspect for any damage, by anxiously pulling plugs from the wall sockets. Then, starting with the server, and working one by one across every computer in my area, I opened the base unit cases, checking for debris. Amazingly, there was very little damage - and most of what was found could be classified as cosmetic. Once I had checked the cabling, and been thankful that we had no computer equipment installed in the wing that was severely damaged, I carefully powered-up the system. The morning greyness was lifting, but another type of greyness still imbued the factory. My thoughts went back, loud and clear, to the mite I had abandoned in the hospital. I worked faster, and checked that everything was 'green to go', just as the office staff arrived, shocked, but ready to work.

I simply shouted "it's all good to go," passing one of the office ladies ascending the stairs, as I descended at double quick time, almost sliding down the wide steps. I headed back to the hospital post-haste.

My son was already looking better, but he was still not well. He raised his head a tiny amount, smiled, lowered his head and returned to the land of sleeping. The nurses had changed shift, and the day shift sister came up to me whispering "You are too dirty to be here, go home and get cleaned up." So, I did.

BOREDOM

My son got well,. My daughter arrived and was doing well, my wife was happy, but I was bored. I lacked challenges. I was used to constant challenges in my life. It felt odd to have everything going like clockwork.

I had programmed the systems at work, helped select new and improved CNC machines, and written some more complex software to manage programming, including programmes that would write programs on their

Wonderful Adversity: Into Africa

own.

Ready for a new challenge, I approached Mr Cigar, telling him of my boredom and desperate need for a challenge. I never expected what would be asked of me.

"I need you to extract everything you can from his mind, before he dies," Mr Cigar was not joking. He had even put his cigar down, and was leaning across the desk, his eyes piercing my very being to the core.

The company had a brilliant engineer, a man in his fifties, who had designed a solution for making a particular type of product, and was able to do the most amazing calculations. Sadly, he was diagnosed with a terminal illness, confined to his house with just a few months to live.

My mission, and I chose to accept it, was to go to his house every day for a couple of hours, for that was all he could cope with, to learn how he did his engineering magic.

Despite losing control of his muscles, and being in a wheel chair, he was ever ready to share the contents of his mind. A mind that was still as young and agile as thirty years ago.

I would ask a question, and he would answer, his mind travelling many times faster than mine, yet pushing me to keep up. I would listen, ask questions, and listen again. Some days I was terribly confused, others it started to make sense.

It would take him around forty hours to study a system. That included looking up all the relevant charts, drawing the relevant parts, working out the amount of copper, tin and other materials. Finally, he would present the solution, and the options related to it, clearly and in a simple written format. Once the system design was accepted, he would create a bill of materials and enter it into the computer system.

Week after week, I learned more. Week after week he grew more and more tired. I would take along my draft ideas, then run sample code with him, side-by-side of his manual work, and finally we produced a working product.

With my version of what was in his head, we could complete each task in less than one hour, with perfect accuracy. With practice, two or three systems could be calculated in just over one hour.

I had succeeded in extracting the man's brains - or at least his knowledge in one particular area, and computerised it. He was thrilled, but weak. Mr Cigar was happy to have the knowledge transfer, if still sad at the impending loss of a valued employee. Most importantly, a company was able to operate smoother, more efficiently and jobs were secured.

A few weeks later, my wheelchair bound friend died. I knew that I had taken out of him a legacy that would live on, running on a silicon chip. Life is fragile, but that does not mean we cannot leave a mark that is visible on this planet long after we have departed.

But I was now bored again. This last challenge had shown me that I could do so much more. Far more than I was being asked to do, and I wanted to push the edges of my operational envelope. So, I went to see Mr Cigar.

He welcomed me into his office, almost offering me a cigar, but he wouldn't, for everybody knew that I did not smoke.

"Yup?" he asked. I never fathomed how he turned that simple word into a question, and always appeared to be laid back in that big leather chair.

"I am bored," I started, hoping that there were no other members of staff nearing death and needing coded before they departed. "I want to start my own business, writing software and developing solutions for companies," I laid myself open for his acceptance or criticism of the idea.

He leaned even further back in his chair, cigar in mouth, hands behind his head. A gentle puff of white smoke lazily left his mouth around the fat cigar. Removing the cigar from his mouth, his face showed no sign of a positive or negative response.

"I agree. You are bored. You should start your own business," he paused for a massive puff on the oversized cigar in his hand. "How much will you charge per hour?"

I had not expected this question, but I told him my planned hourly rate.

"OK," his chirped, sitting upright and leaning on the table, "I will take 40 hours per week for six months."

And that is how my first computer consultancy business was started.

REFUSED PRESENT

The new company started small, working from a table in the corner of the bedroom. I would go in, or at least telephone-in, to Mr Cigar's company most days, just to check on operations, all part of our 'special deal'. Other days I would get to write some code for one unique application or another, develop my back-plotter to another level, or do a demonstration of my own CNC part programme editor, with integrated data transfer - directly from the PC to the machine tool, without any hand held devices. Each time I sold a system, I had the privilege to train the relevant staff to use the software. Most times, I would be able to add extra training in relation to programme writing too.

I started building custom computers, selecting components, receiving them at the house during the day. When the children went to bed, my wife and I would lay out the parts on the lounge floor, build the machines, load software and put them on a 12-hour 'test bench' - or rather 'test floor'. Then,

Wonderful Adversity: Into Africa

before the children would come out from breakfast into the lounge we would pack them up, loading the newly built machines into the car ready for delivery. It was a cottage industry for the computer age!

Machine tools and everything engineering was developing fast, as were the options around them. I was privileged to work on the development of some new machines, upgrading of many old, designing interfaces and solutions to improve production - and of course to make things – lots of things. Engineering is all about making things, making them well - and making them so that they improve the world.

At one site, the machine I worked on was used to make parts for the space programme; at another I worked on racing car parts; another parts for submarines; yet another on oil and gas solutions. I got to enjoy engineering from aerospace to deep sea exploration, and all that lay between the two extremes. Engineering, computing and training was my daily bread. I was having a blast.

I would often work near a small airfield, and the planes were great to watch. I liked to combine weekend sales calls near the airfield with a favourite outing for the family! The children loved to visit the airfield, at least I like to believe so! We would sit together with drinks and ice creams watching the planes take off and land.

One weekend, I had the wonderful idea to purchase a trial flight for my wife's birthday as a surprise. We all walked in to the briefing room chanting "happy birthday, happy trial flight," but, she did not want to take it. Flying was outside of her comfort zone. It is important to recognise each individuals comfort zone. It is also important to use trial flight vouchers. The children were too young to fly, and I thought back on my own RAF rejection, deciding, with encouragement from all around me, to take the trial flight myself!

I walked out onto the grass apron with my instructor. He had ginger hair, making me think of Biggles and Ginger! I may not have been Biggles - but he was definitely a dead ringer for Ginger. The apron had about a dozen little planes sitting on it. All of them were old. The usual collection of Cessna and Piper badges, interspersed with some more exotic planes that I had not seen or heard of before.

We walked around the plane, checking that it was all fit for the flight, and then we climbed aboard. Ginger was happy to answer my six point five zillion questions, and didn't giggle at any of the silly ones. I looked out of the scratched door window at my family and waved. The kids were really excited looking, pointing and jumping, waving and clearly shouting, not that I could hear anything they were yelling.

I was asked to shout the Pilot's pre-start chant of "CLEAR PROP" at the top of my voice, and then Ginger turned the key. 'Whaddyallop, whaddyllllllllallllllalalop' whimpered the engine as it failed to start. Ginger looked at me and said, '"Oh, that's nothing," and turned the key again.

'Whadddlalllllopppp whadyllll --BRRRRRMMMMMMM'. The engine roared making the prop become invisible in its spinning excitement.

I smiled, big and wide. This was a dream coming true. We taxied out to the threshold of the long grass runway. Ginger warned me that there was a dip at the fourth centre line. I had no idea why I should care, but nodded in sympathetic agreement.

"Now, add the power gently," he prompted, and so I did.

Gently for pilot and gently for a non-pilot are not really the same things. I applied the power 'my gently', which was a little too 'violent' for the man next to me. The plane lurched forwards, gaining speed as the propeller bit chunks out of the air ahead. Then we hit that little bump at the fourth centre line marker. It was just enough to get the plane airborne, and for Ginger to grab at the controls. I was happy. He was tense. We were in the air!

We climbed up to about three thousand feet, the countryside spread out beneath us as if it were a carpet and we were sitting on some bizarre chandelier, just hanging there, looking down. I looked over to see the town where we lived, and the hospital where my daughter was born.

There was a brown dirt line all around the the sky, making it look as if somebody had not scrubbed a bath ring out of the atmosphere. I asked Ginger what it was. "It is from the straw-stubble burning. The smoke and dirt sits in a layer," he explained as if it were a normal part of everyday life. He went on to point out cloud types and the rivers... and then, without me realising, we were already descending towards the ground, the runway, with a now visible dip at line four, getting bigger and bigger in the windshield.

Our wheels passed, for me at least, within a few feet of some trees as we seemed to be planning to crash into line four. It was static in the windshield and Ginger seemed to want to make it get bigger and bigger. I dared not speak, for he was Ginger and I was not Biggles!

Just as I thought we were going to keep at the same slope towards the ground, with Ginger wanting to kill line four, he gently, with a pilot gently, pulled the control column back towards him, and continued to do so long after the main wheels kissed the ground. Finally, the nose wheel gave up fighting gravity, placing itself on the centreline. Slowing, we taxied back to the apron.

That ranked as the most amazing day of my life as an activity. To be in the sky, in a little red and white Cessna, free of the bonds of earth. I was truly free, and could move in three dimensions, controlling the machine fairly well, even on that first flight, once I had grasped what 'pilot gently' meant.

The children were over excited, and wanted to hear all about it. My wife stood by my side supportive as ever. There was a lot of hugging and the children telling everybody that "Daddy went up in an aeroplane."

I realised that I had been changed in that thirty-minute excursion from the surface of the planet Earth, and it had also stimulated my children more than any other event they had been to. It was a technical, scientific, fun thing - and it was incredibly special. That one flight had opened my mind, and my ambition. I wanted to learn to fly.

I started to take flying lessons, often arranging work appointments near the flying school at the time of a suitable lesson. Flying became an obsession – more than an addiction. My wife would tell me off for always looking at the sky. I read about flying. I dreamt about flying. I talked about flying, and anything aeronautic, ad nauseam to all I met. Yes, I became an aircraft bore.

Fortunately, business was good and could finance my new found passion. As the company grew, we moved to an office, had a small workshop and I employed a programmer, technician and others. I even made front page of the local newspapers. This was a boom time, a real boom time, and I was riding the wave.

BANKRUPTCY?

One particular company I worked for, in retail outfitting solutions, placed an order for twenty custom computers - and lot of specialist software. It was the biggest order for my company to date. Extending every line of credit possible, the parts arrived; programming, production and input were in full swing. This was going to be the order that would send us all into orbit! I started to think about buying my own aeroplane, realising how wonderful could the world be.

We worked day and night on software and systems build. Testing components and software, working to make it all happen - on time. A buzz was present in the office. It was fantastic.

We were all but ready to deliver the equipment and start training, when I got a phone call. It was the finance director at the client's end. "We are closing down," he said, coldly. I thought it was a joke, but it wasn't. The next 48 hours were spent trying to establish what had happened, and whether we as a company had any recourse. Whichever way we all looked at it, it was bad. It was very bad. There was no way to get money from the collapsing client, we had a lot of 'non-returnable' items in stock, and due dates for payments looming. I had 'pre-spent' some of the profits too, in my excitement.

It was normal to provide credit; 30 days from delivery for payment, especially to a large client with a good payment history. We had never had a bad debt before, and the client in question was a regular, on time payer. I blamed myself, but it was too late, there was a large hole in the side of my boat, blown open by an economic torpedo, and water was rushing in quicker than it could be pumped out.

I would sit late into the night in the office, alone, very alone, looking at the finances. I cancelled my flying lessons and sold one of the company cars. Next, we put our house on the market. Each and every day I sought a solution to selling the overstock and recuperating the calamity in which I had taken my team. It was near impossible. There is a cascade effect from a major company collapsing in any town, and I was caught up in the mudslide of financial despair.

Then, like the final straw on a camel's back, the bank called. "You must understand that the economy has entered a bust phase, and we are calling in our debts from you and others," the stale voice informed me.

Suppliers were already making the same claims. These were not the heady happy days of learning to fly. I needed to learn to swim, and fight a new fight, in the wild ocean of financial desperation, as my business was sinking in shark infested waters.

It was simple, there was no practical choice left but to declare bankruptcy. I spent the weekend at home with the family, trying to have as much of a nice time as possible. At the opening of office hours on the Monday morning, I called the necessary people for a 'Bankruptcy consultancy meeting'. They set the meeting for Friday morning. My fate was sealed. I thought back on my parents losing their home, the goat incident and all that had run up to this point. I had done well, but not well enough. I felt depressed and full of despair. I cried, rather I wept.

I tried not to say much to anybody, but did make a courtesy visit to Mr Cigar. After all, he had helped to start it all, and I owed him an explanation. I was sure he would understand since his business was also hit by economic flak. He sat, listening intently, without smoking any leaves.

"You can come out of this better than you realise," he started, "re-negotiate your debts. You are not alone, and those who you owe money to will be happier with a settlement than waiting for a bankruptcy result. Then, discount sale every asset that you have. You can make it work."

"You mean, call all the people I owe money to, and tell them that we are about to declare bankruptcy?" my stunned response must have sounded rough since I had been crying and sniffling like a four-year-old in his office.

"Yup!" he responded, using his favourite word, leaning back in his chair, adding a smile for good measure. It raised my spirits an almost perceivable amount.

I thought about it all, and although it made no sense to me, what did I have to lose. As I rang creditor after creditor they all understood. The economic collapse of the 1980s was now in full swing, and discounting debts was all the rage. Some accepted back equipment that they had previously refused to, others negotiated to 50% payment and forgiveness of the

Wonderful Adversity: Into Africa

balance. Most impressive were the newspapers and magazines we had been advertising with. They all said "We will forgive the whole debt, in recognition of your honesty." Honesty was paying off again. It seemed that they all realised how a negotiated settlement would be worth more than trying to collect from the receiver.

My balance sheet was tipping in the right direction. But, a business is not just stock, turnover and clients. The staff are what make it all happen. I called them all together and explained to them. "I want to sell you," they laughed nervously, as I went on "I want to sell you to new employers."

Each of them looked at me, confused. I went on to explain that my software rights could be sold, as could different aspects of the business, but if I sold on condition that they took a member of staff, it would protect their jobs. I had a lot of interest in my back-plotter and code generator, and planned to sell the computer side of the business to a competitor, and with each sale, my technical and admin personnel. Amused, and possibly without choice, they all accepted, appearing to find it a rather fun experience.

I started negotiations hard and fast, and was close to a deal for each section of operations, but it was already Friday morning and time for the bankruptcy meeting.

Entering the pastel painted office I sat opposite two lawyers, one male and one female. They dressed in grey and black, almost representing the feeling in my heart as I faced them. They had stern looks on their faces, and asked me to present the papers for their consideration.

I explained, "Since Monday I have re-organised the debts and started to sell assets."

They were furious, how could I? It seems that I may have done something wrong - possibly illegal. Hands started to raise, voices got terser. I tried to keep them on the same page as me, but they were not listening. They treated me like a criminal. I had no idea that being honest could land anybody into so much hot water. Finally, I asked them to look at what I had done, whether it was right or wrong, and to please stop yelling at me – at least until AFTER they could see what I had done... right or wrong.

I showed them the situation on the books on Monday morning... which they in turn described as 'trading insolvent', getting even more excited in their posh, yet dull, clothes, taking notes and referencing little law books. Finally, they accepted to listen to what I had achieved during the week, and to look at the current situation - debts forgiven, goods returned and the offers being made for the parts of the company to be sold off.

Bemused, confused and even amused, they looked at each other, and asked me to leave the room for a moment. They did not shout 'GET OUT OF MY OFFICE', which was a surprise - and a relief!

Five long and arduous minutes passed and I was recalled to the office, like a naughty schoolboy. All the memories of the alcoholic headmaster incident came flooding back.

The She-Lawyer looked at me sternly, then dropped her eyes to the table. The He-Lawyer, face solemn enough to scare a pit-bull terrier, stared at me, analysing me with the customary lawyer look. "You have done an amazing job. You have done better than we would have done in a liquidation situation. Frankly, with what you have presented here, you are within the law, albeit only just. You are no longer in need of our services. Good luck!"

And that was that. I walked out, completed the sale of each component of the company and two weeks later had a little bit of cash in the bank - not a lot, but enough to tide us over to selling the house. It was clear that we would need to sell the house if I was to get a 'normal paid job' again, and so we pre-empted the potential long term issue with an early sale, and moved into rented accommodation. It was all OK. We were together as a family, and supporting each other. We knew of many others in worse situations - for that was the 1980s!

CONSULTANCY

After applying for many jobs, without success, since I was so called 'over qualified', I finally walked into a computer personnel agency, telling them "I need a job and I need it now."

I started the next day working as a consultant for a major computer solutions company, and had a team of eight people working under me.

It was good to no longer be looking for where the money came from - and I was being paid well enough for our needs, our downsized needs, without flying or special treats. I went from contract to contract, working all hours.

I would often have to stay away, and in order to save money, sleep in my car. I would pull into a lay-by, open the window, push back and recline the seat, and sleep - with my feet hanging out of the window. It was not healthy, but, since it kept food on the table, I didn't mind.

One night, a policeman woke me from my slumber with a crisp "Good evening Sir." I thought it was a dream about my previous experience with a police officer whilst in a car.

"Good EVENING SIR!" I heard it again, but louder. I jolted up, and nearly kicked the poor copper on the chin as I retracted my feet into the car. "You can't sleep here, move along please," he advised, and walked away. I learned that the British Police really are amazing, so understated and so correct. So, I woke myself up properly, found my shoes and 'moved along'.

I enjoyed not having to worry about paying staff, and understood the curse "I wish you many staff," much better than ever before.

Eventually, all good things come to an end. Sadly, an end to sustainable contract work was visible on the horizon. With my own business experiences, I could now see when things were not going right, and so, I started to plan the next phase of life, for my family, before impending redundancy came my way.

With the increased mobility enabled by the Common Market, now called the European Union, I decided to apply for work in mainland Europe.

FRANCE

My wife and I flew to Paris to register with a job agency there. I was wearing a suit and tie, and looked terribly British. It seemed that these mainland Europeans were far more laid back, wearing just T-shirts and jeans, so I felt very confident.

We walked into the agency. Looking around, I realised that this was going to be easy. "Good morning," speaking with the very best English accent I could muster, "I have come to register for employment in France." I went on for another five minutes listing my skills set, ambitions and how I could be of use to any European company. It felt that my speech must have sounded so posh and clear, that whatever work might exist in France must surely be mine.

"Quoi?" came the reply from the chap opposite me. "Quoi monsieur?" he asked again, clearly not enabled with any comprehension of the Queen's best English language.

Realising, the situation, I turned to my wife and said "Please explain to him that I am here to register for work in France."

She looked at me, her eyes lost in her scrunched up face of disbelief "What?"

Understanding that she might be affected by the cheese odour and wine vapour filled air of Paris, I repeated myself, louder and more clearly.

She exploded, "You mean you DON'T speak FRENCH!?" with her eyes wide open and flashing some sort of warning message. Well, she never asked me beforehand if I spoke French. I knew that *she* spoke French, and very well, but I never actually studied it for more than a couple of weeks in school, because of that little incident between my mouth and a fist.

She spoke nicely to the man behind the desk, using some strange gestures and wonderful vocabulary, which to this day I have no idea what was said. Then, her shoulders drooped as she exhaled with an exasperated hum before taking me by the arm and leading me outside. There we sat in a little bistro.

"He said, that you need to speak French to work in France," she explained, shaking her head slowly as she sipped one of those children's tea party sized coffee cups that they love in French bistros. They really do not understand the need for hydration, do they?

We went back to the airport, and flew home. Not a lot was said, but I must admit to feeling very British and terribly non-European.

I glanced at my watch. It was a good fifteen minutes past our landing time and we seemed to be flying in circles. It was already dark outside. I looked out of the window to look at the wing and engine of the turbo-prop aircraft we were flying in. The engine cowling looked great, and reminded me of pre-flights at the grass runway where I had started, but never completed, learning to fly. However, the propeller was not spinning as it should. I could actually perceive the blades, flopping slowly around. I looked down to see lots of vehicles on the ground, all over the airport, alongside the runway. There were lots of lights, flashing ones at that.

The announcement came, in that tinny nasally way that it does on aircraft, "Ladies and Gentlemen, we have a slight technical problem and our landing is delayed. Please be patient whilst we deal with the situation."

My wife paled, but I didn't. I found it exciting. I thought back to my flying lessons, long forgotten with the financial woes, and it reignited the passion to be in the air - even in an emergency.

We landed safely, most people never knew what was going on - nor if they had come close to being a part of 'The Ten O'clock News'. I had loved every moment of it - and since the landing was 'uneventful', gained even more respect for pilots – wanting to be one.

We drove home, chatting lightly about my linguistic mono-culture approach. Undeterred, I continued to write to companies I knew of, in mainland Europe, in English, just on the off chance.

A few weeks later I was offered an interview in Switzerland - with a CNC machine tool company! I had to go.

As we discussed the, albeit highly unlikely idea, of moving to Switzerland, the lad started asking awkward questions. He may well have heard his mummy talking about my little linguistic challenge in Paris.

"Daddy what language do they speak in France?" he opened the game with the first move.

"French," I answered, not really wanting to think about Paris again.

"Daddy, what language do they speak in Spain?"

"Spanish," I replied, knowing that I stood little chance of winning this game.

"Daddy, what language do they speak in England?"

"English."

"Daddy...."

"YEEEEEESSSSS."

"Daddy, what country are you going to again?"

"Switzerland," I stated, with a tinge of annoyance in my tone.

"Wow, do they speak Swittish there?" he enquired excitedly, and clearly won the game. I had to laugh, explaining that in Switzerland people speak French, Italian, German and Romansh.

He laughed at himself, as he always did, a happy little chappy, always full of fun. His younger sister wanted another hug, and I enjoyed that trade, teasing her for 'one more hug' repeatedly at each bedtime, until she giggled her way up the stairs.

The day to travel for my interview came, and my little family waved me off. I would fly into Lyon, rent a car and drive to a small town outside of Geneva. I knew that the folks in the company all spoke good English, and that my English and technical skills would be appreciated. After all, they approached me for the interview.

All the way over on the plane I was reading a French phrase book, hoping not to make such an ass out of myself on the mainland, this time around. I probably shouldn't have made the effort, for my fate was sealed very quickly.

Inside the airport it was easy, because I could 'ALWAYS SPEAK IN CAPITAL LETTERS S-L-O-W-L-Y' to make myself understood. That method got me through the car rental arrangements, enabling me to leave the desk with car keys firmly in my hand.

Letters and numbers work in most of the European languages, so finding the parking spot 'C16' for the car was within my skills. I navigated the rows of cars, listening to the Tower of Babel speak going on all around me, oblivious to whatever was being said. Opening the car boot, I threw my bag in, moved to the right hand front door and climbed in.

The car was clearly defective. Nothing was labelled in English... but worse still, there was no steering wheel, no pedals - oh, wait, they were on the other side of the car. It had completely escaped my planning that I was renting a left hand drive car. In the UK all the cars have the steering wheel on the RIGHT side.

I felt as if I was being watched by all those 'mainland people', yet I am sure that nobody really noticed... perhaps. I exited the car, went to the left door and got into a very uncomfortable driving position.

As I drove towards the airport exit, I made a constant mental effort to stay on the wrong side of the road, which was complicated by the window winder being in the place of the gearshift. My muscles pointed my left hand to change gear, but when it found the window winder, it wound the window instead. Whether this was connected to my left arm training in hospital as a child, or whether this was a common experience for those in transit from the UK to European cars, I did not want to find out. I just wanted to stop squealing up the road in first gear, winding the window up and down instead of changing gear.

Finally, I manipulated the wrong hand to change gear and discovered simultaneously that the road signs were all in foreign also. I seriously had not considered this challenge!

For simplicity, and in failing light, I decided to follow the first car out of the airport. It was a good move. The car I chose remained on the correct side of the road, for local rules, therefore, so did I. Eventually, my chosen lead car stopped at a roadside restaurant, and I followed suit. They had no idea that they were leading me into my next adventure, or even that I was following them for my own safety!

Sitting down at a small wooden table, somewhere between Lyon and Grenoble, I was ready to eat. The waitress came over with a cheery "Bonsoir!" I responded with "Bonjour."

It was good enough, even if technically wrong. After some gesticulations that would make a military aircraft marshal during a scramble look lethargic, I had managed to order a glass of water, and obtain a menu.

The menu was in foreign also. Nonetheless, I could point and say "Qu'es que c'est?" which I hoped meant "What is that?"

Waitress was wonderful, she explained what everything was in great detail with such energy and a smile to match. But I did not understand a word. My face contorted with attempts to understand. Finally, with her right index finger raised to the air, as if to hold time still, she left my table.

A few minutes later she returned with her arms full of food items. I hadn't ordered anything... had I? She held each plate in front of me, and then with exaggerated mouth and syllable work, akin to speaking French in UPPER CASE, named each option. I had the 'visual-' and, being French food, 'olfactory-menu'. With a bit of guesswork, along with plenty of "Oui, Oui," I ordered. Soon after, I ate well.

Sadly, I had lost my unmet friends who had led me to this place. They had been able to order, eat and leave long before I had completed my personal 'fiasco de gustation'. It was late, and the restaurant had some rooms free. I checked in and slept quickly, the taste of Fromage Blanc with sprinkled sugar tantalising my taste buds all the way to the land of slumber.

The next morning, I descended to a proper continental breakfast. Croissants took my fancy, and after four or five, coated in rich butter and local honey, along with a cup of hot chocolate - well it looked more like a small fish bowl - I was ready for the road. The question was which road?

In broken English, a local yokel, sadly without a bicycle or a string of onions around his neck, pointed me towards Switzerland.

Well rested, and remembering to enter the car from the left side, it was time to drive 'solo'. No more need to tail a car, just drive towards the sign that says Genève. Yes, the French do not know how to spell Geneva. Shocking and bizarre, but when you realise that the people in Geneva also call it Genève, you must wonder who has it right.

Entering Switzerland was magnificent. Most of the people spoke English. In the restaurants the waiters could often speak six or seven languages - so no need for the 'scratch and sniff menu' there.

For whatever reasons, my interview did not work out. It was a non-event, and clearly not for me. So, with time on my hands, I decided to, once again, look for work in France!

Crossing back over the border, I checked into a small hotel. Prices were low since it was outside of the tourist season. Later I discovered that I was the only guest. It was fine, since I took a long time to communicate anything, and if they had other guests they would not have had the time to play charades each time they communicated with the 'funny English guest'.

With some new words and after acting out my plight in ways that would have driven Shakespeare crazy, I conveyed the idea that I was looking for work. It didn't take long to get an interview with a small CNC production company. They needed an English-speaker, because they suffered from mono-linguistic-syndrome also. Somehow, I am not sure how, we struck a deal and even a start date. Serendipity can be found in the strangest of places, often without any common language necessary.

We were moving to France! Now, that would be an adventure!

CULTURE SHOCK

In order to avoid embarrassing situations in the future, I decided to drive the family car, a Citroen BX, to our new home. Although it was a French car, it had been built for the British market and had the steering wheel on the RIGHT side, and proper English on all the bits and bobs. I helped with some of the packing before embarking on the drive south, but left the rest of the family to complete the task, since they would follow in a few weeks, by air.

The sea crossing was a little bumpy and, once again, I decided to follow the car in front of me to avoid getting into trouble in the first few miles - I mean kilometres... because they don't have any miles in France. The French Autoroute system was incredibly smooth, fast and amazingly well disciplined. Along each of these fantastic, tolls based, highways there were places to pull in and sleep, separate from the petrol stations. This was new to me, and I liked it.

Despite sleeping in the car with my feet out of the window, I was not 'moved along'. Perhaps I could become a European after all! My sense of adventure was alive and well, and this was going to be the new start of lifetime!

As I lowered my position on the latitude count, it was time to leave the arterial routes and wind along the lower class roads. Some of the villages looked like they were still occupied by 'La Resistance', with complete streets untouched since the end of the Second World War. Reaching my destination, I had to find somewhere to stay, find a home to rent for the family, as well as start a new job and learn a new language!

My new boss, or Patron, as they are called in France, was pleasant and helpful, as were his wife and children. I think that they liked having this funny charade man around - I may not have been able to hold a conversation, but I could make for a great hour of hilarity in trying to.

It was arranged for me to stay with a very large Catholic family, slightly into the mountains. Maman and Papa lived in a massive wooden chalet with their eight children - aged from eighteen down to just two years old. I was made more welcome than I could have imagined. Papa spoke reasonably good English, and Maman had studied English in Scotland - so she spoke very clearly, but as if she had escaped from a Glasgow music festival. They were lovely, and decided that they would not speak English with me, unless absolutely necessary. It worked, in some ways.

Breakfast has always been my favourite meal of the day. French breakfast, in a family home in the mountains, made it even more attractive. Fresh bread, croissants, cheese, cut-meats and homemade jam - all washed down with a small bucket of freshly made hot chocolate - with mini-marshmallows floating on the top. It was at this table I made 'small talk', picking up little phrases, and then using them as I could.

I had stayed in the house about a week when I decided to compliment Maman about her amazing homemade jam.

"Maman, cette confiture est tres bon," I ventured, meaning "This jam is very good."

She smiled, Papa nodded and the children all giggled about my accent. So far, so good. But, I had not finished my intended compliments.

"En Angleterre, le confiture est plein de preservatives," I continued, hoping to express "In England, the jam is full of preservatives," but I had no idea of the French word for preservatives, and improvised.

The table erupted. The two older teenagers ejected fresh mouthfuls of baguette coated with jam, soaked in hot chocolate across the table, staining the red and white tablecloth, and scoring hits with blobs of bread on the heads and clothes of those opposite.

The younger children found this amusing and started their usual giggling.

Maman and Papa did not smile. They sat bolt upright - a look of shock on

Wonderful Adversity: Into Africa

their faces. I sat, bemused, confused and lightly dappled with second hand breakfast morsels.

"You mean conservateur," Papa stated, silencing the table with his glare.

I remained silent, confused and concerned at what I had done wrong.

I mentally repeated 'conservateur.... conservateur.... conservateur', wondering what on earth I could have said to cause such offence. Perhaps the jam was not homemade.

Quickly, without further conversation, we finished breakfast in silence. I set off to work.

Learning French was complicated. I had thought I was doing well... but mistakes are inevitable. I shrugged the incident off and continued in my ignorance, hoping one day to understand my gaffe.

Entering the office, I sat at my computer, writing a post-processor - a piece of code that would convert a set of commands from a drawing output to CNC code. It was easy. Of course it was - it was all in English, with numbers and letters. EASY.

Patron greeted me as he entered the room with a hearty "Bonjour!"

"Bonjour," I responded with as much cheer as I could find for being interrupted with sixteen variables running rampant in my head, all trying to make it onto the screen as fast as my fingers could type them.

Patron was wearing an overcoat, and clearly heading out for the day. He started speaking at me, but it was all foreign, and I was in programming mode, so I just threw back the odd, random "Oui, Oui," at him. It had worked before.

As he headed to the door, he said tersely "On y va," in my general direction.

Seeing him at the door, I realised that I should wish him goodbye, and lifting my head, responded "Au revoir," which I knew meant "Goodbye," but he did not go. Instead, he held the door open and yelled "ON Y VA!"

Realising that he may not have heard my first utterance, I sat upright, looked him in the eye and half yelled "AU REVOIR!" very clearly. I was getting good at French.

With a frustrated look on his face, Patron went to the cupboard and took out my coat. He came up behind me and, pulling me to my feet and towards the door repeated, as if his batteries were running low, "ON," pause "Y," pause "VA."

I put on my coat and made a mental note that "On y va," must mean "Let's go." That was easy, I could use that!

We went on a field visit where I worked on machines, whilst Patron spoke French with the client. I didn't need to speak French, machines communicate in binary and hexadecimal which is much easier to understand.

On the way back he took me to a restaurant for lunch. I was able to order pretty well, and felt proud of myself - certain that Patron was happy too. The food was taking a while, so I excused myself to go to 'la toilet'. To take a

British wee wee, not a French Oui oui!

As I entered the toilet, I saw a machine on the wall - a standard issue, well known brand condom vending machine. Nothing unusual in that. However, it had a big sign on it, which made me remember why my shirt still had some chocolate stains from breakfast. The sign said 'PRESERVATIVES'. Yes, the French call condoms PRESERVATIVES. I had proclaimed to the breakfast table, just a few hours earlier that British jam is full of CONDOMS! No wonder the table erupted... no wonder the very Catholic Maman and Papa were so stern. No wonder two teenagers jettisoned their breakfast across the table. I was mortified - for a moment. I started to laugh, finally getting the joke! Finally, I was relieved of my linguistic suspense in a restaurant washroom.

With a flat rented, and the family on their way, it was time to leave the relative safety of Maman and Papa, and to enter the town, a very different place to the mountain chalet.

Both children were enrolled in school, picking up French far quicker than I. My wife integrated to the local community, being linguistically enabled. I, however, was now working on the shop floor, setting up some new machinery.

Here, I would discover 'real French'. My colleagues seemed to plan, each day, to teach me something new for my language skills. They also enjoyed teaching me the wrong word for things, and swear words - as if they were not. I had no idea. To make matters worse, my wife and children had no idea about French swear words. Why would they? They are not taught in school, and genteel ladies are too polite.

One afternoon, a letter came home. It specifically requested that Papa (me) should attend the school for a meeting with children's teacher. La maîtresse d'école was very pleasant, and very French. She was bubbling with excitement, able to sing conjugation songs and say "Ooh la la!" just like a good French teacher should.

"Monsieur, we 'ave a problemmme," she expressed, tilting her head to one side, with a wry smile.

"Oui?" I responded in my best French.

"Oui, oui, monsieur, we 'ave..."

She went on to explain, in heavily French accented English, that the children had some interesting phrases, which did not belong in a primary school. When asked where they had heard the words used, MY NAME came up.

At least the children were honest... but that got me into trouble at school as a child... and now my children's honesty was getting me into trouble at school as an adult. You just can't win sometimes!

I learned, they learned and La maîtresse d'école learned too. What I learned most was that making an attempt was as important, if not more so, than getting it right. Learning by making mistakes - and thankfully being corrected by those with the patience to do so - is an essential skill. Not trying to say something in another language in case you screw it up - or use an inappropriate word - is not the way to learn. Much as in engineering, when we make something that doesn't work, we often learn, as a result, what we need do to do in order to make it work. Mistakes are the fruits picked on the training grounds of any new skill.

For me, at least, it worked. After a few months I was able to teach other people CNC and related skills, in French, without unintentionally insulting them, talking about condoms or shouting "OUI OUI" at everything I didn't understand. I never took any lessons or a course - because my life was the course - and I learned from it every day.

Life was good, I made a good living, and we eventually purchased a little house in the mountains, right on the edge of the ski slopes. I had become more than an Englishman, more than a Brit, I had become European.

ALCOHOL

The village we lived in was small, just a few hundred people. We were the only foreigners and, amazingly, were well accepted. Perhaps because we made mistakes and learned from them, as we tried to fit into village life.

My biggest mistake was to try to integrate into certain French cultural habits.

I had never been a drinker, and never got drunk, nor smoked. Some would say I was a Goody two shoes, but I think that I just did not see the need for stimulants. I got into enough trouble without them!

All the same, I tried never to offend. I found that alcohol dulled my senses, and I did not like lacking full control of myself, nonetheless, I tried to adapt to the alco-culture in a village where they had a communal distillery. In effect it meant accepting glasses of wine with a meal was expected, as well as aperitifs and digestives. I did not enjoy it, and would make each glass last a whole evening, and then leave some. Worse than that was the 'eau-de-vie' meaning 'water of life' but that is not a good name for it. Imagine fire-water, schnapps, moonshine and industrial degreasing agents, along with a little brandy essence - and that was 'eau-de-vie'. I was clearly not a connoisseur.

In the winter, if you went to meet somebody early in the morning, they would offer you some of this liquid rocket fuel - to warm you up! Fortunately, it was served in very small glasses, even smaller than the typical children's tea party coffee cups they used; something more like a little glass thimble. I partook, by obligation and a desire to integrate to the mountain community. It took the back off of my throat every time, and left me a few brain cells shorter than I started. I was not sure if I had sufficient brain cells to keep up this regular sacrifice to the alcohol gods!

As I worked to integrate, I would try to help those 'in-need' within the village, and one old lady, very French and very old, caught my eye one day. It was about a kilometre from our house, and there she was, outside huddled over with a black headscarf around her thinning, snowy white, hair. I asked her in my best French accent how she was. She replied 'not good', in local language. She explained that she had lost all her electricity in her home. I had rewired our house, and had some spare parts left over, so I offered to take a look.

We entered the farm house by the barn door. It was dark, dank and musty beyond belief. Some chickens ran in and out between our legs as she hobbled in, never straightening up her bent form. She pointed to the problem, it was simply wiring. The cotton covered solid copper wires from the 1940's were so deteriorated that nothing was going to work. Her entire 'electrical system' was two light bulbs and one electric socket! I offered to fix it up for her. After all, I had all it would take in my tool box at the house.

Feeling community minded, spirited and integrated, I walked briskly home and collected the necessary items. Within a couple of hours, she had all new wires, new sockets, lights and switches. It cost me nothing more than my time. It gave me a great deal of satisfaction. But the story was not over.

The old lady asked me to meet her sister. Now, I had walked and driven past this house many times, and only ever seen the 'old lady', nobody else. So, I was surprised, but not as surprised as I would be.

She led me into the kitchen, heated by a wood burning stove. Behind the stove there was a bed, and on the bed a seemingly lifeless form. I looked closer, to confirm that it was human. I walked closer, wondering what I was about to discover. It was indeed a very, very old lady. Her skin was wrinkled and there was very little flesh around her bones. I held my breath and watched to see if there was any, even a tiny, sign of life. I watched, waited and then, to my relief, saw a small flinch. Relaxing and resuming normal breathing, inhaling the wood-smoke blended with a strong smell of sausage drying above the stove, I realised that this was, truly, her older sister!

I greeted, or at least addressed, the nonagenarian. Unsure if she heard or understood, I started to make my exit. As I moved back through the barn, with a glimmer of light reaching through the wooden barn doors, my arm was touched gently by the lady I came to help. She told me that I couldn't leave without taking some 'eau de vie'. Reluctantly, and not wanting to offend, I accepted the kindness.

She reached up into an old dresser and brought down an unlabelled bottle of yellow liquid. She filled a larger than usual thimble with the concoction and watched as I drank it. She wanted to see me drink it all. Downing the last drop, and already feeling a little disorientated, I asked her huskily "What was that?"

"Oh, it is the eau de vie from the root of gentian violets," she exclaimed, all pleased with herself, adding "My brother made it."

"Oh!" I responded, rather surprised and feeling less well by the second. "Where is he?"

"He is dead," came the blunt, sad response."He died thirty years ago!"

The next thing I remember is fumbling my way towards the front door of my house. I was not feeling good. I may well have been suffering from 30-year-old alcohol poisoning. Apparently, it took me several hours to make the short journey home.

The next morning, I felt rough, and decided that I had to stop being so polite to everybody. I had lost control of myself from that little drink. I wondered what would have happened if my children or wife had needed me. I would not have been able to drive to the doctor or the hospital. From that day onwards I changed my approach to all alcoholic beverages - even to alcohol filled chocolates!

I never *needed* alcohol to make me happy or to be fun - I could be silly without that! Furthermore, I certainly would never want to go through that feeling again. I had responsibilities, and losing even a little bit of my judgement could mean that I would make a mistake that could harm others - or even result in loss of life. It struck me so hard, I became teetotal.

ACCIDENT

As part of my work, I would get to drive to different parts of the French Alps. It was so beautiful - actually, no, it wasn't. It was much more than that - and more than any mass of words can ever describe. Every day the views would change, becoming more and more engrossing as they shouted out, silently, how magnificent mountain living is.

In autumn the leaves would start experimenting with their pre-death palette of oranges, yellows, reds and browns, weaving their last breath-taking moments into the panorama before they falling to become leaf litter. The scenery would sit waiting, begging for the first fall of snow, to sprinkle a little extra enchantment. It was a time to be cautious on the roads, for many dangers lurked. There was always the risk of deer or wild boar running across the road - and undisciplined drivers cutting the corners! The pending risk of ice and snow, just around the corner, signalled the need for additional care in all manoeuvres.

It was just dusk as I was driving back from the other side of the mountain towards home. I was driving to the speed limit, as generally I did, and certainly did in the mountains. My lights would sometimes pick out movements behind the trees - perhaps a boar, maybe a deer. I hated the cars coming the other way, towards me, spoiling my opportunities to find out what might have been living in the trees ahead by pre-disturbing them.

I descended a major slope, into the valley, mostly in second gear. I had to pick up some speed in the final part of the descent to enable a smooth ascent on the next part of the road. The dip at the bottom was well exposed to the prevailing winds, and twisted slightly before the climb. I had driven it a thousand times before, and knew it well.

Approaching the end of the down-slope, a deer dashed across in front of me, making me smile. I shifted to third and added a little bit of throttle the speedometer started to reflect the increase in speed, but remaining within the limits of the road. I turned to the left on the first part of the bottoming out. As I added the slightest directional correction to the right, ready to mount the slope ahead, all steering inputs failed to gain a response.

My lights no longer illuminated the road, but now the trees. I teased the brakes, gently, trying to arrest the speed that I still had. Nothing happened. I was on black-ice. The exposed piece of road at the bottom of the valley had cooled enough to put the thinnest layer of invisible ice between my tyres and the tarmac. Without traction there was no point in applying brakes. I would have to ride out the energy. With some counter steering, and a lot of luck, I saw the trees pass my left window, and the road started to become visible on my right. I worked the steering to try to regain control, hunting for any traction that might be on offer.

Just as I thought I would make it fully back onto the road, and home to my family, the front left wheel plunged off the edge of solid ground. As the frame of the car contacted the remnant of road edge it pivoted. I was instantly facing downwards, looking at a set of rock steps coming closer by the millisecond. The front of the car impacted a step. My whole body was thrown forwards, straining the seat belt. The back of the car accelerated and passed behind me and to my left, leaving me just swivelling in space. The lights now shone on a solid stone wall, which appeared to take a bite out of the remaining front end of the car, and with it both the front lights went dead, and the engine stalled. Silence.

Time stood still, but it was not over. What felt like a second or two later, there was a loud bang, as the back end of the car slammed home and lodged onto the steps. My body slammed back forcefully into the chair, my knuckles hurting with squeezing the steering wheel. The ride was over. It had all come to a standstill. I knew that I was in a bad way. No cuts and no bruises, but my back was on fire. I could feel that familiar hand grenade exploding - but this time it had been accompanied by a Claymore mine and some sort of small nuclear device!

I just sat. I could not do anything else. As I sat, I contemplated whether I was dead or alive. Concluding 'alive', simply by the pain shooting down my legs and exploding out of my toes, I realised, once again, that I had to 'embrace the pain'.

A door in the side of the wall opened, allowing a shaft of light to reflect off of the freshly exposed sheet metal that used to be my car. An older gentleman came up to my door, opening it against bent metal, torch in hand, and asking if I was OK. Realising that I was not, he called the emergency services.

There were some occasional glimpses of the inside of an ambulance before I woke up in hospital. The weeks that ensued were filled with tests, x-rays and suppositories. Yes, the French health professionals love suppositories. I decided not to ask why.

CAT scans showed the worst. My back, at the site of the operations many years ago, had been destabilised. Doctors drew lines and marked angles. More tests. Dye was injected into my spinal column for some special x-rays, and it all seemed to run together, one day into another. The pain medication was very strong, which was good in some ways, but it dulled my mind to a similar level to that of my drinking the last thimble of eau-de-vie in an old lady's barn. I couldn't do anything. I was as useful as a three-week old cabbage.

One day a man came along and took the hospital bed, with me on it, off to a room, deep in the hospital basement. There in the middle of the room was a noose - similar to that which is used for hanging people who had done something wrong. I was positioned beneath the noose, raised to a standing position, the noose was placed around my neck and slowly tightened with an upwards pull; my back felt tight and I screamed. There was no point in screaming, this was a long way from the wards, and nobody came running.

Then two men stripped me all but naked, and started to coat me in plaster of Paris. From my armpits to my hips. They left me hanging there, saying something as they left the room, but it made no sense. The feeling in my feet was impaired, but I was certain that I still maintained some contact with the cold floor. I fell asleep, the drugs preventing my eyelids from remaining open. When I awoke I was back on the ward. The plaster was gone. Perhaps it was just a dream.

A few days later the hanging man returned. He had a large plastic bag, with what looked like the torso of a human being in it. Indeed, that was the contents of his bag. MY TORSO. He had formed a plastic corset, so hard and strong that it would allow me to return to standing up without compression of my spine. He had needed the plaster-cast in order to mould it.

I was told to roll on my side, and they slipped the medieval-torture-looking-device under my body. Rolling me onto my back and showing me how to pull the six straps tight, locking my upper body into a rock solid casing. Tears ran down my cheeks, but I did not let out any whimper or scream, for I knew this was a necessary part of my life now.

Once strapped in, breathing was possible, just. Any twisting or bending of my spine was impossible. This was my prosthesis, my ticket to standing unaided. In order to exit the bed, I had to rock myself onto my side and swing my legs over the edge of the bed, keeping them bent as if already sitting down. Using my hands I could push-and-pull myself into an actual sitting position.

From there, I would learn, once again, to walk. The pain was omnipresent. The challenge of moving each leg forwards taking more concentration than that required to dissect out Malpighian tubules from a Rhodnius Prolixus.

Finally, I was discharged from hospital, with a letter. It stated that I would not be able to work again. I was eligible for early retirement on medical grounds. I was able to return home, and asked to remember to move slowly. I could only get out of bed comfortably whilst wearing my prosthesis.

I wanted to drive, and technically there were no reasons not to. However, no matter how I tried, my left leg would simply not depress the clutch and sustain the pressure. Each time I tried, it fired scud missiles up my legs and into my lower back. I refused to give in to this limitation, and pushed myself day after day, month after month. With time, I learned to drive again, but only an automatic. We changed our car to a smaller one, with an automatic box.

I could no longer work in the factory, and my wife had taken two jobs to keep the family fed. She taught in a local school during the day, and washed up dishes in a local guest house in the evenings. I had to do something. I had to return to being the breadwinner. But how?

I could not sit, for more than about ten minutes, in a normal chair. At home I used a special sitting device, which basically let me sit on my knees, with my thighs at 45 degrees to my body. It was comfortable enough to be able to work at the computer for a couple of hours at a time. So, I returned to writing software on contract. I got a few simple contracts - mainly for some of the many small CNC workshops, scattered around the mountain side. I had good days and bad days.

One good day was when the children had their friends over to play. I could not pick the children up, nor have them sit on my lap. Kicking a ball was out of the question. So I had to find other ways to share special moments with them.

I took an old computer circuit board and hid it inside my shirt. Then, walking like a robot, went towards the children complaining that I had a 'circuit failure'. Being compassionate children, who had not watched any Hollywood disaster movies about robots, they all gathered around. I started to tap my chest and sides - all solid from my prosthesis. They too started to tap me, and found it fascinating. Then, faking a total 'systems failure', I pulled out the hidden circuit board and declared "SYSTEMS SHUT D O W N," standing motionless with the board in my hand. They loved it. My daughter lovingly replaced the circuit board inside my shirt, and I 'returned to life'. Such is the way to have a good day in such circumstances.

DEPRESSION

The bad days were black. Very black. Very, very black. My personal life was gone. I had become hard, remote and removed as a husband. I couldn't stand any touching of my body, and I hated my physical condition. I was not earning enough to enable my wife to stop working two shifts, and the finances, once again, were getting too much. The pain was dulled by medication, but my neurons fired salvo after salvo of debilitating shock-waves in the unending battle of damaged bones, cartilages, muscles and nerves.

With my 'never work again' letter, my limited walking, limited driving, constant medication, coupled with my resultant snappy and irritated personality, I felt ready to die. Dark thoughts entered my head daily, then hourly, and finally they started to consume me. I was clearly depressed, but I did not let my dark thoughts out to the public. I would still smile when 'on display'. Nobody knew the pain I went through to walk, to slowly go down three steps or to wipe my own bottom. I allowed nobody to realise just a sneeze was like a volcanic eruption of agony, running from my back in all directions. Nobody could possibly understand the sores beneath the prosthesis - or the frustration at having to put it on, before leaving the horizontal, and only being able to remove it at the end of the day, once back in bed. I felt as if those wanting to encourage me, were simply looking on and saying "OH you are doing so well," without any inkling of an understanding. I may have been doing relatively well physically, but mentally... mentally I was worse than a mess, I was scrap metal, twisted and rusty, waiting to go to the furnace.

One night, as I lay painfully awake, after taking far too much medication, and creating a chemical storm in my own brain. I lay considering my limited

options. I contemplated into the depths of the worst thoughts any man can have.
   a. I could continue, being a burden to my family
   b. I could leave them and live a miserable life alone or
   c. I could die and release them.

At that point, death was the most welcoming option. However, my rational mind was still functioning, albeit off of normal logic through the mist of the medication. I reasoned that, if I committed suicide, it would mean no insurance pay-out, and shame on my family. I could not do that to them. So I started to contemplate the perfect suicide. A suicide that would not look like one.

There had been a recent suicide nearby on a particular mountain road. A young couple had driven over the edge, holding hands, leaving life behind, simply because their respective parents had forbidden their relationship. Much as it was sad, it gave me an idea.

All I needed to do, was simply drive that same road, and to have an easy, guaranteed fatal, accident - off the edge of the mountain. I realised the law required that I wear a seatbelt, and would therefore need to ensure that the impact would be sufficient to complete the termination of my life, regardless of the seat belt.

I carried out some rough calculations in regards to the speed that I would need to leave the road at, making sure that it would be still be within the speed limit, to ensure that the insurance company could have no excuse to refuse pay-out.

I needed to make sure that the car was in good condition, insurance - motor and life - premiums paid. I would also need to ensure that there was no sign of depression at home; no letter; no tears; nothing should be out of place.

Each day I thought about it, time and time over, imagining the transient pain, and the potential escape from my torture - perhaps there was an alternative. Whilst the children were at school, and my wife at work, I considered all of the options again and again, but in my depression, and pain medication stupor, could only see death as a viable way out.

I decided it would be best that I carried out the deed on a weekend. It would mean that the three of them would be together, mother and children. They would be able to support each other. A Saturday seemed to be the best choice, at least they would have a bit more time to adjust before the school week started.

My chosen day arrived, and after breakfast I told everybody that I was going to get something from the bottom of the mountain. I insisted on going alone. For obvious reasons.

I gave everybody an extra hug and left the house, keeping a stiff upper lip, not looking back. Setting out, and driving carefully, I headed towards my chosen road. As I drove, I looked around me at the mountains, the cows in the fields, the bee hives, the rivers - it was so beautiful. But I could no longer appreciate it, in my condition.

I had reasoned the whole act out. Descending the mountain, I prepared myself for the end. The pain in my legs seemed to intensify, almost wishing me to hurry up and complete the deed.

I set my speed, coming around the last corner and could see my exit point ahead. Momentarily, I glimpsed a little family walking by the side of the road. The children were about the same ages as mine. I closed my eyes. I shook as if having a convulsion. The world, blurred by the tears flowing freely, spun around me. I hit the brakes, quite hard. I did not want to die. For a moment I thought I would not be able to slow enough to prevent my own demise. But I did, just. Shaking, I continued down the mountain road, unable to carry out the act.

At the next lay by, I pulled in, blocked upright in my plastic cocooned torso. I looked in the rear-view mirror. I did not see myself. I saw a coward. A red eyed, puffy, sad and miserable man. I had planned to do the most selfish thing anybody could do. Perhaps I was driven by pain, perhaps my judgement was affected by the medication. Either way, it was a close call.

Time ticked by. I sat, watching myself, contemplating what I had nearly completed - or rather nearly ended. Pulling myself together, I decided that I would push on. After all, I had overcome so many challenges in the past. I could overcome some more. I drove home. Entering the house I spoke to no one. Entering the bedroom, I prostrated myself on the bed, crying. After a while I lay on my back, staring at the ceiling, feeling, and knowing, that I was a bad husband and an awful father.

Suicide would have been the most selfish thing I could have done. Not just for my family then, but for all people that were still to come into my life.

INVERSION

A few weeks later I had to travel to visit a company about a software contract. Strapping myself into the plastic torso, I headed out. It felt good to be going on a meaningful, money earning, mission. Every time I drove down the mountain I remembered what I had nearly done, and felt like a coward, a really bad, selfish and miserable person, deep, deep inside.

The client meeting went well, and despite the cold weather, including snow heaps on the edge of the road, I knew that I would overcome my challenges. Setting off home, I decided to take the autoroute, it would be faster, and put less load on my back, compared to the twisting country road. The slip road to join the main carriageway, at the junction I had chosen, had a very tight curve, practically a hairpin turn, and I still had summer tyres on the car. I thought it would be OK, but it wasn't.

As I tried to turn, a little fast for the conditions, the car went sideways. There was a brief moment of driving on two wheels, and then sliding along the grass reserve area on the side-door, and finally, a short distance on the roof of the car. It was almost like ballet - but in slow motion, without any music. I watched the whole world rotate in the windshield, and come to rest in the Australian position - upside down.

I hung in my seatbelt, waiting... thinking... expecting that somebody would come and help me. Several cars drove by, unable to see me, for the car was tucked just out of sight.

Amazingly, I felt little pain, but a lot of stupidity. A few weeks ago, I had wanted to do something worse than this, on purpose, and now I was in a real accident. Another car passed.

Thinking about my long-ago flying lessons, I remembered Morse code for SOS, or Save Our Souls, the international distress beacon.

Beep beep beep... beeeeep beeeeep beeeeep.... beep beep beep, I sounded the horn.

I repeated the signal, seemingly forever, but surely for less than ten minutes. A young man bent down to the side window, swinging his head upside down to look me in the eye with a "Ca va, monsieur?" meaning "Are you alright sir?"

In hindsight, that must have been the dumbest question anybody ever asked a driver hanging by their seatbelt in an inverted car. Nonetheless, his assistance and concern was much appreciated.

I explained that I could not just un-strap myself and exit, since I was in a prosthesis, and scared for my back. Without hesitation, he went to call for the Sapeur Pompiers - or ambulance/fire brigade. Remember, mobile phones were still rare - and expensive - at that time.

He returned, waiting patiently with me, suggesting from time to time that he should rock the car over, with me in it. I shook my head, violently. I imagined the unexploded ordinance waiting in my lower back for such an event to release its pent up energy.

The red camionnette of the Sapeur Pompiers parked near the scene of the upside down vehicle. They also wanted to extract me - until I tapped my solid chest and explained my compromised back. Without argument, they deployed a system to right the car gently, with me inside. Then, with the dexterity of a midwife delivering a breach baby, they extracted me from the car without any pressure to my back. I felt nothing. I was scared to even try to move my toes. I wondered how much more damage I may have done to my body.

Lying in the hospital, awaiting yet more x-rays, I pondered on the amount of radiation I had been exposed to in all of my exploits. I decided it was best to stop thinking about it, after exceeding one hundred x-rays in my mental counting.

A few hours later, I was asked "Try to stand up Monsieur," I complied, gingerly. The medical team were standing by, concerned about something that may have been missed in the examinations. As my feet contacted the floor, I braced for the electrical storm that would normally be associated with such a movement. But it did not come. I felt better than before this accident. My first ever experience of coming out of an accident with less wrong than before the accident.

Smiling, I thanked the team, as they told me I could go home. The Sapeur Pompiers had even checked out my car, finding it safe to drive, even if a little scratched, and had driven it to the hospital for me. I drove home, with another tale to tell.

Each morning I exited bed expecting the nerve fuelled explosions of sciatica to rip me apart, but they didn't. I had tingles, numbness, pain, etc - but less than before. I started to gain hope.

It appeared that the 'rolling a car and hanging upside down in it for thirty minutes' therapy, may well have put something right in my back!

My usual doctor pooh-poohed the whole idea. I knew that I could do more, and had hope, but I didn't know where to turn for help in shedding my plastic torso, and regaining my life. A friend suggested that I visited The Wizard.

WIZARDRY

The Wizard was a proper, certified, medical doctor, with a reputation of being terribly, openly and crazily unorthodox. He lived in an isolated house on the side of a mountain. It was known that he would carry out minor surgery on humans and animals as the need arose. I am sure that some of what he did was beyond his medical licence. Some viewed him as whacky, others as a miracle worker. Hence, his local nickname of The Wizard. What could I have to lose in visiting this strange fellow on the other side of the mountain?

I arrived in his waiting room, it was full of magazines. Not just any magazines. FLYING magazines. Clearly, this wizard flew! I sat, number two in line, to see the magical medical man. About twenty minutes later, he popped his head around the heavy wooden door and called "next." I could not see his body, but his head was high up the door. Either he was standing on a chair, or he was a tall fellow. He was clean shaven, meaning that he was not Gandalf, and had a warm smile on his very French looking face, which reassured me.

An hour later, yes, a full hour later, he had finished his session with the previous patient. I know this, not because I was called, but because I could hear him at the front door and waving off the patient. Not just saying "goodbye" but more of detailed discourse, as saying goodbye to a family member. It was very strange behaviour for a medical doctor.

The front door closed, and instantaneously the door to the waiting room opened a head-wide crack. Seeing me, flying magazine in my lap, he opened the door fully, standing in the doorway. He was tall, there was no chair nor stool beneath his feet. He was thin, with, what appeared to me at least, incredibly long arms.

He walked into the waiting room and sat down next to me. I still took a lot of time to be able to stand up, so he was sitting beside me before my backside could even separate itself from the wooden seat that I was perched upon.

We must have spent a good fifteen minutes talking about aeroplanes. Then, with his assistance, I stood and we made our way into his double door-ed office. I commented on the double doors. "For privacy," he responded, bluntly. Blunt was this man's strength.

Once again, I found myself on a leather chair, and this one made body noises freely, especially with my plastic encapsulated, robotic movement restricted torso. The Wizard laughed as I made a fake fart on the back of the leather. He giggled and laughed more than any other doctor I had ever met.

He asked me to tell him about my back. But he was not satisfied with anything I told him. He wanted to dig as far back as he could - right to my birth! Then, over two and half hours later, he looked me in the eye.

"What would you like to be able to do, that you cannot do now?" he asked, leaning forwards and peering into my head, seemingly looking for cogs and gears whirring between my ears.

"Fly," was the simple, one-word answer.

He slowly, carefully, and fully in control of his movements, leaned back - well back in his chair. His overly long arms wrapped their way upwards, as if in slow motion, until his hands locked behind his head. He threw me a verbal spirit dampener. "In France, you will never be able to get a medical to fly a Cessna or a Piper light aircraft," he explained. It worked. He had raised my

Wonderful Adversity: Into Africa

spirits with a question, and then dashed them on the rocks of despair with his response to my answer. But he had not finished his game.

"However, you could fly *ultra léger* without a medical," he tossed the words out, as if they were inconsequential, but they were not. They grabbed a hold of some sort of mooring rope for my soul, and secured something inside of me.

He went on to talk about the ULM movement in France, that of the Ultra-Light Motorised aircraft, and how they were catching on as a lower cost, lower medical restraint, way to fly.

We chatted, and chatted, but I knew that even getting into, let alone out of, a small plane was not a possibility in my plastic prosthesis.

Suddenly, and without warning he blurted out "So, if you really want to fly, you will learn to overcome zat plastic thing and to be fit and 'ealthy again!"

"Yes, I would love to.... but how?" I sighed, even though he had me hooked on his crazy idea.

"It will be tough, and you will go for *balneotherapie* twice a week for many months. AND do exercises every day. But if you have the goal of flying, you will succeed," he prescribed. Without a pause, he picked up the phone and called his friends with a special underwater physio treatment centre, booking my first appointment. He was almost as excited about it as I was!

We exited his house-cum-surgery and moved towards my car. He pushed me away from the car, and guided me down the hill outside his house, towards a hedge encompassed field. The Wizard had some strange ways, but I liked him, so I accepted this kidnapping detour. In the corner of the field stood a stable. He kept pushing me towards the stable, and I kept moving towards it, full of trust. Then, as we rounded the corner to the front of the wooden construction, I realised that it was not just a stable - but rather a stable for about fifty mechanical horses. A tiny fifty-horsepower two-stroke engine sat on top of the simplest little aluminium tube covered aircraft I had ever seen. The Wizard smiled fully, doing a little excitement dance on the spot. He stopped being a doctor and became a passionate aviator. Prancing, leaping and almost teleporting himself around the small airframe, he explained how he had built it, and enjoyed flying it in the early mornings, when the wind was calm. This was 'ultra light flying'. His enthusiasm rubbed off onto me - it was as if we were in a special open market, and he just sold me a dream, for free... well, not quite.

Slowly, for that was the only way for me to walk up a hill, we returned to my car. I drove home, imaging my car was a small plane, and gazing longingly at the mountain tops, wanting to soar once more. Despite the pain, I had a purpose. I was going to fly again. I had to, and really did, believe it.

A few days later I arrived at the balneotherapie centre. The glass door opened and a jolly, stout, man reached his hand out, guiding me into the building. Once inside, he sent me to change into swimming shorts. I had to remove my torso prosthesis, and therefore needed help into and out of the small swimming pool treatment zone. Once in the water, I realised that is was not just water, but salted and scented water. I felt free, weightless and able to move around. But my chest started to get tight, my breathing harder to complete. I must have been allergic to something in the water. A wheeze started, and then I knew that an asthma attack, a large one, was on the way.

Breathlessly, I asked for my Ventolin inhaler, from my pocket in the changing room. The stout man obliged rapidly. He handed it to me as I squeaked like a dog's toy being attacked by a bull mastiff. Grabbing at the blue inhaler I started puffing away on it - taking many times more than the recommended dose, all the time hanging onto the edge of the pool.

Stout man asked me many times if I wanted to stop and leave the pool. "Non, non, non!" I stated, each and every time. I was not going to let an asthma attack stop me having this treatment. Eventually, the attack started to subside.

With the asthma almost under control, and the inhaler within reach at all times, perched on the edge of the pool, the process began.

Using a car-jet-wash like contraption (actually I think it was just a regular pressure washer for cars) I was hosed down, along the muscle lines, under-water. The pressure line working around my inflamed, bruised and raw back. It hurt. Oh, boy did it hurt. But I was not going to let that be known to my hydro-masseur! Then, came some water-borne exercises. I could move in ways that were impossible on land - building muscles, strength and endurance. Archimedes principle worked in my favour - giving me the ability to move and train muscles that would otherwise be impossible. The water provided a work-load that adjusted to the speed of my movements, the faster I moved the greater the work load, just as in aviation, we call it drag!

Then, some more jet-wash massage and a massive help out of the pool. I was exhausted. It took me over an hour to get dressed, torso-wrapped and breathing well enough to drive home. But I felt happy. This could be the way to fly again.

That night I slept the best I had slept in well over a year. It was a sleep of fatigue, exhaustion and exhilaration. I had not exercised freely on the land, and had not pushed myself physically, that hard, for a very long time.

The next day, my muscles tormented me. Sciatica pulsed down my legs. I chose to stay in bed. I doubted the prudence of my chosen course of treatment. As I lay, I thought about the little plane in The Wizard's stable, and all of its sixty horses! It made me smile, and then I slept some more. That evening I decided to get out of bed, and slid my prosthesis under my body, strapping into it as if I were some sort of monster. I felt a bit more 'able to move', but it may well have been psychological.

An hour of being vertical was enough, and the horizontal plane called me back. I did not sleep well that night, not due to pain, but because I was thinking of flying. Would it be possible? Even if I could manage it physically, what about financially?

For my next balneotherapie session, I dosed up on asthma medication, in large quantities, in advance. It helped, but did not stop me making little tortured mouse-like noises, from the depths of my chest. The stout man jet washed me whilst making me do exercises. It got easier each time I visited.

After three weeks, I was feeling so much better. It was as if the jet wash was massaging fluids that had pooled around my injuries away. I still had pain, but it was controllable. I even started to reduce my pain meds. It was time to visit The Wizard again.

"Tres bien!" he exclaimed, just looking at me "I can see you are standing better - and moving better!" It is amazing how we do not perceive daily changes in our own posture and freedom of movement, but those who have not seen you for a few weeks, notice it instantly. He examined me.

"Now, we must get rid of that plastic monstrosity," he declared. He devised a schedule to slowly, very slowly, rid me of my prosthesis. It was coupled to the underwater jet therapy, and some very tough exercises.

Weeks turned to months and, eventually, I no longer needed to wear my support at all. I moved carefully, never twisting from side-to-side, and I took each step as if I walking on broken glass, but I was regaining my freedom of movement. Physically, I knew that flying would be possible again... but now to fix the finances.

FLYING

One of the clients I had been writing software for proposed a business partnership. It seemed like a good idea at the time. He had resources, and I had a head full of programming code. He brought the business, and I wrote thousands of lines - no, tens of thousands of lines of code. Every day, I would sit at my computer and type. I wrote financial software, stock control, bill of materials and everything to manage any type of enterprise you can imagine. I was good with numbers, code and solving problems, and loved doing so.

As I got stronger, I travelled to clients all over Europe, installing and training - as well as designing complete systems, and building the odd specialist computer too. The money was now good enough for me to find a flying school, an Ultralight flying school. It was time to discover the little planes.

I asked The Wizard, and he pointed me in the direction of a small school about an hours drive away, relatively close to Mont Blanc.

One weekend, we drove as a family to the airfield. A field would have been a better description. It was a muddy field, at the bottom of a mountainside, with a marsh at one end of it, and massive high-tension power lines at the other. One side had a row of Poplar trees, the other a row of little planes, covered in tarpaulins, two wooden shacks and a little play park, populated with two swings and a slide. The children saw the little play park, inspired to get out of the car. It was cold, damp and one of the greyest days of any year.

We parked, letting the children run towards the swings. A large brown dog stood between them and their goal. He made sure that they stood as still as statues.

"Hélice!" meaning propeller in French, was shouted loudly, and the dog responded, leaving his guard position, and allowing the children in. We walked towards the skinny man, fumbling a pack of Gauloises cigarettes, with one perched precariously between his fingers. It was he who had called out the dog's name.

"Oui?" he asked, tersely.

"Can I learn to fly here?" I enquired, in French, but with a discernible British accent..

"Oui!" he snapped, entering the first wooden shack.

We followed. Inside it was totally disorganised. Nothing like the British flying schools I knew. It was more like the bedroom of an overgrown teenager. Magazines and unwashed, well used, coffee cups were covering every horizontal surface. Photographs and magazine clippings of aeroplanes covered the vertical ones.

Sticky cigarette tar plastered the wooden ceiling, and the suspected smell of two-stroke fuel-soaked floorboards was confirmed by the half-disassembled - or half assembled – two-stroke engine in one corner. A broken propeller occupied two of the seats in another corner. This was a fun place!

"Would you like a baptême d'air?" he poured the thick French accented dressing over his salad of two languages, trying to accommodate my origins.

"A what?" I asked, confused by the terminology.

"Baptême d'air you know, errr it is like ze baptême in ze church - but in ze air," came the so French and so unclear to me explanation. A few moments later I realised that the French call a 'first flight in a plane' a *baptism of the air*. So, I agreed to embark on the spiritual experience.

My instructor was a well known pilot, with lots of international awards. Apparently he was famous, but I had never heard of him, not coming from the ULM denomination of the religion of aviation. All the same, he waxed lyrical in broken Franglais about his awards, and I listened, impressed.

We squelched through some mud, up to the side of a little cloth covered collection of aluminium tubes. It looked like it had fallen out of some Hollywood comedy about early aviation. Inside, the panel was sparsely populated, with just a few instruments. An aluminium tube affair hung loosely from the top of the cabin, above and between the seats. I had no idea as to its purpose. The outside of the aircraft looked like some used bed-sheets pulled half-tight around a collection of tubular greenhouse tubes. The engine sat up-front, above the wing. It had no cowling, being totally exposed to the weather, with a little black plastic handle hanging down at the back, reminiscent of the starter handle for a lawnmower. I wondered what I was doing even considering this flight. But, this is what I had come for, and so, I would partake, at least once, of this form of aviation worship.

It took me a while to climb into the pilot's seat. It hurt, but I could cope. Excitement, mixed with trepidation, overcame the pain sufficiently for the event. I glanced back to see the children and my wife in the play park, along with Hélice the dog. I reassured myself that they would be fine.

"Pull on zee tube," I was instructed, as he pointed to tube I has spotting earlier. So I reached up and pulled.

"Zat is zee brake for zee wheels," he pointed out - but I had already grasped the idea.

Hanging off the apparent hand brake, I was left a bit confused as to why the famous instructor was still outside the plane. Then he reached up, grabbing the plastic handle next to the engine, with his left hand.

I frowned whilst twisting my head to look up at him.

Reaching into the cockpit, with his right hand, he flipped what looked like a bicycle gear changer, clamped to the side of the plane, forwards. With second movement of his right hand he pulled another, rather long white-painted lever back hard. As he moved this lever a corresponding component, on my side of the plane, also moved. I watched, concerned.

Then he leaned forwards, gathered his strength and recoiled backwards yelling something incomprehensible. The engine started with a VROOOOOOM. This plane had no electric starter. It was, indeed, started in the same fashion as a lawnmower. Over the noise of the engine he yelled at me "'old ze brakes," So I did.

He vanished behind the aircraft. I sat, alone, in the cockpit, unaware of what was going on around me. I glanced again at my family, wondering if I would ever see them again.

Then, as quickly as he had disappeared, famous instructor, jumped into the seat next to me and shouting "ON Y VA." My memories of Patron flooded back as I remembered that 'on y va' meant 'Let's Go!'

Reaching across me, he pushed and pulled at things, then snatched my hand away from the brake handle above our heads. It was noisy and blustery - more like sitting on a badly maintained sit-and-ride mower in a wind storm.

The plane had no doors, and the windshield did not cover to the top of my head. My hair was fighting to retain connection with my scalp. But it felt good.

Famous instructor was clearly in a showing off mood, a common state of affairs for pilots, and one that I had encountered before. He was yelling at me, the wind snatching his words rapidly away. I was not grasping ten percent of his discourse. There were no headsets, and it was not the best place to chit-chat.

He applied some power, using the long white lever, which I now identified as the throttle. The plane started to taxi, a few metres later, he literally U turned the plane spinning on one wheel. We were at the marsh end of the field, looking straight at the high-tension power cables. Before I could even assess the situation, he pushed forwards on the throttle lever. The little plane instantly started to roll, gaining speed much more quickly than a Cessna. I was petrified. There was no way we could possibly be doing anything other than kill ourselves by flying into the best Electricité de France transmission lines.

Before I could object, a miracle happened. The plane leapt into the air! Seriously, this plane could fly. We were airborne in a matter of meters - about twenty percent of the best take off roll a Cessna could dream of. Then we climbed, turned and climbed some more. We were rapidly well clear of the power lines, up into the crisp mountain air.

I felt more like a bird than a human flying in plane. I was flying - really flying - integrated fully to the air. The plane rolled, pitched and yawed exactly the same as the Cessna I had been learning in years ago - but with more grace, more crispness, more excitement - and a lot more wind in my face. It felt so amazingly fresh, free and fulfilling.

We climbed to a few thousand feet, looking out, up and down at the Alps. Stunning would be an understatement. Famous instructor threw the plane into near aerobatic manoeuvres, all the time with me bracing my back in case something should happen. I loved the negative G, being pulled out of my seat as I lost all of my weight, but retained my full mass! It felt GOOOOOD on my back. Adrenalin was pumping and I had the biggest smile on my face in many years. I was alive and free. Feeling as if there were no constraints on where or how I could move, Famous instructor gave me the controls. Within minutes, I had integrated and became a part of the machine. I had total control of where I went and how I got there. I was re-invigorated with a reason to live a long life.

Then, without warning, at about three thousand feet, right above the marshy end of the field below, famous instructor reached forward and hit two big red emergency stop buttons. The engine spluttered and stopped. Silence filled the cabin. As my ears adjusted to the removal of the decibels from the engine, I heard a whoosh of air in the wings. Famous instructor

Wonderful Adversity: Into Africa

said, "Now ve can talk!" the plane turned into a bad glider, with Famous explaining everything that I had worked out, without hearing him, earlier. He continued to throw the plane around, as we constantly lost altitude - without any thrust at the front end to help us. If we wanted to restart the engine, one of us would have to get out and pull that handle. That was not going to happen.

Without warning, he pushed us into a dive, down the side of the vineyard covered hillside, heading towards the marsh. This pilot didn't like marshes in the same way Ginger didn't like the fourth white line on my first runway. I tensed up, feeling the wounds deep in my back. There was not enough field to land on, I was sure. Just as I was certain we were going to land in the marsh, he pulled the stick back towards his stomach - and held it there. Our wheels were skimming the top of the marsh reeds. I could even hear them tapping on the tyres.

As we came towards the end of the beginning of the runway area, the wheels kissed the fields' grass, and the plane rolled forwards. Famous reached up, hanging on the upside-down hand brake. We stopped, with a bit of a wobble, but we stopped.

I was the happiest man on the planet, actually in the cosmos. I had flown again - and it was good. By the time I had extracted myself from the plane I was very sore. I would not share that fact with anybody, for fear of being allowed to fly again.

We returned as often as we could. In just a few weeks, and around five hours of instruction, I was solo. With a further twenty hours, I was ready for my exams. However, I learned that the written exams would be in French. Well, why not, we were in France.

I sat and passed the exams, with a good mark. My flying licence was, in due course issued. To top it all, I even managed to purchase an aircraft kit, participating in the building of my own aircraft. It was tough, but it was worth it. That little plane would sit at the airfield waiting for a flight each week. Whenever possible, the family joined me to go for a weekends flying. We even based a caravan near the airfield for comfort breaks. It was magical.

The rules for VFR (Visual Flight Rules) are very clear, and we had to all be on the ground before thirty minutes after sunset. It did not always happen, and there were occasions when car lights would be used to assist a late arrival in finding the place to land. As long as the officials never found out, it was OK, or so I was told by Famous.

One beautiful autumn evening I was out flying, and forgot about the time. I was busy watching the orange glow reflected by the snow capped Mont Blanc. I circled at around five thousand feet, chilled in the evening air, and very open cockpit. As the orange dissipated, I realised that I should dive for home. Normally, a late arrival would have some kind soul out with their car lights to help them in. Not that night.

I picked out the shadows of the vineyards, and set up my approach slope parallel to the hillside covered in grape vines. I knew that I had to miss the marshland, and I knew that I could not go-around because I would not be able to see the pylons at the other end of the field.

As I rounded out, I could see the reddish glow of cigarettes being puffed near the wooden shacks. All the same, nobody came to help me. I found the threshold and put the wheels down in the post-dusk evening. It must have been a similar feeling to that felt by the pilots during wartime, landing without lights in some field in France. Still unable to understand why nobody was coming near me, I taxied, shutdown, tied-down and pulled a tarpaulin over the engine.

The cigarette lights started to scatter in all directions. I was confused. Famous came up to me, about six inches from my nose and yelled at me in English, which was odd since we normally spoke French together now. "I ave told you about ze time we must all land!" he chastised me.

I responded in English "Sorry, I lost track of the time," knowing that others did the same on a regular basis.

"You English people, you will never learn," he screamed, shrugging his shoulders and walking away. A few seconds later the sound of wood hitting wood hard echoed across the darkness, as he slammed closed the door to the office. I followed slowly, silent, unaware of my misdemeanour and the reasons behind his outburst.

A few moments later a car started up and pulled out of the car-park, just as I was within a few metres of the door to my anticipated sanctioning. Famous burst out of the shack laughing heartily. Teasing me in French, he explained that a Civil Aviation inspector had been at the field, and asked if all the planes were landed, within the legal time frame. I was the only one airborne, and since we did not use radios, nobody could warn me.

Apparently, he had lamented to the instructor that "It is only the English who were still up, because they cannot tell the time," and that "It is a waste of time waiting to speak to him, because he doesn't speak French."

It saved my bacon, and taught me a lesson. I made a mental note to keep a better eye on the time. After all, that landing in the dark was a real challenge - and if anything had gone wrong, it would not have been my licence I would be worried about, it could have cost me my life. A life I dearly wanted to live. Experience is a fantastic teacher.

I had many wonderful (daylight) flights, and even had a good number of landings in fields, both intentionally, and not so intentionally. Most times there were no challenges. I did make some mistakes.

One field I landed in, just because it was there, and that was perfectly legal with the approval of the owners, who I knew. It was not far from my home, and the farmer was very pleasant.

I came in slowly, and touched down - only to discover that the grass was much, much longer than I had remembered, or noticed. The plane slowed

Wonderful Adversity: Into Africa

rapidly, and came to an abrupt standstill as if landing on an aircraft carrier, caught by the arrestor cable.

I got out, chatted with friends, and then it was time to head out again. Together, we all pushed back the aircraft to the far end of the field. Then we walked up and down, compressing the grass in front of the plane, as I planned my exit. At the end of the field there was a slight upwards incline, and then a ditch before the road. After that a barbed wire fence, then another field.

I started the engine and powered my way towards the ditch. I was not gaining enough speed. I hit the brakes, and shut down. We all pushed the plane back again. I would have another go, with friends cheering me on for good measure.

This time I hammered the engine hard, desperate for the speed to build, but it was not coming fast enough. Just as I thought about giving up again, I realised that I could not stop before the ditch. I had no air under my wheels and my indicated airspeed was nowhere near what it was going to take to get airborne. The pressed down grass was grabbing the undercarriage, as if trying to stop me leaving that field.

I knew that I was probably going to end up face first in the ditch, but I had no choice but to keep the throttle at maximum. The grass on each side of me, at my eye height, was just beginning to blur. I managed to get the nose wheel off of the ground about foot. Hitting the edge of the ditch with the main gear, I braced myself, waiting for the impending impact.

The whole plane lurched into the air, still below flying speed. I pushed the elevator control to try for some level flight, perhaps hoping to make the road - or the next field. As I did so, without the drag of the grass, my airspeed increased just enough for me to skim the tarmac of the road, thankfully without any cars passing. The barbed wire fence was my next obstacle, and I had to give up some airspeed to climb a foot or two. My wheels must have clipped the wire as I passed over it, pushing forwards on the stick just a little, heading down towards the next field. There were cows in this field. A large brown cow, about 100 metres from me, lifted its head and looked me straight in the eye. I continued to gain airspeed, and thankfully for the cow, and my aircraft, had enough speed to climb out, up and away, to live another day.

I learned more from that experience than I could possibly have learned from all the books in the British Library. My heart beat strong, and my eyes were wider than dinner plates, but I lived through it. I learned through it.

I loved flying, all things flying, all things engines, all things airframes, and all things about the skill, risk management and technicalities that flying has associated with it.

My children would fly with me from time-to-time, but it never attracted my wife. She was the sensible one, with her feet, literally, planted firmly on the ground. It was probably a good balance.

WHATEVER YOU MAY CALL IT.

My business partner and I did not always see eye-to-eye, but we were doing a good turnover, with excellent profits. I would put some of his 'ways of doing things' down to 'being French', rightly or wrongly. We had our fights, disagreements and challenges, but overall we got along. Although working in a different culture brings a variety of unexpected issues, generally it worked.

Family life was good too. The children were doing great in school, my wife no longer needed to work, the house was warm, the woodpile well stocked and everything as it should be for a stable and happy life. Amazingly, even the teachers no longer called me in for vocabulary clarification lessons.

We would eat our meals at the kitchen table, French style. A tomato salad drenched in homemade dressing starter, some French style main course, followed by a yogurt or two and some pungent French cheese on fresh bread - lovely food, and very tasty. My weight increased. With the amount of dairy foods being consumed, I was not surprised!

Then one spring evening, I sat at the table, eating heartily with the family, when I had the strangest of feelings. I always believed in following my gut, and whether you want to put it down to faith, religion, human interconnection, coincidence or just plain craziness, what happened next is as true as my blood is red. It was as if something came over me. A cold feeling down my spine. My heart beat faster. I opened my mouth and stated "We have to go to Ghana."

It was the weirdest thing. None of us knew where Ghana was. I thought it was in South America. Quickly we put the idea to one side and finished the meal, right down to the wonderful cheese course!

The children went to bed, and my wife and I discussed the silly nonsense that had ejected out of my mouth. We looked in an atlas, discovering that Ghana was in West Africa. Neither of us had visited sub-Saharan Africa before. Giving the idea ten more minutes of consideration, and having discounted the whole idea as preposterous, it was forgotten.

An hour or so later, we switched on the TV. There, straight in front of us, was a documentary about Ghana. It was spooky. It resulted in chills doing somersaults along my spine, and goose bumps practising the Mexican wave up and down my arms.

The next morning, I booked plane tickets for the whole family to visit Ghana, without consultation with my spouse. I had never heard of Ghana Airways, but they had good prices, even if they only flew from London. Sometimes you just know that you have to do something.

Contacting the Ghanaian embassy in Paris, I took an appointment for visas. Driving to the embassy took nearly four hours. I kept talking to myself,

Wonderful Adversity: Into Africa

out loud, in the car.

"What on earth are you doing now?" I asked myself.

"What you feel you must do," I responded.

"You must be crazy," I explained. This conversation continued with some slight variations, repeatedly. But I kept on driving, persuaded by myself or some other power which was outside of my control.

The ambassador himself met with me. A pleasant chap. He seemed surprised that somebody from France wanted to visit Ghana at that time. We chatted, he told me the history of the country, and treated me with such kindness, promising that we would have a wonderful time. Happily, I left with four visa-stamped passports in my hand.

The children were hyper-excited at the idea of visiting Africa. We researched, we talked and we planned. It was terribly surreal. It was simply something I knew that we had to do. Soon the day was upon us. It was time to head out on our two-week trip to Ghana. Ghana here we come!

EXPLORATION

We would drive over the French border and then fly from Geneva, Switzerland to London Heathrow, spend the night and then head on to Ghana. I was a little worried because we had not been able to get a phone call or any other form of communication through to book a hotel in Accra, the capital city of Ghana. Nonetheless, I was confident that we would find something when we arrived. My wife sat looking very concerned at the whole expedition, for it had become just that. We were heading out, all dressed in walking shoes with backpacks, going to a country we did not know, where we knew no one, and where we had no reservations or even contacts. In hindsight that was not a smart move, but I was riding a wave of inspiration. Acting without thinking it all through had a knack of paying off for me. Little did I know what I was getting my family into.

The flight from Geneva to Heathrow was smooth. The children getting more and more excited. We checked into a little hotel close to our departure terminal, and settled down for the night. We needed to be at the airport for 10am to book in for the next leg, so we had plenty of time to lounge around in the morning. Or so we thought.

At 5am, fire alarms resounded through the corridors and in the rooms. The hotel was on fire. Shaking the children awake we rushed out into the car park, waiting for the fire-brigade to give the all clear. It was a cold and crisp 'summer morning'. That was not unusual for London. I had pulled my shoes on, but none of the rest of the family had managed to collect their footwear during the evacuation. I allowed the children to stand on my shoes, taking it in turns, to help protect their feet. Many others around us had also forgotten their shoes, hopping from one foot to the other trying to prevent their lower extremities from chilling.

By 5:30am we were allowed back to our rooms. The incident, caused by a smouldering hair dryer, had been contained. We tried going back to bed. However, with children on their first trip to Africa that day, it was not going to happen. They would not settle and just seemed to ask between every other breath "Can we go to see the planes?" It worked as an idea for me! Consequently, we decided to simply go early to the airport and watch the aircraft movements, to while away the time before our flight.

It was barely 8am as the taxi dropped us at the correct door for Ghana Airways. It was easily two hours before check-in would open. We entered, backpacks on, walking shoes stoutly attached to our now warm feet.

As we pushed open the door to the terminal, we were met with a sea of black faces. I had never seen so many dark skinned people in one location in my life. The children asked "Are we in Africa now?" It was quite understandable, for it really looked like another country!

We tried to weave a path through the mass of tightly packed people, all apparently with more bags than they could carry, and some with oversized carrier bags packed to within an ounce of bursting. I overheard two people in the huddle discussion their trip to Ghana. Intrigued, I asked, "Which flight are you waiting for?"

To my utter and total disbelief the response was "Ghana Airways."

Laughing, I explained, in case they had not understood, "But check in is not for another two hours!"

"If you want to get a seat on Ghana Airways, you have to line up early - because they oversell all the seats," a helpful lady informed me. She appeared experienced in such travel.

Around her, those listening in echoed "Ahaaaaa" nasally, showing accord with the information shared. These were regular travellers with Ghana Airways, and it was clearly prudent to listen to the advice.

The night had been short, and our arrival at the airport early, through circumstances beyond our control. It appeared that serendipity was playing her hand in our favour. Learning as we went, we joined the back of the huddle-like queue.

I had not planned on queuing for hours to check in. But then I had not travelled to Africa before. We were swallowing new experiences, and with them knowledge of a different culture. It was a steep learning curve.

My family represented the only white faces in the queue. It was fun, and we did not feel too out of place. There was a lot of lively banter, joking and

Wonderful Adversity: Into Africa

speaking in strange languages. The lady in front of us had a little girl similar in age to our daughter. The two girls played well together as we waited. The girl was lighter skinned than her mother, more caramel than chocolate in tone. Both mother and daughter were happy to chat, educating us about the wonders that lay on the other side of a seven-hour flight.

After about forty minutes, the mother asked us to watch Caramel girl whilst she went to the desk. We obliged. Ten minutes later, she returned in tears.

"What's the matter?" I asked

"They won't allow my daughter to travel," she lamented, explaining, "They have changed their unaccompanied minor policy, and now I need to find somebody to agree to look after her on the flight." Tears were rolling down her chocolate cheeks, her ivory white smile no longer visible.

I didn't stop to consider my next offer. "We can take her for you. After all she is happy playing with our daughter."

My right hand was suddenly in a death grip from my wife, who was shaking her head. She tried to pull me away, but I was in Good Samaritan mode, and could not imagine anything other than the best in people.

Caramel was happy and laughing, her chocolate mother now relieved. I felt good too. My wife was clearly not happy. The mother excused herself to write a quick letter of consent, permitting us to take her daughter on the plane. She was to be met by her grandfather at the destination airport.

As soon as the mother moved out of earshot, my wife decided to release her pent-up concerns, rather like a machine gun in rapid fire mode.

"What if she is carrying drugs?"

"What if she is a stolen child?"

"What if we can't find her grandfather at the other end?"

"What if there is a problem?"

"What if... what if... what if..."

Her last bullet was fired with incredible accuracy, hitting be between the eyes, "We shouldn't do this."

Much as I realise she had asked a lot of different questions, they were fired so quickly, and without pause for response, I guessed that the only question I should ask myself would be "Why did I open my mouth, again?"

Without doubt, for normal thinking people, she was right. However, I was committed to the deed. I did not see a way to back out, and I really couldn't imagine any problems. With mother's letter in hand, and a promise that Caramel would be able to identify her grandfather at the other end, we checked in, two adults and three children to Accra.

Chocolate mother was happy, I was happy, the three children were happy. Wife was definitely not. Right or wrong, time would tell.

We stood in the line for passport checks. It came to our turn. The passport control man looked at the two white and one caramel faced youngsters, asking "Are these all your children?"

I replied "Two are, and the third is travelling with us. I have a letter from her mother," hoping that I sounded confident.

"Step aside please, sir," he insisted, adding "We just need to carry out some additional checks."

We stood to one side of the line. Waiting, whilst a seemingly endless flow of passengers passed. The officer was checking a list, holding each passport in turn to the light, whilst making a large number of phone calls.

"I told you we shouldn't do this," my wife whispered to me, repeatedly.

"Don't worry," I replied, trying to sound confident. I paused, glancing left and right to make sure I could not be heard, then whispered, "It will be OK," doubting my decision.

Finally, five passports were returned to my slightly sweaty palm and we moved on to the security check. "What if she has drugs in her bag?" my doubting wife whispered in my ear.

Laughing, I responded in hushed tone, "They bring drugs from Africa to England, not the other way around," and waited for the security check to clear us all through.

In the departure lounge, we sat, playing games and telling stories. Finally, we boarded a DC10 with a bright red, yellow and green tail. The registration made me smile, 9G-ANA.

Our seven-hour flight was uneventful, but rather long for children. I invented more stories and played even more games with the kids, because the in-flight entertainment system was not working. Nobody else seemed surprised at the lack of an in-flight movie. Apparently it happened quite regularly on this route. Well, the tickets were not expensive... so, no worries, as long as the plane was safe.

It was good old DC10, solid and reliable... after they had fixed that annoying little problem of engines falling off, some years back.

We were less than an hour from Accra when turbulence flicked at the aircraft. Thunderstorms were visible all around us, with black anvil-headed fury, all the way up to thirty-five thousand feet, illuminated by the strobe light effect of plasma bolts bursting across the sky. The plane started to shake, and we noticeably changed course to fly around the challenging air. I thought to myself "Welcome to the tropics!"

As we commenced the descent, my mind started to catch up with my mouth and my actions. How would we really know who we would be handing Caramel over to? What if she couldn't recognise her grandfather? What if the grandfather did not turn up to the airport? Where would we go to stay? I remembered that we did not have any hotel reservations.

I suddenly realised that I had taken my family, at full-speed, into a badly thought out adventure, complicating it along the way by taking on responsibility for another minor. I shared my concerns with my wife. She had that "I told you so," look on her face that most women appear to be born with as a standard feature.

Wonderful Adversity: Into Africa

Remembering that 'women have many faults, but men have only two - everything they say and everything they do...' I decided to sit still and keep quiet. My wife had been incredibly supportive of the trip, but now she was looking decidedly anxious. She did not like flying at all, and this was a very long flight - with a very different set of people to which either of us was accustomed. Not many wives would have entertained such an escapade, especially this far.

The plane slowed, the descent was well underway. Children - lots of children - all over the place, were still not strapped into their seats. There was crying, moving of bags around, people leaning over the back of chairs to chat to friends behind. Amazingly, it was all very convivial. It had the atmosphere of a flying village or a massive family coach holiday to the seaside. I smiled, almost giggled. It was refreshing to see so many people, most of whom did not know each other, being a family. As we descended through the three-thousand-foot mark, minutes before the flight would end, crew rushed through the cabin, ensuring as many passengers as possible were strapped in.

The wheels touched down with a screech. The passengers cheered and clapped. It was already well past sunset, and we could barely pick out the lights of the city. Ghana had only just entered 'The Fourth Republic', and was in full reconstruction mode. I knew that infrastructure was going to be a challenge on this trip, but I had expected to see a few more lights.

Before the plane came to a standstill, and long before the 'fasten seat belts' sign had been extinguished, the aisles of the plane were pulsating with bodies. Overhead compartments were opened and contents distributed, hopefully to the correct owners. But nobody could exit the plane until the cabin doors opened. Our little group of five sat still, with me reassuring the clan "We will all get out safely, don't worry. They won't take off again until we have left the plane."

For small children it must have seemed like total mayhem. Some of the adults on the flight were fully fledged West African market women, coming back from merchandise purchasing trips. Their bags were crammed with stuff, and their body shape reflected the same shape as their bags - bulging all over. Genetic or diet, some West African trading ladies can truly have well-endowed upper front and lower back padding zones.

Finally, steps were pushed up to the side of the plane, and the door opened. People spilled out, whilst we sat. After all, we had nowhere to go, and it was our first time here. We would follow the crowd.

Eventually, we waddled to the door opening, stepping out onto the top of the access steps. West Africa hit us all in the face.

The temperature was high, coupled with a sticky humidity. The perfume of the night air, blended with acrid sweat odour, tickled our nostrils. The overwhelming sight of a developing nation airport burned indelibly into my memory. The sounds around were very different too.

A meandering river of people wandered from the plane to the terminal building. Each person loaded with several pieces of hand luggage. Some carried seemingly heavy load on their heads. Everything was different to Europe. These sounds, smells, tastes, and perceptions were so intense that our senses were overloaded. As we walked down the old steps towards the apron, our skin poured sweat, our clothes mopping it up as quickly as it could - but losing the battle. We followed the weaving, wandering conga line towards a big AKWAABA sign at the entrance to the terminal building. Caramel told us excitedly "Akwaaba means welcome in Ghana language."

Inside there was a throng of people. It was more like entering an already overpopulated sardine can than an airport. I never knew people could be packed so closely together. Some were clearly passengers, others were officials, and others seemed to be looking for a friend, or perhaps a pocket to befriend.

"Hey, friend, can I help you?" we were asked incessantly as we tried to shuffle towards the immigration counter. I held children's' hands, and tried to cover my pockets at the same time. I was not feeling very comfortable, but could not let that feeling be shared with my travelling group.

In the distance, I could see a man wearing some sort of crown. He was really well dressed and surrounded by others wearing some sort of traditional wear. He was looking into the crowd, searching with his eyes left and right, up and down. He was the only one wearing the funky headgear, so I guessed that he must either be important or part of a cultural display of some sort.

The children could not see much, being so low down, out of the line of sight. Together we shuffled forwards, passports in hand. Unexpectedly, Caramel shouted "Grandpa!"

I was quite taken aback, Grandpa was supposed to meet us after we had cleared immigration and customs, or so I thought. Perhaps the girl was confused.

Letting go of my hand she ran headlong towards the man in a crown. He bent down and grabbed the child off of the ground, smiling and hugging. A well built lady was standing next to Grandpa, clearly Grandma, for she was quick to get the second hug and would not let go of her captured prize.

We approached, rather unsure of the procedure that was unfolding Hollywood style around us. "Good evening," I proffered, "Are you Caramel's Grandparents?"

As I completed the sentence, Grandma relinquished Caramel to the ground and enveloped myself, wife and children, sequentially into full bodied hugging. Hot, sweaty, but full of care, family loving hugging. Welcome to Africa... or Akwaaba as they say in Ghana!

We became oblivious to the hoards around us, and handed over the passport for Caramel, accepting thanks from the Paramount Chief of an area of Ghana (for that is who Grandpa was), for bringing such a precious cargo

Wonderful Adversity: Into Africa

to the homeland. The international politeness of "Oh, do come and visit us if you are near our community," was extended. Of course, neither phone number nor any address was shared with us. So it was our first taste of the politeness of Africa.

After what seemed like hours we exited the crowded airport. The strongest blast of stale human sweat odour rolled over us all. It was acrid, but it was to be expected in the heat, even more so when you realised that most people were wearing tank tops and flip-flops. I had in my mind to find a taxi and go to the nearest hotel. That is how naive I was.

Fortunately, serendipity was wide awake and looking out for us all. A smartly dressed lady tapped me on the arm, asking "Where are you going?"

I responded "We are looking for a taxi to get to a hotel."

"Which hotel?" the smartly dressed woman asked, innocently, her accent mixed with English, French and some other flavoured intonations.

"No idea. We are new in town and could not make a booking before leaving home," my 'clueless white man for the first time in Africa' response rolled flawlessly out of my mouth.

Smartly smiled, laughed nervously, and asked "Seriously?" her face looking as if she was meeting aliens for the first time.

It really was totally unbelievable, but it was, incredibly, true. "Oh, yes, seriously," I responded, rather proud of myself. My wife nodded slowly, without a smile, in the background, confirming my lack of mental stability and poor judgement. Meanwhile the children were mesmerised by the throng of people, smells and the whole experience.

Smartly said, "Then follow me," and so we did.

In hindsight, the stupidity of it all was beyond logic and should not be carried out by others. It worked for me, but please never travel to Africa without a proper plan.

We followed Smartly to a small mini-bus, where she bundled us all into the back. It was not air-conditioned, but it was clean. She jumped into the front passenger seat and spoke some guttural sounds at the driver. He understood, but we were completely lost in this new culture. The vehicle started to move. I breathed a sigh of relief. We were going to a place with somewhere to sleep. We were all really tired, having started the day with a fire alarm and encountered so many unexpected episodes over the past eighteen hours. But, of course, unexpected episodes were not over for the day.

The mini-bus drove along the pot-holed roads of the city, with the occasional clunk as a wheel dropped into a hole large enough to swallow a small refrigerator. Eventually, we pulled into the courtyard of a hotel. Palm trees, flowers and large glass doors. It was an international chain name - but this was not to the standard of any international hotel I had visited before.

Accepting of the situation, we entered the establishment. The cool air, relatively speaking, of the reception area soothed our damp bodies with a contrasting temperature.

Sending the children with my wife to get some refreshments at the bar, I went to check in. Smartly informed me of the price per night. I laughed, and my wallet had a heart attack. I actually think that my wallet wanted to run back to the airport and fly home. My face must have said it all.

"Umm, this is the normal price for an international hotel in Accra," she offered, almost apologetically.

"Well, this is about four times what I had expected," I pleaded.

"Don't worry, just pay cash for tonight. We will do you a good deal. Then I will find you another hotel in the morning," she offered as an instant, and very acceptable solution, although I am not sure that it was altogether kosher.

I paid over some crisp US dollar bills. I had not changed any money to local currency since it was not possible to purchase Ghana Cedis outside of the country. I walked over to join the family, placing the key fob for the room on the table, innocently.

We drank our soft drinks and headed up to the room, ready for a good night's sleep. As we entered the hotel room, the room phone started to buzz. Dropping bags, I picked it up.

"Good evening!" I exhaled, my cheer falsified, over extreme tiredness, for the benefit of the caller.

"Gud evenin," came a broken ladies voice, "Wud you like some company for dis night?" she asked.

"Ummm sorry?" I asked quizzically, unsure of what I had heard.

"Wud you like me for company dis night?" she offered, trying to glaze her voice with honey.

Unsure of what was going on or being intended, I countered with, "Actually, no, I have my wife and family with me for company."

Her next response finally kicked in my realisation of the 'type of offer' that was being made. "For da right price I don't mind," she giggled.

I hung up quickly, and must have blushed every shade of the rainbow. I wondered how the person knew we were entering our room at that specific time? How did she know the room number? Then, my logic circuits, adjusting to African logic, realised that I had seen some ladies, who could not afford clothing to cover their bodies decently, downstairs. One of them must have noted our room number and decided to try her marketing skills. That was a big lesson in keeping room numbers and keys out of sight in the future.

We all slept like babies, woken the next morning by bright West African sunshine pouring through the curtains, traversing the textiles as if it they were made of transparent plastic, spilling across the bed sheets. Drawing the curtains, I realised that the sky was much brighter than the grey of London we had left just 24 hours ago. The world here looked very different to our home in the French Alps. It was my first experience of an African sky, and it looked good.

It was a new day, without fire alarms. What could possibly go wrong now, we were in Africa!

ACCRA

We went down to the buffet breakfast, where magnificent three dimensional, pastel coloured masterpieces composed of pineapples, bananas, pawpaw, and other tropical fruits awaited us. As we tucked into the fresh fruits of Ghana, Smartly came to the table.

Bending down and whispering in my ear secretively, she told me that we should hurry out of the breakfast area and that the minibus would take us to our new hotel, at a much better rate. Excitedly, we grabbed our rucksacks and headed out front.

Our first stop was a small shop called a 'Forex Bureau' where, in a six-foot by six-foot space, money changing took place. I had no idea if it was a good rate, but at least we now had some local money.

We were not in the bus more than fifteen minutes, but in those minutes of driving in daylight, we saw the challenges of West Africa in full Ultra High Definition. Beggars, hawkers, shack stalls, children running barefoot, rags instead of clothes. My heart went out to them, but I found it hard to contrast with the new 4x4 vehicles on the roads, men in suits and women in stunning multi-coloured cloth fashion parade - intermingled with the signs of poverty.

Our new hotel was just that, new. We were the first, and only, guests in this six bedroom facility. The hotel was either not finished yet, or this was as finished as it was going to get. Our room was massive, and the bathroom big enough to sleep in. It was magnificent. We waved goodbye to Smartly, thanking her for such amazing help.

The hotel had two staff, Old man and Young lady. Old man kindly asked us what we would like for dinner that evening, showing us a menu full of delights. Having made a choice, we were just about to leave, when he asked "Please Sir, can you pay for it now, please."

Old man was clearly trained in the colonial years. He had pride in the way he stood, spoke and interacted. I queried his demand, but he explained that he would need to purchase the required food items for the evening. Not knowing the local customs, I paid him a large number of local bank notes, but that was not necessarily a large amount of money. He went to purchase the evening meal, as we set off to explore the city.

We walked into a major downtown market area, where the hustle and bustle of London would be considered calm in comparison to the day's goings on. Women were walking around with entire shops balanced on their heads. Everybody weaved in and out of each other. Piles of stinking rubbish adorned the ground. People were jumping open drains and avoiding the missing lumps of pavement. If it had been a video game, it would have been a smash hit. I do not think that either Super Mario or Sonic the Hedgehog could have coped though, especially since these players only had one life.

We entered a small textiles shop at the edge of the market, to look at the amazing cloth strips called Kente. Spectacular hand woven compositions of colour and texture hung around the shop. Thinking, as strange as it seemed, that I had heard Caramel, I swung around to see where the voice came from.

In a second I had disappeared. Lost in the warmth of a Grandma hug. I am glad that I had inhaled before she enveloped me, it possibly saved my life. Caramel and Grandma were out shopping before returning to their community in the bush-lands. All of us were in a better position to talk, no longer in the crowded immigration hall at night, but now in a crowded market in daylight.

"What are the chances of meeting these people in this market?" I asked myself, almost out loud. There was something special going on, but I had no idea what.

"You must come to the village and visit us!" Grandma stated, thrusting a small piece of paper in my hand, with some sort of address on it. It had no street name, no house number, but a 'location'. I thanked her, slipping the paper deep into my sweat lined trouser pocket.

They continued shopping, Caramel looking back and waving repeatedly. We set off to lunch in an open air restaurant, called a 'Chop Bar', inside the market area.

To make the service easy, we ordered four plates of fish and chips. The waitress was so excited at the little white family eating in her Chop Bar, she ran off to the kitchen in double-quick time. We drank coke from glass bottles that appeared to have been stolen from the Happy Day's set in Hollywood. After twenty minutes, waitress returned and said, in very broken English. "Da fish no got," I thought about the structure of the sentence, and the words used - rearranged and found "Got No Fish."

Smiling, I said, "OK, we will take chicken then." It was a tough call, since there were chickens running under all the tables in the eating area, picking up scraps, jumping up and down into the open ditches. A few minutes later we heard a chicken being killed. At least we knew that lunch was on its way, and it would be fresh.

Twenty minutes later waitress returned. Smilingly, she uttered "da chips got finished."

I translated to "They have no chips," for the benefit of the family. Frustrated, I turned to her asking "What do you have?"

"Yam!" she exclaimed, as if having just found gold after a month of trekking through jungles.

"Yam then, please," I acknowledged, learning fast that things here were very different to France and England.

Finally, food arrived. However, it was not exactly, how might one put it, edible. They had covered it with some black sauce. I asked what it was called, to be told gleefully "Shito."

I had another name for it "Fire and brimstone with a hint of fish." It was way too spicy hot. It burnt our lips, our tongues and that which entered our stomachs burned even more. It festered inside us, like molten lava in a rumbling volcano. It was time to head back to the hotel, where we hoped that Old Man had managed to purchase some food that we would be able to eat!

DESTINY

Old Man was at the reception desk, apparently waiting for us, fast asleep, head laid upon his folded arms. I coughed loudly, repeatedly, until he raised his eyelids sufficiently to reveal his bloodshot eyes. A few seconds passed, as if he was trying to remember who was who and where he was. Old Man jumped to attention, shouted "Yes Master," and welcomed us, his smile overcoming any irritation that I may have felt.

After dropping the day's purchases into the bedroom, with its two massive twin beds suitable to accommodate our little clan, and a quick clean-up from the dust of the market, it was soon 6:30pm, time for the evening meal.

Being so close to the equator, the days in southern Ghana are approximately 12 hours long, every day of the year. The sun kisses the ground each morning between 05:30 and 06:00, and bids the surface 'goodnight' at around 6pm each evening.

The dining room was dark, partly because the sun had bid adieu to this part of the planet for the day, but also because of the decor and the lack of electricity. It provided a massive contrast with the bright daytime kaleidoscope of colours. The lack of light would make seeing the food more difficult, but we would have to manage.

Several rounds of soft drinks, in 1960's style glass bottles, were delivered to the table, along with straws to sip from, plus a few litres of bottled water.

I had not realised how thirsty I was, let alone considered the hydration challenges for my children.

Finally, Young Lady came out from the kitchen with our ordered food of Chicken Club Sandwiches with chips. Imagine our surprise at the food before us; sweet, yellowish, cotton wool textured bread, spread with some sort of margarine, sprinkled with chicken skin covered with a thin layer of chicken meat, and some leaves that we were informed was local lettuce. The chips looked like they had been fried earlier in the day and reheated - several times. I smiled, and we all thanked Young Lady. She curtsied, and took her leave.

Hungry, we ate what we could. Still hungry retired to our room for the night. It was not late, but we were all tired, falling asleep without any rocking, despite the rumbling tummies.

It could not have yet reached 10pm, when I awoke. My abdomen felt as if there was a full blown performance of Riverdance taking place inside. Sensing the worst that could happen probably would, I darted for the bathroom. I tried putting the light on, but the power was off. Taking my seat upon the Throne of Glory, in the pitch black of the night, my rear end exploded, playing the Thomas Crapper anthem at full volume, with harmonics. Between the gas and liquid that exited my system, seemingly at speeds approaching Mach 1, sounding as if they had, and the agonising cramps in my abdomen, I felt as if I was about to either enter orbit or die from being blown inside out.

Groaning, I doubled up, believing that my destiny was to remain glued to the rim of the toilet for ever. Then I heard a little voice at the door. "Daddy, I have a sore tummy." Quickly, I carried out an interim clean up exercise, and allowed the seat of power to be used by my daughter. She too emptied the contents of her little alimentary tract in seconds - and just as well, because there was a groan coming from the bedroom. Over the next ninety minutes we all took it in turns to attempt to foul up the entire waste system of the hotel - if not Accra. Finally, it appeared to have come to an end, with all four of us, bowels empty, standing in the bathroom - wait, three of us, for one had fallen asleep on the floor. Now we understood the need for a large bathroom in this part of the world; for toilet parties.

Whether it was the festering Shito or the Club Sandwich, nobody will ever know, but it was gone now. This trip would require a different approach to nutrition - and a lot more hydration. With everybody tucked up into bed, sleep took each of us away, one by one.

The next dawn was that of Sunday. As soon as the sun peered into our room, I was up. The rest of the family slept as if in suspended animation. Knowing that I was responsible for the trip, and had only brought the clan here on the basis of a 'feeling', I decided to explore the neighbourhood, solo.

Pulling on some clothes and slipping my feet into walking shoes, I crept out of the room, down the stairs and past a dozing Old Man with his head on a desk. Young Lady was sleeping on the bare, cool floor, covered in just a large piece of cotton cloth. He raised his head, looked at me, and returned to his dream land. She did not stir in the least! Leaving the compound of the hotel, I breathed the cool morning air. Cool is a relative term in the tropics.

The street was busy, people fetching water from a standpipe, ladies carrying children wrapped onto their backs with a piece of cloth. This was a hustle and bustle of a 'getting ready' nature, as opposed to the buy and sell mayhem of the market. I passed a walled off area with some wooden shacks in it. In the middle there was a small camp fire arrangement, with tree branches for fuel and a large aluminium pot sitting on top of some large rocks. There, guarding the food pot, sat a woman wrapped in just a piece of cloth with a net over her hair. She was stirring the contents of the pot, using every bit of strength in her body, stopping the pot moving by holding it down with two metal bars, using her feet. Next to her, a goat with two kids wandered around accompanied by some small bantam like chicken. All over the compound, people were moving, getting dressed, brushing their teeth, combing hair. It all took place in the open air. I realised that these people lived in the wooden shacks, and with a little extra visual scanning, I noticed that they slept on mats on the floor. This was not just a small walled off area with wooden shacks in it, this was somebody's home. The camp fire, well, that was the kitchen. My attention was moved away from home viewing by a man peeing into the gutter just a few yards away from where I stood. Realising that I had just discovered their bathroom, I decided to walk smartly on, feeling embarrassed at having innocently invaded the privacy of a family or two, or perhaps three. Further on, I noticed a growing smell of faeces, reminiscent of my past evening's toilet party. It was coming from a piece of shrub land, and therein were people squatting, albeit discretely, doing their business, al fresco. I was beginning to understand how people lived, or perhaps survived would have been a better term.

I kept on walking, wondering what to do with the family that day, when I came across a church. Although I had been brought up by a lay pastor, and been subjected to many long sermons, we did not attend church regularly as a family. Don't get me wrong, there is nothing wrong with church, but I believed that faith was more important than religion, and still do. All the same, I wondered if a visit to an African Church might be a fun thing for the family to do that morning. The notice board stated that the service would start at 10am. Armed with a plan, I went back to the hotel.

Old Man and Young Lady had relinquished their sleeping spots, and were busying themselves caring for the establishment. I greeted them, and they responded politely.

Upstairs, the family were almost stirring. Children much more so than my poor wife, who had taken the worst battering of her digestive system of any of us. Brightly and full of energy I proposed a 'trip to church', which I promised would be 'fun'.

An hour later, the crew, almost feeling human, were ready to descend the stairs for breakfast. One look at the breakfast table, and the whole idea of feeding the rumbling tummies, with more material for rapid ejection, was not as welcome as we had hoped. We sipped some water and nibbled on the corners of some toast. That was enough for that meal. The motion of just going back to bed was tabled, and rejected. We were going to church.

Walking past the al fresco family compound was now very different. They were all dressed in party clothes. Frilly dresses on the little girls, collars and ties on the boy-children. Men looking smart and ladies dressed in, what was obviously, their Sunday Best. I spotted the lady from the cooking pot, amazingly transformed into the most well presented woman in the country. I realised at that point that many Africans, regardless of their poor conditions of living, are full of pride and a determination to put on a brave and colourful front. If I had not witnessed the scene of a few hours earlier, I would never have believed that these beautifully presented families lived in abject poverty. I felt for them, respecting them enormously.

Arriving at the church, we made quite a stir. The doorman showed us to a pew and we sat patiently listening to the church organist practicing on an electronic keyboard. Well, I thought it was practice.

The church filled - to the point where no seats were left, and then, amongst the sea of black faces, a white chap walked in with his wife and four children. It is amazing how you instantly feel an association with a person of the same skin colour, especially when you feel as if you are in the minority. I had never known that feeling before, but now I did, and in buckets. I smiled, realising that he had also noticed that there was only one other white family in the whole place. An understanding of being a minority permeated my body for the first time. The other family were in the front row, whilst we sat at the back.

After the first song, the other white man stood up and addressed the crowd. It was no longer a congregation, it was a crowd. People were hanging around the open doors, and standing at the back of the room, this was not like a Church in the UK or France, where the empty seats outnumber the occupied ones by ten to one.

He was the preacher. He preached a simple sermon, with some translation into local language going on. It made the whole sermon twice as long - perhaps longer. The translation was clearly not 'altogether precise'. For each one sentence from Preacher, the translator made about four sentences. Sometimes, the Preacher said something which was not funny, but when translated into local lingo the crowd giggled.

A folded note was passed over my shoulder, and dropped into my lap. It was like being back in school where notes were passed from desk-to-desk without the teacher knowing.

Surprised, I opened it. "My dear brother, God has sent you to me. I need a sewing machine and some money to start a business," the note was written in well formed, cursive script. I refolded it, and slid it into my pocket, hoping that Preacher had not noticed me being naughty in his classroom.

Then, another note arrived "My dear brother, God has sent you to me. I need a bicycle and some money." I refolded it and hid it away, trying to ensure that I did not get caught. The handwriting was incredibly similar to the first note.

As the final hymn was sung, a group gathered around my little family. I felt uncomfortable. Everybody wanted to be our friends, and they all needed something. More notes, and a plethora of verbal requests for help. I rubbed my head, checking that I was not wearing a cap with 'FREE MONEY HERE' embroidered on it. All the same, I had to understand that, for them, we had everything. My morning expedition had taught me that many of them had nothing. Wealth really is relative.

Eventually, the cavalry came. Preacher broke through the circle of new friends and wannabe recipients of sewing machines and bicycles, and pulled us clear. He invited us back to his home for a 'cup of tea'. It is amazing how welcome that phrase can be.

The children all played together, whilst Preacher and Preacher's Wife sat and chatted with my wife and I. Preacher asked me "So, why are you in Ghana?"

After a long pause, I replied honestly "I don't know."

That was a bit of a show stopper. Silence hung in the air. Nobody quite knew what to say. Eventually, I proffered. "A couple of months back I felt compelled to come to Ghana, without any rhyme or reason. It was such a strong feeling that we came."

For a man of God and lead by faith, the look on his face was, well, rather doubtful and disbelieving. After all, nobody just goes someplace because they felt compelled to. Or do they?

In an attempt to humour me, and the women folk, he asked "So, what do you do for a living?"

"I work in information technology and engineering," I responded, realising that my skills were several light years ahead of the conditions that the local folks lived in.

Shaking his head, he asked me to elaborate.

"I work with robots, CNC machine tools, write software and even build computers and install them, as well as creating the software needed for whatever needs done." It was not rocket science, but he was clearly having difficulties understanding my English accent, my motivation and my skills set.

He shook his head again. "You won't believe what I am going to tell you," he sighed, and told a story.

Apparently, around the time of my 'inspiration to visit Ghana', the church had been donated a batch of computers from the USA, for the creation of a computer school. The idea being to upgrade the skills of the local people. Sadly, when they tried to set them up, nothing worked. So, the congregation had told Preacher that they wanted to pray to God to send somebody to fix their computer school. They had a prayer meeting and that was that.

I had realised long ago that mankind is connected. Thinking about somebody and then they call you... Travelling far from home and meeting the next door neighbour... Needing something to eat, and somebody dropping by with exactly what you needed...

If you connect with humanity and the planet, through whatever means, humanity and the planet will connect with you.

Some people attribute these things to coincidence, others to the supernatural, some to religion, others blame aliens. Whatever you put life's serendipitous moments down to, it is real, and it is there for everybody, if they will only connect with it. Despite my father's attempts during my childhood to indoctrinate me with very passionate views on a particular denomination of a particular religion being the only right way, I had a different approach. I believe that Faith is more important than Religion. Faith is a belief in something, whereas Religion is a man made set of rules used to bind that Faith to a culture. I had, and have, a strong Faith and realised that this meeting was not a coincidence, it was destined. We were connected. How, why and by what did not matter.

"Well, I can take a look at the computers for you," I offered. Preacher had no idea who I was, but he trusted me, for some reason. He took me to the room with the computers in. It was a mess. The machines were badly in need of some tender loving care, software and configuration. It was all possible, with time and effort, and I knew that I could do it.

"I can fix some of these machines up for you. Tomorrow perhaps?" Once again, my mouth worked independently of my responsibilities. I gave no thought for my family, but focused on the need that I could address, thinking in the here and now.

Returning to the manse, the women folk and children were happy together. Both sides finding solace in soul mates, playmates and instant friendship. It was as if we had always known each other.

Before long, Preacher's Wife had a spread of food on the table, soft-tummy-friendly-food. We all tucked in, heartily. During the meal, Preacher informed the table of our plans to fix up computers the next day. Amazingly, everybody was happy.

Preacher's Wife gave hints and tips on food that would be safe, and shared stories of their family settling into the challenges of the country. It was good to know that we were not alone in experiencing tummy troubles. There are 'good foods' and 'bad foods' in every culture, and those travelling to new areas are best to find out, before experimenting, which ones are safe and which ones are likely to send you to hospital with a prolapsed bowel.

Time flies when you are making friends and sharing stories. Before we knew it the clock had fast-forwarded to bed-time, and we headed back to the comfort of the hotel.

Wonderful Adversity: Into Africa

COMPUTERS

I entered the computer room with Preacher. He was terribly correct and well mannered. I was a little rougher around the edges. A local chap was in charge of the computer room, with the title of 'Computer School Manager'. He nearly jumped through the ceiling with joy at the sight of this 'sent from God' man who was there to 'fix all the problems'. Whether I was sent by God, or called by their belief and passion for a solution, that is up to each individual to decide, but the fact is, they prayed and I arrived. I did not feel like an 'answer from God', no, just a human doing what I felt I should do. Whatever it was, there was a need. I could, and should, meet that need.

The hot room was a challenge to work in. Louvre blade windows and a slow spinning ceiling fan worked together to suck and blow hot and dusty air over my sticky, sweaty body. I opened each machine up, discovering that not all of the machines had RAM, and some connectors were simply lose. Some had blown power supplies, and others were clearly the victims of old age, beyond economic repair. It is amazing that people will donate clearly broken items to regions where repair is nigh-impossible.

Working like Dr Frankenstein on steroids, and with the help of Manager and Preacher, we pulled parts out of some machines and fitted them back into others. It was spare-part surgery, at board level! Sometimes it worked, sometimes it did not. There were a few sparks here and there, and a few choice words from my mouth, that got a stern look from Preacher. Regardless, by lunchtime, five machines were actually running.

Pastor's wife fed us all, again. We were feeling thankful that God had sent her to save us from starvation! In my opinion, no man or woman should ever feel that 'cooking and hosting' is 'just' a job or a duty. Providing food for visitors, hosting travellers and caring for the family is the most important role on the planet. It is far too often overlooked and rarely given the credit it deserves. As I ate another mouthful of tummy safe food I was more thankful than the Manager could ever be for his computers working.

That afternoon I searched through the available floppy disks, found some suitable software and loaded it all up. After providing a small training course to the excited and ready to learn 'Computer School Manager', my job was done. The new computer school was ready to start operations.

Feeling incredibly 'Mission Accomplished', and all of us feeling better for eating well, including learning what was, and was not, safe to eat in this part of the world, we bid the Preacher family farewell. We realised that we had met, shared, helped, been helped and now it was time to move on. My reason for travelling to Ghana satisfied, we were free to travel inland, as tourists, before heading back to our French mountain home.

PEUGEOT

Having taken advice about 'tummy-safe-food' from Preacher's wife, we stocked up on crackers and water, packing our things carefully in our trusty rucksacks. We were ready to take the bus from Accra to Kumasi. We had been told that the STC (State Transport Company) bus was the safest way to travel inland, and we were ready to give it a try.

Waving goodbye to Old Man and Young Lady, we took a taxi to the bus station. Ignorance is bliss, and if I had known how chaotic it was going to be, I would never have headed there. Everything was as unclear as possible, queuing for a ticket was not straightforward, nor was getting one. Finally, after being in the wrong queue for a while, some shouting and a lot of frustration, we were aboard a nice 'clean looking' bus.

We filed in along with the many passengers. My wife and I sat on one pair of seats, with the children on the two seats in front of us. The bus quickly filled. To my amazement extra seats were added, to fill the aisle. One-by-one each seat was occupied, and every inch of space consumed either with human beings, baggage or merchandise. It became obligatory to breathe the mixed spice filled air, pungently laden with the smell of local foods.

The bus sat, heating up in the sun, as if waiting for the passengers to be cooked before delivering them to their destination. Then, without warning, the overloaded vehicle lurched forwards, out of the yard and onto the road. We were on our way. The welcome breeze from the window helped to cool and refresh the bus - a much needed process for the general health of the half-cooked folks aboard.

The road in the city had some potholes, but once out on the intercity highway, it got rough - to say the least. The driver knew the road, and demonstrated his familiarity by driving creatively. Whereas in the UK vehicles drive on the left of the road, and in France on the right, I quickly discovered that, for the sake of comfort and protection of the suspension of the bus, our driver chose to place his wheels on whichever side of the road had the least potholes. This led to some incredible weaving, and the occasional emergency 'side-of-road-change', either for the avoidance of oncoming traffic or to circumnavigate a broken-down vehicle on the side, or in the middle, of the road.

We saw all sorts of vehicle skeletons, smashed up and rusting away, tucked away in the bush to the side of the road. I realised that travelling on a bus in a developing nation carries a few more risks than any other form of transport in the world.

There were other, non-life-threatening risks of being aboard 'high-density-seating' transport. When the children asked for a biscuit, their mother opened a packet, taking one each for us. However, before it could be passed to our hungry children, the lady squished next to me reached in for her share. Shocked but unable to say anything through lack of cultural and linguistic understanding, it was obligatorily overlooked. Quickly, the packet was passed over to the kids. Being polite, after taking one biscuit each, they offered the chap next to them, shoe-horned into the aisle seat, a biscuit. Before a moment had passed the packet was mobile and being passed around the bus until empty. I learned never to share food in public in a developing nation, unless you are ready to share widely.

Of course, it was not a one-way deal. When those around us opened their food, of a local nature, they would kindly say "You are invited," with a smile. Based on past experiences of local food, and being in a confined, inescapable location, it was best to decline anything that might cause embarrassment through any potential interaction with our delicate digestive systems.

Finally, reaching Kumasi, the Garden City as it is called, we discovered what humidity really is. If we had thought Accra was humid, then Kumasi was a walk-in swimming pool. You could practically drink the air. Every single step resulted in a trickle of water down the back. I had to blow sharply to disperse sweat from running off my lip, into my mouth. It was exhausting. Consequently, we asked for a taxi to take us to an economy hotel.

The hotel had a proper swimming pool, which we all enjoyed. Furthermore, there was working air-conditioning in the rooms. This was the life! Africa at its best. To round off the day, the hotel had a proper Chinese restaurant, run by a friendly oriental chap. Rice, with chicken and cashew nuts was the order of the day. It went down well, and stayed in the right place.

The next morning, we did the family orientated tourist things that there are to do in Kumasi. Visit the zoo, watch wood carving and enjoy the markets. By now we had all become accustomed to being called 'Obruni'. Obruni means 'foreigner', but is often used to mean 'white person'. It was not intended as an offensive term.

With the family relaxing by the pool, back at the hotel, I wanted to do some things, just for me. One was to visit the Magazine, a renowned market place where used and patter car spares were sold. Furthermore, the

Magazine had a substantial engineering, or rather bush-engineering, centre. I also wanted to visit Kumasi Airport.

I started with the Magazine. I was barely into the first five stalls of salvaged car parts, when a young man 'attached himself' to me, rather like a tick. No matter where I went, twisted or turned, he was by my side, calling me 'Obruni'. Irritated by his constant fascination with me, I asked a market lady how to refer to my parasitic friend. She informed me that 'Obibini' meant African, or 'black person'. From then on, every time he would 'Obruni' me, I responded with 'Obibini' hoping for some release from his attention. It did not work; in fact it attracted more local youngsters, all wanting to hear me call them 'Obibini' in response to their calling me 'Obruni'. My frustration finally gave in to amusement, and I abandoned seeing any more of the magazine, laughing my way into the front passenger seat of the first taxi I could find.

It was a rather bashed, faded blue, Peugeot 504 estate. Not a modern motorcar by anybody's reckoning. The driver was a skinny, small chap, with a massive smile. His command of the English language was poor, but he quickly understood that I wanted to go to the airport.

He dropped me at the entrance. I paid him and he smiled widely. Entering the terminal building, I realised that this was a little used airport. My very presence created a stir, and the airport manager was called to meet the Obruni man who was asking questions about aeroplanes.

Inviting me into his office, he started on the offensive. "Do you have security clearance to be here?"

"Umm, no, I am a pilot and I like aeroplanes and wanted to see the airport," I ventured, wondering if I was in trouble or not.

"What do you want to know and why?" he came back snappily.

"I fly small planes, with two seats, used for teaching people how to fly, and I just wondered if you had any planes to rent here, and how often this airport is used?" I gave him my most honest answer, remembering that honest had gotten me into trouble in the past, but knowing that it was the best policy.

"Well, this is Ghana, and we don't have that sort of thing. We used to under Kwame Nkrumah, our first President, but now flying is for the military and airlines only," he replied, but he had not finished, adding, "But, umm, I think that we need to call National Security about your asking these questions."

I had no idea how my honest interest could get me into trouble so quickly. Feeling a little uncomfortable, I sat there and waited. Two pleasant chaps turned up and started to ask me questions. They also wanted to look at my passport, and any other pieces of identity I had on me. One of the men shared with me that in the 1960's Ghana had a programme run by a pilot called Hanna Reitsch, from Germany, for teaching people to fly, but that it was stopped by the coup in 1966. They explained very nicely that there were no small planes in Kumasi, and that there was no flying for the general public in Ghana. It was all very cordial. I was allowed to leave without any charges being brought against me.

Breathing a sigh of relief, I left the terminal building. To my surprise, Peugeot driver was waiting for me. He had decided that I would never get a taxi if he left. He was probably right. I got into his taxi, glad to be back with a smiling, friendly face. Without any chatter, he took me back to the hotel. I thanked him for his good service, and wished him goodnight.

The next morning, we planned to head to Tamale, in the North of Ghana. We would go to the bus station for another exciting episode of STC road weaving. As we exited the hotel, Peugeot was sitting outside. On seeing us he jumped up and waved. I was pleased to see him, and took the family over to meet the happy chap. We piled in and I asked him to take us to the bus depot.

"Why master?" he asked, in his thick accent.

"We are going to Tamale today," I explained.

"I take you Tamale. Peugeot strong car for Ghana road," he offered.

It never occurred to me to take a taxi half way across the country, but he was willing and had already shown care taking of me the day before. He drove well, and missed more potholes that the STC drivers! So, after some negotiations, a deal was struck. We had our own private taxi to Tamale, for about the double the money.

It was a good decision. Biscuits lasted longer, there was more space, and the children slept across the rear seat. I sat up front watching out for pot holes, broken down vehicles and the many other challenges of the road to the north.

Peugeot was great, he didn't understand much of what I asked him, but he always gave an answer. Often that answer was just a simple "Yes please Master," even if the answer had no possible relevance to the question I had asked. It reminded me of my learning to speak French. I had a lot more sympathy for Patron and those who had struggled to understand me and my constant "Oui Oui."

Tamale contrasted Kumasi. Here the air was dry. Our lips were already suffering from the dry heat. We were closer to the Sahara Desert, and although a long way away from it, that proximity could be felt in the air, and sensed in the clothes of the people. This was a much more Moslem area, but also an area that had a less dense population. Everybody treated us so well. We were welcomed like celebrities wherever we went. The hotel was thrilled to have clients, and gave us outstanding treatment, within the confines of the resources available to them. It was basic, but it was safe and clean.

Water did not flow from the taps, but rather dribbled. We all learned to fill a bucket, slowly, and take a bucket bath. It was refreshing, especially after the long day on the road. I paid for a room for Peugeot, and we all settled for the night.

At 4am the world exploded. Somebody was chanting outside our window. "Ohhhhhhh laaaa Laaaaaa Ohhhhhh Laaaa" I thought I heard. Jumping up, wondering if it was a fire alarm, I listened more intently "Alla-hu akkkkkbar, alla-hu akkkkkbar," and looking out of the window saw the minaret of the mosque - just outside our window. It was just the morning call to prayer. Wife and children had started to stir, wondering what was going on. I explained, and they all placed their pillows firmly over their heads, seeking the remnant of their night's sleep. I joined them, wishing no disrespect to the religion and custom around me.

When the real morning dawned, we discovered that Tamale had little to see. So, we decided to head to Mole Game Reserve, a place where we had read about elephants, lions and antelope living freely. Apparently it was possible to walk amongst them.

Peugeot loaded his trusty wagon, and we all waved goodbye to the very pleasant hotel manager. Along the way, I saw a sign for Tamale airport. Commenting on it was enough for Peugeot to interpret that "Obruni want go da airport," and without my knowing detoured to a reasonably sized airport, parking right out front.

The temptation was now too much for me, I had to go in and ask about light aviation. In the same way as my visit to Kumasi Airport. The manager received me, asking "What are you doing here?" however, he did not threaten me with the security services.

He confirmed the story from Kumasi, but also suggested that I visited the Ghana Civil Aviation Authority building in Accra. He was far more positive and made encouraging noises about the possibility of flying light planes in the country. We shook hands.

Returning to the trusty Peugeot, we once again headed towards Mole, guided by our faithful driver.

The road to Mole was a long and dusty one, the surface covered with compacted red laterite. Compacted may well have been an ambitious word for the condition, since we seemed to leave a red dust cloud behind us, and drive through such clouds from the oncoming traffic.

Our windows were wide open, in an attempt to reduce the temperature inside the car. It was an exercise in futility. Whatever we did, we could only hope for a fraction of a degree respite. What we did manage, was to coat our bodies, clothes, bags, hair and every nook and cranny with fine red-laterite dust.

Exiting the car on arrival at Mole, we looked more like sunburnt American Indians than British people with fair skin. At least the dust acted as sun screen, so it was not all bad.

Mole was clearly not a very busy place. The visitor centre was built on a raised area, looking down over the forest and watering holes. The guest house had magnificent views, but not a magnificent swimming pool. That was a half-full, squirming green mire of algae and frogs. The rooms were simple, but the water supply was not great. Upon opening the taps, the a brownish wet stuff trickled out. It was clearly not 'safe', based on my experiences.

Getting clean was going to be a challenge, as would hydration. We had consumed all of our water supplies on the road, planning to replenish stocks at the game reserve. So, full of good cheer, I headed to the guest house bar, to purchase some water and soft drinks.

"We have one bottle of water, two bottle of coke and plenty of beer," came the response from the bartender.

My face must have looked a picture, not only covered in red laterite dust, but shocked at the lack of facilities at this tourist destination.

He added, "But we will get more tomorrow morning. Tomorrow we send for supplies before dawn." I guess that they had been busy or badly stocked... or perhaps both!

I took all the non-alcoholic beverages that I could, and added one bottle of beer. We tried to clean up, without much success. The children drank the coke. I planned on using the beer for adult teeth brushing, and we tried to make it all go around as fairly and safely as possible.

It was already late, so we all settled down for the night, especially since there was no electricity to our room. The windows had no curtains, and some of the louvre blades were missing. At least we had nature's night-time display of sparkling stars. Standing at the window, I could pick out the tree tops of the forest below, aware that some amazing wildlife was living just metres from our window. It was exciting.

The night was hot, and I awoke, thirsty. The only 'safe' to drink liquid was the beer. It had been open a while, and was very warm, but it was wet. I took a sip. My head exploded, it had been a long time since I had taken any alcohol into my system. I felt woozy from just one mouthful, and put the bottle back down, leaving it reserved for teeth brushing. Thirsty, and a little disorientated, I went back to bed. Tomorrow had to be a better day, surely.

ELEPHANTS

The next morning, the bartender brought bottles of water to the room, permitting us to thoroughly refresh ourselves. Later, we went on a foot-safari around the park, accompanied by a game warden. It was stunning. Antelopes, crocodiles, elephants, wart-hogs, baboons and more birds than you could count. It was so magnificent. If this had been the only reason for coming to Ghana, it was worth it.

Exhausted from the trek, we settled for a second evening in our basic room overlooking the canopy of the forest.

Deciding to take an early trek into the park the next morning, we set out before dawn. There is nothing more amazing than walking through the West African forest as the sun rises. The colours, temperature changes and sounds all come together in a magnificent symphony to start the day. A secretary bird crossed our path, looking at us as if to say "Humans don't wake up this early!" We saw tracks of many animals, fresh from their nocturnal meanderings. At one point we got really close to a young elephant. It was so amazing to see such wildlife in close proximity. The young elephant's mother was not so impressed at seeing humans close up - which resulted in a rapid retreat by our group at one point. I now know that nobody ever runs fast, until one is being chased by a cow elephant!

Later, by the watering hole, the children played close to the baboons - in hindsight, way too close, but at the time it looked cute. It was a magnificent experience.

We rested for the afternoon, and planned an early return to the south the next morning. There was just one more 'must do' on our list, before leaving the country, and that was visiting the Akosombo Dam.

NEW NAME

Peugeot told us that he would be happy to drive us all the way back to Accra, and that he knew where Akosombo was. Full of confidence, we set off early in the morning, heading south.

It took longer than planned, and we had to spend a night in a hotel along the way, finally reaching Akosombo in the early afternoon, a day later than planned.

In the 1960's, Akosombo hydroelectric dam was constructed, creating the largest man-made lake in the world, and a legacy of power production. With a surface area of over 8,500 square kilometres (3,280 square miles) and a shore line estimated to be approaching 7,500km (4,660 miles), it is one of the wonders of West Africa.

We sat on the balcony of the Volta Hotel, eating salad, and enjoying really cold water from a glass. It was sheer luxury compared to the previous week of adventures. We could look down on the dam wall, watching the water swirling downstream, after passing through the massive turbines, powering

Wonderful Adversity: Into Africa

the whole country. A work of engineering art, a masterpiece and something to top off the day.

Conscious of wanting to be back in the city before the day was over, we extracted ourselves, embarking on the final leg of our trip. About twenty minutes along the way, I spotted a road sign for a town I remembered from somewhere. I fumbled in my collection of cards and bits of paper accumulated since arriving. Sure enough it was there on a small scrap of paper. It was the location on the piece of paper that Grandma had given to me in the market.

I showed the paper to Peugeot, and he stopped to ask directions. It was a detour, but it was an exciting idea for us all to go and see Caramel, and her grandparents! After all, what harm could a quick drop-in visit in the African bush do?

We seemed to drive for a very long time, finally coming across a large house with a wall around it. An officious looking man came to the gate. I explained that we had come to visit Grandpa, Grandma and Caramel. He was not impressed. "You need an appointment to see the Paramount Chief," he barked, his face crumpled through frowning.

I was not going to be chased away so easily. "Please tell him that the family who brought Caramel to the country are here to visit," I requested.

He went away, and a few minutes later a small group of people, including some children, ventured onto the balcony of the building. Moving clear of the obstacle of the gate, which obscured a clear line of sight, we all stepped back in order to get a better look at the balcony, and to be seen more clearly.

Something happened on the balcony; jumping, shouting, exclamations and proclamations in all sorts of languages. It was Caramel, Grandma and some other locals, looking to see who was at the gate. Upon seeing us, they entered into jubilation mode, West African style.

The gate bolt clunked open, and the gate swung welcomingly wide. The gate man transformed into a smiling and welcoming soul.

We climbed the concrete steps, joining the family on the balcony. Apparently Grandpa was busy, but would join us soon. Hugs all round, and that included the enveloping Grandma hugs, requiring a large inhalation prior to participation.

The children played together, smiling, looking at some recently born kittens, playing with dogs, running, skipping and generally doing what kids do best.

Grandma took my wife and I into a long room, with sofas and chairs lining the two long sides, and a wooden ceremonial stool at one end. In due course Grandpa came in, draped in a large piece of cloth, and sat upon the wooden chieftaincy stool.

He smiled, welcoming us to his palace. Yes, we were in his palace. No wonder the gate man had been so cautious. Asking questions of every kind about our trip, he absorbed everything we had to say. Grandma raised her hands with excitement at many of the incidents, and we all laughed a great deal.

One of my random statements, probably not fully thought through before I opened my mouth, created a massive reaction.

"I enquired in Kumasi and Tamale about light aviation, but was told that Ghana has no small planes or General Aviation," I lamented, omitting my interface with the security services.

"I flew in a small two-seat plane just last week," Grandpa stated, correcting my ignorance, and adding "I flew with the President. He is a good pilot."

I was taken aback. I had been asking about aviation around the country, and the answer lay with the man who we had first met on arrival, the man whose granddaughter we had accompanied from the UK.

Grandpa went on to explain that a local Italian man had a two-seat cloth covered plane, and that the President would sometimes fly it at the weekend. Grandpa was privileged to take a short ride in it, with the President, between the time of our arrival in the country and the time of us sitting in the palace with this Chief. Apparently, the President wanted to see active light aviation in the country, but apart from military and commercial aircraft, there was only this one little two-seat plane that was active, to his knowledge.

He went on to describe it. It was clearly an Ultra Light! My mind was blown. A few sentences further on, Grandpa looked at me, asking "Which day of the week were you born on?"

"Ah, that is complicated," I responded, "My birth certificate indicates a Saturday, but my mother insists that I was born on a Thursday. She always tells me that 'Thursday's child has far to go', and that is why I live in France and travel to Africa."

"Well, your mother is always right," he pointed out, adding "You will now be called Yaw, meaning boy born on a Thursday. Yaw Obruni."

He paused for a moment, then added "But you fly aeroplanes. Hmm. You are a captain. You will be called 'Captain Yaw Obruni'."

The next twenty minutes involved me dressing in traditional cloth, sitting on a wooden stool and being inducted into my new African family. I felt very at home. Perhaps I was born in the wrong place on this planet.

Before we left, another piece of paper was thrust into my hands. This time it was the contact details of the Italian pilot who operated the small plane. I was so happy.

Once outside, we realised that the night was falling fast, and we still needed to make it to Accra. The car's lights were not great, so, I asked Peugeot to take his time, which he did. It would have been a shame to end our trip in an accident, for we had witnessed too many along the sides of the roads already.

As we drove down the rural roads towards the main highway, the sweet smell of neem trees in flower permeated the air. Even at night, the heat was still suffocating, especially once we hit the edge of the city. The concrete buildings act as storage heaters, absorbing the sun's rays during the day, and releasing the heat back to the otherwise cooling night air. The smells changed as we entered the city too. Open drains, open defecation and free range urination combined to give the night air a perfume that climbed aggressively through the car window. We could have closed the windows, if only we did not seek the relative cooling effect of the blowing air. Unfortunately, Peugeot did not have the benefit of air-conditioning in his car.

We checked into a different hotel, much closer to the airport, for we were due to fly out the next day. We paid Peugeot, more than we had promised, and hugged him goodbye, thanking him for his careful care of us across the tarmac spotted potholes of Ghana.

One more night, and we would be going home.

SERENDIPITY

The next morning, I tried to call the Italian Pilot, but the number simply did not go through, despite my prayers to Strowger for a miracle on the erratic exchange network. After breakfast we took a walk out from the hotel along the street. It was a completely different part of town, far more built up, with walled homes and no visible signs of poverty.

Suddenly, a car honked loudly, screeching to a standstill next to us. We all jumped out of our skins. It was Preacher.

Leaping out of the car, he was clearly happy to see us all. We shared our stories of travelling around the country, and he updated us on the success of the computer school, which was now enrolling students. Furthermore, he gave us the number of his newly acquired mobile phone. Mobile was a bit of an exaggeration, since his phone was about the size of a house brick, and not much lighter.

We now had a way to keep in contact. He drove off smiling, as we all waved, happy to close the circle of the visit. We enjoyed our last day with a shopping trip to the amazing Accra arts and crafts market, and then headed to the airport. Our time in Africa was over.

Jonathan & Patricia Porter

HAPPY MEALS

Once home in France, and back to work, my mind was still constantly on Ghana. It was as if I had left something behind. It was a weird feeling. We all spoke fondly of our rather unorthodox holiday in West Africa, realising that we had not only had an amazing time, but also done something beneficial for the people whilst there. In fact, we had done a lot considering we did not make preparations before leaving. Following gut instinct and embracing serendipity had turned out quite well after all.

About six weeks later, I could contain myself no longer. I needed to go back to Ghana. This idea was not well received by those around me, especially my business partner. All the same, I made it clear that I would be gone for another two weeks.

I managed to achieve a distorted phone call to Preacher's mobile phone. The land lines were hopeless, but the 'new mobile network' actually worked, after a fashion. He was ready to help with accommodation, and also would meet me from the airport. I asked what his children missed most from the USA, and he glibly told me 'Mc Donald's'. Laughing, we hung up, looking forward to seeing each other very soon.

I collected some computer parts together, and stuffed my bags with goodies for the Computer School. On the way to the airport I stopped at a McDonald's and purchased four Happy Meals, *without* the burgers, fries or drinks. The person behind the counter could not understand why I was content to pay full price for a meal without the food. I had a plan. Collapsing the Happy Meal boxes, and carefully stowing the toys along with straws and napkins, I was ready to develop my scheme.

Arriving in Accra, I had two large suitcases with computer parts in, my laptop computer and my pockets filled with items that I did want to check in. In my left jacket pocket I had a box of ten floppy disks, loaded with software for the Computer School.

Customs stopped me on the way through, asking what I had in my case. I responded "Items for a computer school that I am donating to," playing my honesty card. They opened the case, and could only see some old circuit boards and cables. Shaking their heads, they waved me through, certain that I was not all together in control of my senses.

On the outside of the terminal building I could see Preacher, bobbing up and down, at the back of the pressing crowd. International airports in Africa seem to have some of the largest crowds imaginable, all waiting for some loved one or other. I started to push through the crowd, when I felt something odd on my left side. I turned to see a young man holding my box

Wonderful Adversity: Into Africa

of diskettes. "What are you doing with those?" I asked, indignantly.

"They looked heavy, so I was carrying them for you," he swiftly responded, handing me the box and slipping away into the crowd. That was the last time I carried items in jacket pockets.

Preacher welcomed me with a hug. We climbed into his car, after fighting the failing door mechanisms and drove back to the Church compound, where I would be staying in a small guest room. Preacher's wife and the kids appeared pleased to see the funny Englishman, and I felt very at home.

Once again, Preacher asked me "So, why are you here this time?"

I responded, honestly, "I don't know," at which point he dropped his head in his hands and shook it, whilst I added, "but his time I need to find out WHY I am here."

Preacher, being a man of faith, seemed to accept this weird explanation; after all, I added some amusement to their lives. The next morning I made a call to the Italian Pilot, and he was thrilled to hear from me. He had heard that a British pilot had been asking about flying, and was himself keen to see General Aviation grow in the country. We agreed to meet the next day in a town called Akuse, about ninety minutes' drive from Accra.

For the rest of the day, I added hardware and software to the little Computer School, and provided whatever assistance I could. It was fun, easy, but fun.

That evening, I asked Preacher to allow me to treat the family to a take away meal. He agreed. I grabbed my small bag of hidden goodies as we set out to the only 'tummy safe' take away restaurant close to his home. The menu had two options, either fried chicken with fried rice or fried rice with fried chicken. We ordered fried chicken with fried rice for everybody. Preacher was still confused, and kept asking what I had in the bag.

The chicken and rice was finally delivered to the counter and the bill settled. Once back in the car, I had to reveal my plan. Opening my little bag, I removed the Happy Meal boxes, toys, etc. and together we made up special fake Mc Donald's Happy Meals for the children.

At the manse, it was pure pleasure to watch four youngsters, all separated from their culture, excited at the concept that 'Mc Donald's' was sending them special happy meals. If I achieved nothing else from this trip, that moment, that special and forever etched in my mind moment was worth the plane fare.

The Preacher and his wife shared a great deal of useful knowledge, based on hard learned experiences, about Ghanaian culture, and the associated challenges of living as ex-pats, especially with a family, in Ghana. Preacher was not much of a 'God Squad' chap, taking a far more a pastoral role in his work, caring for the whole community and its needs. I enjoyed his down to earth approach, and the fact that he did not ram his religious views down the throats of others. A very different approach from many preachers I had been unfortunate enough to deal with in the past. We laughed a lot, and he accepted my occasional slip of language. I suspected that he put it down to my being British, or an engineer.

Getting to bed very late, I started to get excited about actually seeing this small plane I had heard about. I tried to find some sleep, it evaded me, hiding behind my imagination running rampant with ideas of being in the air over Africa.

ADVENTURE

Setting out at dawn, in a local taxi, I headed out into the bush lands where the Italian Pilot lived and worked. The same location where the little, still to be confirmed existed, plane was supposedly hangared.

Ghana had just one motorway, only a few kilometres long and nearly fifty years old, which we took to Tema, the principal sea port town in the country. From there we headed north, the road deteriorating rapidly as we moved away from the urban sprawl of Tema's so called 'planned community' structure.

As we drove my eyes were feasting on all that was to be seen. The last time I had been on this road, I was southbound, in the dark and in a Peugeot 504. This time, I could see the shrub land, the coastal savannah, and with it a very different Ghana to that which I had witnessed travelling to Kumasi and Tamale a few weeks before. This was like another country within a country, and it seemed to tear at my soul.

We passed two rocks perched precariously on the top of a rise, whereupon the driver explained "Twin rock - where mankind was born. We came from the middle of the rocks."

I didn't know if he was making it up, but it was plausible as a folk story. Every culture has a Genesis story, and we must all respect those different views, especially since for some it has a deep meaning.

A few kilometres further along, baboons were playing by the side of the road, seemingly oblivious to the traffic. Eventually, I spotted a recognisable landmark; a large, by local standards, mountain standing alone on the plain. I say large by local standards, because at just 1000 feet tall (300m), the peaks altitude above mean sea-level was far, far lower than where I lived in France, part way up a mountain! Compared to the French Alps, it was practically a mole hill!

My driver started telling me stories about the Krobo tribe, after whom this mountain was named, 'Krobo Mountain'. His history lessons of the tribe and how they collected heads, engaging in a major war with the British in the mid 1890's, intrigued me. He concluded the lesson with the Krobo's losing the mountain to the British, after a long siege and negotiated settlement wherein the British purchased the mountain and relocated the tribes to new villages. Remembering that all things are relative to the experience of a people, I listened, trying not to comment or pick out any potential inaccuracies in his tale. All tales have some component of truth in them, and I would simply store his, to compare with others later on.

Finally, we arrived at Italian Pilot's home. It was a simple two bedroom bungalow. He was so excited to share stories of flying in Ghana, and to discuss anything aviation with me as he could. He spoke fast and loud, as most Italians do. I missed some of the words he spoke, but managed to keep up with the general gist and direction of his discourse.

Finally, all the excitement of meeting each other and sharing flying stories gave way to the stimulated need to visit the aircraft. My driver was fast asleep in his taxi, so we took Italian's white Nissan pickup for the short drive to the edge of a lake. It was not the Volta Lake, but a smaller lake, formed between two hydro-electric dams, those of Akosombo and Kpong. A small dirt strip ran perpendicular to the water body. At one end a make-shift hangar stood guard, with a small plane inside, sitting patiently, waiting for my discovery.

The plane was not like anything I had seen before. It was an aluminium tube frame with cloth covering, the same as my own plane, but there the similarities ended.

The cockpit resembled a small cable car cabin with an engine bolted behind, strapped underneath the wing. It was fascinating. Italian was dancing with excitement and already pushing the plane out of the hangar for the sunlight to be able to praise its form.

We did a thorough walk around the plane, with every little detail being explained in rapid fire Italian seasoned pseudo-English phrases. Then we climbed inside and started the engine. My new friend was pleased to wax lyrical about aviation - and everything about this plane with its Italian production styling.

With a suspension that was hard, the air being hot and the surface rather rough, I was concerned about the taxi and take off, but the little plane did not seem to mind. We lined up on the runway, facing the lake. It was quite clear that, if we did not make a good take off, we could get a quick wash in the warm tropical water ahead. There were two little fishing boats on the lake, watching us, perhaps waiting for us to take a dive.

Adding full power, the little engine spun its three blade wooden propeller with its all it had. Being behind the cockpit there may have been less free air available, for we did not accelerate quickly. Dust flew up behind us, and we moved forwards, slowly. Once we reached a certain speed the plane gained pace, but the water was getting closer! I could see that we were close to flying speed, but the plane was simply not getting into the air. Finally, with the lake filling my field of view, Italian yanked back on the stick. I was surprised at how suddenly and violently he made the control input. The nose wheel lifted off of the ground, rapidly followed by the main wheels, and we watched the water pass underneath us, separated by just a few feet of hot and humid air! It felt good. It felt more like a scene from a Hollywood movie than real life, and I felt far very much like Indiana Jones at that moment - all it needed was an octopus to reach a tentacle out of the water below and spin our tyres.

I was on another plane of existence. Italian handed the controls over to me, and I flew us to about 800 feet about the surface. It was beautiful. The water, hills, mountains, villages, dams and a magnificent arched steel bridge over the river. We hung in the air as if suspended on bungee cords. On occasion, we would be yanked ever higher by a thermal, and then plunge back towards the surface as we exited the rising air. Flying here was very different to flying in the UK or France. It was challenging, surprising and incredibly special, calling on all of my flying experiences in a massive and intense manner.

Coming back to land on the little waterside runway we touched down firmly, dropping from a flying machine to a ground machine in a second. It may not have been terribly graceful, but it was amazing in every way. We pushed the little plane away and headed back to the bungalow. There we found my driver, still fast asleep, oblivious to our excursion.

Italian gave me a piece of paper, on it the name of a man at the International Airport. "Go see him. He need people like you," he advised me, his Italian twang making the words smile as he spoke them. I thanked Italian, proceeded to wake my driver, and headed back to Accra.

The days are short in Ghana, and there was no time to follow up on the new lead that sat, hot as a potato, in my pocket. Tired, but happy, I headed back to see Preacher. The children were outside playing and made my welcome very special. That one counterfeit Happy Meal did a lot for making friends amongst those kids.

Entering the lounge, I was introduced to a larger than life American lady, who was visiting my hosts. She lived and worked in a village a few kilometres outside the urban sprawl of Accra. I quickly assessed her as a 'New Yorker', for she was loud, in ya face and up front. Nothing wrong with that, but clearly a stereotypical New York lady. As she shared her stories of challenges and successes, I was left wondering why a New Yorker would even dream of coming to Ghana. She seemed very out of place. I tried to sit quietly, which even on the best of days can be a challenge for me. But I tried, only letting slip the occasional comment, which was probably politically incorrect. To keep me in check, Preacher kept looking over at me, clearly aware that I was being a little irritated by some of the commentary coming from New York, and obviously wishing that I would keep my little comments to myself.

All that she uttered came across as complaints. It was too hot during the day; too sticky during the night; the power was erratic at best; the water never flowed; the roads were full of bumps; the shops were never full of anything; etc. Well, I had gathered that in my first visit, that is why it was called a 'developing nation'. It was not something to complain about, but something to accept and work around. It was an opportunity to be a part of positive change. However, New York went on to complain about her staff, her driver, her cleaner - actually, just about everything in the country. I was left wondering why she did not get on the next plane out of the place, if she found it that intolerable. I will admit that she was grating on my nerves - a lot. Then New York had a wildlife story to tell.

"So, there I was in the house when I saw a large snake crawling across the floor," she embarked animatedly upon her next story. I cringed wondering what would come next, but had no idea of how ridiculous it could possibly be. "So, I jumped on the couch and called out GET ME AN AFRICAN and quick!" I am sure that there was more to the story, but I could not contain myself any longer.

I erupted into laughter, Preacher followed my lead. The Preacher's Wife looked at both of us in horror, telling us off with flashes of her naughty boys look. I leapt to my feet and ran to the other side of the room, in total giggles, my shoulders rising and falling as if attached to a high speed oscillating drive. Preacher followed me. I know that I started it, so did everybody else in the room. I would have to take the blame.

We tried to stop our giggling, but we couldn't. The more I giggled, the more he giggled, and that made me giggle more. Tears started to flow down our faces. I reached for my inhaler as my asthma kicked in, but that only made us both laugh even more. There we were, two grown men, exhausted from New York's tales, frustrated at her constant complaints, but amused beyond belief at her clear need for the people she had been complaining about.

I had in my mind, this woman standing on the couch calling 'GET ME AN AFRICAN' pleading for one of those people she complained about so much, but needing one to beat or chase a simple snake. Preacher and I built on the image in our heads, going from the sublime to the ridiculous - and we giggled uncontrollably some more.

Preacher's Wife came to tell us off, or calm us down... I am not sure which - but that only made it worse. Clearly, I was not a good influence on this man of God.

New York collected her things and left, unsure of what had happened, possibly, actually probably, offended by my behaviour. I am sure that it was all put down to my being British.

Life in the 1990's in Ghana was clearly simple, tough and a challenge, but it was what you made of it. You got out what you put in. If you complained a lot, you would be unhappy, but if you were ready to embrace the enormous challenges, you could find satisfaction on a daily basis. At least that was my take.

IRRITATION

With my fresh scrap of paper in one hand, and my laptop computer in the other, I took a taxi to the airport. There, a new cargo village was being built. Ghana had excelled in increasing what they called non-traditional exports. Traditional exports were things like cocoa, manganese ore, bauxite, timber, gold and diamonds. Non-traditional exports included vegetables, textiles, processed food stuffs, handicrafts, pineapples and other fruits. Exports, coupled with the growth in the country's economy, fuelled the freight movements by air. The country's air trade routes were growing exponentially, and thus a new cargo area was about to be opened at the international airport. That was where I was heading!

At the gate I showed my precious scrap of paper, and was directed to a basic porta-cabin like arrangement. Inside, it was all new, relatively bare, basic and functional. In a side office sat the man I had come to see. He was a well-built man, an outstanding business fellow, sharp as a laser honed razor blade - and very busy. He was Ghanaian by passport, but middle eastern by appearance. He had built up the pineapple cargo business and was helping to set up operations for cargo plane handling.

Mr Cargo was a little brash. He did not use five words when four would do. He had a cigarette close to hand at all times, and a smile that would flash on and off during every conversation. Several things were clear; he knew his business, he knew air cargo and he knew Ghana!

"What do you want?" his blunt opening question was launched at me.

"'I was sent here by the Italian Pilot, just to explore opportunities," I responded, redirecting a wanton drifting cloud of cigarette smoke with my hand.

"Well, I don't have time for you. We have our first cargo coming into this facility TONIGHT and we still don't have our systems set up as we need them," he lamented.

My mouth has this unusual habit of making offers before my brain has processed the implications, and so it did again. "I can write you software to handle that if you need it," I slammed my offer on the table, almost as off-

Wonderful Adversity: Into Africa

hand as Mr Cargo would have.

Pulling his cigarette out of his mouth he laughed, adding "What do you know about aircraft and cargo, and how can you solve a problem so quickly?"

He then puffed deeply on his cigarette and slowly grew a wry smile, before exhaling acrid smoke through the corner of his mouth. He had a point, but I was not going to let my proposition down, I had to back it up somehow, adding "I am pilot, and have written more business packages than you can imagine. BUT you are right, it is a big risk. So, let me use a desk in your office for a couple of hours, and just see what I can do - no charge, just let me try."

Laughing and shaking his head, he directed a member of staff to show me to a spare desk, giving me the relevant papers related to their needs of the moment. I unpacked my state of the art 80386 laptop computer and started to build an application using morsels of old, proven code, some new and a lot of creative energies. I was having fun, and proving a point.

Having written a lot of software and being used to rapid prototyping I was not overly worried by my claim. That coupled with my knowledge of the working of airports, aviation and a lot of reading about it all, I soon put together something that would meet the immediate needs of the new operations at the cargo village.

After about two hours I called Mr Cargo over. He came, an almost mocking smile on his face, disbelieving that I could have anything worthwhile to show him. His face changed to one of disbelief and satisfaction combined as I demonstrated a simple, effective and most importantly functional, robust, solution to his immediate needs.

True to my word, I made no charge. Shaking his hand, I bid him adieu and headed towards the door. He called after me "When do you fly out?"

I called back my fly home date and airline, walking briskly away from his office, a little irritated, but content with my delivery of the goods whilst under pressure.

I had not liked the manner of Mr Cargo, but I had shown him what could be done with a little effort and appropriate technical knowledge. I hoped that he would be successful with his projects, but doubted that I would ever see him again. He was a very good business man, something that I knew that I would never be. A simple fact of life I had come to accept.

I had many other meetings with a variety of folks, trying to find why I felt so strongly that I should have come back to Ghana. I had been stimulated by solving that problem for Mr Cargo, and realised that I could solve many problems in this developing nation. I had the passion, the ability and was ready to bring my skills to the continent. But, despite many efforts, nothing came together. Perhaps I had only come to provide some Happy Meals and create some stop-gap software for an air cargo start-up.

My last day arrived, and I resigned myself to leaving Ghana for the second and last time, returning to the beauty of the French Alps, my business and a comfortable life-style. I needed to put this apparent foolishness of 'needing to find why I came to Ghana' behind me. But that was all about to change!

BOGATA!

I sat in the departure lounge, waiting for my plane to be called. That aluminium bird which would take me home had to be nearly ready. It was hot and sticky. Seemingly more so than usual, since the air-conditioning was not working. Even with the terminal building windows wide open, the night air was not giving any breeze to soothe the weary travellers. I watched many passengers, all waiting to climb inside the oversized Pringles tubes with wings on, heading out across the planet. Most of the folks were clearly business people, with a smattering of family visitors, and perhaps one or two tourists. I sat near the back of the room, avoiding the high density human heat that clearly existed at the embarkation end of the building.

We all had our boarding cards, so it did not matter who boarded first or last. We all had a seat allocated and the plane would not go without any one of us, provided we were in the boarding lounge. Well, that was my logic. I had no idea how accurate it might be.

A voice came over a poor quality speaker "First, business and passengers with children may board now."

The human herd surged like a wave forwards, I remained sitting at the back, avoiding the risk of drowning in human sweat. Just as I was about to stand up to follow the masses, I heard Mr Cargo's voice demanding "Hold that plane!"

He was walking towards me with a well-dressed, official looking, gentleman of South American appearance. My mind jumped into overdrive. Had my software failed? What could I possibly have done wrong? Should I make a run for it? Why didn't I go to the front of the queue? But it was too late - he was upon me.

Cargo spoke to the crew and asked them to wait for me. Yes, for me. I started to get really worried now, but dared not show it. The two men sat down, one on each side of me, The South American man started to speak...

"I come from Bogota, Columbia, but I work for USAID, the United States Agency for International Development," he paused, smiled reassuringly and

Wonderful Adversity: Into Africa

continued. "We have a policy development unit looking at how Non-Traditional Exports can help reduce poverty and increase national wealth in Ghana."

His accent had a little Spanish twang hidden in certain syllables, and he spoke without punctuation. I listened to his words, heard and understood them, it was very interesting, but I could see no relevance to anything I had done, right or wrong. The mention of Columbia had me a little worried in case he was about to ask me to carry drugs. Fortunately, that was not the challenge he had brought me.

"We have a lot of corrupt data from the current system, and I was telling Mr Cargo about it just now. He said we had to come and speak to you before you leave the country," he swirled the words out of his mouth, sprinkling them in front of me as a conundrum.

OK, so now I was intrigued. Bogota waved a little collection of floppy disks in my face. "The corrupt data is here, but I realise that you are flying out, and there is no time to look at it," he explained, shooting a sideways look at Mr Cargo.

I took the disks and quickly inserted them into my laptop, one by one, reconstituting the master record on my screen. Cargo and Bogota chatted at me, but I heard nothing. When I am writing or coding, my ears become disconnected, I am literally oblivious to all around me. Occasionally, I lifted my head to make sure that my flight was not leaving without me, but I really wanted to see this corrupt data.

It was really bad. I had worked with a lot of corrupt files, but this one was special. It was almost as if it had been corrupted on purpose. I looked at the data in binary and hexadecimal, looking for a pattern. Then, once on the scent of a possible relationship between damaged records and the underlying file image, I started some simple manipulation. A quick parsing routine, followed by writing every good record out into one file, and every bad one into another. Two files created, one of clean records and one of dubious records. About fifteen minutes had passed. Cargo and Bogota had stopped speaking, realising that I was too rude to even listen to them.

"I can tell you what is wrong," I offered, giving a summary of the issues.

"How long, and what would it take to fix it?" Bogota chirped in with a much more cheery voice than he had started with.

"I have fixed it, what format would you like it in?" I proposed.

"Can you do Paradox and DBase II?" he asked. Cargo sat back smiling, having been the instigator of a solution.

Within minutes I returned his disks, added some new ones from my own stock, and saw a very happy man with usable data. Perhaps I had found the reason for my visit after all, and now I could go home.

We all shook hands, exchanged business cards, and said our farewells, whilst the airline staff waited at the end of the room for their last passenger to join them. Home was just a few hours away now, my mission over, nothing else could stop me.

I had barely taken five steps, when Bogota shouted after me "If you come back to Ghana I have lots of work for you to do here!"

Cargo added "Call me if you are coming back, I can help with transport!"

I kept on walking, thinking that I would never be back. I had passed a frustrating couple of weeks, realised the challenges of the country, and not managed to find my niche. I had done my wild goose chase, clearly not even found a gosling, and now abandoned the hunting trip. I boarded the plane and settled down to sleep for the overnight flight back to Europe. No more trips to Ghana for me.

I must have fallen asleep long before take-off, because the next thing I remember was looking out of the window onto early morning mainland Europe. My mind was fresh, and I was ready to go home to resume a normal life.

I heard a little echo in my mind, "IF you come back to Ghana I have lots of work for you to do here." The word "IF" echoed more loudly than the rest of the sentence.

The Columbian accent seeped out of the memory as it repeatedly bounced around my cerebral cortex. It was like some sort of call of the wild, the migratory instinct of the swallow or the need for an annual stampede of bison across the plains. It was irritating, persistent and yet somehow meaningful.

Every hour the call felt stronger. "IF you come back to Ghana I have lots of work for you to do here!" I knew that I could do so much to help improve lives in Ghana, but how? Now there was an apparent route. Much as I could sense the need and the route to Ghana, how could I sell that route to a family living in France, enjoying a lovely little village at the bottom of beautiful ski-slopes.

DECEPTION

I walked out of the airport and into the arms of my little clan. Hugs and squeals, as are normal when a husband and father makes his return from an African adventure in one piece, abounded. My wife would soon squeal some more, but not necessarily good squeals.

"I have a job offer in Ghana," I proffered, before we even got home. The silence was rather loud. So, once it had a chance to sink in, I repeated myself "I have a job offer in Ghana."

It may not have been the total truth, but it was not a total untruth either. The next day I spoke to my business partner, and offered that he could buy me out. He readily agreed. We were seeing less and less eye-to-eye on certain business practices, and my heart was far more into 'doing things because they have a purpose' than his approach of 'doing things because they have a profit'. I was not a good business man, but I was a good problem solver, and I loved adventure.

I called Cargo, telling him that I wanted to come back to Ghana, set up somewhere to live for the family, ready for when we moved there. He was shocked, but quickly arranged for me to fly on a cargo plane from Luxembourg. This was going to be my make sure I was not crazy trip.

Arriving in Luxembourg, I met the flight crew at their hotel, travelling together to the airport and passing through crew security to get onto the DC8 cargo plane. I was not the only passenger. A ship's Captain was also hitching a ride to Accra. Talk about tall, he barely fitted through the cabin door. He had not been to Ghana before, and we chatted about all sorts of things. Flying 'crew' on a cargo plane you are sitting on a jump seat. There are no 'passenger seats', and as a hitch-hiker you are expected to look after yourself. Without any in-flight entertainment and definitely no meals service, you must be self-sufficient. Furthermore, such aircraft operators do not even try to make it comfortable, even for their crew. The pilots, once on board, relaxed, undoing their shirt buttons, losing their epaulettes, and just flying. It was very different to a passenger plane operation. Cargo planes are functional. They need to carry goods to market, and that is that. Simple, no frills.

Our route took us to another West African country first, to deliver some crates from the hold. I had never been to that particular country, but had heard some pretty amazing stories about the challenges of working across West Africa from the crew.

Landing at our intermediate airport, we taxied to the apron and waited for steps to be pushed up to the side of the plane. I was to be allowed to open the door, which had me excited to say the least. Pushing and turning the handle, and then manipulating open that massive door was not easy, but it was satisfying. Unexpectedly, I saw a soldier coming up the steps towards me. I was not too worried, to start with.

He was wearing full combat gear, AK47 in his hands, but when I looked down, he was wearing flip-flops. He looked me straight in the eye. I could see red capillaries bursting throughout the whites of his eyes. Opening his mouth, he spoke with an alcohol induced slur "You are under arrest. You and this aircraft... all of you are under arrest."

I started to get worried, very worried. The loadmaster slipped away behind me, leaving my body as the only barrier between the soldier, with his AK47, and the interior of the aircraft. Flip-Flop soldier looked at me, working on getting a decent focus, repeating his statement about arresting us all. At that point, the loadmaster returned with a 'spruced up' first officer. White shirt well buttoned, a Windsor knotted tie, braid clearly visible on his shoulders and his cap on his head. The flight crew had not looked like that when we landed.

"What's the matter SOLDIER?" he demanded, snapping to a false attention before the Flip-flop man.

With less conviction the soldier repeated "You are under arrest, you and this aircraft... under arrest," as he waved a vague circle with the barrel of his gun.

The first officer snapped loudly, "No we are not. You are not supposed to be here. We are. Now, bugger off, Soldier."

I stepped further back inside the plane, planning my possible hiding place in case bullets started to fly.

Flip-flop looked, shifted his weight from one leg to the other, then, pulling himself almost to attention, saluted and stated "Yes, Sir," turned around and ran down the steps. I could not tell if any financial incentive changed hands, but I do not think so. It was simply a case of incredible brinkmanship, played by a pilot used to the situations into which he flew.

Two hours later we took off to complete our journey into Accra. Before I even made it to the bottom of the steps I had become a walking swimming pool. Sweat was escaping from every inch of my body. I must have looked as if I had just swum ashore from a fishing vessel, not landed in a cargo plane!

Mr Cargo was waiting for the tall maritime Captain and me at the bottom of the steps from the plane. Smiling and waving his hands and arms around freely, he called "Welcome to Ghana." He must have said it at least half a dozen times. Tall-Captain did not say much, but his head was on a constant swivel, taking in the panorama around us, assessing everything he saw.

Handing over our passports to be stamped by immigration, we jumped into a waiting 4x4 with air-conditioning running at full blast. My clothes started to chill, and I started to feel human again. Pausing at the cargo office, we were each gifted large bottles of cold water, which we consumed as if they were thimbles filled with water. Thirsty was not the word for our condition.

With my passport returned, I thanked Cargo. Saying goodbye to both him and Tall, I headed to find Preacher.

Preacher's family greeted me with gusto, I felt at home. This was the right place to be headed to. I explained that we were moving to Ghana, and that I had a job offer. They were surprised, yet thrilled, and helped me to find a small house to rent at a reasonable rate on the outskirts of the city.

I tried to make contact with Bogota but he was out of the office for the whole time I was able to stay, which was less than a week, after all.

I reported back to the airport, where Mr Cargo had promised me a return ride in another DC8, this time flying pineapples to Luxembourg. It was a

Wonderful Adversity: Into Africa

direct flight, which pleased me, since I did not want another drunk flip-flop wearing soldier encounter on my itinerary.

As we lined up on the main runway out of Accra, there was an active discussion between the crew. "Number three is not right," said the flight engineer, adding a few moments later "but it should be OK."

Discussions about fuel, alternate landings and more were running quickly between them. Then, decision made, they pushed the thrust levers forwards. The plane started to accelerate. I saw the terminal building pass on our right, but our wheels were still on the ground. Then I saw the cargo building flash past, but our wheels were still on the ground. I knew that the wheels had to leave the ground before the end of the runway, or I might not be going home, ever.

The crew mumbled some options between each other and then, as the runway disappeared, we parted company with terra firma, climbing over the trees at the end of the runway. Sitting in the cockpit, I was not sure by how much we cleared the trees by, but I was sure it was a close thing. I made a mental note to check for twigs in the main gear on landing. We climbed very slowly, and turned over the coastline, silence filled the cockpit.

After about fifteen minutes and with a good altitude attained, conversation returned. It turned out that one of the engines was not performing quite as it should. The crew informed those on board, all six of us, that it was affecting climb, and may affect cruise also. Plans for an alternate landing in Libya were started.

Libya may not have been terribly friendly with Europe at that time, but this aircraft carried a West African registration, and Libya was very friendly with all the West African nations. It was as good an alternative as any.

At thirty-five thousand feet over the Sahara desert the first officer excused himself from his post to take a comfort break. As he passed me, the captain offered for me to sit in the right hand seat. I don't think he had finished his offer before I was settled down and strapped in.

"If we have to go into Libya, we need to burn some more fuel, so I want to let you do that," he proposed, flicking off the autopilot.

"You can fly, so take her over," he said nonchalantly. So I did, as he added, "be gentle, but get a good feel."

I really could not believe what was happening, but embraced it as my destiny. I pushed the column a teeny bit, pulled a teeny bit, and watched the altimeter dancing in response to my inputs. Then I tried the ailerons, changing course a few degrees and back again, repeatedly. Before I could play with the rudder pedals, the captain stopped me with "Don't worry about the rudders, I have yaw damper on."

For the next thirty minutes I hand flew the course, not very well, and burning that extra bit of fuel. Whether it was truly necessary, or just for me, I will never know. Frankly, I don't care about the reason. I flew a DC8 over the Sahara desert, and nobody can take that away from me.

As we approached Libyan airspace, the crew made the decision to press on to Luxembourg, where we landed without incident. The aircraft did need attention on engine three, and I could not find any twigs in the undercarriage. All is well that ends well, and adds to our life experiences!

MORAL GHANAIAN

We loaded our household possessions into a forty foot long shipping container, and then followed it to the airfield where my little plane was parked. Removing the wings, we slid the plane into the container with furniture and toys. It looked great as they closed and sealed the lock on the sea-faring steel box that would take a couple of months to catch us up.

We arrived in Ghana between Christmas and New Year. Preacher and his family looked after us. My wife was happy to have a friend to chat to, the children friends to play with and I somebody to laugh about New York with.

We moved in to a basic home, with barely any furniture, in coping mode, waiting for the container with all of our goods and aeroplane to arrive. Meanwhile, I needed to finalise my work with Bogota.

The New Year was full of promise. I walked into Bogota's office to a warm and cheery reception. "Take a seat, tell me why you are back in Ghana?" he smiled warmly.

I reminded him of his statement about coming back to Ghana to work for him. He paled, his smile melting away as if it had been made of chocolate, suddenly exposed to the heat of a flame gun.

"Ummm, but you are not Ghanaian," he offered as an excuse for his lost smile.

Well, that was no surprise to me. I did not look like a local, and when he met me he knew that I was not. So, where was the problem?

"Hang on," I ventured, "you need my skills, my experience and my general abilities, but you can't use them unless I am a Ghanaian?"

"Absolutely. YES!" he exclaimed, relieved that I was bright enough to understand the complicated situation we both found ourselves in. Well, my situation was a bit more complicated than his. I had a wife and children in a house a few kilometres away and all the household possessions, and an aeroplane, on the high seas, being told "Ummm, but you are not Ghanaian." All he had was a data challenge he needed to find a solution to.

Thankfully, my mouth overtook my brain by ejecting, "Can you employ a

Wonderful Adversity: Into Africa

Ghanaian company, since that is a moral being under Ghanaian law?"

"Of course!" he replied, sliding down in the chair as if attempting to hide behind his desk, clearly realising that this 'totally new to West Africa person' had no idea of the complexity of bureaucracy and how complicated something that sounds so simple can be.

"Then if I create a Ghanaian company, you can employ that company to solve your problems," my mouth offered succinctly, whilst my brain was still working on what was going on.

Bogota sat bolt upright in his chair, "You can do that?" and without waiting for an answer from either me or my mouth, he added "If you can, then I have plenty of work for you."

So, I set out to create a Ghanaian company under the Ghana Investment Promotion Council rules. The staff there were very helpful, and within a couple of weeks I was in possession of a bona fide 'Certificate to Commence Business'. I was now a Director and employee of a moral Ghanaian company, and able to start solving problems for the betterment of Ghana.

I took the certificates to Bogota with a cheery smile. He clearly did not know whether to be shocked that somebody could register a company and get their paperwork so quickly, or happy that he had access to a problem solver. He readily accepted the latter.

Inviting me to his side of the desk, he showed me some of the challenges he was up against. I left him an hour later with more than enough work for a year.

Week in, week out, more work came my way. Then I was given a desk in the Ministry of Trade and Industry, working side by side with the data teams. I was being given the opportunity to train Government personnel to write computer programmes, collect, analyse and interpret trade data, use spreadsheets, and much more. That sounded easy. Of course, I knew nothing of what was really being handed to me on a platter. It was a much more massive meal, with more diverse flavours, textures and chewy bits than I could ever have imagined!

FLYING BICYCLES

Eventually, the container of household goods, and aeroplane, landed at Tema port. Several weeks later it was cleared for delivery, and we even got permission for the contents to be inspected by customs, during un-stuffing, at our home. Every single container coming into the country was fully inspected. Every single box and every single item imported was up for some sort of tax or duty. Concern over illegal items was high, especially firearms and ammunition, for obvious reasons.

The team of three customs officers gathered around the doors of the container as the seal, placed in France, was, after serial numbers were checked, double and triple checked, finally cut. After all, we did not want to open the wrong container only to find something not acceptable to Ghana inside.

As the doors swung open, there stood my little plane. Her three blade propeller just a few inches inside the container, and the wings stowed nicely, one on each side. The customs officers had never seen anything like it.

Understanding that the manner in which I answered their questions would determine my fate, and that of the goods inside, I waited until they had finished their huddle and approached me.

"What is that?" came the simple demand, accompanied by a waft of the hand towards the airframe.

"A small plane," I responded truthfully.

Laughter amongst the three officers abounded. Then, with a dead pan face came the follow up. "No, seriously, what is that?"

"It is what we call an ultralight aircraft, it is not a certified aircraft such as you see at the airport, but a small plane, normally built by individuals for their personal training and learning," I made a valiant start.

"But can it fly?" asked customs officer number two.

"Yes, it can, but not as high as the other planes. Nor as far," I responded helpfully, adding some education.

"But there are no seats," chirped up officer number three, the only female amongst them.

Confused, since I could see two seats, I offered "There are seats for pilot and co-pilot only, but not for passengers, at the back, like there are in the bigger planes."

"So it is more like a bicycle for the air," she proffered, with a sunny smile.

"YES, YES!" my glee escaped me, "YES, it is JUST like a flying bicycle. You can learn on it and go relatively short distances."

Well, it seemed like a valid explanation to me. Customs officer one, held his pen over the little blue Landing Account booklet that he was obliged to fill in. He looked at his shoes, then raised his eyes to look at the sky, then gazed inside the container at the strange object.

"One...' he paused, looking at both of his colleagues and completed, "...flying bicycle." He must have looked at the entry for a good thirty seconds before commanding "Well, unload it and let's look at what else is in the container," clearly relieved at having classified this strange object that Obruni had brought into Ghana.

Nothing major came up after that, apart from repeated requests to see my fire-arms. However, I had not brought any fire-arms with me, which confused the customs team. We all shook hands, paid the obligatory food allowance, and they headed off to their homes.

Stage one of getting a plane to Ghana had been completed. I would now need to register that plane with the authorities.

I called Italian, who was more than thrilled that another small plane had entered the territory. I asked whether I could assemble the plane and test fly it at Akuse, which was eventually agreed. I had the plane all together, but still needed a registration and an approval to actually fly it, so Italian and I went the Ghana Civil Aviation Authority together.

Italian knew everybody there, and when he told them that I had brought my girlfriend to live in Ghana, it got a lot of attention.

"He bring his girlfriend here for me to try. I let him try my girlfriend. He like my girlfriend. I want to try his girlfriend. Then we take both girlfriend together for adventure," he explained, in his thickest Italian accent. Sadly, much as I understood his humour, those in the office were thoroughly confused.

I explained rapidly, "My girlfriend is my plane. His girlfriend is his plane. We are too busy with our wives to have girlfriends other than planes," not knowing if I was making it all sound worse than it already become.

Finally, one of the staff caught the joke, laughed and explained the whole pantomime in Twi, one of the local languages, to his colleagues.

A few hours later I was given a registration ending in DR or 'Delta Romeo' and an appointment for an inspector to come out to see 'my girlfriend', as the staff in the office had now decided to refer to my plane.

On the designated day, at roughly the designated time, Inspector came along to the little lakeside strip in the Eastern Region of Ghana. He climbed out of his official car, wearing really nice shiny shoes. He was not in the best attire for a visit to a muddy remote air-strip, but he did not appear to mind.

With a clipboard in one hand, and chewed pen in the other, he started to walk around Delta Romeo. It was clear from his facial expression that he had never seen anything like it before.

Eventually, he asked me "Can it really fly?"

"I can show you if you like," I offered, in response.

With a surprised look on his face, he agreed. I offered he could be a passenger, but that was declined as quickly as if I had offered him an arsenic laced cocktail. Unperturbed, I strapped in and set up to fly a quick routine.

I had not taken into account the heat, and the effective Density Altitude or DA. Aircraft performance is generally given based on what is called the ISA (International Standard Atmosphere), which states that 'standard' sea level conditions are 15ºC, 1013.25hpa and an air density of 1.225kg per metre cubed. Of course, that is not, in one way or another, too far off an average day in Europe... but it was far from the conditions that I was about to fly in at just 6 degrees North of the equator, and practically on the prime

(Greenwich) meridian!

The strip was about 180ft above sea level, but the air-on temperature was close to 40°C, dew point was at least 35°C and the pressure setting on my altimeter showed 1016 hectopascals or millibar, which would make the air interact with the aircraft as if it were taking off at over 3,500ft above sea level. Of course, this is all based on relative conditions. The bottom line is that an increase in DA affects both engine and aircraft behaviour and responsiveness, negatively.

As I added power, the prop struggled to grab enough air to give me the performance I was used to, flying in the cold crisp air of the Alps. All the same, I hung on in there, advancing on the growing lake, watching those fishermen at the end of the strip. Finally, my Delta Romeo leapt into the air, and started to climb. I constantly adjusted my inputs to suit the conditions. She put on a marvellous display, with stalls, steep turns and a couple of touch and go's. We landed, me and her, happy as could be. I had a big smile on my face. The inspector had a bigger smile on his. Italian, with a wide grin, invited us all to celebrate with some grappa. I declined the grappa, but they indulged in some southern European pleasure!

My permit to fly was issued the next day, along with a jibe about how beautiful my girlfriend was. I was now able to fly in Ghana. With the fresh permit in hand, I would now need to move Delta Romeo from the remote airstrip to Accra, closer to my home. I was advised to base her at the Kotoka International Airport, or KIA for short.

With permission to land in Accra in hand, my wife drove me to Akuse, where I prepared for the flight to KIA. Plans went awry quickly, due to some unforeseen maintenance problems. One of those was related to the radio. In France I never flew with a radio, but it was obligatory in Ghana. I had a handheld radio adaptation on the instrument panel. It was a bit Heath Robinson, but it worked, after a fashion.

Time was ticking. I told my wife to go on ahead of me, and meet me at KIA. Italian, who was armed with his own hand held radio to listen in and track my progress, offered to go with her and the children.

It took me even longer than expected to prepare the aircraft, and it was getting late. I quickly calculated the time it would take to make it to the international airport, realising that I would have about twenty minutes of daylight left when I got there. That should have been ample.

Once again, I lined up facing the lake and opened the throttle. This time I adapted my procedures for a smoother departure and climb.

I was flying solo, and it was my first cross-country flight in Africa. Magic, magnificent, fandabbywabbydoozie, splendiferous, awesome and WOW, even if all rolled into one, would not come close to describing how it felt. The air, blowing through the open sides of the cockpit, felt warm on my arms and face. The view below went beyond breath taking. This was the life. What more could I ever want.

As I got closer to Accra, I made a couple of calls on the radio, but got no response. I was now definitely inside the terminal area, and could see the international airport growing slowly ahead of me. I had decided to approach at right angles to the airport, to keep out of the way of the commercial traffic. It is never a good idea to get on the approach to an airport in an Ultralight with an Airbus or Boeing established at the same time. This, it turned out, was a good decision. I could see the lights of an airliner in the distance, with less than five nautical miles left to run, meaning we would soon be risking collision if I did not do something.

I made another call on the radio. Nothing. After another ten attempts, I decided to put myself in a position where the tower could give me a non-radio clearance to land. This is a standard procedure, learned during training, using lights shone from the tower. Today, for the first time, I would put it into practice.

On the ground, wife, kids and Italian were getting worried. They could see Delta Romeo flying in tight circles making 'big wing' signs to the tower, showing that I wanted a light signal.

I turned the plane around and around, watching the sun disappear fast behind the horizon, checking all the time for my expected solid green light from the tower, to indicate that I could land.

It did not come. The lights of more aircraft on final for the main runway could be discerned in the distance. I realised that I would be soon be completely out of daylight, and flying outside of my approved conditions, if I waited until the aircraft on final for runway 21 landed.

I knew that there was a little used cross runway, orientated 25/07. I could see the windsock, and although it would mean a cross-wind landing, I estimated that I would be able to land on the threshold of runway 25, and stop well before the main runway, sort my radio out and then taxi to the hangars on the other side of the runway. I also realised that the area I wanted to land in was part of the military base.

Runway numbers are related to magnetic alignment. Runway 21 means aligned at 210 degrees (plus or minus 5 degrees) and runway 25 means aligned at 250 degrees (plus or minus 5 degrees) on the magnetic compass. 21 if landed on the from the other end, become 03 and 25 if landed on from the other end become 07, as in 030 and 070 degrees magnetic. Consequently, the two numbers for any runway will always give 18 if subtracted from each other, because they represent a straight line, at 180 degrees opposed on the magnetic compass.

I did not have much time to consider all of these options, and so, without radio, alone in a small plane a couple of kilometres to the East of one of West Africa's busiest international airports, I had to make a solo decision.

Deciding to land on 25, and handle the military consequences, I started to position my aircraft. The car with my mobile ground support team were busy watching my antics, realising by now that I had no radio, since they could not contact me either. They watched Delta Romeo line up for 25, and decided to head to the military base, fearing the worst.

Landing, and rolling out to a standstill, hundreds of metres before the intersection with the main runway, I sighed with massive relief. A Boeing landing just a few minutes later, confirming my sigh was well earned.

Before I could shut down the engine, I had about fifteen soldiers standing alongside the plane, looking at the unexpected aircraft, wondering what was going on.

I pushed the two ignition switches down with a single swipe of my hand, abruptly killing the engine. Climbing out of the cockpit, I greeted the welcoming committee. They were all well-presented and well-armed, but nobody had drawn a weapon. The group pulled to attention, as if I had been expected. I checked to see if any of them were wearing flip-flops. To my relief, they all wore shiny parade boots. Impeccably presented, friendly faces, without weapons drawn, that made me feel better.

"Good evening," I opened my discourse with the troops, "I suffered radio failure and needed to land here." I hoped this would be a reasonable opening statement.

"You are welcome," came the crisp, well-spoken response from the lead soldier. "How can we help you?"

"Do any of you have a radio I can call tower with?" I pleaded, feeling rather silly.

At that point I could see Italian running across the apron, looking for his worth as if world as if the sky had fallen on his head, shouting, "It is OK. It is OK. He is allowed."

Breathlessly he burst between the soldiers and me. The soldiers smiled and shook his hand. They obviously already knew him. Italian handed me his air-band transceiver, and instructed me to call the tower, which I did.

"Taxi to the intersection and call again for clearance to cross the active," a controller instructed.

I quickly thanked the soldiers for the courteous welcome, shaking hands and smiling. After all, they had given me the most amazing welcome to Accra.

Taking Italian's radio, I taxied to the hold, shut down my engine, in order to hear on the portable transceiver, and awaited crossing clearance. Once cleared, I started up and made it to the hangar for the night.

Italian had been worried that I might get arrested. But I didn't. No matter how many times I went over the scenario, I still came out believing that I had made the best decision possible under the circumstances. I learned that at times we are not able to communicate with others, and those watching us from the ground may get concerned, but they are not in control of the situation. They do not know all the things the PIC (Pilot in Command) knows. I guess that is why the role of a pilot, and the resultant personality set, is misunderstood all over the world.

HANGAR CHANGES

I didn't get a chance to look at the aircraft radio problem as early as I would have liked, since I had to travel to Takoradi Sea Port for work. Takoradi was the site of the first landing of an aircraft in Ghana in 1928. Sir Alan Cobham, during the first circumnavigation of Africa in a sea plane, landed in the harbour there, soon after it had been completed. Even on my first visit, I realised that Takoradi Port was an amazing time machine. Wood panel lined walls in the arrival hall dated from before the Second World War, when sea travel was still the only way to get between continents. Out in the harbour the logs of mahogany and other tropical hardwoods were being floated to their transport vessels, whilst a manganese ore carrying cargo train dumped more rocks into waiting ships holds.

Takoradi was fun, but I still wanted to get back to my plane. All the same, I worked on the data systems for exports and learned much from the helpful staff at the port.

Fortunately, by Saturday morning I was back in Accra and in the hangar. To my shock, Delta Romeo had been tampered with. Nothing major, but it was clear that somebody had been 'tinkering', perhaps not with bad intent, but it still worried me.

I called Italian, and he told me to not worry, but to focus on fixing the radio instead.

The BNC connector to the antenna had come apart, which explained my lack of radio communications. It didn't take long to fix, and I was soon able to carry out a radio check with the tower. I then focused on some other little maintenance items that needed done. Being an aircraft constructed out of aluminium tubes and cloth covers, it needed maintenance of some sort after almost every flight. Engineering is as much fun as flying, so it didn't bother me in the least.

Italian called me and told me to request 'taxi to the military base'. I queried the instruction. "Don't argue. Go taxi to the military base NOW," came the accented order.

With my newly working radio, I obtained a start-up clearance and taxied to the military base. There, I was met by the chap in charge of fighter jet maintenance. He drew his hand across his throat, indicating that I should shut down my engine. I complied, a little bewildered at what was going on.

Before I could climb out of the cockpit Jet maintenance was shaking my hand. Jet was excited at seeing another aircraft, and could not stop talking about everything engines and airframes. Finally, Jet told me that my aircraft would be parked under the wing of a larger aircraft inside one of the military hangars. I was not going to argue.

A tall, thin Wing Commander, wandered down some metal stairs, a thin moustache barely visible against his West African complexion. "Akwaaba," he welcomed, "You must be Yaw Obruni."

Italian had briefed WingCo about the situation on the civilian side of the airport, and he offered to provide Delta Romeo hangar space within his facility.

"You can hangar your bird here," he said with a smooth but incisive voice, reminiscent of somebody who had been through Sandhurst Officer Training in the UK. "But I want you to share your passion for flying with the boys too. You know, show them your machine and stuff."

It was the sort of deal that would make any aviator smile. My little plane was to be hangared opposite the fighter jets, and underneath the wing of a military version of the Islander twin-engine aircraft, called the Defender.

Jet and WingCo helped me to push Delta Romeo back into position. As I was about to leave, WingCo handed me a clearance letter, giving me access to the military base. I felt very privileged.

I managed to fly from the military base most weekends. Sometimes I would fly up to Akuse, to visit Italian. I learned more and more about the various aircraft and who flew what. Most importantly I was able to exchange ideas and skills with the very well disciplined and polite members of Ghana's Armed Forces, especially the Ghana Air Force.

TRAINING

Most of my working week was taken up with training staff from Ghana Customs, Excise and Preventive Service, or CEPS as they preferred to be called, and the team at the Ministry of Trade and Industry or MOTI. Together we worked on data collection and analysis solutions, to support the USAID Trade and Investment Programme. It required setting up data collection at three major ports, two sea (Takoradi and Tema) and one air (Kotoka International Airport). In addition, the office in downtown Accra would receive the overland entry forms from all around the country, ready for data input to the computers.

Collating the data was a challenge. Units of measure could easily be confused between tonnes and kilos, units and boxes, metres and millimetres. Country codes got mixed up; Austria and Australia were commonly confused, but not on purpose, rather through a lack of working geographical understanding. Sometimes, the local names of things added to the challenge. For example, a local fish called salmon, which is nothing like the salmon

Wonderful Adversity: Into Africa

described in the international coding, also known as the Harmonised System, or HS code, which easily leads to misclassification.

Little by little, an intense programme of education and training led to increased learning on everybody's part. Eventually, a working system was established. Error rates dropped, entry quality improved and more usable data was coming out of the system.

I loved going out on field work, and would use a motorcycle to get to and from the various locations. I found that I could travel quicker and cooler on the bike, plus it was a lot of fun. That is until I had a mishap.

On the way back from Takoradi, a taxi lost control knocking me off the motorbike, fortunately, at a relatively low speed. It would have been worse had I not foreseen the potential and been in 'avoidance mode', having applied my brakes heavily. Nonetheless, the front wheel of my bike was destroyed, as was the skin on my left hand and arm. Blood dripped freely. As luck would have it, the accident happened in front of a Police Station. As bad luck would have it, the taxi driver was related to the Police Officer on duty. I pointed out that the taxi had no working lights, no working brakes, no insurance sticker, and no road worthiness sticker. I then requested to see the driver's licence.

I was wasting my breath. In the case of an accident in remote parts of West Africa, it is important to note that 'The white man never has right of way', and that was becoming abundantly clear.

I decided to restate my position. "Well, listen, it is just my bike, and I can get patched up, so, let's not pursue this any further," adding for effect, "I hope that your brother, the taxi driver, can get back to work now."

It was like magic. The taxi driver disappeared, with his taxi. However, my bike was taken into a police yard. I was told it would need to be tested before it could be returned to me. I asked "Tested for what?"

"In case you brakes has failed," the police officer answered in his stilted English, smothered in a large dash of West African smile.

I was flabbergasted, I had brake marks on the road, the taxi had none. The collision was on MY lane on the road. Anybody could see that it was not my fault, and that my vehicle complied with the regulations – and that the taxi did not. It was not worth fighting this particular battle. I was also aware that I needed to work on dressing my cuts - and get the trade data from Takoradi Port back to Accra. Leaving my details and bike at the station, I hitched a ride back to Accra. I had dealt with the police in many countries, but this was clearly very different.

Rather than go straight home, blood stained, I decided to clean off the worst of the blood and carry out basic dressings at Bogota's house. I did not want to arrive home and create unnecessary concerns.

It was getting late, and the night was very dark. I knocked on Bogota's solid wood front-door. Opening, he beamed a massive smile. "Come in, come in," he proclaimed, standing back and semi-bowing as if in a medieval play.

I showed him the diskette with the data on, saying "I have the data from Takoradi, but I have a problem also," with that I raised my blooded arm.

The next hour was spent in his kitchen, trying to clear mud, blood, stones and some glass from a variety of puncture wounds. There were more that I had realised and we picked out debris from my arms, knees and legs, where I had simply not felt the damage due to historical nerve damage and perhaps a large dose of adrenalin.

Bogota drove me home, looking much more presentable than I had arrived at place.

The next day, Bogota arranged for the collection of my bike and 'disappearance of any issues from the Police'. I had been in the right, and I am sure that the Policeman knew that his brother was very much in the wrong. Unfortunately, things are not always that simple. I never asked how Bogota made the problem 'go away', but I am sure that he did so in an official manner.

CHAINSAWS

Much as I enjoyed working hand-in-hand with the good folks within the ministries buildings, I found the working methods and bureaucracy frustrating. Generally, attitudes to work were good. However, there was a lack of fact and knowledge sharing between teams, who should have been working together seamlessly. I spent most of my time between two neighbouring offices. They were separated by a simple wooden partition wall, which could have been made out of six foot thick solid lead, and have had no less impact on communications between the teams in each room.

To get between rooms it was necessary to walk out of one office, along a corridor, and into the next. For me, it was a two minute trip. For my colleagues, their offices could have, at times, been on different continents. Part of the challenge being that 'timely and efficient' were missing sentiments in their working practices and expectations. In my naivety, I proposed that the two rooms should be knocked into one, thus creating a more productive team spirit and with it, increased productivity for the staff. I would be more productive too. To me, it seemed like a good idea.

My liaison officer listened to the proposal. Unable to find any valid argument against it, he suggested a meeting with the relevant Minister. I was up for that, and we went upstairs to visit him.

The Minister was very supportive; he listened to my arguments,

Wonderful Adversity: Into Africa

supported by my Ghanaian colleague. Finally, he pronounced, "OK, I will issue a works order."

I was thrilled. That must have been the quickest decision made by any politician in the history of democracy. My colleague collected the approvals slip, hand written by the Minister. I could not believe the efficiency, so I decided to clarify. As we moved towards the door, I turned to face the minister, asking "How long will this take to implement?"

"Minimum six months, probably twelve to eighteen - these things take time to happen," the Minister answered, dryly, frankly and absolutely honestly, as he dropped his head to read the next request on his busy desk.

Frustrated, and unable to control my mouth, I asked "In any case, you are happy for the work to be done then?"

"Why not?" he retorted in the standard Ghanaian official 'alternative to commitment' response. It was enough for me.

The next morning, I took my chainsaw to work. I had brought it with me from France, where it was used to cut logs for firewood. I had found no need for firewood in Ghana, so the chainsaw was about to find a new application; Government building remodelling.

I briefed my colleagues in each office that we had approval to make a common work space, and that I was authorised to remove the partition. They all understood, and agreed to move their desks away from the wooden wall. In fact, they seemed rather excited and became readily co-operative. Perhaps the fact that something was happening in a timely manner was already bringing a change to attitudes.

I started up the chainsaw. 'Vrooooommmmmm' it yelled, filling the corridors of the building with its subsequent echoes.

Plunging the saw into the wooden partition, I proceeding to cut a massive hole. The wooden shape falling to the floor with a crash, releasing dust and debris, accumulated over decades, across the room. I stepped back, covered in red wood chippings. I revved up the machine, plunging again and ripping sideways, cutting through wood and old nails as if they were butter.

In less than ten minutes I had removed the partition completely. I was satisfied. My colleagues were, to put it mildly, 'less satisfied' at the condition of the room. Wood chips, dust, debris and a lot of my sweat could be found in many parts of the room – and on co-workers. It was a bit of a mess.

The noise had alerted those on the upper floors to some 'unscheduled maintenance activity'.

The Minister burst into the room, to be greeted by a sawdust coated Obruni, wielding a chainsaw. His mouth dropped open, eyes darting from left to right, ceiling to floor. He could not believe it.

I decided to speak first. "You approved the work, Sir," I offered, "and now it is done."

I was hopeful that he would embrace the result. But that was not to be the case. "You have not heard the last of this." he blurted, bursting out of the room as quickly as he had entered.

We all laughed. Staff from both rooms laughed, I laughed. We all laughed together. It was the making of a team.

"Listen up," I ordered using my best Sergeant Major's voice, "WE have to make this OUR working space. WE have to clean this up. WE have to build a BETTER office. WE CAN DO IT."

Whether the dust of the wall falling down had some hypnotic effect, or whether the shock of my action had knocked the staff into a different realm, I will never know, but they all stood by me from that point onward.

The ladies took the curtains down and home to wash. The also cleaned the louvre blades - probably for the first time in ten years. Men and women worked side-by-side clearing up the rubbish. I chose two good chaps to come with me to the wood market in order to purchase paint, plywood and nails for the renovation. We then detoured to another shop, purchasing maps of Ghana and other posters to decorate the walls.

Together, we redecorated the office, and laid it out as a combined operations room. Over the next week it all came together, and looked magnificent, which was just as well.

A reporter from a European newspaper had heard about the new data collection systems and reports, and wanted to write a story about it. She was in this recently created office, interviewing the resident staff about their roles, when the door burst open.

The Minister filled the doorway with his impressive form. His eyes darted around the room, as if hunting for prey, then locking on mine. It was if he locked on ready to launch Exocet missiles. He stepped forwards revealing two uniformed officers behind him. The entourage entered the room and moved towards me.

"Minister," I declared bringing his attack force to a standstill, "Glad you are here." He looked through me, his sentiments towards me clearly not positive. Before he could utter a word I continued, "This journalist would like to interview you about the new joint operations room. She is interested in how data collection and reporting is improving from the Ministry." It was the only card I could play, and it would either be a trump card or I was about to fold.

To be fair, the Minister had not expected to see the room back in order, a team working together and a journalist. Forever the politician he gave a wonderful interview, and ended by whispering to me on the way out of the room "You need to redecorate my office next." The uniforms left with him. I sighed with relief.

We worked together after that, without ever mentioning the incident again. Most importantly, it improved teamwork and work output growing in quality and quantity.

Yes, I had overstepped the mark. Yes, I was severely admonished by Bogota, and others. BUT it had worked. It was one of the wonderful occasions where the means clearly justified the end, and nobody managed to shout 'Get out of my office' at me.

FLYING IN GHANA

Although I used my plane mainly for giving air experience flights to friends and family, I also shared a lot of flights with a British chap from the gold mines. Gold was an enthusiastic fellow. He beamed that enthusiasm several kilometres ahead of himself. He was just full of energy and passion for absolutely everything.

We met one day at the airport. He sauntered up to me on the apron, beaming a wide smile. I was carrying out a pre-flight check on Delta Romeo, in preparation to take Preacher's Wife flying. Gold had just exited a Beechcraft 1900D, having come back from one of the remote goldmines. He started to stroke my aircraft, with tenderness, admiring her as if she were a Fabergé Egg. His smile grew and grew, finally braking through the sides of his face as his eyes widened above the top of his head. After a brief introduction of himself, and some British chit-chat about the weather, he asked "Can I learn to fly with you?"

It was not what I had expected as a question, but it was a welcome concept. I told him I would ask the WingCo, and offered that he could take a flight with me if he waited until after I had flown Preacher's Wife. Jiggling with more anticipation than a four-year old, he agreed.

I strapped Preacher's wife in and we headed out to the main runway. Since the main runway, 21, was about 3000m long, I declined the option to go the beginning of the runway for take offs, opting instead to use just the last 1000m from the intersection of the much shorter and rarely used military runway 25.

Preacher's Wife was looking forward to her flight, and smiled most of the time. Of course, most people are not used to flying in small planes without any doors, and being subject to every thermal and gust of wind. It takes people by surprise. The feeling of being one with the air is increased as they are bumped about in the cockpit. I explained that the air in West Africa is like the roads, full of potholes, and we just keep on riding over and through them. The analogy is valid for the most part.

I called the tower for a re-join to land, requesting runway 25, but they declined, insisting on making me use runway 21. I did not mind, since landing on a runway that is more than ten times longer than needed is always fun. What the tower had forgotten is that my little plane approached at barely 50kts and they had me set up on a full pattern, just like the larger planes.

Finally, I sat on standard final approach, progressing slowly towards the runway ahead. It was very pleasant watching the city slide beneath our wings as the long runway inched closer to us.

Over the radio, I listened to the other traffic. A Hercules C130 military aircraft had now also set up on finals to land, for the same runway as us. Not a problem, except that he was approaching about four times faster than Delta Romeo.

With less than mile to go before the beginning of the runway, I pushed my head out of the open side of the aircraft and looked behind me. I could clearly see the giant gaining on us. Realising that I had been on approach for so long that the Air Traffic Controllers may have forgotten about me, I made a quick radio call.

"Delta Romeo request immediate landing on taxiway instead of runway 21," it was not really a request. I could see the taxiway, it was clear, I knew that even if we landed on runway 21, we could not possibly clear the runway before the Herc' landed. Furthermore, even if I gave full power and landed on the end of the runway, the C130 could still eat me up on his roll-out.

There was a pause in radio comms. I waited no longer, and moved my aircraft to the right of the approach path, pushing the nose down and adding full power. I was running close to the VNE, or maximum speed before failure of the airframe. As the ground rushed towards us, ATC approved my already executed manoeuvre. The Preacher's Wife was enjoying looking out at the red and white water tower that had suddenly become a lot closer, oblivious to the large machine chasing us towards the ground.

I touched down well into the taxiway, and allowed the plane to roll forward as far as I could, moving as quickly as possible to clear the taxiway for any other ground traffic.

Before we could clear the taxiway I heard the sound of the Herc' coming behind us. Looking out to my left, the C130 had already landed, and was slowing down as it passed us. The First Officer was waving to me.

I taxied back, and unloaded Preacher's Wife, who appeared to have not even noticed that we nearly became breakfast for one of the greatest military aircraft ever built.

Gold climbed aboard and we set off, again from the intersection of 25/21. Gold explained that he flew regularly, as a passenger, for his work, in mid-range aircraft. Making it clear that he really wanted to learn to fly, he fiddled with the stick, nonchalantly. I put him on the controls as soon as we were clear of the city airspace. He loved it. He took to the air like an eagle, his enthusiasm expanding by orders of magnitude.

Wonderful Adversity: Into Africa

Coming back towards the airport, I made a radio call to re-join for runway 25 - but the radio was not working. I pressed the PTT (Push to Talk) button, and looked for the transmit indicator to come on. We were not transmitting. The last thing I needed was another radio problem. Having personally installed the radio, I had an idea that might just enable us to fix the problem. Leaving Gold on the controls, I pulled my Swiss army knife out of its leather belt pouch. Wiggling the PTT switch out of the joystick using the knife, I was subsequently able to access the wires. I cut off the PTT switch and bared the two conductors that had been soldered to it. It reminded us both of the children's TV programme, 'MacGyver'. We both felt very MacGyver-ish at that point.

Hoping that my plan would work, I touched the two bare wires together, and the transmit indicator came up on the LCD display. "Delta Romeo requests re-join on long final for runway TWO FIVE," I added a lot of emphasis to the TWO FIVE.

Without any hesitation, the Tower came back with approval for the shorter runway, probably remembering the near incident from less than an hour ago.

We landed, smiled and went to see WingCo together. I asked about the procedure for teaching Gold to fly. WingCo told me "Go ahead and teach him," followed, after a short pause, with a simple "Why not."

We agreed that I would teach in English, but could still use my French teaching syllabus, and since Gold was bi-lingual English/French also, he could share my books. Once trained, he would need to be examined by the Wing's friend who was a flight examiner for the Ghana Air force. We had a plan.

From that day onwards the Tower never hesitated to allow me to use runway 25. It was a great day of learning for me and the team in the Tower. We were all learning together on how to integrate light aviation into the commercial and military dominated airspace.

A few weeks later, needing to visit Kumasi for some meetings, I decided to fly myself. Gold had wanted to come with me, but couldn't due to his work commitments. For me it would be the longest cross-country flight I had done in my little Rotax two-stroke powered plane, but I felt confident.

With no up to date maps, no reliable weather forecasts and a few hundred kilometres of flight over ostensibly hostile terrain, it was a brave mission.

I arrived at the airport before dawn, filling the fuel reservoir with two-stroke mix to the very top of the fifty litre fuel tank. I climbed in, my out of date map in hand, without any GPS, since they were not generally available at that time, basically flying with just a watch and a compass, as in the early days of aviation.

Tower gave me a clearance to depart from 25, and I headed out following my compass heading, hoping for the best. I climbed to 2000 feet, before nearing the bottom of the clouds. I had hoped to get higher, but being on

VFR, (Visual Flight Rules, meaning 'staying within sight of the ground') and never having flown 'VFR on top' (meaning flying ABOVE the clouds, but never in them - i.e., able to get on top and back underneath through breaks or holes in the clouds), I remained at 1800 feet.

I felt a million dollars. Delta Romeo was flying beautifully, the little engine spinning sweetly. I was burning a bit more fuel than planned, but that was OK, I had reserves. Onwards we flew, leaving the city behind us, heading towards the rain forest. That was when things started to go awry.

I had not understood that early morning mists come up from the rain forest. As the sun rose, the water vapour in the forest turned into mist, shrouding all but the largest trees. My points of reference were rapidly disappearing. I had planned to fly in a straight line to Kumasi, but without any visual references to relate to my map, I would have to revert to some old fashioned feature following navigation.

I knew that the main Kumasi road was to my right, or east of my track, and changed my heading to try to find it and then follow it. I decided to fly in that direction for up to fifteen minutes. The time went, but I saw no roads. Realising that I must have missed the road, I changed heading towards the west. Time passed, fuel burned, and I was now sitting above the mist of the rain forest, with no usable references, an out of date map, no navigational aids, and out of radio range of either Tower. I was alone, above the sea of mist, watched by the occasional massive tree that reached above the main canopy and its deathly white shroud. I thought of climbing to get a better radio signal, but that was not possible with the solid layer of cloud just a few feet above my wing. This is what the pioneers of aviation must have lived through. I just hoped to live through it too.

I had to decide whether to turn south and head back or to be creative. If I turned south, I would be able to hit the coastline and then find Accra easily, but when I looked at the fuel, I was already pushing towards the half tank level. With the wind coming from the south, heading back could be a disaster in its own right. The nearest airfield was Kumasi. I had to establish a new plan.

I decided to fly lower, right down to about five hundred feet above the surface. From there I could peer through the mist and pick out some larger dirt tracks and follow one to intercept the tarmac road to Kumasi. It worked. Much as IFR (Instrument Flight Rules or flying by suitable instruments when not in sight of the ground) was unavailable to me, I did manage to find my way via poor man's IFR - I Follow Roads.

Confidently, I followed the highway, ticking off landmarks on my map, wishing that I had taken action sooner. About an hour before reaching Kumasi, the mist had started to lift, increasing my visibility and hopes of completing my adventure safely.

I glanced behind me at the, barely-transparent, fibreglass fuel tank, and tried to guess the remaining quantity of fuel. My best estimate was that

Wonderful Adversity: Into Africa

Delta Romeo had just enough fuel left to make it to the planned destination of Kumasi.

I could just push on and take the risk, hoping to land on fumes, knowing that if I ran out of fuel over the city of Kumasi there was nowhere to land. Alternatively, I could make a precautionary landing in the heavily forested area, look for fuel top up, and then continue the journey. I really regretted the high fuel burn of a two-stroke engine. Wishing I had bigger fuel tanks and a four stroke engine would not change the situation, and it is not possible to upgrade either the engine or fuel tanks on an aircraft in-light. I made a mental note to not undertake such an adventure with this engine and fuel tank combination again.

Option two carried the least risk to others, as well as for Delta Romeo, and so it was time to start looking for a suitable landing area. Time ticked by, as did the kilometres. Then, with about thirty minutes of fuel left, I spotted an opening in the canopy below. It was a school field. In fact, there were two, one small and one large.

I decided to go for the larger field. Flying over it in order to assess the best angle to land, I noticed two palm trees which would be directly in line of my approach. They were tall also, very tall. Making a trial approach, I rocked the wings enabling the plane to go between the two palm trees, and passed over my intended landing area at about fifty feet. I looked down, reckoned that the field should work fine, added full power and climbed away, ready to come in to actually land on the next pass. Turning and setting up for the field again, I looked out of the cockpit to discover that it had disappeared.

What had been an empty school field was now completely packed with human beings. Young, old, men and women, all had come to stand and cheer in the field into which I planned to land. My emergency landing area had become a sea of bodies. With time and fuel running out, I headed to the smaller landing area. Turning to set up an approach, I realised that Delta Romeo had become an aerial Pied Piper of Hamelin. The entire community, far larger than imaginable for the location, were following the plane.

Thinking in the air, I decided to circle the smaller field until it filled with people. They were cheering, waving with full jubilation and generally celebrating the mechanical bird over their homes. Once they were all assembled, I flew hard and fast, at full power, back to my original choice of field. I turned and headed between the two palm trees, faster than I would have liked, but I needed to move fast, since the townsfolk were already rushing at full pelt towards my precious landing area. The plane rocked to sixty degrees as I passed between the fronds of the palms, and I then pulled the engine back to idle. Slipping the plane with full rudder and opposite aileron, I was practically flying sideways, trying to kill speed and lose height simultaneously.

With the edge of the field barely ten feet below my wheels, I kicked Delta Romeo's rudder straight, levelled the wings and simultaneously switched off the engine. I was committed. The main gear kissed the ground as the propeller stopped turning. I held back on the stick as long as I could, before lowering the nose wheel and practically hanging off the brake handle. Just before the energy was completely spent, with crowds rushing towards the plane, the nose wheel hit a stone and collapsed. The nose of the aircraft lowered rapidly, just enough to break one blade of the propeller.

Quickly, aware of the impending arrival of hundreds of people, I unstrapped myself, and climbed out of the damaged plane. The wave of bodies was upon me in seconds.

Two men rushed to the front of the crowd carrying spanners, shouting, "We can spark it for you, Master." meaning that they could fix it, or so they thought. Needless to say I didn't bother asking for their qualifications before declining their kindness.

The next twenty minutes were very confusing. A group of ladies formed an impromptu choir near the plane, giving thanks to God for my safety. In another corner a chicken was being slaughtered and a Fetish Priest thanked the ancestors for looking after me, and the children hung around me as if I were sent from heaven.

It was hot, I was tired, frustrated, and trying to work out how to get myself out of this little mishap. The crowd parted and a large man, with an entourage, all clearly important arrived. It was the Chief.

Chiefs generally have a linguist to translate for them. In the Akan tribes, this person is called an Okyeame. The chiefs Okyeame spoke to me in perfect English, "Welcome to our village. How can we help you?"

Taking a deep breath, I absorbed the atmosphere and spoke in the way that I thought might best extract me safely from my condition.

"Greetings, and thank you for welcoming me to your community," I started, not knowing what to say next. My mind processed the hundreds of options that could be spoken, and after a pause that felt like a lifetime, I added "Your playing field has been put here to help me in my time of need. I was low on fuel and needed a place to land. Your field was the best available, and I thank you and your people for making such a wonderful place in this beautiful forest."

I paused, looking around at the height of the trees and wondering how on earth I had managed to land without any personal injury. "Unfortunately, I have some minor damage and will need to take my aircraft to Kumasi by road now. Would it please the community to help me to carry out that challenge?" I breathed in, hoping that I had not offended whilst waiting for Okyeame to translate for the Chief.

The Chief spoke loudly, whilst I awaited the needed translation. "We had thought that you were President Rawlings. My people wanted to greet him. That is why we came to greet you. However, we thank God and the ancestors for your safety. How can we help you?"

Well, that went better than I had ever expected, apart from being

Wonderful Adversity: Into Africa

mistaken for the President of Ghana. Over the next twenty minutes the community arranged for wooden benches from the school to be placed in a circle around the plane. The children sat on the benches to stop anybody going near. During this time, a runner was sent to look for a taxi. Finally, the taxi, arrived. It was a little beaten up, but it was a taxi, with most parts attached, more or less.

One of the community elders came with me, and we drove down the bumpy roads for what seemed like days. It was probably no more than an hour, before we came to a larger town, with trucks. With the Elder translating, I managed to hire a truck. Being ready to head back to collect the plane, and then drive it to Kumasi, the Elder grabbed my arm, whispering "You must take back Schnapps for the Chief."

"I don't purchase alcohol," I countered.

"It is for the pouring of libations and it is our custom," he stated, without any room for negotiation.

Elder knew where to buy the best Dutch Schnapps, which I purchased before we could head back. On the return journey I realised how dense the rain forest really is, and how lucky I was to be still breathing.

I had hoped to head straight to the impromptu airfield, where Delta Romeo was patiently waiting for me, but alas, I had not understood the procedure.

We parked in front of the Chief's Palace. It was a mud construct home, larger than those around, with lots of chickens making dust baths in the dark soil. The Chief and his esteemed entourage were waiting for me.

Sitting opposite the Village Team, I was accompanied by Elder.

Elder whispered to me "State you mission."

At this point, for me at least, my mission was clear. But I realised that I was now into tradition and way, way out of my depth.

"I come to thank you and your people for your kindness and support to me in my time of need. Your village has saved my life, and I wish to thank you," I offered as a mission statement, adding, as if an afterthought, "and to collect my aircraft to take to Kumasi Airport."

Translation was given to the chief and then all went quiet. Elder pushed my shoulder, whispering "Drinks."

"As part of my thanks I bring this bottle of Schnapps to you," I mumbled, uncomfortable at handling alcohol at all, especially such strong liquor. I held the bottle out and it was taken by one of the Chief's aides.

Elder was not satisfied, and in the uneasy silence prompted "Add some money."

Reaching into my left pocket I pulled out a wad of cash and, quickly passing it to my right hand to avoid cultural offence, offered it with "And I bring this money towards the expenses of the community and as a thank you for your kindness."

I paused, money at arm's length, nothing happening.

Elder nodded at the Chief, and after some internal communication the same aide came and relieved me of my cash.

Then the Chief spoke to me, in English. He spoke excellent English, but had not done so directly to me, before tradition had been completed. He thanked me and then allowed us all to move to the aircraft landing site.

Time was spent taking the wings off, and trying not to lose any parts to the many helpers insisting on being involved with this momentous occasion. Eventually, the truck was loaded and we set off to Kumasi Airport, where I hoped to be able to secure Delta Romeo pending repairs.

Children chased the truck for a good few kilometres, their numbers dropping slowly, until the last one stood and waved at me, for I was sitting in the back of the truck holding the tail of the aircraft.

My problems may have seemed less, but they were far from over.

The red dust from the laterite roads billowed up around me and the plane, camouflaging us as we drove along.

It was nearly dusk when we arrived at Kumasi Airport. I asked for a place to park the plane. My last visit to this airport had me interviewed by the National Security Service, just for asking about aircraft. Today was going to be no different.

Two dark-suited men watched as we unloaded the plane, reconnected the wings and tied the aircraft down using my lightweight drive in anchors, off to one side of the apron, on a grassy area.

I paid the truck driver, and as he drove away, the two dark-suited men came along side me, one on each side.

"Come with us," they ordered in unison.

I was taken into an office, sat on one side of a desk, whilst the Suits laid charge against me with "Why were you impersonating the President of Ghana?"

I laid out the whole story in great detail, "I was flying from Accra to Kumasi..." and so on and so forth, I explained everything, adding at the end, "You can check with the Wing Commander in Accra if you like."

"So, you were not trying to impersonate our President?" was the only response generated by my long explanation.

"No," I offered simply, wondering if I would get free accommodation in a barred room, without a bed, for the night.

They took all my details, and allowed me to call my wife. I reassured her that I had arrived in Kumasi, with a little detour, saving her the full details.

Suits spoke amongst themselves in a local language, whilst I sat contemplating my future, if I even had one.

They stood up, and shook my hands, offering me a ride to whichever hotel I wanted, clearly satisfied with my story, and probably having confirmed who I was with the Wing Commander. As we left, the Airport Manager came out and carried out a short exchange with Suits.

"We will watch your plane for you. Come back when you are ready,"

Airport Manager offered to me, obviously happy this time with the fact that I really was a pilot, and really had a plane.

I slept very well that night probably through sheer exhaustion.

GHANA AIR FORCE

I carried out my necessary meetings, taking through necessity road transport back to Accra. I went through the required paperwork, regarding the incident, with the Authorities, and then needed to order spares to repair Delta Romeo.

Gold was amazing, he came up with an idea. "Don't just fix it - make it better," he proposed. So we made a plan. Upgrade the engine and the prop at the same time. Sometimes, just putting things back as they were is OK, but why not take advantage of a mishap to create something better.

Parts were ordered, and we planned to fly to Kumasi together, to repair the aircraft in situ, before flying it back. However, WingCo had a different idea.

One morning I received a phone call. "Get to the airport now, and take some tools with you," it was WingCo. He had a transport plane about to depart, taking some items to Kumasi, and it would return empty. If I could fit my plane inside, they could fly it back to Accra.

I practically teleported myself to the airport, and was more excited than an electron in the CERN HADRON supercollider as we flew to the place where Delta Romeo sat patiently waiting.

Once on site, it took minutes to get the wings off and inside the small transport plane, but the fuselage would not fit with the engine on. I could not hold up the team, since I was hitching a ride - and providing some engineering exercises for the military.

Believing that we would be changing the engine anyway, I took a pair of pliers and snipped the various umbilical cords that connected the engine to the airframe, and with just six bolts removed, the engine lifted away.

We tried the airframe again, and it fitted, just, but it fitted. The military personnel strapped everything down with true professionalism. My admiration for the skills of the Ghana Air Force grew by the second, then burst through the roof when I was invited to sit on the jump seat all the way back to Accra.

Jet was waiting for our return, with his team of engine experts. Together we unloaded the airframe in double quick time, even refitting the wings.

A couple of weeks later the spares arrived. It only took a few days to install the upgrades. Now Delta Romeo sported a bigger engine and a shiny new three-blade, carbon fibre, propeller. Each blade was painted a different colour; red, yellow and green, the national colours of Ghana. She looked resplendent, and was now a true Ghanaian aircraft. Gold and I must have looked at her, paying her compliments, for at least twenty minutes before being able to leave her in the hangar.

Gold continued to build hours in Delta Romeo, between his trips to the various countries in West Africa as his job permitted.

Arriving back from one of his many trips, Gold called me one evening. "Can we do a flying lesson at first light tomorrow morning, before I fly back out in the afternoon?" he pleaded.

At 4am, I headed to his house, the morning sun still hiding-out in East Africa. We planned breakfast together before driving to the airport. Gold opened the door with a big welcome. I stepped onto the terrazzo floor of the entrance hall just as the lights went out. Part of the 'joy' of living in Ghana was the erratic power supply. Unperturbed, using flashlights, we headed to the kitchen and set up bowls of muesli as pilot fuel, ready for our morning mission. We ate in darkness, as I briefed Gold on the detail of the training. I hoped to send Gold solo that morning, but he did not know that. Just as I completed going through the planned exercises, excluding the 'solo' part, the power returned.

We both looked into our nearly empty cereal bowls, across the table, and then at each other's beards. Ants were everywhere. It seems that the muesli box had become home to a few thousand ants. Furthermore, they had become a part of our breakfast, and facial hair.

Rapidly, we washed our faces, wiped down the table, threw away the remnants of our ant flavoured breakfast, and set out to fly.

Once at the airport, the sky was clear, East Africa had finally decided to share sun with the West, the warm rays gently rubbing our arms as we fuelled-up the plane.

After three circuits I asked Gold to land, telling him that I needed the toilet. I blamed it on the ants.

As soon as we landed, I explained that he was being sent solo. His face did not know whether to smile or frown. He was happy, scared, excited and pensive all at once. I refastened my seatbelt to the empty seat and stood back, with a hand-held radio at the ready, just in case he needed a few hints to get back down safely.

He fired up the engine and rolled forwards just a few metres before the aircraft leapt skywards. I did not need to see Gold's face to know that it was beaming with a greater intensity than the sun.

He came back ten minutes later and made a most beautiful landing on runway 25, backtracked and shutdown the plane by my side. He shook his head, then put his head in hands, waved, slapped his face and finally screamed "YEEEEEES."

Gold was on his way towards a pilot's licence.

FLYING JETS

As part of my work in Ghana, I would prepare documents that made their way to all sorts of magnificent places, including the various Ambassadors desks, and the seat of Government.

One evening I was sitting at home when the phone rang, "You will be picked up from your house for a meeting at Osu Castle. Be ready in fifteen minutes," the dry and factual announcement squawked out of the crackly phone handset.

Osu Castle was where the President and his team operated from. The President's official residence lay within its old colonial slave fort wall. I had no idea why I was going to the Castle. I was not shocked, but I was concerned. My work had ruffled a few feathers, but my job was to give facts, not to make friends.

A dark car collected me from our home on the outskirts of Accra, and I set off into uncharted territory. Driving through the streets in the dark, at fairly high speeds, I kept wondering if this would be my last night of freedom. There were so many stories and rumours about what happens in African Governments. Was I being set up? Had I overstepped some hidden line in the sand?

We pulled up to the outer gate, which opened as if automatically, but was actually powered by two well-armed guards. Approaching a second gate, the car headlights were switched off as the driver switched on the interior courtesy light. The barrel of a gun could be seen through a slit in the wall to the right of the black gate. My heart beat as if it were playing an extremely long drum roll in preparation for the next circus act.

A soldier peered through the half-open car window, and finally nodded. As he did so the interior gate opened, and we disappeared into the inner sanctum of the President's abode. It was terribly impressive, even if a bit awe-inspiring and even frightening.

We exited the car and I was shown up some stairs to a small room. In the room was a large television, a collection of couches and a couple of armchairs. It was not plush, looking more like a family room for a working class family. At the other side of the room a door was open, giving a glimpse into the next room. Children could be seen playing happily on the floor.

There were two, clearly visible, people and another whose feet alone could be seen, their body blocked by the open door. As I was ushered further in, and the door pulled closed behind me, I came face-to-face with the man behind the door, President Jerry John Rawlings.

Despite never having met me before, he greeted me as if I were a long lost friend, using my first name, and offering me a seat. I had not expected this. Introductions were made all around. A journalist from Europe, a businessman from Ghana, and little ol' me, sitting with the President, whilst his kids play next door.

The questions flew back and forth about my work, and what the challenges in different areas were. I answered to my fullest everything asked of me, and then sat back as other discussions took place.

Becoming bored by the political conversation, I wandered next door to play with the children. Youngsters were far more my cup of tea than grown up political talk. I told the children some stories, we played several games, and then I taught them to catch coins off their elbows.

Suddenly, the President called me and the children into his room, for the children to show him their new trick. I could see the human, father side of the man. I could see that he was not a politician. Definitely not. He was a man of passion, who cared for his children and his country. He may have done some wrong things, and go on to do some more - but don't we all? We can all find bad in anybody if we want to, but when the good out-shines the bad by hundreds or thousands to one, it amazes me that folks still hang on to the negatives that they can find. We all have to make our own minds up, and there and then, in his presence, in his home, I could see into the man's eyes, right down to his soul. His heart was clearly big and full of care, not only for his family, but also for Ghana. I was deeply impressed. I decided to accept the man for who he was, a family man. I discounted the stories and rumours, and took him for whom he revealed to me that he was.

The President asked the children if he could try to catch coins off of his own elbow, and the whole room went silent. The President was ready to potentially fail in this game, with his children, in front of people he did not know. I was impressed. I was more impressed when he caught the coins first time, so much so that I exclaimed "Clearly a pilot, Sir!" We all laughed.

With that, the President asked me straight up "Of all that you have seen in Ghana, what have you liked the most?"

That was a tough question. There had been something I wanted to comment on. Now I could, to the President, "Well, Sir, I think that Jet and the Aermacchi pilots are doing a great job. I have enjoyed seeing the improvement in the formation flying of the fighter jets recently, at the Air

Wonderful Adversity: Into Africa

Force base."

He looked at me, head tilted a few degrees to one side, and reached for the phone. The conversation was in hushed tones, fast, and quickly over. He then barked at me "Be at the Air Force base, Sunday afternoon at 4pm."

With that, our meeting was over, and I was heading back home.

On the Sunday afternoon, I headed to the Air Force base with the family. Unsure of what exactly would happen, Jet led me into a locker room where I was fitted into a military green 'G-suit' and given a briefing on the Aermacchi. Leaving the air-conditioned briefing room, the hot afternoon sun slapped me in the face as I was led onto the apron. Jet showed me how to climb aboard and then strapped me firmly into the rear seat of the single jet engine plane. Unsure of the exact plan of action and what would come next, I sat held securely in the military jet.

Jet's briefed me on 'ejection seats' and having to remove the arming, pin once the canopy was closed. My pilot for the pending flight walked out. Confidently, my 'jet training instructor for the next hour' marched across the apron and climbed into the front seat. He was unmistakable. He was the President of Ghana himself. I swallowed hard, politely whispering "Good afternoon, Sir."

He nodded and started the pre-start checks. For the next hour, he was not the President, he was a fellow aviator, and my life was in his capable hands. The flight was incredible, a blur, but incredible. We flew along the coast, up the River Volta, over the Akosombo and Kpong hydroelectric dams, did some aerobatic manoeuvres and back to two touch 'n' go circuits at Kotoka International Airport, before landing. No better 'thank you' for my work in the country could have occurred. I contemplated what I would say to the 'big man' when we landed.

Before I could un-strap myself, and fumble the helmet away from my beaming face, the President/Instructor was out of the plane, across the apron, marching head-on towards my two waiting children. He barely paused, his step simply adjusted by a partial pace, to make a simple, one sentence statement to them as he passed by, "Quite a pilot your father," and he disappeared into a waiting, darkened window, car. Chuffed would be an understatement of how I felt.

A few months later, I had the privilege of flying the President in my own plane. He simply walked up to Delta Romeo on the apron, handed over his belongings to his security detail, 'removed his Presidential title', attached his 'fellow aviator title', and we went up for a flight, short but sweet. He could fly, really well. On landing, he exited and disappeared, making a brief complimentary comment about my small tube and cloth plane. My respect for the man grew.

Jonathan & Patricia Porter

CHANGES

My contract for working on trade data was coming to an end. One project was closing and another not scheduled to begin for six months. Bogota explained that he would have no work for me until at least a few months after a new project started, and that all the support for the staff in the combined operations room would have to be suspended.

I told him my mind, straight up, "International Aid must be sustainable, and the team need support still. You cannot just switch it on and off like that."

He explained, with his gentle, firm and factual voice, "I don't make the rules. This is the way it works in International Aid. One programme finishes then we negotiate a new one. Until we sign an agreement between the two Governments we must suspend our operations. You can't change the system."

It irked me that every single aid programme had to be 'agreed with the Government'. There was no thinking about the needs of the people, continuity or sustainability. It appeared to be all about ticking boxes.

On my way home I thought about my team in the office. They had come so far, but they were still learning and still needed support. I made the decision to continue to work in the office for as long as I could, even without pay, knowing that it was against the rules. It made no sense to work for free, but it made less sense to watch all of the efforts laid to waste by bureaucratic delays. I realised that my proposed actions could get me into trouble, a great deal of trouble. That would be nothing new.

For the next six months I went into the office at the Ministry of Trade and Industry every day, continuing the much needed support to the hard working team.

Then, one overcast day, Bogota walked into the office. The look of shock on his face when he saw me was precious. "What are you doing here? Whose contract are you on? How? Why? When? Where?" It was as if he wanted to spew out as many questions as possible without waiting for an answer. I was not sure if he was happy or sad to see me. He was certainly surprised.

I explained that I couldn't let the unit down, and had worked off my own initiative pending a renewal of the support programme. Amazed, he immediately offered me work on the new project for one year. I accepted. I never worked those six months for money, it was for the team and for the support of Ghana's trade programmes. I was inspired by the amazing flight in a jet, presented by the President himself, but I did it mainly because I simply believed in what I was doing.

At the end of the year, the team were practically self-reliant, and so it was time to see what came next. There was no more tangible support coming for the work that I had been involved in, and no more areas that

Wonderful Adversity: Into Africa

required my inputs at that time. Change was on the horizon.

The children were at critical stages of their education, and my wife missed the UK terribly. When I failed to find another contract to follow on with, and unable to work another period of time without being paid, we took the tough decision to move back to the UK. We set the wheels in motion. It is never easy to move from one country to another, and this would be no different.

At the Ministry, the team were keen to find a solution to keep me on. After a lot of negotiation, we agreed a package for me to consult directly with the Government, three weeks on, and two weeks off. With the house nearly fully packed, and the inherent insecurity of working for a Government in a developing nation, I agreed to travel back and forth between the UK and Ghana to work.

Gold agreed to look after Delta Romeo, and was all but ready for his final practical exam to obtain a Ghana Pilot Licence, in the coming weeks.

At home, we packed as much of our lives into boxes as we could and set out to the old country. I would be gone for two weeks, just to set up the family, then return to work in the Ministry. With the children set up in their new schools, and a temporary home rented on the South coast of England. I headed back to the warmth of the tropics.

Gold met me, taking me back to his home. Gold had readily agreed to provide accommodation for me during my times in Ghana, so that we could talk flying even more.

Once there, we found that his wife was very unwell. She was in bed, howling in pain, clutching at her belly. I looked, touched her abdomen and watched her writhe in agony. It was appendicitis.

We rushed her to the hospital. Once there she was taken to surgery. It appeared that her appendix had burst. Knowing that blood may, even on the off-chance, be needed, and that I was a suitable donor, I waited at the hospital. Soon, an older lady, wearing clackity court shoes, came into the room, choosing the seat next to me.

"Hello," she spoke with a thick German accent, "are you here for Gold's wife?"

"Yes," I replied.

"Good. Me too. We can wait together then," she added, in a matter of fact tone, lacking any audible emotion.

We chatted about all sorts of things from the weather to aviation. Then, out of the blue she asked me the strangest question.

"What do think about Adolf Hitler?" her eyes piercing deep into mine, clearly not wanting the standard British response.

I thought for a moment, not sure of what or where this lady was coming from, but certain that I was in a tough place. I hunted deep in my memory, recalling some of the history lessons from my ex-SAS teacher and documentaries. Eventually, I answered, as if writing a balanced essay for a jury of international examiners.

"We must remember that he was elected democratically. He was at one point the choice of the people. He did many, many bad things. History has recounted endless times the bad things that occurred under his rule. Things that the people never expected when they voted for him, and then regretted having elected him. Things that the people were horrified at," I fumbled my answer.

I was clearly digging my own deep hole, so I added "But he stimulated aviation and rocket technology that we all benefit from today. After the war, it was the German scientists who helped the Russians in their space programme, and the Americans in theirs."

My heart stopped beating, I felt scared. I did not know why, but I did. I hoped that my speech was helping me to balance the scales that I had clearly tilted precariously. In the dim light of the hospital room, I could see that her face was still twitching, smile now converted into a tiny hyphen of tightened lips.

After a seemingly interminable silence I added "The work on computers done in Germany before and during the war is often forgotten, but the Zuse computer is still being used in Zurich today." That was all I could manage in my attempt to answer this woman's tough, anti-personnel-mine laden question.

Finally, after deep and contemplated thought, she responded, "You give a good answer. You are not like others. You see more than the headlines. Now, let me tell you something."

My heart was pounding; I felt a little scared of this frail old lady and her clackity shoes. I had no idea where she was from, nor what she would throw next into my path. Learning closer to me, her face barely six inches away, eyes locked in their gaze into mine, she whispered "My father was an SS officer. He worked closely with Adolf Hitler."

I was not sure if she was proud, or ashamed. But she seemed relieved to tell somebody about this hidden fact. Her eyes leaked a little as she unlocked, and then disengaged, her gaze from mine. She dropped her eyes to focus on the floor. She had wanted to tell somebody about this secret, but needed first to know if it was safe to do so.

We sat in silence, practically able to hear each other's heartbeat. We had a connection, but I could not determine what sort. I knew that it had helped her to state those two last sentences, and that I must learn from it.

I contemplated the last ten minutes of discourse. Realising that we never know what is really behind the smile of the people we meet. They all have something hidden, something never said, something that chews on their being, silently, waiting for a moment of exposure, only to be returned to that little pocket of solitude. Nothing happens without a reason, but the reason for that conversation, at that time, eluded me completely.

Gold burst into the room. My heart nearly exploded through my shirt with surprise. His wife was out of surgery, and she did not need blood. It was all going to be fine.

The old lady nodded as she left the room and her clackity shoes echoed away down the hospital corridor. Gold and I set off, back to his home to get some rest. I did not share my strange encounter with him. It simply seemed inappropriate.

Each morning Gold and I went to the airport to work on his flying skills, generally between 6 and 8am. From there I headed to the Ministry and worked on improving the various systems and a new software solution that would improve operations at Tema port.

As I got towards the end of my first trip back to Ghana working directly for the Government, I felt pulled in two directions. The need I felt, to stay and do what I was so clearly good at, and the need of my family, to travel back to the UK to provide support for my little tribe, as they settled back to British life.

I worked hard to get Gold enough solo time for his final flight exam, which was set for two days after my departure. Gold was more than ready for his final flight assessment, and I was so looking forward to hearing that he had received his Ghana Pilot's Licence. Before he took me to the airport for my flight home, we took a picture of Gold pretending to eat the keys to Delta Romeo, whilst sitting at the table. He chuckled with excitement, and his wife tried not to laugh, for her stitches still hurt from surgery.

Gold hugged me with great force when he dropped me off at the airport that night. Contemplating the challenges of my two continent life, I flew to my other home, and to my family.

Back in the UK, excitement was rampant. I listened to stories of school and the differences between Ghana, France and England, realising that the best gift I had ever given my children was the gift of living in different cultures. My wife had found a car that we could afford to purchase, and was clearly happy to be back in her home country. She had been shopping, and made a great deal of successful effort to re-integrate the family to UK life.

In the afternoon, we purchased the car she had spotted, a large green Ford Grenada, naming it the Skylark. No real idea why, but it seemed like a good name for the car. On the way home we stopped to eat fish and chips, out of paper, sitting on the promenade, British style. It was sort of normal, but nothing like the life in Africa. I felt torn between the two continents in the very depths of my soul.

I called Gold, wishing him luck for his flying test the next day, and making him promise to call me as soon as he got his licence.

That night, I was so excited for Gold. He had the keys to Delta Romeo and would soon be able to take her flying on his own, whenever he wanted.

Waking up early, I worked on my computer, preparing for my return to Ghana in a couple of weeks. My eyes flicked onto the telephone regularly, expecting a call about Gold's flying test results. The phone did not ring, which I simply, and negligently, put down to the poor phone lines in Ghana.

With the children home from school and supper eaten, finally, the phone rang. My wife was closest and picked up the phone. When I arrived by her side she was ashen. He voice was trembling and the word "Dead," was being repeated, solemnly.

I snatched the phone. "What has happened?" my voice reaching down the phone and across the continents desperate for an answer to my probing.

"Gold... is... dead..." came back the reply from his wife, tears of grief coating every syllable.

My mind envisioned Delta Romeo stuck in tree; upside down in a lake; crushed under another aircraft; and many more images of what could have happened to snatch Gold from the planet. My mind's ability to envisage the worst possible scenarios exceeded all expectations.

"He was sitting at his desk..." the weepy voice continued, "and then he... just... died."

After that the words became unintelligible. My own eyes sprung a major hydraulic leak. My heart felt as if it had stopped. Denial, anger and bargaining from the Kübler-Ross model of the five stages of grief, bit me simultaneously.

After a while, sobbing and sharing had done as much as it may or may not do to help, and with our multiple goodbyes said, we both hung up.

I couldn't speak. The loss of somebody who you have been so close to, who is not a blood relative, is hard to express. He was only a few years older than me, in his mid-thirties. When I found my voice, all I could say, repeating twenty times in a husky tone, was "WHY?"

I realised that I treated so many things in my life as constants - forgetting that very little is.

FUNERALS

Flying back to Ghana, my first port of call was to Gold's house. His widow was forlorn. We hugged, shared our loss, mine nowhere near hers, but both of us shared that common thread of losing a dear friend. Tears and tissues were found on the floor in abundance. We then sat for a seemingly interminable time, just next to each other, without words.

Drying her eyes, she told me the full story of how she had found Gold collapsed at his desk, barely alive, and rushed him to the nearest hospital. Sadly, once there, they did not have the needed supplies, even if they had the skills, to deal with his condition, and so he died soon after. The doctors

Wonderful Adversity: Into Africa

put it down to a heart-attack, but nobody would ever really know. He had departed this realm, and no matter how much denial, anger, bargaining and depression is spent, it must always end with acceptance. Acceptance does not mean happy, acceptance means ready, no matter how reluctantly, to move on.

We sat some more, as I desperately searched my seemingly empty head for things to say. Remembering the ant flavoured muesli story, I recounted it, with exaggerations and actions. We both laughed, tears of a different sort now flowing down our cheeks. Memories of the good times smeared across the surface of our distress.

Human emotions appear to be laid out on a Möbius strip, inside our heads, and therefore, if we keep on moving we will always move from one emotion to another, covering every possible angle, without ever changing the side we started on. Always coming back to the beginning. Surprisingly, grief and laughter are parked next to each other on our emotive list, and thus we can move between the two in an instant.

It would take time to sort out Gold's estate. We agreed to sell Delta Romeo to provide funds to ensure that Gold's widow did not have to worry in the short term. A buyer came forward with a poor price, but it would keep her in funds pending things getting sorted out.

After we had laughed and cried some more, I offered to speak at Gold's memorial. It was a sad day, one where I realised that being in Ghana can mean that medical care is simply not available, as it is elsewhere.

After another cycle between the UK and Ghana, and back to the UK again, I had a major consideration to make. I had not been paid by those who were supposed to pay, and was catapulting my bank balance heavily into the red. I simply could not pay another ticket to Ghana out of my own pocket. Much as the pay for my work should come in due course, I personally could not bankroll a foreign government.

Pressure from home was for me to get a job, in the UK, and so I applied to teach in a college. I was surprised to be offered a lecturer position, as Course Leader, for an Advanced Information and Communications Technology course.

If I accepted the lecturer job, I would not be able to run between two countries. It was going to be a tough decision.

That decision was made for me with a rather threatening phone call. The call came from Switzerland, from a person who commuted between Switzerland and Ghana, on a similar project to mine. I knew the person who was calling, but I did not know the side of him that came over the phone that night.

"Yaw," my Ghanaian name was spoken frankly and with a snap, "What would it take for us to ensure that you NEVER go to Ghana again?" Menace hung on every word. I knew that his company was not happy with my working on the customs systems. They had other ideas, for their own ends.

My work had highlighted certain issues in his company, which was a large one. But I never imagined a call like this. Once again my mouth worked ahead of my brain, "There is nothing that will ever stop me from going to Ghana. But, I am going to work in the UK for a couple of years just now."

Whether my brain had processed the veiled threat, or whether that call was simply the serendipitous moment I needed to push me down on one side of the fence, for the time being, I will never know. But it made it clear to me, and to my family, that I needed to step back from Ghana for a while.

The Swiss chap, sounded much happier as he hung up the phone. For me, it placed a firm punctuation mark on my decisions for the next couple of years.

TEACHING & LEARNING

As a teenager, I had not gone to University, due to the goat incident. To be teaching alongside the academics was going to be interesting. Everything was so formal compared to industry. Staff rooms, fixed times for everything to happen, and lots of meetings... more meetings and seemingly endless paperwork. Proper lunch and coffee breaks felt funny. It was nothing like work, as I knew it.

Then there were the personalities.

Snappy lady; she was the boss of the unit. She always walked into work each morning with a pretty little patent handbag, held in front of her 'Queen style'. She walked and talked with a snap. Her claim to fame was working with COBOL at some point in history - comparatively recent by the human time line, but ancient in computing terms. She knew the theory of computing, very well, but lacked the practical experience. She was an excellent team leader, even if a bit starchy at times. I got on well with her, in a working sense, even though we had different approaches to teaching and learning.

Plaid Shirts; the nerds of computing. Some had worked in industry in fairly recent years, but tendered to be terribly keen on 'doing it by the book'. These folks loved the theory, and could teach it very well, albeit too dry for my liking. Humour was something which they used, but it was focused on a plane of existence that few could align with. None of them liked wearing office clothes, but all seemed to enjoy the tartan patterns in their shirts and, whenever possible, created contrast by wearing brown corduroy trousers and open toe sandals, with socks. I enjoyed the technical and theoretical discussions with these chaps.

Enthused Apps Ladies; the goddesses of applications. These ladies made the creation of Word and Excel documents look like fun. Adding images, drawings, changing the size of the margins, all presented as if they were doing some form of keyboard aerobics. They seemed to like wearing darker clothes, and walking briskly. They were wonderfully full of energy and had passion for teaching. They were great fun to work with, and ready to learn, always full of banter and fun.

All of these wonderful personalities had a common fuel: Coffee. The staff room was dominated by a coffee machine. On arrival in the morning a coffee cup had to be safely in hand, and some of the brownish liquid ingested, prior to chit-chat. Between each lecture session it was not unusual to see a small flock of teaching staff sipping around the coffee machine, as if it were some magical bird bath for lecturers. Before leaving, the 'one for the road coffee' was practically obligatory for all members of the holy order of coffee worshippers.

I had never been a coffee drinker, but I did try their method for a week. It was not a good idea. It gave me the shakes, shivers, sweats and generally made me commit more acts of dubious reason than normal. So, I gave up coffee and tea, as I had already done with alcohol years ago. After all, I managed to be lively, enthusiastic and able to climb on tables without ever imbibing any chemical additive to my system.

Although I was a team leader, I was not terribly well accepted. I did not hold a degree, and I had little 'institutional teaching' experience. My teaching was from the cutting face of industry, not the chalk face of a classroom. I would have to prove myself.

I quickly realised that the course I had taken on was struggling to achieve results. There was not the student retention, nor the student achievement expected, especially in the Plaid Shirt subjects. I looked at the students, and could see why. To me, in my ignorance, I saw them as bored and lacking challenge. Yes, they were learning, but the material was not exactly stimulating. Apps Girls did better, but they often lacked the respect of students in the male dominated classroom. Out of the two year groups, there was one girl, in the second year of students, and four in the first year group, out of a total of around fifty students.

The girl in the second year was in a wheelchair. She was a tough cookie. Her upper body strength was enough for her to hold her own against the lads. Those in the first year group were all lightly built, but with quick and sharp tongues. All of the girls struggled to achieve real integration in the male-dominated-geek-zone.

My delivery style was a little different to the norm. I preferred to use real-life examples over book scenarios, which students seem to prefer, but that is not where my approach variance ended.

I noted that a standard lesson/lecture is one hour long, and students get bored, disruptive and annoying during that time. However, they will sit through three hours of a movie, or play a video game for even longer, without losing interest. I believed then, and still believe now, in several basic rules of the learning environment:

1. A good student will often learn with a bad teacher.
2. A bad student will often fail with a good teacher.
3. Most students are not in the above two categories, and they need support to maximise their achievements; They need learning opportunities.
4. Teaching can take place in a room without learning taking place. This is the worst kind of teaching, but all too often found in technical topics.
5. Learning is what should take place in a classroom/lecture theatre, over and above teaching.
6. If a teacher decides to become a learning facilitator, things change in the dynamics of education.
7. Education has to compete with TV, Cinema and video games.
8. We all get bored and distracted.
9. Each of us learns in a different way.
10. Learning facilitation requires a lot of energy. Most of that energy does not equate to an instant usable result, as in an internal combustion engine, so a lot more energy has to go in than would be imagined to get something usable out.
11. Hands-on experiences are essential in learning and retaining knowledge.
12. Education should be like a bakers shop. Bakers bake the cakes that their clients need, not what is easiest to produce. Bakers have to sell their cakes. Education is about producing employees. Employees that employers want. Employees that are useful and can produce on day one of a new job.
13. The most disruptive students are often the best.

With this in mind, I decided to experiment within the educational establishment for which I worked, consciously and with a hint of mischief. Probably not a good plan for a long-term career, but a good plan for the students at the time.

I found that too many lessons were dry for the students:
- introduction
- deliver a speech on the topic, using visual aids if available
- practical hands-on
- answer questions
- end lesson

That was not my style... my normal lesson would involve what I like to see as a cinematic performance.
- dramatic introduction to grab class attention
- detail, a story that gets the topic across

Wonderful Adversity: Into Africa

- practical hands-on
- handle the issues, one-on-one and as a group
- dramatic group attention direction
- ensure learning took place
- end on a cliff-hanger

This requires a quick-thinking approach and a lot more of being in tune with the class. Most days it worked. It appeared to be more popular with most students than the traditional 'chalk and talk' style of teaching. Those colleagues who embraced it were fantastic, generally those with a similar approach to mine, just needing a bit of encouragement to go that bit further.

I remember teaching database theory, a much disliked subject, to a particular group. The group were propped up against their desks, some already having hacked into the college network for nefarious reasons, others sleeping, most trying to play a game without anybody noticing, and failing miserably.

The workstations were laid out in a row format. Consequently, when standing at the front of the class it was impossible to see the screens, but easy from the back. Sadly, the time to get from the front to the back down the aisle was long, since it was a minefield. Students would ensure that the walkway had bags, papers and legs to impede progress, allowing those little devils at the rear to look like angels upon arrival of the warden, I mean lecturer.

Nobody had their eyes forwards. Nobody was really interested in the topic of the day. So, it was time to shake it up. In my best Sergeant Major voice, borrowed from years of watching Windsor Davis in 'It ain't 'alf hot mum', I yelled "Right, you 'orrible little people," which distracted about 30% from their other matters.

"Heads up, eyes forwards," I added with a snap, collecting another 20%. Those at the back were not ready to engage. "Today we are going to look at database theory..." I added, equally loud, obnoxious and military style, gaining about 10% more.

Without 100% I was not going to continue. Leaping onto the desk in-front of me, I pounced from desk-to-desk until I was standing on the furthest away desk. I stood at rear edge of the surface, my toes tucked under and behind a particular students monitor. Leaning over, my body arched, neck twisted rearwards to enable my wide open eyes to drill into the skull of the offending student, I looked through the offender. His chair moved rearwards, whilst his arms and body pinned themselves against the wall. All he could see was me. He sat frozen, looking at me as if I had just popped out of Sigourney Weaver's stomach in an Alien movie. It got his attention. I dropped my head to inspect his computer screen. It was porn. No surprise there. Without a word, I reached down to the keyboard and closed the application. The room was silent. I stepped sideways, off the desk, dropped to the floor and walked over the minefield of bags back to my delivery point. I had 100% attention.

"He can't f$@%ing do that," came a barely audibly comment from the second row.

I stepped forwards, lowering my head and retorted in an equally low tone "Yes I f$@%ing can."

I had their attention. "Now, back to databases..." and went on to talk about work I had done in Ghana, painting every detail and personality, adding the data in along the way. I was telling a story, it had highs and lows, a bit of exaggeration and drama added, in true Hollywood style. It ensured that the audience stayed with me. It was probably the first time the Harmonised Code for international trade had been used as an introduction to databases.

Then, over to the practical stuff, and it happened as it should, more or less. The students were able to transform an idea into a database, a database that actually worked. I was happy. My teaching colleagues were not so happy.

In the staff room a Plaid Shirt collared me. I avoided stepping on his sock covered toes, peeping out from his sandals. He laid into me about Codd's Laws of Normalisation. "You have to teach them Codd's laws..." he commenced and spent twenty minutes drawing diagrams and arrows.

When he had finished, I thanked him and showed him how I had been achieving the same result, reliably, efficiently and in less than five minutes. It was not good enough for him. "You have to do it Codd's way," he snapped, then shook his head violently.

He had a point, since the students would need to be able to explain Codd's laws on database development in their exams, but I felt that it was best to be able to solve the problem first, and then explain it later. It seemed to work, since the students got good results. In fact by the end of the first year of my being a lecturer there had been rumblings at the QCA.

QCA, or Qualifications and Curriculum Authority, oversaw all courses and the outcomes. Somebody may have told them that I was unconventional. For whatever reason, they sent an inspector to visit one of my classes.

My co-ordinator was worried. I was not. If I was sacked for delivering practical skills, even if unconventionally, I would simply return to industry, earn double or triple the money and be fine. I had chosen to teach, but was not obliged to stay there.

Inspector Lady met me in the staff room. "Good Morning. I have come to observe your teaching methods," she proposed dryly. Together we walked to the classroom. I looked out of place, wearing a large blue tie with an aeroplane on it, including a 3D rotating propeller. She looked totally in-place, clipping along in her tiny heeled closed shoes, beige stockings, well pleated kilt, cream blouse and a cardigan.

As we entered the classroom it erupted. They all laughed at the blue-rinse haired Inspector. I turned and snapped "Take your seats for another exciting ride in the learning adventure of I...C...T..." They conformed, for the most part.

I settled inspector in the front corner, so that the students could see her, hoping that they would be more co-operative with the newcomer in sight. That was a mistake.

"Today, we will consider a problem at a factory in relation to managing data for production," I began.

Used to my style and technique, a student called out "What is the name of the company?"

I responded with the name of a company in the flavours and perfumes industry, located relatively close to the college. Just as I took a breath to continue, I noticed a hand shoot up. This was unusual since they generally just yelled out questions.

"Yes?" I asked, happy that the mob was cooperating in my assessment.

"Do they make the flavours for condoms?" he asked, trying to look innocent, but darting his eyes at the Inspector in the corner.

The class collapsed in giggles, Inspector, blushing profusely, silently dropping her head.

"Alright, alright," I sighed. Then, looking at the offending lad, as he grinned from ear to ear, I walked slowly and very deliberately towards him. With as straight a face as possible, I asked "So, what is your favourite flavour condom?"

I won on the resultant uproar. Laughter filled every head, apart from Condom Boy's. He looked back at his keyboard, a slight pinkness in his cheeks, and soon the lesson was back underway. But I was not to get off that lightly.

As if to try to get me dismissed and out of their hair for good, two lads at the back started to fight. Chairs went sideways, a monitor nearly met its end on the floor. Bodies writhed in teenager slapping and swearing mode. I scrambled over the bags to stop them, and then stood between them.

"CHAPS," I yelled, loud enough to hurt their ears. "If you have so much energy, you should compete with me in a push-up match." Hush crawled through every inch of the room. Inspector looked at me her face twisted, mouth almost opening and then sealing tightly as if preparing for a bucket of water to be thrown over her. She was clearly wanting to ask whether that was 'allowed' or not, but decided to refrain, watch and understand the outcome. She remained quiet, looking non-committal, as she tried to blend into the fabric of the room.

With the two offenders now at the front of the room, just a few feet from Inspector, and the whole class on their feet watching, I explained the rules of the game. I was certain this would be my last ever lesson, so make it a good one.

"You two have so much energy you want to fight in my lecture, well, I will cut you a deal," I proposed. They looked at me, quizzically. "We, all three, do twenty press-ups, and whoever completes them the quickest can run this show."

The body of students cheered and clapped. The Inspector rolled her eyes so far back into her head I am sure that they did a complete 360 degrees and returned from her lower eyelids.

I had to stop the clapping and chanting so that we had silence for the challenge about to be undertaken.

The two students and I were poised, hands-on the ground, back straight, lifted to locked elbow, ready to commence. I counted down "Three.... Two.... One.... GO."

For the first five they were neck-and-neck with me, the body of the class shouting the numbers out at each return to arm-lock. Then, as I pushed the pace, they tried to keep up. By twelve the first student dropped to the floor complaining about his arms. The second student held his own, but did not complete before me, dropping in a similar condition to his friend on the count of twenty.

I stood, composed myself and continued with the lesson, hiding my breathlessness and sore arms as best I could. Two tired young men dragged themselves back to their seats compliantly.

When the lesson was over, the class poured out excitedly, wanting to share the craziness of their last hour with other mates. Some were more polite than others, but they were overall better than normal. The room was now a cage with two persons in it. The predator and the prey, or rather the Inspector and me.

She sat, her ankles crossed, hands folded together, like crisp white linen, in her lap. I sat down opposite her and waited. I could hear a metronome, that was my heart, it was slowly being drowned out by the million thoughts racing through my head as I feared the worst. Then she spoke.

"I... I..." she stammered then paused, following up with, "I have to tell you that this was the most different lesson I have ever sat through." In chess there are twenty possible first moves, and this was clearly 'The English Opening'.

Unsure of her next more, I went for 'The Symmetrical Defence', and responded "This is the first time I have had an inspector in a class. That was a little different for me too."

She smiled and leaned her body forwards, leaving her hands parked in her lap. Smiling, she broke her porcelain face into a thousand cracks of laughter lines, and continued "That was rather fun. I liked the way you handled all of the problems. Clearly, lots of learning was taking place."

I relaxed, allowing a light smile to show on my face.

In an instant, she stopped smiling, and her face returned to pure chinaware, decorated with thin red line of lipstick, adorned with crystal blue eyes. "If I report what I have seen in this classroom today, you may lose your job. You are not conventional," she admitted.

I knew exactly what she meant, but decided to simply remain still, attentive, hoping for some better news.

"But I won't write down what I saw. I will report that it was a good lesson and that you are an unconventional, but successful, lecturer," she punctuated the final syllable with a sharp, single nod of her head.

We stood up as if choreographed, shook hands and headed back to the staff room. I knew that I was out on a limb with my style, but I also knew that it was getting results.

One of the students was from China. He spoke little English, and was not interested in anything more than meeting his visa requirements. He had ability, but lacked application. At the end of a particular term, I wrote a long report listing his attitudes, attendance rate, and laziness. Basically making it clear that he was playing at learning. There was no need to read too much between the lines that I felt that his family were wasting their money keeping him in education. It was a harsh document.

Early in the next term there was an open evening. Parents and friends were invited to come and see what the students had been doing, and better understand the learning process. I went through a number of casual interactions with students and their family members, laughing and encouraging, complimenting and complaining. Some parents would complain about me, but many more were happy with my approach to teaching their offspring. I accepted that you cannot please all of the people all of the time.

Just as we were about to close the event, the door was filled with a gaggle of Chinese faces. They shuffled in, walking towards me. At the back of the group, my Chinese student stood with his head hung low. If he had been blessed with a tail, it would have been tucked between his legs.

A Chinese translator came forwards and explained that the parents of the lad had seen my report, and wanted to meet me. No worries, I thought, and greeted the crowd with "Nee men hrao," a group greeting in Mandarin, probably with an awful accent. An older lady stepped forward and spoke at me in syllables and sounds that meant nothing to me at all. The translator just stood there. At a natural, I think, pause in the lady's incantation at me, I interjected with "Wo bu dong," continuing in English, "I do not understand. I only know a few phrases in Chinese."

The translator spoke for a few moments and laughter filled the bellies of the crowd, all of them that is, apart from my student. Never greet in a foreign language unless you are ready to handle a full conversation in that language.

The translator then explained that the parents had wanted to meet me. They were part of a wealthy Chinese family. Never had any of their son's tutors or lecturers dared to write what I had written about their beloved only child. I stopped smiling, but they all kept big grins on their faces, some nodding slowly, shallowly and almost in unison. I wanted to disappear, but I had to face the outcome of my written summary of this young man.

The older lady, apparently the mother of the lad, continued speaking in raised and accented tones.

The translation came next, "She thinks that you are very handsome."

I was sure that the translator had that wrong, and looked at him quizzically.

"I mean, she thinks you are very right," he clarified.

Handsome or right, I would take both, and responded with my best "sheea sheea," or thank you, nodding a little and trying a semi-Chinese partial bow from the waist.

The student was pushed forwards, made to stand in front of me and apologise. The mother interrupting and the father looking angry, but the message was getting across. We all exchanged a few more pleasantries and the family exited.

The next day, that Chinese student came to me, thanking me for my support to him. He then attended far more lessons and achieved a bit better. He could have done more, but he did enough to please me and his family. It made me feel good, especially the 'handsome and right' part.

The international students were fantastic, and I enjoyed them, remembering my time in private school as a child, and living in the international community of Ghana. Most were very pleasant; a few scared the socks off of me.

After 9/11, and with the growing international tension over Iraq, there was a lot of nervousness amongst certain factions of the student body. The West had made a lot of negative comments about Saddam Hussein. One late afternoon, after the main body of learners had left the buildings, a group of students from Iraq and surrounding areas approached me. They timed it, or so it seemed, to coincide with my being in a dead end corridor. Six large, far stronger than I, young men, all in their early twenties, stood in a semi-circle, herding me against the wall, but without physical contact.

"Hi Chaps. How y'all doing?" I offered. But they had no time for pleasantries. My mind raced back to the incident at school with my colleague from Iraq... I remembered the knife and looked rapidly at each of their hands. Not all were visible, some were held behind backs. I worried, but tried not to show it.

They exchanged some comments in Arabic, which I had no idea about, then one of them, the Leader, asked, almost spitting in my face, and jerking his head as he spoke threw a question at my throat. "What do you think about Saddam Hussein?" he hissed.

Oh my, what a question. Should I comment on Weapons of Mass Destruction? Should I crack a joke? I was flummoxed - a rare occasion, but it happens. Then as the breath of these men could be felt coming closer to me, I remembered being asked about Adolf Hitler, and how I had handled that question in hospital half-a-world away from here.

"Well," I paused, hunting for words, sentiments and an ability to express myself clearly "the leader of any country is to be decided by the people of that country." They moved back two or three centimetres, the Leader cocking his head to one side as he jutted his jaw towards me. "I believe that there was an election to appoint him as the leader, and therefore, it is not my concern, but that of the people of Iraq," I had a flow going now, and two of the lads started to nod. "All leaders do good and bad," the word bad had not been a good choice and I could see it on their faces, "but we judge each leader on the balance of good versus bad." I used bad again, evoking a rise in the shoulders of my pseudo-captors. "British Prime Ministers have done bad things, as have American presidents," I kept on using bad, but now against the leaders of the West, which had a placating effect. "However, we cannot change the past, but only shape the future, and that will be what determines were we all go from here." I had dug my bunker, or possibly my grave, I was not sure which.

The group pulled away from me, and huddled, exchanging their thoughts. Leader turned to me and said "You answer well. Thank you," and with that, they walked away, as if nothing had happened. I breathed in, shook a little in my shoes, and then walked a good distance behind them hunting an open, busy space.

A few weeks later, I was asked to take over for an absent lecturer. The same group of young men were in the class. I had heard, and could believe, that they were a challenging group, but I was ready to tackle them. Leader showed me full respect, and did not allow any of his 'group' to harass me. I covered a few lessons until a replacement lecturer could be found, leaving me wondering what happened to the original member of staff. They seemed to listen well, and learn, so I had no complaints. Cultural differences need to be embraced, if success is to be achieved. My international schooling and travel had taught more than any anthropological studies could hope to.

INNOVATION

At the end of my first year of teaching, I was asked to get involved with a new qualification. The Inspector from QCA had taken to my style, and wanted something new in the pot. Meetings were held in London, most of which shocked the socks of off me. The main idea was to develop a course that the available teaching staff of the country could deliver, not what the industry needed. A few of us tried to move that goal-post more in line with the long-term economics of the students as opposed to that of the teachers, but it was not easy.

I was told to try understanding that colleges cannot always find suitable staff for some of the more 'in-demand' skills, because those with the skills do not work in education. The argument was put forward that the employer should train them at work, and colleges should simply get them ready to learn. I found this a bit odd, but quickly realised that it was a reality, both practically and economically, for the education of young people.

Due to my verbal outpourings at meetings, I was asked to work on a standards handbook. I had no idea what that was, until somebody sat me down and showed me an example, telling me "Just produce work to a top, middle and bottom grade, as if you were a student, and then explain in an accompanying text why it met those criteria."

I had a better idea, "Why don't we ask students to produce the work for the standards handbook, and then annotate that?" I half-asked, half-proposed. It was as if I had let off a flash-bang grenade in their midst. The clock ticked loudly, waiting for the first person in the room speak. Finally, the chairman of the group broke the silence with "Why not."

I selected three students, one male and two female. Each was shown the new performance criteria for each of the grades, and then asked to work towards that grade. For the sake of argument, we will refer to those grades and students as A, B and C.

A worked on the top grade, he produced an endless stream of top quality outputs.

B wanted to work to the A grade, but she had to be held back so as not to overachieve.

C was annoyed at having to work to the lowest grade, but finally managed to get something together.

The day came to go to London. I took A, B and C with me, as well as their work and my 'marking advice'. The assessment team sat around the table, excited at the prospect before them.

That is where it all went wrong. A was accused of going way beyond the requirements of the assessment criteria. B was accused of achieving an A, and C was accused of achieving a B. I disagreed.

"A has done work that we would never expect to see from a student," came the comment from an older chap sitting at the end of the table.

"He is a student," I muttered under my breath. We argued for hours, literally pulling sheets of the students work out to reduce the quality to the so called 'required standard'. I watched, dumbfounded at the whole process. This was work produced by real-life students, in a realistic time frame, to the new standards, with only minimal guidance from a tutor.

I started to lose confidence in the education system. Not for the masses, but the very able students. For the masses, it was great, it enabled them to get a good grade, but it certainly was not being designed to stretch the top students.

To ease my frustrations, I flew more, finally achieving my British PPL, flying in the Cessna 172 and Piper PA28. These 'standard' aircraft did not excite me as much as the more interesting aircraft. After a while I started flying with the Tiger Club, out of Headcorn aerodrome in Kent. The Tiger Club was an amazing operation, with a broad range of classic aircraft and remarkable pilots. I was only a baby pilot compared to the giants who flew there, but they offered encouragement and training. Soon I was flying the Piper Cub, Jodel D150 Mascaret and even the Tiger Moth. These aircraft all gave me thrills. It was a therapy, for they helped me to cope with the frustrations of working in education.

The students didn't frustrate me. My frustrations came from a system which lacked ambition for real-life skills teaching, that had lost its way from providing top youngsters with employable skills, and started to focus on lots of certificates. In comparison, flying is not forgiving; it does not care about your certificates or getting the answers right in one hour, on one day, on one paper. Flying cares about your skills, every hour, every day and in every aircraft. I cared more about skills than certificates, and so, flying was my escape to reality. I had some wonderful flights, enjoying the company of some of the most amazing personalities in British aviation.

One particular pilot wore bright red boots. He had a wonderfully British accent, and could easily have just walked off of the set for 'Those Magnificent Men in Their Flying Machines'. Red was a true aviator. He could fly, tinker with the engines and also tell stories, lots of stories, sprinkled with very British guffaws.

Red was the sort of chap you had to be wide awake to have a conversation with. He bubbled and jiggled as he spoke. There was never a dull moment. He had a strong command of the English language and I often felt that he should come with a glossary, or at least a quick reference guide. All the same, I enjoyed his wild stories.

Flying with Red was also an experience. He took me for my first ride in the Tiger Moth. It is an open cockpit biplane, with the most basic of instruments, and yet it was the primary trainer for the British Royal Air Force for many years. We stood next to the old lady, whilst he recanted a dozen wondrous stories that would put most flyers off. It just excited me even more.

Finally, he fitted a leather helmet onto my head, within it my headset was held. I also wore some funky flying goggles and Red showed me how to use a flaky, musty, rubber mask over my mouth. It was not for oxygen, but to enable my voice to be heard on the intercom, due to the amount of air that would be flowing over my face. Being excited, I may not have listened to all the instructions as well as I should have.

We climbed aboard, I took the rear seat. It was like being transported back fifty or sixty years. The Tiger Moth is a real time machine. Then it got better, as we called the ground crew to hand swing the large wooden prop. The Gipsy Major engine spluttered, coughed and finally roared. The blast of air over my face took me by surprise. I was glad of the flying goggles, since even with them on I could feel the blast on my eyes through the small gaps between the leather seals and my skin.

Red signalled for the chocks to be pulled and started to taxi, or rather the Tiger Moth did, since there are no brakes on this plane. It was necessary to move to a place where the wooden skid at the tail end had enough friction to enable the plane to warm up safely. Warming up is done on time, since there are no temperature gauges in the Tiger Moth.

Red said something to me over the intercom, but it was lost amongst the clanging of pistons, rushes of air from the prop, the sound of my own blood pulsating in my ears and an emotion so strong that it cannot be described, painted or transmitted to another soul.

Suddenly, we were taxing at a pace. Weaving left and right to see over the massive cowl that obscured our vision. I knew when we were lined up, simply because I could see the runway markers each side of me. The runway line was only present in my imagination. A word from the tower, reassuring us both that the runway was clear, and the throttle eased forwards.

We rolled, the main gear well in contact with the surface whilst the tail skid bounced a few times, until Red pushed the stick forward just enough to lift the tail, but not so much as to nick the ground with the prop. Now the speed built quickly, and we were soon heaving away from the ground. It was not like any other plane I had ever flown in, it was more like sitting on a magic carpet, with a noisy tiger roaring at one end. The Kentish countryside slid beneath the lower wing, as the clouds raced to join the panorama over the top wing. I wanted to smile wider, but the icy chill bit at my face as if telling me to keep a stiff upper lip. We climbed to about three thousand feet, almost to the could base. Red handed me the controls.

The Tiger is a pleasure to fly, all added to by the ability to look at the countryside from an open cockpit. I carried out some gentle manoeuvres, treating the machine with care, knowing that she was older than me, and as a mark of respect for her engineering. It was way too gentle for Red.

Red took the controls back, instantly rolling the plane in a perfect barrel roll. I was thrilled. It was fantastic. Then, he went for a loop, pushing the nose over, making the ground approach at an ever increasing speed, then, with the dexterity of a surgeon, he pulled up to the top of the loop, totally inverted, and held it there, for about a second. That was a second too long for me.

I was hanging in the seatbelt webbings, feeling a little vulnerable, and tilted my head back to see the earth beneath my inverted form. At that very moment, my helmet and headset decided to respond to the attraction of the planet, assisted by the force of the air blasting across the top of my head. I had not, as hindsight now informs me, tightened my helmet enough. In an open cockpit aircraft tight is, well, TIGHT.

The wind had found enough space to enter the leather cap, and, with the assistance of Isaac Newton's friend Gravity, work towards disavowing me of my communications and head protection. Just as nature felt it had won, and the ensemble detached from my skull, I grabbed, and at that same moment Red began the final part of the loop. With the changes in forces in the airborne ensemble and my hand hunting to retain my chattels, I miraculously won in keeping my equipment, but it was a close run race. Red offered that I try the same manoeuvre, unaware of what had occurred behind him during his exploits.

I tightened the chin strap, retightened my seatbelt and carried out the same manoeuvre, without the hesitation at the top of the loop. It was a dream come true. We played in the sky, dodging clouds and playing with the birds, for another twenty minutes before it was time to land.

The approach in the Tiger Moth is slipped, to enable a view of the runway, and then kicked straight with the rudders, taking away any possible view of the landing area before rounding out. The pilot makes use of peripheral vision, focusing through the cowling at an imaginary runway ahead. It is amazing how the brain manages this, and even more amazing how the airplane flies.

We did a beautiful three point landing, touching the mains and the tail skid at the exact same moment, with lowest possible flying speed, rolling out waiting for the friction of the skid to slow the aircraft to a standstill. After taxiing back to the apron, Red and I climbed out, shook other's hands and smiled the smile that only a pilot of an open cockpit bi-plane can ever understand and appreciate.

CENTRAL BANK

The phone rang, I answered it. "Hello Yaw," came a familiar voice, "How would you like to spend a couple of weeks in Ghana, helping out with some training at the Bank of Ghana?" It was Bogota.

The timing was perfect. I was frustrated at college, and a bit of extra cash would come in handy, very handy. A deal was cut, and I flew out to give some training in numerical modelling for those in the research department at the central bank.

As I stepped out of the British Airways 767 into the humid, Africa scented air of Kotoka International Airport, every step down the stairs onto, and across the apron left a tear dripping from my eyes. I felt at 'home'. I realised that 'home is where your heart is', and that Ghana, West Africa had truly stolen my heart. It was not something I could put into words, but something that can only be felt in the core of one's person.

I enjoyed the team that needed training, for they were as thirsty as sponges abandoned in the Sahara for a month, soaking up every drip of information that was shared with them. I found the passion to learn and apply a big boost, and felt my efforts were far more useful than when teaching in the home counties of England.

We closed the training early one day, due to an internal meeting at the Bank. Taking the opportunity to visit my friends in the Ghana Civil Aviation Authority, I was informed that light aviation in the country had all but disappeared. Sadly, it was due mainly to politics, coupled with the migration away from Ghana of the aviation minded ex-pats. We shared some stories, laughed and even cried together. Then, something bizarre happened.

The Director of Safety Regulation posed a blunt question. A question that would seal my fate.

"What are YOU going to do to restart light aviation in Ghana?" he probed, looking at me across his desk with a face as serious as an oncologist delivering bad news.

ME? ME? The implications of this question were massive. What could I do? He was not joking. This really was a life or death question, not for me, but for light aviation in Ghana.

Once again, my mouth engaged, revved and set off without waiting for my thought processes to catch up. I heard the following words spilling, in all sincerity, across the man's desk, with my voice attached indelibly to every syllable. "The only way to see light and General Aviation work sustainably in Ghana is to build aircraft in West Africa. Aircraft built by West Africans, for West Africans, built here in Ghana for Ghana. We need an indigenous light aviation industry."

I watched myself as if from the ceiling fan spinning wearily above, wanting to grab my jaw and hold it closed, but the words were out. It was the truth, yet the 'official reaction' took me by surprise.

I have rarely seen any Ghanaian, or other nationality, official laugh uncontrollably, but that day I did. I swear that he actually left his chair and bounced off of the floor twice at one point. Between his chuckles he blurted out "We don't even build bicycles in Ghana - let alone... aircraft."

I swiftly responded, not sure of why he was laughing so strongly, "BUT Aircraft are easier to build than bicycles, it is not rocket science." After all, I knew that I could build planes, but I had never even dreamt of building a bicycle.

I thought back to the honour I had been given of a flight in the

Aermacchi, by the previous President of Ghana. I spooled at high speed through my many hours of flying over small villages in my own little plane in the recent years. I realised that the words that I had spoken in those few minutes, albeit interspersed with tears and laughter from the Director, and a few nervous chuckles from myself, were words of truth.

Before I left his office, we shook hands heartily and he promised to support any ideas that could be brought forward to make 'aviation for the people' a dream come true. He shook his head as I looked back before closing the door behind me. I even heard him laugh one more time as I walked away.

Unknowingly, I had set a challenge to myself. A major challenge, but one that I was determined to give my all to make work. I if I did not, I would never be able to forgive myself.

I finished the training programme at the Bank, and was dropped back at Kotoka International Airport, for the BA flight back to the UK where family waited patiently for me.

As I sat in the hot and clammy waiting area for my flight, I felt my heart bleeding for the lost light aviation opportunities in Ghana. It occupied my complete thought process. I entered into the denial stage of grief. I could not accept that light aviation could be snuffed out by a simple change in government. It could not happen.

Sitting at 35,000 feet over the desert, I started to imagine what could be done. I imagined every scenario I could. I became angry at the lack of light aviation in Ghana. It was unjust. But it had happened.

As we entered European airspace I was ready to negotiate a solution, to find a bargaining chip that would enable light aviation to flourish, and I realised that in order to give that a chance, I would need to move back to Ghana.

FAMILY BARGAINING

Once back to our family home, a beautiful four bedroom detached executive home, in a highly desirable area of the South of England, I broke my news.

"I want to go back to Ghana to work on getting light aviation working," I stated quietly one evening just as my wife had switched off the light for us to go to sleep. It seemed like a good idea at the time, but in hindsight, it was not the best choice of moment.

The light was returned to full intensity, as were my wife's face and eyes. "WHAT?" it was an honest response and totally understandable.

I explained that I felt that it should be possible to sell up everything and head to Ghana to establish a team of like-minded aviators, stimulating a working light aviation industry.

Unsurprisingly, it was not seen as a totally acceptable concept. The discussions, which went from cool through warm to very hot, and back again, went on until dawn's glow started knocking on the curtains. The conversation was closed, at least verbally, but not mentally for either party.

The next day, tired from lack of sleep, and after getting home from work, we left the teenagers downstairs and sat on the edge of the bed. I had a piece of paper, pen and a large dose of conviction. My wife had a stern look, logic and reason.

We wrote down all the options, and we were both set in our ways. This exercise was repeated over several days. Finally, all credit to my wife, she agreed. It was not going to be easy, but we were both ready to go into the venture lock stock and barrel. It would be a make or break of our finance and relationship.

Sitting with the two teenagers we jointly explained the plan. It was as if I had failed to read the instructions on my own M18 claymore mine. 'This side towards the enemy', was pointed at me. I felt a thousand pellets of anger, anguish and upset. It was understandable. My son had just started a new job, and my daughter was about to start college. They made it clear that they would not be joining us on this adventure.

As we explored the idea further, I was offered a fresh contract working on a different government project in Ghana, funded by USAID, which would make the move a thousand times easier. That helped us to take the final plunge. We put the house on the market.

With two bed-sits rented for the kids, and the house under offer, we were ready for the wildest plan I had ever conceived.

As we got closer to our last day in the UK, I called Red. "Hi Red, I am leaving next week to live in Ghana, West Africa," I informed him.

"What would a chap like you want to do in a country like Ghana?" he enquired with his most inquisitive and British voice.

I gave him the rough outline about the idea of setting up a light aviation industry in the region. After he had finished laughing he told me "I have flown in every country in Africa except one, and that one is too small to speak about. I have flown for Governments, military, private corporations and even rebels, and I will tell you now... *you are crazy*."

It was an honest assessment. He then asked "What class of aircraft are you planning on using?" I explained the concept of using the Zenith CH701 Short Take Off and Landing (STOL) Light Sport Aircraft as a basic model, and adapting it for medical and humanitarian uses also. His reaction took me aback.

"Bravo. Bravo. That is the perfect type of aircraft to use there. It is light, easy to build, doesn't need much infrastructure, great to teach the locals in - and perfect for reaching those little African villages. Wonderful stuff," and then he added, in his 007 secretive tone, "You know that my wife is African, don't you."

He went on, "I know the risk that you are taking. If you come back in ten years with your life and the shirt on your back, you will have succeeded." We both laughed, heartily and with every ounce of British-ness that we could muster. I knew that I would miss Red and all the other personalities that make the British aviation scene so fantastic.

HOTEL AND A MORTUARY

Arriving in Ghana and planning to make it your home, is a massive moment. It was all made easier by the work with an international aid organisation. A hotel room was provided, and very comfortable it was too, at least for the first few weeks.

In order to facilitate moving around, a vehicle would need to be procured, at a suitable price. We settled for a Korean built 4x4 semi-off-road Land Cruiser copy as our car. It was affordable, basic and it worked.

Living in a hotel is no fun after a while. The lack of privacy, or ability to determine one's own schedule, wears on the nerves. All the same, it was a welcome kick start, but not a long term solution by anybody's standards. I would have to start looking for a longer term base, for my own sanity, as much as for my wife's.

I knew that very few places would be suitable for starting an aviation operation in Ghana. It would have to be outside of the International Airport Control Area, with easy access to the city of Accra and Tema sea ports, for administrative and shipping logistics. Furthermore, it should be close to an established highway, with a good road surface. Taking a map, I drew a circle to represent the Kotoka International Airport control area, and then added a parallel circle, a few kilometres out, to represent a 'suitable' zone. As if it were destined to be, the most ideal location of all that were now on offer was the very area where the Paramount Chief, Caramel's grandfather, was living. It was time for a road trip.

The next weekend, my wife and I set out to visit the Chief. He and his wife welcomed us as if we were long lost members of the tribe. The hugs and jubilation took me quite by surprise. Just when I thought it was all over, Grandma came over to me and hugged me with all her worth. If she had squeezed for a few seconds longer, I would have surely passed out.

I sat and explained the reason for being back in Ghana, and the long term vision that was in my confused head. The wise old man shook his head repeatedly, telling me that he did not think it could be done. I sat resolute in my determination, and gave him assurances that I was crazy enough to make it work.

Finally, he agreed to help. He provided contact with a Landlord renting out a bungalow, and also of another Chief with land to rent, that may be suitable. We hugged some more, and then set out to find the man with property to rent.

The directions were simple. Go to the town mortuary, and ask for 'The Landlord'. So we did.

Landlord was a welcoming chap. He had run a very successful business for many years, which suddenly went down the tubes during one of the country's economic hiccoughs. His abandoned factory, and workers housing, were nestled in a neat little compound, just behind the mortuary.

The bungalow was simple, but it would do. So we struck a deal and a few weeks later moved in.

The commute to the city for contract work was a bind, but at least I could scout for land suitable for an aviation project more easily. Getting up early was essential. The early mornings are cooler than the regular daily peak of temperatures above 35C (95F). It was made easier by the herd of cows that moved past the windows of the bungalow, accompanied by a Fulani herdsman, at first light.

Within a month we had found a plot that could be made into a home-workshop-personal airstrip, about ten miles from the mortuary. The idea, in my mind, was to build a plane, fly it, and prove that it could be done, in the hope that it would trigger support post proof of concept phase. My logic seemed sound, to me at least.

Realising that the 4x4 would not do on a construction site, we also procured a small Chinese-built half-tonne pickup. Much as it was basic and tinny, it would make a great work-horse, and it would be needed if this plan were to be realised.

We continued negotiation on the land, and finally agreed a suitable deal with the chief of the family owning those lands. His title was Nene (pronounced 'ney-ney'), the local name for a chief, but it suited him down to a tee. He was well into his seventies, had a fantastic smile and a proliferation of hair growing from his ears. He was almost magical in his appearance and way of talking. I took to him, and he took to me. Life poured out of his every movement and he laughed at every opportunity. It was a pleasure to work with this man and his family.

When sitting in his summer house to finalise the contract, the chickens, ducks and goats gathered around, walking between us, as if to consummate the deal with Mother Nature's approval. Nene explained that he would use part of the proceeds to put his son through University, which I approved of wholeheartedly.

In true West African tradition, a land deal needs a ceremony - on the land. So, the date was set for the slaughtering of a sheep, and pouring of libations. I decided to spice it up a bit, and arranged to arrive riding on a horse, wearing the traditional costume of Kente.

The entourage of Nene were thrilled. They squealed with delight, totally unaware of the precarious position the white man was in, atop his mount. Getting onto a horse in traditional dress is easy, but getting off without losing, what is all but a large sheet of material wrapped around one's body, takes a bit more care.

As they gathered around, I had no choice but to abandon my plan of decorum and simply slid off of the horse, trying to catch whatever parts of the traditional wear I could. It was not a pretty sight, and I was thankful for wearing a sturdy pair of shorts under my Kente cloth. Instead of causing upset, it created a fresh atmosphere of carnival like celebrations. I was the only one embarrassed, and upon realising so, I re-wrapped myself in cloth and placed my perceived humiliation in a mental box, to be revisited at a later point in time.

Nene sat with elders from his family on one set of benches, and I sat on the other with my wife and a local friend. We exchanged the formalities of welcome and trade, and established the reason for our being together. We all knew why we were there, but that is the custom.

Then as the libations were poured to the ancestors, and the sheep ceremoniously slaughtered, the land was assigned to me and my wife. I was now a long-term leaseholder in Ghana. It should be noted that foreigners cannot have freehold of land in Ghana under the constitution.

The sheep was being butchered and each person present given some choice morsel to take home, so that we could all remember what had happened, and that the blood of the sheep had been spilled on that land as a seal on the deal. It was incredibly emotional, and the first step on the road to creating a light aviation operation in Ghana.

THE GUN

The land was very remote, and apart from the risks from potential thieves, there was a considerable risk from snakes. Under the advice of Nene, I investigated purchasing a gun. Unable to find a gun shop, I went to the Police Headquarters in Accra. After being shuttled around several offices, I was led to an office with a tatty 'Firearms' door sign tacked to it.

Entering the room, three police officers raised their heads from tables, covered inches deep in papers. "Can I help you?" enquired the officer in the far corner.

"I would like to purchase a gun," I stated bluntly, never having done so before.

"Can you shoot?" he retorted.

"Yes, I learned in school from an ex-SAS officer," I hoped that my long-ago experience would count.

"Good. You can purchase a shotgun," he offered.

"I am used to firing a .22 rifle, Sir," I counter offered.

"No, you can have a shotgun," he concluded.

"OK, I would like a shotgun," my response raised mumbled sounds of congratulations, on my acceptance of the imposed decision, from the other officers in the room. I just needed a simple solution. Simple is not the way of buying a gun in West Africa.

I was handed a form to complete, it asked for masses of detail, including 'Use of weapon'. I asked "What should I put for use of weapon?"

"Put self-defence and hunting," the officer instructed.

I complied, singed the form and handed it to him.

"That will be $1,000.00," he stated bluntly. I was not in a position to argue.

"That seems a lot?" I proffered, in an attempt at negotiation with the police.

After a pause he looked me straight in the eye and without blinking asked "Do you want the gun or not?"

I paid the money and was presented with a beautiful, new, pump action, pistol-grip shot gun, and one hundred rounds of ammunition. I was actually a little scared, having imagined a double-barrel hunting gun.

"You can conceal this easier, should you need to," he suggested, as he demonstrated the loading and unloading of the gun, adding "remember to let off a couple of rounds every week at night, to let the locals know that you are armed." It was a moment of realisation that there were greater dangers in this adventure than I had contemplated.

That weekend we visited the land and tried out the gun. The Russian ammunition making louder bangs than I had expected. We also looked around the plot we had purchased, and laid out plans for how to set up the project.

BUILDING

The first challenge was to build a home, a workshop and a runway. It was a massive task, and one that involved a lot of paperwork. The approval for the runway was the most difficult, and I knew that it would take over a year. During the process, the house and workshop were to be built.

Being in a rural area, it was more cost effective to produce our own building blocks. The local concept of a 'block' consisted of sand and cement pounded into a mould. First of all, we needed steel or wood to make a mould. The local saw mill was a basic affair. Barefooted men walked on piles of sawdust, built up around sixty-year old machines, all operated in the least health and safety aware manner imaginable. The concept of maintenance was limited, but what did happen was mainly through cannibalisation of other machines. It is not that Personal Protective Equipment (PPE) was ignored as a concept. Such equipment was simply not available or even known about. I met the Sawmill owner, a cheery chap, with bits missing off of two of his fingers, and scars over his feet and legs. Clearly, he had entered into battle with his own equipment on many occasions, and so far managed to win, without too many personal losses. He beamed a smile at me, asking "What canna I get you Massa?"

I did not like the 'Massa' or 'Master' part, but knew that it was a term of respect, hanging over from the colonial days. "You do not need to call me Massa or Master," I explained, adding, "My name is Yaw, and I need some wood for mould making." I used my Ghanaian name, hoping that it would stick.

"OK, Boss Yaw," he replied, adjusting his reference to retain respect for me, and also his culture, "We no do have mould wood here."

I could see suitable wood lying on the floor and pointed to a long rough cut plank. "This will do nicely. How much is it?" I enquired, hopeful of a swift exchange of business.

"Massa Boss, dat is not moulding wood, it is good wood," he retorted, making me realise that I had not expressed my self well. Words can sound the same but mean very different things.

"Chief," I decided to play him at his own game, "I want wood to make a box, to shape blocks for my house."

"Ah, I got," he sighed, walking up a pile of half decimated chunks of tree. Grabbing a long plank from the rear side of the pile he proclaimed, "Dis be good. Dis be Ofram," and he cascaded back down the pile with the plank balanced on one shoulder.

Dropping it in front of me, a small puff of dirt spilled over my shoes, and a strong smell of fresh wood rushed up at my nostrils. It was a pale wood, with dark veins running through it, beautiful in texture, but not planed or presented as I was used to in the builders merchants of Europe. I went to pick it up, discovering that it was much heavier than it looked, probably because it had not been dried, still carrying a lot of sap.

We haggled over price for a few minutes, and loaded it into the pickup. Back at the building site, I had employed a handful of locals, all of whom had their own construction ideas.

The challenge was to establish a working balance between what they knew and used as a benchmark, physics, and my own experiences in building.

Proposals of building with cement tainted mud blocks, using steel to make a mould and making a single wooden mould were offered; each with relative merits. One of the younger workers, Kojo, stood back and looked at the wood, almost lovingly. I approached him and asked, "Kojo, what are you thinking?"

"Boss, we have lots of blocks to make, and you say you are making one mould. It will take long time," he offered, with a better than average command of the English language.

The standard block was about eighteen inches long, eight inches high, and six inches thick. I looked at the plans for the buildings, realising that we would need several thousand blocks. It was a bigger project than I had anticipated. Nonetheless, it was my problem now, and it had to be done.

I sat on a stone with Kojo. The heat of the stone was burning through my trousers, whilst the sun's rays scorched my back. I needed to find a solution. I had a plank of wood, a pile of sand and twenty bags of cement. What I did not have, was a plan to convert that all into the start of building.

"Boss, we can make two blocks at once with double mould," offered Kojo.

That was the moment when the angels started to sing in my head and my mind either had a brilliant idea, or one of total stupidity. "Let's make six blocks in one mould," I suggested.

Kojo looked at me, almost speaking what was in his mind, his eyes whispering to me quietly "It won't work," but his mouth said "I can try."

Over the next hour we built a simple, break-apart, six-block mould and tried it. It worked. Kojo grinned, happy to have achieved the task at hand.

Blocks take about ten minutes of sand and cement mix being pounded into them, then a short break before the mould can be broken away, followed by a full week to set in the sun, before use. I ordered more sand and cement, and started the block factory close to where the house and workshop were to be built. Kojo and the other men worked hard, really hard. Blocks were coming out thick and fast. We needed to produce over one hundred per day, to keep building on schedule.

After a week, there were blocks ready to be laid, and the team split, moving construction forwards impressively.

The men worked so hard, that I had a brilliant idea. I would reward them all with a company bicycle. They walked from the local village over five miles each morning, and back again at night. The dirt track was poorly maintained, and the risk of a snake bite from a puff adder was high.

To make it more exciting, I took the men in the back of the pickup to Tema, in order to choose their own bikes. It was like Christmas, Eid and a Durbar all in one. Each chose a bike, and after I had paid for the fleet, they held each one tightly to their bodies, in the open back of the pick-up, all the way home.

The next morning, it was like a fashion parade for bikes, as each one had been personalised. I felt good. They looked happy.

Less work was done that day, and at the end of the day, they asked collectively for a pay increase. I was taken aback. No, I was offended. I had just spent more than an entire months payroll on obtaining nice bikes for each of them, and now they wanted a pay rise. I declined their proposal.

Over the next few days work slowed. I was confused. I took Kojo to one side and asked him what had happened.

"Boss, you showed us that you have money. You bought us bikes, so now we need more money to work here," he expressed with his calloused hands presented to me, showing his openness.

I did not understand. Calling a good friend who ran a local plantation, I shared the story. He laughed heartily. "I made the same mistake a few years ago. You have not heard the end of it. You must learn that this is not Europe, and the culture is very different. You will only learn by your mistakes," and he hung up, clearly amused at my naivety.

Bewildered, I tried to get the maximum work out of the team, but it was not going well. I was suddenly resented, because I had the money to buy them bikes.

At the end of the month, I called the staff together and issued their pay packs. I added about ten percent in bonuses, hoping to address the issues at hand. I did not expect what came next.

Kofi, a rather large and aggressive worker, with rippling muscles, walked up to me and presented a large number of slips of paper, stating "You must pay these too."

I looked through the papers, all from a small bicycle repair shop in the nearby town. Each had the name of a member of staff and poorly inscribed details of repairs carried out to bicycles.

"I am pleased to see that you are taking good care of your bikes. Maintenance is key," I proclaimed, adding the local language for well-done of

"Ayekoo." It was the only logical statement to make.

The group huddled and spat words at each other in local language, leaving me feeling even more isolated and confused.

Finally, Kojo came forward with an explanation. "Boss, you have cost us these repairs. If you had not purchased us the bicycles, we would not have these bills. Working for you is costing us money."

Flabbergasted, I looked at the group, my mouth fell wide open, and my heart sunk to new lows.

"I am sorry, but I thought I was helping you," I offered. But it was not good enough. Three of the team quit, taking their bicycles with them. I had truly failed to grasp the reality of my new life in the West African bushlands.

The remaining staff met with me the next morning, and we agreed a pay increase, and that I would not repair their bicycles. They also agreed to help find replacement staff for the building that was dragging on, and well behind schedule.

The next morning they all arrived without their bikes, late to work. I was frustrated and shouted a great deal. This was not what I had expected of them. I felt abused. I shouldn't have done, for I had brought this upon myself. A local employer would have paid them less, expected more and not taken care of them, let alone provide bicycles. I was at fault for breaking the status quo.

During the day, Kojo came to me and stated quietly, "You must not mention the bikes again. We have all rented them out now to make money."

There was no thank you, just a statement of fact. I was trying to learn on a curve that climbed almost vertically.

POWER AND WATER

The building plot had no water and no power to it, as is standard for most parts of the developing nations. In order to make blocks, concrete, etc. we had been using river water. Water was fetched in drums in the back of the truck, from the river about three miles away. It was a thankless task, taking several trips per day. It was clear that we needed to get water and power to the site. The time had come to engage with bureaucracy.

The utilities in Ghana are government owned and operated, ostensibly, in the interest of the people. Unfortunately, some of those in their relevant offices may have missed the memo on 'in the interest of the people'.

Wonderful Adversity: Into Africa

Starting with ECG (Electricity Company of Ghana), I asked about running power poles to the site. I knew it was a long shot, and would probably not be cost-effective, over a generator, but asked all the same. The estimated cost came to over fifty thousand US dollars. The chaps were pleasant, and may have inflated the price a little for a foreigner, but all the same, it confirmed that a generator would be on the agenda.

Modern gensets burn as little as two or three litres of diesel per hour, and can be linked to a simple inverter system to store power in batteries, for the 'low hours of consumption', overnight. The total cost would be less than a quarter of the ECG quote, and it made sense. I also considered the option of solar power, purchasing a small panel to try it out. I had doubts about the effectiveness, both electrically and cost wise. Being close to the equator, the day length is roughly equal to the night time, all year around. Add to that the cloud cover, and the three or more months of sand filled air, carried in the Harmattan trade winds each year, and you do not really get that much power yielding sun.

My estimate for a return on investment, after some trials, was more than fifteen years. I also estimated that the panels themselves risked damage or theft, deciding against adding solar to the power mix.

Next, water. The land was less than a mile and a half from a water main, which offered the easiest water solution. I visited the local water office, and completed of a mass of forms. Ten days later, a clean shaven, middle-aged chap came out to survey the site. He arrived in a white Toyota Hilux, wearing a navy polyester suit. Most of the government offices and cars seemed to be air-conditioned to sub-arctic temperatures, which accommodated wearing a suit. Out in the bush, a pair of sturdy jeans and a T-shirt would be more suitable attire. He started to melt inside his suit; beads of sweat suddenly appeared on his face and hands, and started to run wildly down his dark skin.

"Good morning," I greeted the chap, "you are welcome." It was standard practice to ensure that a visitor knew that they were welcome, even if they clearly looked uncomfortable. "Thank you for coming to visit us today," I really was thankful for the thought of water coming to the desert. "We would like to run water from the main line over there," with a wave of my hand, "past our land, and also to the next community."

About a mile further down the track a small group of people lived in mud huts, fetching their drinking water from the river. The children were often sick with diarrhoea, one of the most common causes of infant death in the area. To my mind, it made sense to pay for the line to come past our land, and on to their village, as a social component of our living in the bush. My visitor did not agree.

"If you pay for the pipe to the village, who will pay their water bill?" he semi-sneered at me. I had not considered that.

"I am sure that the people will. It would be better for their children," I countered.

Shaking his head, my visitor looked me in the eye, proposing "You will need to pay for the pipe, the connection and something for me to prepare the quotation."

"Something for you... to prepare the quotation?" I was confused.

"Yes, if I process the papers for this work, then I am doing you a favour, and you need to recognise my value," his bribe request being laid out blatantly in front of me.

Raising my voice, in anger and shock combined I exclaimed "YOU have to be joking? I want to run water to my land AND to your people, and you want a BRIBE?" My volume was loud enough to bring Kojo and Kofi running. They took up positions on each side of me.

The visitor looked at Kojo, "Tell your Obruni boss, that I do not care for the people living in those huts along the track. If *Obruni* does, then *Obruni* will pay me one thousand Cedis to process his request," his demand being more than his month's salary.

Playing his game, I also spoke to Kojo, "Tell this man that I will not pay a single pesewa of bribe for the provision of water, not for me and not for any other person. *He* must take responsibility for *his* job," my indignation clearly displayed.

Clearly, there was no need for Kojo to say a word, as we could all hear each other perfectly well. The water man turned and headed to his car. I called after him my instant bluff, "I will send Kojo for the quote in two weeks. If it is not ready, then I will simply drill a borehole."

I turned smugly, believing that this man would simply go ahead and prepare the quote anyway. He had to be bluffing about not caring about water to the people and their families along the track.

Two weeks later I sent Kojo to see the water man. He returned empty handed. "The man says you are difficult. You have to pay him to prepare a quote. He wants two thousand Cedis now," Kojo was clearly upset by his visit, but continued, "and you must be responsible for any bills for the other people on the line."

I fumed. I really fumed. My heart beat faster. My fist clenched. I swore... a lot. Then, I asked Kojo and Kofi what they would do.

"Boss, We just try not to deal with these big men. They always want something. Even if you get the water laid on, they will switch it off and ask for money to switch it back on again," Kofi explained and lamented at the same time.

Speechless, I ran the scenario in my head.
1. Pay, or rather bribe, the man to do the quote.
2. Get the quote, after a long delay and possible additional payments.
3. Pay the quote.
4. The workers would arrive to carry out the work, but may want some 'incentive' above the agreed price.

5. Water would go on, hopefully.
6. Water would be switched off, as soon as the workers or the bosses needed more cash.
7. If water went to the families down the track, I would probably be liable for their water bills.
8. The locals may leave the taps running wildly, or use the water for their crops too, which I would have to pay for.

Bottom line, this was not a viable option. My bluff may be my only solution.

Contacting a borehole company, run by Germans, I was given a quote, a date to commence work and passed an agreement, in the space of ten minutes. It was a good bluff, and one that should pay off.

They arrived on time and bored a hundred foot deep hole. The sweetest water ever came out, and nobody asked for a bribe. Sadly, the volume of water available was only enough for the site, not enough to provide to the needs of the community along the track. My conscience was clear, but I hoped that the water man's conscience bothered him. It was a wasted hope, but I spent it anyway.

A septic tank was dug. Now, with water and a septic tank, we finally could imagine a flushing toilet to replace the long-drop latrine we had all been using. Progress was being made.

NEVER ENDING BUILDING

The building crew were making progress, albeit slowly, and I hoped that if I could show them my gratitude, they might pick up the pace a bit. Unfortunately, I seemed unable to find a way to demonstrate my thanks to the staff for working. Provision of free meals was met with a refusal to eat by some, since the food may be poisoned. So, we scrapped the meals. This led to a claim for the money for the value of the free meals.

I gave in. It was easier. I stopped trying to show them my gratitude, and got a bit more work out of them.

A study, carried out by an American university team, found similar issues in the cities. One particular case, that of a Chinese employer who gave certain members of staff a pay increase, reflecting their increased transport costs, after a transport fare hike. The next day he was asked by a member of staff for a similar pay increase, due to the increase in transport fares in the country. Since the employee was given free accommodation, within walking distance of the company, the employer refused. This led to the young man arriving late to work each day. When questioned, the young man explained that he had to walk to work, and did not have the transport money. Regardless of whether he used transport or not, his perception of what his employer should do was different to the thinking of his foreign boss, who had simply hoped to help those living further away with their increased costs.

It was apparent that foreign employers tended to try to help their staff, without understanding the culture. Local employers treated all staff the same, often not as well as the newbie managers.

I had to harden up fast, or I would run out of funds to complete the never-ending building.

The roof trusses were made by a local carpenter. As soon as they went up, I could see that they were wrong. He insisted that they were right. The roof leaked, and so, to his complete disgust, I insisted that he take it all down and do it again. Fortunately, I had not paid him all of his monies. He asked for even more money, and I refused. It was as simple as that. Take a hard line, as one of his countrymen would have done. I then showed him how to calculate the angle for each piece of wood, and how to set the trusses using templates. He stood back, half-watching, barely listening.

Kojo whispered in my ear "He does not care for your method. Just do it, do not explain."

I did not listen, and carried on explaining, my words falling on deaf and uninterested ears. The carpenter completed the job, more or less, took his pay and left. I had been teaching, but he had not been prepared to learn. My frustrations grew, but at least the building was progressing.

Kojo and a couple of others were willing to learn, but most just wanted money. I joked that they all wanted a salary, but not a job. The truth was hidden in there somewhere.

I continued doing occasional contract work in the city for the international aid agencies, and raised these concerns with the management of a well-known organisation. The lady, with a Masters in some obscure social field, explained it to me. "You see, the West gives money for projects. The people see that they get money for projects, and whether they do a good job or not, sometimes not even completing the project, they are paid."

The look on my face must have shown confusion, so she continued, "Do you not understand? If aid money really worked, we would not need it any more. What happens is, when we give money, we create dependency. So, when you give more to your employees, they want even more from you." She looked at her watch and excused herself.

I refused to accept it, deciding to try one more incentive to create opportunities on the building site. I called a meeting and told the crew what I had been told by the educated lady in the city. They all agreed with her. Exasperated, I tried to get them to understand the need to seek personal satisfaction in doing the job, doing it well, on time and for an agreed sum. They laughed. I decided to outline my master plan for building site domination.

"OK, chaps, I have a proposition to make to you," I was about to lay out what I saw as a stroke of genius. "We do not have much work to complete this house and workshop, but if we can complete it within three weeks, I will create a building company, with you all as shareholders in the company."

It was a bold offer. After the laughter calmed down, Kofi, muscles rippling came forwards and asked, "Will it be MY business?"

"No, it would be OUR business, we would share the work and the profits. I can help set up work, and all the official papers. You can do the work and together everybody will benefit," I explained, hoping that my words would appease the strongman in front of me. They agreed to think about it.

The next morning I was all set for a determined crew, ready to break the land speed record of building. I was to be disappointed. They arrived late and worked slower than I had ever seen before. I walked out into the bushlands and cried.

I was trying so hard to help these people, but they did not want help. Whatever I proposed, they deposed, and it was getting me down. My wife was getting frustrated at the house never being ready, and living behind a mortuary. It was not what we had expected. Fate was about to take a hand in it all.

That night there was a local uprising against our Landlord. Swarms of people gathered outside the gates, and gunshots echoed sporadically as the crowd called for blood. It appeared that there was a chieftaincy dispute, and the Landlord was in the middle of it.

We did not sleep on the bed that night, but rather on the floor, hoping to be out of the line of fire for any stray bullets that may happen towards our bungalow.

I slept, or at least tried to, with my hand on the pump-action shotgun, loaded with a full eight rounds. Just before dawn I heard two shots, coming from entrance gate area. Minutes later, two more shots rang out, closer to our bungalow, then one more, very loud shot close to our bungalow. Scurrying to the front window, gun in hand, I peered through a slim gap in the dusty curtains. There, walking towards our home, was a man wearing shorts and red T-shirt, holding a shotgun, aiming it at a point to the side of the building, Rambo style.

I did not recognise the man approaching, but he looked menacing. I drew an imaginary line in the sand, about ten metres from where I squatted. If he were to cross that line, I planned to fire the gun. He approached the line, without crossing it, raising his gun. The first ray of the morning sun kissed the barrel as he pointed it above his head.

I slid down a bit, trying not to be seen. Two loud bangs were emitted in close succession. I shuddered. He had fired shots over the roof of our refuge. My wife entered the room at that same moment, throwing herself on the floor, shaking. Raising the barrel of my gun to eye-level and using the muzzle to nudge the curtain aside, I took aim at the red T-shirt, trying to forget that a man was inside it. He was two metres from my 'trigger line'. I slid off the safety catch and lay my trigger finger alongside the guard.

In my rifle training, it was emphasised to never aim a gun at a person. This was the first time that necessity dictated that I should break that rule. I heard my ex-SAS teacher in my head, calming me down, readying me for what might happen in the coming minutes.

Preparing to take a shot at a human being, albeit in self-defence, released a whole new set of feelings. Bad feelings. What had I gotten myself into? What worse situation could I get into if I pulled that trigger? What if I did? What could happen if I didn't? A plethora of possibilities swirled around inside my mind, leaving me giddy, scared and breathless.

My heart was beating faster, my breathing rapid but shallow. I would have to hold my breath to steady the gun, if and when that dreaded moment came. A bead of sweat dropped into my sighting eye. I dropped my head to wipe it away on my shoulder.

A deep voice called from the gate side of the compound. The red T-shirt turned and walked away from the house, towards the compound entrance. I slid down, my back to the wall beneath the window and re-engaged safety. My wife, understandably, cried.

MOVING TO THE BUSH

I was not feeling great about the situation my decision making had brought us to. A short discussion with my wife, led to the decision to move into the unfinished house. She started packing. I went to see Landlord.

It turned out that the man with a gun was a 'hired security man' whom Landlord had taken on less than an hour ago, to keep the masses at the gate in check. He had been instructed to walk around the compound and let off a few shots. I asked why we had not been informed before he shot over our bungalow. Landlord failed to see any need for such action.

I could still hear a large, angry-sounding crowd at the gate, and prepared myself for the rapid relocation to an unfinished property in the bush.

Different dangers would exist in the bush, but at least they would be under my control. The lack of self-determination, living in a compound where

Landlord could order an armed man to wander around, letting off shots, without alerting me, was too much for my personal risk management acceptance levels.

We loaded both vehicles with all that we could, the pick-up loaded high and a bit excessively, and headed towards the compound gate. My wife went first, in the hope that a white woman could appease the crowd. I sat behind in the truck, with the loaded pistol grip pump-action gun slid under my seat, ready to let off warning shots and to keep an eye on her progress. It was the safest way to exit the gate, and avoided the possibility of her getting cut-off behind me by the crowd, or even the gate men.

The gate opened enough for her car to nuzzle out, surrounded by the aggravated crowd. They erupted in rage. Then, as we had hoped, the sight of a white woman, smiling and waving, led to the parting of the masses. I followed close behind, practically welded to the car in front, ensuring that no human being could fit between the vehicles at any time. I was subject to some name calling, but still managed to keep moving, pretending that I had no idea what they were so irate over.

We arrived on the building site to the building crew sitting eating breakfast, as usual. I did not understand the concept of these men walking five miles from home, to sit and eat breakfast during paid time, at the workplace. I had tried to challenge it, but had come to accept it as a cultural practice that I could not change. The number of working practices that appeared impossible to change were too many. They were getting me down.

Kojo and Kofi, wiping hands on their T-shirts to get rid of food debris, came over to the loaded vehicles and asked what had happened. They had heard about the uprising, and the death threats to Landlord. They seemed unfazed by it all.

I called the group together. "Tomorrow will be three weeks since I proposed a reward of setting up a company if you could complete the work in three weeks," I sighed long and loud, "but you have not completed the work. Therefore, I will not create a company for you."

My words seemed to have no effect on them as a group, for they had never wanted to be a part of a company. I entered preacher mode. "You have so much potential. Each of you can do amazing work when you want to. Each of you can achieve great things. Each of you has let yourself down. Each of you could do more, make more and be more. If only... you... wanted... to..." my voice trailed at the end, as I realised the reality of my last sentence.

The phrase 'You can take a horse to water, but you cannot make it drink' came to mind. I also remembered being told in school 'Give a man a fish, feed him for a day. Teach a man to fish, feed him for a lifetime.'

I decided to return to my bush pulpit. "We have come a long way, but you do not seem to want any more than you have already. Those who no longer want to work on the house, please raise your hands, I will pay you up to today and you can leave."

To my utter astonishment, all but Kojo and Kofi raised their hands. I paid them and they left. My wife was distraught. I was angry.

"Kofi and Kojo, come with me, and help unload the truck. We will fix up one room to be safe enough to sleep in for the night," I snapped. It was a bold, perhaps stupid concept, but a necessity.

That night we slept inside the room, without plaster on the walls, without a ceiling, under a mosquito net, with louvre blades wide open for air flow. We slept well, serenaded to sleep by the sounds of the bush, woken by the dawn chorus. It was basic, but it was home, and there were no hoards seeking blood or retribution.

PLANE TROUBLE

Although the house and workshop were not completed, it was time to make the next step in the whole crazy plan that was well afoot. I ordered an aircraft kit from France, not the planned Zenith CH701, but a tube and cloth X-Air Falcon. Tube and cloth planes can be built really quickly, and it offered a low-cost, low-risk option. After all, this was a proof of concept package. For the engine I chose a relatively unknown Australian brand, which was also a lot cheaper than my preferred Rotax engine.

I revisited my friend in the Ghana Civil Aviation Authority (GCAA). He was pleased to see me, but also informed me that he was retiring. His replacement was not so keen on aviation for the people, but he promised to help me in the quest that was now underway.

I needed to complete some forms for approval to build an aircraft, and for the bush strip that we would operate out of. It seemed simple enough.

Taking the papers back to the never-ending-construction site, I sat filling them out. With the genset now working, there was power in the house, even if the plastering was dragging on. It smelt damp, which attracted more and more mosquitoes, which feasted on my blood at every opportunity.

I returned the necessary papers to the GCAA, paying the relevant fees. There was no request for a bribe, and everybody was very helpful.

The aircraft kit arrived, and eventually got through customs, with a lot of paperwork and a substantial payment of duties and taxes, some of which seemed excessive and unjustifiable.

Back in the bush, the aircraft started to come together – much quicker than the house, at any rate. Within a couple of weeks it looked like a plane, which is the biggest advantage of the tubular-frame construction method.

Just as I felt that success was on the horizon, I fell ill. My temperature soared, and sweat ran in rivers from my body. I shivered, and melted on the bed. The pain in my back, between my shoulder blades told me that it was malaria.

Malaria treatments are readily available from any chemist in most parts of Africa, without a prescription. For the next three days I took a full course of Artemether and Lumefantrine combination therapy. They tasted disgusting, but quickly killed the parasites in my blood. Much as I recovered from the Malaria, I was left weakened. I felt the need to chat to my son.

There was only one spot near the house where a mobile phone signal could be captured reliably. It involved climbing on some rocks and leaning precariously off the edge. From that vantage point, I called Matt to update him on the progress being made, omitting my recovery from malaria.

"Dad, it is not right. It is simply not right," he complained, "You are the old man, and I am a young man. You have more adventures than me. It's just not right."

I laughed and replied, "You chose not to come out to be a part of the adventure, but you are still welcome."

We chatted for bit, and then a scorpion ran over my shoe. Laughing, I updated Matt on the transit of the large black monster over my footwear.

"That does it," he stomped the words down the phone, "I am coming out to help you."

A few weeks later we drove to the city to collect him from the airport. It was hot and sticky, as always, and the wait seemed interminable. You never know what to expect in a developing nation at the airport, and this day was to be no exception. Watching many passengers from his flight leave the arrivals hall, and with time ticking methodically by, I started to get concerned. Then, I saw Matt, without his bags, walking towards us.

"They don't believe your address," he stated, "the immigration officers do not believe your address."

It was not unusual for immigration and customs officers to find creative ways to hinder the passage of foreigners, in the hope of some 'facilitation funds', and this was no different. On the arrivals form, visitors are required to write the address where they will be staying. Clearly, writing that you would be staying on a farm, in a rural part of Ghana, whilst also being white, was a bit of a stretch for the man in charge.

"Welcome son," I greeted him, and walked with him back to the immigration station. My story was only believed because I was clearly more confident and better prepared to the coercion ideals of the day. The truth is not always easy to grasp, especially when it involves westerners willingly living in the bushlands.

Matt walked out with me, his bags in his hands, and greeted his mum. It was a great moment. The feeling of being a family, and having support, in both directions, was invigorating.

The next morning, once Matt had recovered from his trip, he joined Kojo and Kofi on the construction tasks for the house. They loved it. He loved it. Much was achieved, and I smiled.

Over the weekend, Matt helped me to prepare the plane for a test run down the runway. The plane was all but ready, and a few runs up and down with the aircraft, on the makeshift bush strip, would boost our moral.

Matt cut out the registration marks for the aircraft, and carefully stuck them in place. Her registration was 9G-ZAA, the 9G related to the Ghana register of aircraft, the Z to the fact that the aircraft had been built in Ghana and the AA just the first aircraft registered under the new register. Using the phonetic alphabet, the aircraft was christened Alpha-Alpha, after her last two letters of the registration. She looked resplendent, seducing us with her desire to fly. We could hold ourselves back no longer.

Excitedly, we pushed the plane onto the strip and fuelled it up. I was running around with a handful of tools and Matt was being a great son, looking for things for me to use some tools on.

"What about this bit?" he shouted, and I went to his indicated location to take a look. Between us we checked every nut and bolt about twenty times, giggling and laughing in the same way as when I had helped him build Lego kits years ago.

Eventually, it was time to put procrastination in my back pocket and to try out the machine. I put on my 'bone dome', and climbed into the plane. It had been nearly two years since I had flown, but the stick and throttle fell to my hands, as if I had been born with them there. As my feet slid onto the rudder pedals I did not feel as if I was sitting in the aircraft, but rather wearing it.

Matt and his mum stood watching as I yelled "Clear prop," and pressed the start button on the panel in front of me. Nothing happened.

Another round or two of troubleshooting, and we were ready to try again. This time, my battle cry of "Clear prop" was fired into the air with the added propulsion of a spinning prop and roaring engine. It worked.

Those who have never built an aircraft will never know the feeling that goes with creating a flying machine, and hearing the engine run for the first time. It is a magnificent feeling that courses through veins of the creator like pure adrenalin. At the very moment the engine caught, and the 'suck, squeeze, bang, blow' cycle of the pistons in their cylinders got underway with a roar, it was as if I had been granted a second heart. I felt the engine pounding, as if it were in my chest. It felt good. It brought me more revitalisation than any health spa could ever achieve.

Trying the throttle movements, the plane responded, yearning to move. I decided to let her move under her own steam. Gently at first, we held each other closely as we taxied at walking pace up and down the strip. As we got

Wonderful Adversity: Into Africa

to know each other better, we picked up the pace. On one of the runs, her nose wheel picked up off of the surface, tempting me to push her into the air. I resisted.

We carried out a few more runs up and down, before I reluctantly flicked off the ignition switches and let the engine stop. It was sad. I had wanted to do more, and so did she, but we could not without taking the necessary precautions.

Safety is everything in aviation, and so another round of checks, especially around the engine, was clearly necessary before going to the next stage in our relationship.

There were no oil leaks, and the warm engine felt good under my hand. Another check of the fuel systems and it was time to try her again.

This time there was no holding her back. As I applied power she reared up, her nose wheel far from the surface. If I hesitated now, I would be at risk of running out of runway. I opened up the throttle, all the way. Her main gear left the surface, and we were airborne.

She climbed into the sky, and I went gladly with her. It was as emotional and sensuous as any moment in my life. I needed to drag myself away from the pleasure and focus on the business of the moment. This was a test flight, and I had to make sure that she was flying as expected. We found some stable air at around one thousand five hundred feet above the ground, and five hundred feet below the cloud base. Here we could meander left and right, at varying degrees of bank, feeling for any signs of bad behaviour in her airframe. As we entered a sixty degree turn, there was a loud cracking noise from the wing above me. Startled, I looked up and along the under-wing surfaces. Minor wrinkles in the cloth, that had been present on the ground, had suddenly disappeared, as the cloths seated into an even better position. I smiled, knowing that she had spoken to me, expressing her satisfaction and pleasure in flight.

As I completed the in-flight test programme, I grinned, smiled, laughed and chuckled all at once, a sort of 'grismilauchuck', if such a thing exists. But only for moment, for now I would have to land this creation, back on the narrow and rather short strip, near the house.

Lining up, I realised that the strip really was short. I came in too fast, and there was no way I would be able land. Without blinking, for my eyes were wider-open than ever, I added full power and we went around. Four more attempts, and I wondered if I would be able to land this machine before running out of fuel.

I broke out from the circuit, climbed back to fifteen hundred feet, and practised landing on an imaginary runway in the sky. It was much easier; no trees, no rocks, no strip, and the landing was simply a thousand feet off the ground. It gave me the confidence and feeling for this wild bird, and how to get her back onto the ground.

Setting up on a long, long approach, I coaxed her gently towards the surface, slowing her down to 'stall speed plus a third', allowing her undercarriage to skim the tops of the long grasses before the threshold of the strip. Without her realising, I had reduced the engine to idle, and her wheels kissed the ground sweetly. At that moment, unsure of her intentions, I switched off the engine and pressed firmly on her brakes.

Together, we slid to stop at the end of the strip. Exhausted, happy and enthralled at the success, albeit only just, of the flight.

Before I could exit the plane, Matt was there, ready to help me disembark. That evening we celebrated the realisation of the start of a dream.

The next afternoon, Matt and I decided to carry out another test flight. It was much warmer than the previous day, well into the high thirties in Celsius (over one hundred in Fahrenheit) but I felt confident all the same. Matt set up a camera to take photos, and we were very buoyant about the next phase of testing, which would hopefully involve some easier landings.

Once again, I added full power, and the plane leapt into the air, but not for long. The engine sputtered and started to lose power fast. I looked down at Matt, watching me with a wide smile; his eyes shaded with his hand to getter a better view.

Sometimes, when things go wrong in flight, time slows massively. Everything happens as if on a different plane, and you feel as if you are watching yourself from outside the cockpit, at least that is how it felt that day.

I watched myself pushing the throttle further forwards, bending the stop. I watched Matt's face turn from happy to grim. I listened to the engine cough, and watched the prop slowdown. I witnessed the loss of airspeed, failure to maintain climb rate and feared the impending stall, all at just fifty feet above the surface. I watched the end of the strip disappear beneath plane, noting that the aircraft too low for a turn around. I saw the trees reach up their leaf covered fingers, trying to grab hold of the undercarriage of their prey.

Back in the cockpit a phenomenon occurred. I heard the voice of my instructor, from years ago, yelling at me "PUSH. Push the nose over."

Reflexes from my training kicked in and I sought to maintain enough airspeed to control the machine. Looking ahead, I could only see a small clearing in the trees, and that was my only option.

There was no time left to make assumptions or calculations. I had to just do three things.
1. Fly the plane.
2. Fly the plane.
3. Fly the plane.

And so I did.

At first it was surreal. Without any engine sound coming out of the power-plant, I was free to hear the leaves scratching at the undercarriage, followed by twigs breaking as they lost the fight with my wing-tips. An instant later there was a louder noise, as the undercarriage engaged with the rough undergrowth in the thicket. The roll-out was short, and shortened more by the aircraft becoming wedged between two trees, at the exact wingspan of the little lady.

I reached behind my seat and turned off the fuel, before evacuating the cockpit. I could not feel my heart pounding in my chest, and so quickly took my pulse to check if I was still alive. It was a pleasant surprise to find that little 'bumpity bump' on my wrist. Looking around, I tried to imagine how we would get the airframe out of its new nest. The aircraft looked at me forlorn.

"Dad. Dad. Where are you?" Matt's voice was coming towards me, calling frantically.

"Over here," I called, my voice sounding a little shaky.

I could hear his foot-falls on the twigs and the sound of the long grasses brushing against his jeans. His eyes finally found their way into a line of sight with mine. We both smiled.

He ran up to me and hugged me. My eyes sprang a small hydraulic leak, and I stated to shake. The shock was finally setting in.

"Don't worry Dad. We can fix it," came the reassuring words of my young man.

NIGHTMARES

After any accident, it is normal to have nightmares, and to doubt one's self. Each night I relived that flight, or rather lack of it. The aircraft had been partially disassembled and returned to the workshop for inspection. Although there was no major damage, it was a blow to my confidence, and something which left me wondering about my life choices.

However, every time I started to think about throwing in the towel, the words of my son boomed in my ears "Don't worry Dad. We can fix it."

If he had the belief that we could fix a plane, after a rather unfortunate incident, then I had to have faith that I too could fix the challenges of completing the house, and to getting a working light aviation industry underway in Ghana.

It did not stop the nightmares, but it did give me the strength to overcome them, and to imagine better days.

A few weeks later, the plane was back together again, and ready for flight. I had looked over all the systems, and found nothing amiss. The only thought I had was the temperature on the day of the incident. I believed that the engine had suffered from vapour lock in the fuel system. It was clear that the aircraft didn't like the higher temperatures of that second almost-flight.

Consequently, the next test was done in the early hours of the morning, before the temperature rose above the thirty Celsius mark (mid-nineties Fahrenheit). Despite some minor worries, it all went well, and an operational limit was mentally set in place for the engine operations.

Much as this flight stopped me having nightmares about the engine, the nightmare of bureaucracy was only just about to begin.

With my proof of test flight and other documents all in hand, I set off to the Ghana CAA (Civil Aviation Authority) building, ready to seek the necessary approvals to operate.

"Hmmmn hmmmmn," the new GCAA director hummed like a slightly out of balance motor, "you will have to send the aircraft out of the country to be tested now." The words were said without his eyes leaving their gaze onto the surface of his paper strewn desk.

"What?" I yelled. I could not help it. It had been one full year since the project had begun, and all papers submitted, invitations made, happy smiles given and explanations offered. I had done everything they had asked.

"We do not have the expertise in Ghana to look at your aircraft. So, send it back to France. Have them check it. If they say it is OK, you can then re-import it," his logic was beyond comprehension.

"There has to be another way?" I asked, stated and pleaded all at once.

"You can write to the Director General, but he will only ask me for my opinion," he responded dryly, lifting his eyes, but not his head, to look at me from under his bushy eyebrows.

I left, annoyed, angry and disappointed. Matt was waiting in the car. As I briefed him on the meeting, his excited calmish waters of anticipation turned to high powered angry storm, blowing off in all directions. I drove away, as we both let off varying degrees of exasperation, in colourful language, that Mr F would have been proud of.

The next day I started a campaign called WAASP, the West African Aviation Solution Proposal. Literally leaving the idea of sending the aircraft out of the country, or even flying, I decided to create a presentation programme, to educate ministers of state, technocrats and GCAA staff about the importance of light aviation.

It focused on the concept of affordable aviation, and skills enhancement. I started with the Director General, who demonstrated total disinterest, probably influenced by my latest nemesis. Undeterred, I took the proposal to the Minister of Trade and Industry, Minister of Tourism, Minister of Transport and Minister of anything I could think of that might help fight cause.

One day, I took the proposal to seat of Government, known as the Castle. I drove to the old slave fort in Osu, and walked to the main reception. There, I was met by some faces I recognised, and who knew me, from years ago. These old acquaintances made me most welcome. Even though they were reception and security staff, I gave my shortened speech about the WAASP concept. They were enthralled and full of enthusiasm.

"Let me put you through to the secretary for the Big Man," came the offer from the young lady at the desk. I was thrilled; perhaps this would be the breakthrough I needed.

She handed the phone to me. After the usual introduction pleasantries, I went into sales mode. "I have come here to explain how we can build aircraft in Ghana, perhaps setting up a small flying school with aircraft built in Ghana, by Ghanaians..." I was in full flow, but she cut me off.

"If we want things like that in Ghana, we will do them ourselves. This Government knows how to do these things. We do not need you," venom clearly detectable in her tone. It was blunt, cold and harsh killer to my passion. I heard the click of her handset going down before I could even respond.

My friends around me were shocked, but could do nothing to support me other than offer the cultural "Sorry-oo." I left, feeling battered and beaten.

I was injured by the comments, and knew that the Government had no intentions nor desire to enter into the concepts that I was touting. So, I did not give up.

Over two hundred letters, and with more than fifty presentations to various officials and dignitaries, and lots of annoyance, later; I felt that I was getting nowhere.

I pondered the differences between patience and perseverance, and found that I was demonstrating both. I began to doubt if my mind was even in the right place.

A few days later I received a call to go to the 'Castle Annex', or 'Blue Gate' as it was known locally, to make a presentation. I had written to them a long time ago, but had given up on ever getting a response.

Behind the Blue Gate, lay the offices of the Head of National Security, and the plethora of Bureau of National Investigation officers. It was rumoured that folks got invited to go there, and were never seen again.

Having come so far, it would have been remiss to not take up this invitation to enter the heart of the security services, delivering my vision for a light aviation industry in Ghana.

The night before the meeting I lay awake in bed. My head was swimming with ideas and worries. In the early hours of the morning my eyelids gave up the fight with my swirling mind. Sleep grabbed me by surprise.

Normally, I do not remember dreams, but that night was to be very different. I dreamt vivid dreams, and they did not enjoy encouraging or pleasant outcomes. Nightmares are scarier, but they were certainly amongst the 'bad dream' class of nocturnal vision. I relived my many near misses in aircraft, and imagined worse outcomes than the reality had shown. To top it all, I experienced a long and detailed sleep experience, feeling very much as if it were real.

I dreamt that I had to take off, in a small plane, from a street in a city. Once airborne I could not gain altitude due to the many telephone and electric wires that crossed the street. The colours of many shops whizzed past me, but I could not look into their windows for fear of crashing. Cars disappeared under my plane, as I hoped that my undercarriage would not touch their speeding metal frames. My eyes hunted for a gap in the cobweb of plastic coated copper wire traps above my plane. I saw no hope of ever climbing to a safe altitude. Trucks zoomed towards me, and I had to slide my craft between them in knife edge manoeuvres. I breathed in to help reduce the size of my flying machine, without effect.

As I flew out of the city the trees took over, and the avenues left no option for my plane to get above their thick, leafy canopy. No matter how I tried, I was stuck having to fly wherever the road led, and would not be able to climb above the restrictions of the city- and country-scapes around me. The dream seemed to last forever, longer than any fuel tank could have afforded in flight.

Finally, I saw the sun blasting directly at me, straight ahead, blinding me, creating rainbows and diamond-like stars on the windshield. I could not see where I was flying, for it was far too bright.

I awoke to the sunshine beating on my face through the windows. Looking at the clock, I realised, much like the white rabbit, that I was late, very late, for a very important date. There was no time to say hello or goodbye, just to throw on clothes and drive to the city, rather fast.

BLUE GATE

Amazingly, I made it to the city, and parked outside the blue gate entrance to the Castle Annexe, with two minutes to spare. I was scared, excited, worried and hopeful. If this meeting went well, it could mean permissions to operate and do more with aviation.

Much as I was on time, the processing prior to admission to the inner sanctum of the security services was detailed, and time consuming. Forms to

Wonderful Adversity: Into Africa

fill, body searches, and then a long walk across the courtyard and up concrete flights of steps, before finally reaching the waiting room for the Director of National Security.

The room smelt musty. A television chatted away to itself in the corner. A pleasant secretary waved at a plush suite of heavily padded furniture, indicating that I should sit. So I did.

The wall had a photograph of the President, hanging slightly crooked. I felt his eyes piercing my soul. I wondered if he knew that I was there. I wondered about straightening his picture, but decided against such action, for fear of upsetting anybody, especially the President.

The time for my meeting passed without any indication that my presence had been noted. I prompted the secretary about whether I was at the right place for my rendezvous. She reassured me, telling me "Wait. You must patient yourself." It was more like an order.

A feature length film was starting on the television. It was some comedy about cowboys and time travel. I started to watch. The plot was good, and the jokes fell through the dialogue frequently enough to keep my mind off of waiting.

Just as the credits started to roll at the end of the film, the secretary called me over. "He will see you soon. He has just arrived," she smiled, as she spoke, giving me some glimmer of hope.

I was not overly surprised at the tardiness of the Director. After all, I had waited six hours past the appointment time at one official meeting.

Soon, I was called into his office. The Director of NatSec was a tall man, thin and bespectacled. He commanded respect with every inch of his being. The office was large, but poorly lit. We sat at a dark wooden table.

"Thank you for seeing me..." I started to speak, but it was not my turn.

"So, you are the one who is talking about helicopters and flying in my country?" NatSec voice was quiet, but his words spoke volumes, vibrating to the depth of my being.

"Yes..." I wanted to say more, but it was still not my turn to respond.

"You have made presentations to ministers, the GCAA and even tried to speak to the Office of the President. You want to jeopardise the security of my nation with machines that can be used to carry weapons and threaten our people," he summarised my activities as if they were accusations.

He was clearly aware of who I was, and my recent activities of information, but he had also taken hold of the wrong end of the stick.

"Well..." I tried explain, but without success.

"President Rawlings had a flying club, and we shut that down with the change of government. Now, you come along and want to start again..." he continued to try intimidation tactics, building a wall of fear in my mind.

I was not going to be subdued any longer and forcefully spoke through my personal wall of fear.

"Sir, I understand you concerns," I launched, and as he tried to cut me off, I raised my volume, "BUT I have no political affiliations. I am not a terrorist. I love this country. I want to make things better. I believe that light aviation has a place in building up the young people, opening opportunities, creating jobs and reaching the remote parts of the country with medical care and education." I ran out of breath to continue, and before I could inhale enough to recommence, NatSec seized the opportunity.

"SO, if I grant you permission to fly, build aircraft, and other things what guarantee do I have that you will not let enemies of the state access these flying machines?" he questioned. It was clearly a big question, so he paused for moment, allowing me to answer.

"Mobile phones," I started, wondering why, and seeking some link to the statement to solve the question asked. "Mobile phones can be used to communicate, to save lives, to buy goods and services, to help doctors and more. They can also be used to co-ordinate criminal activities," I felt it was going well and then spoilt the run with the closer of "and trigger bombs."

"What size bomb can your plane carry? What if you flew into the side of one of our buildings?" the interrogation flowed seamlessly as he leant across the table, allowing his gaze to jeopardise my ability to control my bladder.

Seizing control back, of my bladder and the situation, I offered "There is no point in carrying a bomb in a small plane. You do not have the inertia. If you tried to, you would simply blast yourself away from the surface. It is not like nine-eleven and the twin towers, those were airliners. No, this is about SMALL planes doing good, helping people, your people, to a better life." I stopped, wondering if I would be arrested.

Standing and walking around the room, seemingly aimlessly, NatSec charged the atmosphere in the room. I decide not to speak again, unless asked a question.

"So, let me ask you a question," he started, clearly understanding my position. "What would you do if ex-President Rawlings came to you to use one of your aircraft?"

It was a trick question, for I knew that this NatSec had some personal, negative feelings for the ex-President. I chose to answer with caution.

"Sir, knowing your personal feelings about the ex-President, I would tell him that it would not be in the interest of aviation and development in Ghana for him to fly at this time," I breathed deeply, hoping that I had given an acceptable response.

NatSec stopped, looked me in the eye and nodded, a smile creeping into the corners of his eyes, but excluding his mouth from any sign of softness.

I continued, "However, it only seems fair to me that, if you do not want me to fly the ex-President, then I will not fly the current one either... until both are allowed to fly." It was a bold statement, but one that I would live or die by.

NatSec stood motionless, whilst I held my breath. I felt him listening to my deepest whirring thoughts about never leaving Blue Gate again.

"You really are sincere, aren't you?" he stated, sitting down again. "Come back tomorrow. I will have a letter of approval for your flying operations. One copy for you, and one for the GCAA."

We shook hands and I left the premises, relieved, but desperately needing to find a toilet. Throughout the meeting my stomach had been turning, and now it was ready to initiate an evacuation.

Driving to the nearest hotel, I rushed into the toilet, off of the foyer. There the world dropped out of my bottom, relieved, scared and exhilarated. It must have been the anxiety and excess of adrenaline which finally caught up with me.

I shook, smiling and tears forming in my eyes. I never imagined the go ahead for light aviation taking so much time and effort, nor it culminating in my relief in a hotel toilet cubicle.

Pulling myself together, I drove home and informed the home-team. We were all thrilled, not really knowing what monster we had unleashed upon ourselves.

REGULATIONS

The excitement of picking up the 'approvals' letter gave me a feeling of hope. However, the reality of taxiing to the runway of a flying dream was not going to be as easy as I had hoped.

I thanked the young lady at the Castle Annexe reception for the letters addressed to me and the GCAA, and hurried back to my car to read the contents. It was simple, and answered a lot of questions. The phrases 'no objections to the development and operation of an airfield' and 'no objections to the building and operating aircraft' opened my eyes to the situation at the GCAA. No matter how much the good folks at the Civil Aviation Authority wanted to see light aviation develop, it was not able to permit it, unless an express 'lack of objection', came from the Director of National Security.

My lack of understanding of the basic functioning of a developing nation's infrastructure, slapped me in the face. Every minister and every GCAA official I had made presentations to, right down to staff in the Office of the President, none had any real power to enable the progress of light aviation without the express 'no objection' from NatSec.

I had written to NatSec very early on in my quest, but they had not responded for many months. Not until I had made an absolute nuisance of myself to ministers, technocrats and the seat of Government. I wondered if there would have been a quicker way, but realised that it was unlikely.

Feeling satisfied that I had reached the top of the mountain of challenges, I drove to Kotoka International Airport, finding a space in the public car park right in front of the Tower. With a spring in my step and enthusiasm seeping out of every pore, I took the freshly printed letter of 'no objection' to my nemesis the Director of Regulation.

I entered his room, to find his face characteristically pointed at the surface of his desk. "I hear you have a letter for me," he stated flatly.

"Indeed I do," came my enthusiastic response, as I placed if firmly in front of his downward facing eyes.

The next thirty seconds seemed to last forever, but I did not care. I was so happy at my success, I was flying at ten thousand feet in bright sunshine, and nobody could burst my bubble.

"Hmmmn hmmmn," his out of balance fan motor sounded from within his body. "Well, we will need to write some regulations now, in order to allow you to operate," he spoke flatly, not even hinting at how he felt about the situation.

The force of his word-missiles hit my high-altitude, soaring spirit and I fell ten thousand feet in a millisecond. I had operated an aircraft in Ghana under the previous government, so what had changed?

It took me a moment to find any words, and then, quietly, I offered "I do not understand." It was all that I could find to say.

"We have new L.I.s and there is no provision for what you want to do," he answered cryptically.

"Ummm, L.I.s?" I quizzed.

"Legal Instruments, Acts of Parliament. The laws that allow us to operate. We just need to write some regulations for what you want to do," he offered politely.

Anybody who has heard the term 'write some regulations', knows that it invokes the spirits of darkness, the realms of all that is unholy, time-consuming and barrier raising. It is a term that makes the bravest soldiers cringe and cower, and it gave me little hope.

"Can I help?" I offered, wondering if I could join the forces of darkness in their quest to regulate.

"Hmmmmn, hmmmmn," he droned, "why not?"

Unsure of whether I was cursed or blessed, I smiled and leant forwards, placing both elbows on his desk, "How?"

Without answering, he picked up his phone and called for one of his section heads to come to the room. A few moments later, the office door swung widely open and a beaming face entered with a "Yes Sir."

"Can you work with this man to set up regulations for Ultralight aircraft. Use other countries regulations as a guide," he invoked.

Wonderful Adversity: Into Africa

"Can I just clarify one thing," I offered, and continued without waiting for permission. "Ultralight means one thing in the USA, and something else in the rest of the world. FAR 103, is the American definition of an Ultralight, which is single seat, In France, an Ultralight, or ULM, is up to two seats and four hundred and fifty kilos, more if you have a parachute. Perhaps we should also look at what the USA call the LSA, or Light Sport Aircraft regulation which covers two seat aircraft."

Flashing my limited knowledge of regulations gave me confidence, and I hoped would endear me to the team I was about to join.

The new face offered, "Why don't you print out all the different regulations, then we can have a meeting to discuss them."

It was agreed that all parties needed four weeks to research, and then a team meeting would be held to advance the regulations. I may have been brought back to earth, but I was not giving up to the enemy of paperwork and bureaucracy, especially having found a way into their ranks.

On the day of the meeting, I had printed out the French, British, Brazilian, Canadian and American regulations. Furthermore, I had carried out extensive cross-referencing, made proposals, and even had a basic regulation document adapted to the needs of Ghana of my own to offer. I was well prepared.

Entering the meeting room, there were at least a dozen people around the table. Some I recognised, but the majority were new to me. I sat with my ream and a bit of print outs in front of me, ready for battle.

In front of each seat, roughly placed on the dark table, a six page document waited for each participant. The meeting began, and we were instructed to read the document in front of us. It was a proposed regulation.

Confused I tried to question the methodology, "But, we have not discussed it yet?" my voice trailing off as I realised my lack of understanding.

"We have taken the standards from another country and adapted them to our needs," the meeting chairman continued.

As the 'regulations' were read aloud, I sat and tried to listen. I held my breath over "such aircraft shall not be allowed to fly more than eight nautical miles from their base" and tried to remain focused on every word. Then, reading ahead, I prepared myself for the proposed regulation for aircraft construction to be voiced.

"Documents which must accompany an application for the issue of a Certificate of Airworthiness for Microlight Aircraft. 1. A Certificate of Erection signed by an Engineer holding current Indian Aviation Medical Examiners Licence confirming that the said aircraft has been assembled in accordance with the manufacturer's instructions."

I sniggered, and all the faces in the room lifted in unison to stare at my face. They had all been reading, but not listening to what had been written down.

"Um, Gentlemen," for there were no women in the room, "I do not think that this is what you mean. Why would we need a medical examiner to issue a certificate of 'erection' or rather 'build'?"

Discussions flew left and right, in local language, leaving me blind. Without further ado, the meeting was called to close. I was called into the Directors office with the Chairman of the group.

I was ordered, "Explain what is wrong with the statement?"

"First of all, part of the regulations proposed are taken from India, and refer to using Indian personnel. Secondly, you do not normally give a certificate of airworthiness to such aircraft, but rather a Permit to Fly. Then there is a clear misunderstanding of the term AME. AME can mean Aircraft Maintenance Engineer or Aviation Medical Examiner. Also, the use of the term microlight is confusing for our neighbouring states, which are all Francophone, and may prefer the use of the term Ultralight, to be in keeping with the regional terminology," I was shaking as I spoke, and could hear it in my own voice.

The Director read aloud "A Certificate of Erection signed by an Engineer holding current Indian Aviation Medical Examiners Licence," and turned his face squarely on the chairman. "Do not make a fool of this office. Now, go and consider all the regulations, and listen to what this man has to say." He gestured towards me, indicating that I was the 'this man'. My nemesis had morphed into an ally.

Chairman and I exited the office together, agreeing another meeting date. I left him my ream of papers and my proposed regulation outline, without any mention of erection, or Indian personnel, within it.

At the next meeting, the retired director, my friend, was present, acting as adviser to the chairman. All parties interacted positively, and over a four-hour session bashed an outline regulation together. It was a workable document, and gave a maximum take-off weight of five hundred kilos. It was a really good compromise, if only it would be accepted.

A month later, I was called back to the Tower. A final document entitled 'Chapter twenty-five, regulation for Ultralight aircraft' was read by the team. It covered licensing, building, training and operating sub-five-hundred kilogramme aircraft in Ghana. It had some constraints, but was overall a workable document, and one on which a company could be formed to build, operate and train on such aircraft. It offered a suitable base for the use of such aircraft for humanitarian purposes also. I felt that a breakthrough had been made, proving that patience coupled with perseverance can be a powerful weapon in development.

BUILDING A FIELD

Relieved that all regulations were finally in place, now it was time to form a company, and find a proper site for an airfield. The work could now begin.

As a matter of courtesy, I visited a number of the Ministries buildings to inform the technocrats, who had been supportive in the quest, of the approvals, and implementation of working regulations.

In the Ministry of Transport, which held responsibility for the aviation sector, the Chief Director received me with a big smile. "I heard that you are able to begin your project," he beamed.

"Yes, thank you," I responded, unable to hide my excitement, "but now we must choose a company name." I went on to list several names under consideration, looking for his input.

Laughing he responded, "We call you the WAASPs people. For so many months you came to this office with your WAASP presentation, West African Aviation Solution Proposal. For us, you will always be the WAASPs people."

Locally, there was an insect called the Potters Wasp (Ancistrocerus), and such wasps were renowned for building mud nests everywhere. They were a nuisance, albeit industrious. I looked back at the smiling, fun filled face of the Chief Director and responded, "WAASPS it will be then."

Later that day, the company WAASPS Ltd was formed at the office of the Registrar General. When the clerk asked what WAASPS stood for, I was a bit flummoxed, for it did not need to stand for anything, it was 'a nickname' from the Ministry of Transport. That would not suffice for the prim and proper registration staff. I stammered out an idea, "West African Aviation Solutions and Provider of Service," it was clunky, but it was accepted.

I knew that I could not do everything, and also that such a company would need funds. Consequently, my son Matt, some friends and acquaintances joined in the creation of the business, mostly as passive shareholders, all with a desire to see light aviation grow in the sub-region. All hoped to make a bit of money, but also realised that the risks were high, and if they didn't, it would not be the end of the world.

One of those shareholders was a flying instructor, based in a nearby country. I did not know him very well, but he came highly recommended. Moving to Ghana, he took on the role of director and Chief Flying Instructor. He brought many positive experiences to the company and helped to select a suitable site for the building, of what was to become known as, Kpong Airfield.

The selection of the site was, as always in land deals in West Africa, fraught with conflicting claims of ownership. However, the land owner, a local Chief called Nene, held a Supreme Court judgement in his favour.

The land was covered in trees, and had a cattle farmer in a corner of it. Just a mile off of the main road, but far from accessible power, it was perfect. About three thousand metres from the planned threshold of the main runway, there was a mountain, or rather a hill, standing at about a thousand feet. Nene assured us that the cattle farmer, or Cattleman as we nicknamed him, was an illegal squatter and that he would move him on.

When the authorities came to visit the site for their inspection, they were shocked. "You cannot fly here, there is no runway, and a mountain in the way," exclaimed one of the inexperienced team members.

An older chap, retired from airline flying, admonished him with "These small craft can fly from grass and even climb over that mountain."

Captain Inspection appeared to be a supporter of our concept. We made a note to keep on his good side. Despite not being happy about the cattle corral close to the intended runway threshold, he understood that it takes time to evict squatters.

We started work on clearing the runway areas. It was a mammoth task. Employing local people in groups of ten per day, we often had all the workers quit by lunchtime, because the work was too hard. It was hard. The sun was scorching, and we needed the trees removed with minimal disturbance to surrounding soil structures. The work needed to be done to a standard, and many of the local workers struggled to understand the end purpose of the work.

One day, Matt managed to borrow a bulldozer from a friend. It was a magnificent, albeit very old, Italian machine. There were bits of wire holding things together, and it came with an operator by the name of Citroen. When asked where he got his name, he responded "I work Citroen cars once."

Citroen was a great operator. When the machine broke down, which was practically an hourly affair, he would jump down and fix it. Come to think of it, 'fix it' was probably a bit too descriptive for his methods of 'somehow repair it'.

My co-director stood watching the repairs, his Gitanes smouldering in his hand. I hated the smell, adjusting my position in relation to the wind for comfort. Gitanes commented at each 'repair', "You think this machine will last?" Fortunately, Citroen appeared to be a miracle worker, raising the machine from the dead on a regular basis.

One day, Cattleman, who was being evicted by Nene, ran out from behind some trees and stood about fifty metres ahead of the moving bulldozer. He raised his hands above his head, holding a clay saucer, shouting something, and then stooped to place the saucer on the ground. I could not hear him shouting, but rather just see his mouth moving, as if shouting. The noise of the bulldozer and my distance from the site prevented me knowing more.

Within moments, the bulldozer came to a standstill. All the workers dropped their tools and everybody walked away from the site, towards me.

Watching from a distance, I wondered what had happened. From my limited experiences of reasons for a rapid withdrawal from the field, I postulated that a snake had been released. Imagine my surprise when Citroen told me "He has put juju on the land, we cannot work anymore." It was a flat, factual statement, collaborated by the other workers.

Looking across the field, I watched Cattleman, walking away, clearly smug about his coup. Placing curses through Juju is a major part of the culture in West Africa. Rumours of politicians and football clubs burying live animals and making sacrifices are not uncommon. I remembered a case of a man being arrested for trading his daughter to a Fetish Priest, for ceremonial purposes, in return for a chain saw. I could not make light of the beliefs of my staff, no matter how alien they were to me.

"I understand your fears," I launched, with my face sternly set, "but I must assure you that this man's juju will not work here." Their faces twisted in confusion. "You see, I am protected by my God, and he will not let this man's juju stop this project," I reassured.

Gitanes looked doubtful at my attempts to rectify the situation, wandering away from the group for yet another smoke.

"My father was a man of God, and he taught me to pray against these things," I bluffed, for my old man had never prayed against juju in any of his church services.

Relived faces rose around me, giving me confidence to carry on. Being raised by a lay-preacher had given me the grounding in 'impromptu prayers'. This was the most important time in my life to call upon that ability and God.

I asked all the men to hold hands, mentally preparing my prayer, feeling the power of faith in the men around me. Gitanes looked on in total disbelief at my approach.

"May the God of Abraham hear our prayer," I launched, appealing to the three leading mono-theistic religions. Muslims, Jews and Christians, all believe in the same God, that of Abraham, as portrayed in their respective teachings. I continued, "We beseech thee to stop all evil from stopping the work on this airfield today, and that all juju laid in front of the bulldozer should have no effect on the machine or the workers," I paused, wondering if that was enough, both for God and also the workers, before closing with "AMEN" as loudly and pastor-like as I could manage.

The men all rippled "amen" around me. We let go of each other's sweaty and callous filled hands. Confidently, I started to walk towards the bulldozer, only to find the workers still standing where we had finished praying.

"C'mon chaps, let's get back to work," was the only encouragement I had left to offer, as I continued to walk briskly towards the cursed machine and saucer. I did not look back again, but as I got closer to the juju site, I could see bit of dead bird and a pool of blood. For the first time, it scared me. Feeling my face lose all of its blood supply, I breathed in deeply, and held it. Trying not to think about what was going on, I forgot to breathe out. My head started to buzz with a lack of oxygen, and I wondered if the juju was affecting me. Above the sound of a memory of my father praying the Lord's Prayer, I heard the sound of the men coming behind me. It jolted me back to reality.

Exhaling, as quietly as I could, I turned and ordered boldly "start the machine. We continue."

Sheepishly, Citroen got into the cab of the dozer. I climbed up alongside him. He started the engine, and a billow of black smoke blew down and over the cab ominously.

"Drive," was the only instruction I could muster. It must have been barely audible over the roar of the engine.

The rest of the workers stood back, watching. They were clearly both scared and excited at the same time. The 'dozers tracks rolled forwards, the pushing blade approaching the saucer of sacrificial blood. To my relief, the machine that broke down so often, continued over the saucer and worked non-stop for the rest of the day. My act of faith had worked, and had inspired the workers of the day.

That night I pondered the extent to which juju was both practiced and feared. I was especially thankful for my upbringing by a lay-preacher who taught me how to pray, as well as sell things in the market.

Eight weeks later, enough area was cleared, levelled and stabilised for a basic runway of about three hundred meters by twenty, a car park and reception area. It was enough to start operating, and importantly open a flying school.

FLYING – A NEW PERSPECTIVE

There had been a lot of interest in learning to fly from the ex-pat community, and a lot of interest in the idea of flying from the local population. The concept of cost effective flying, even that which is offered by the microlight/ultralight/Light Sport category of aviation, remains relatively expensive. The cost of flying, regardless of the size or category of aircraft is limited to those who are prepared to make the commitment, investing both time and money. Even with all the time and money in the world, it can be a futile pastime if it is not laced with passion.

Those who succeed in learning to fly are generally the obsessive type, compelled to run to the window and look at an aeroplane passing, even if they have seen the same one hundreds of times before. It requires the same

Wonderful Adversity: Into Africa

passion, practice and dedication, as learning to play a musical instrument.

The ex-pat community, thankfully, included a number of individuals who had always wanted to learn to fly, had disposable income and spare time. A few phone calls to selected acquaintances, and we had four students ready to sign up to the new flying school. With only one aircraft, Alpha-Alpha, and with an engine that complained at the heat, we had to book carefully. No more than two lessons, each early morning, per day. Cautiously, we booked two for the Saturday morning and two for the Sunday morning.

It was exciting, even if the runway was just dirt. The only safety fence we could muster was series of sticks, cut from local trees, pushed into the ground, with a line of bailing twine as a barrier to access.

I flew Alpha-Alpha from home to the airfield. Circling the hundred-acre site, an appreciation for the magnitude of what we had taken on, and what was left to be done, filled my available mental bandwidth.

The field was mainly trees, with our short, dirt runway looking like a scratch on the surface. On the approach, it would be necessary to fly over one corner of the Cattleman's makeshift corral, before touching down on the more than adequate runway.

Gitanes had already parked at the airfield, and was waiting, smoking his pungent cigarette. I really detested that smell, possibly because I had never smoked. Furthermore, I loathed having to remind him to put the cigarette out around the fuel canisters. Laughing, he told me that "In my country, we sometimes smoke in the cockpit. But only after we have drunk enough wine to make sure we fly straight."

I was not impressed, for this was not what I had expected from him based on prior exchanges. My indignation was cut short by the sight of a teenager wandering across the runway in the direction of the plane.

"HEY YOU," I yelled, "GET OFF THE RUNWAY."

It was a wasted outburst, and I should have known better. How could any of the locals appreciate what a runway was, let alone consider a compacted dirt line, in the middle of trees, as anything resembling a place for aircraft to operate. Nonetheless, education begins with the first person to walk across the preciously graded dirt.

"Come here," I yelled, as he wandered at the same pace towards the aircraft, avoiding my gaze. Frustrated, without proper reason, other than being stressed at the first day of opening a flying school, I ran over to him. He stood motionless, about ten metres from the airframe, staring at the monster before him.

"Can I help you?" I asked, hoping that my change of tone and approach might get a better reaction.

"Where you go put the spirits?" he asked, without taking his eyes off of the machine.

My first thought was that he meant to ask where we put the fuel for the engine to run. "We put petrol in the fuel tanks, which are here," I pointed to the tank visible behind the seats, hoping that my words were making sense.

"No. Where go spirits for fly?" he asked, scrunching his face tightly.

He was dressed in the usual 'young man of the bush' attire, His trousers and T-shirt had both seen better days. They were probably second-hand, from a local 'bend-down-boutique', so called because the clothes are laid out on the ground for you to inspect by crouching or bending down. His flip-flop clad, visibly scarred feet were sprinkled with dust from walking through the bush. I finally grasped that he was asking about the supernatural reasons for flight, and had probably never seen an aircraft close up before.

"There are no spirits. This is an aeroplane, and it flies by generating lift from the aerodynamic forces of air going over the wings," my proud description was lost between leaving my mouth and finding ears into which to fall, and be understood.

Blankly, our intruder turned, making eye contact for a brief moment, before continuing through the bush, away from the airfield.

Gitanes had finished his cancer-stick, clearly amused at my attempts to educate our passer-by. "You cannot explain these things to people like that," was his only comment on the event.

There was no time to further contemplate the situation. The first flying school client pulled into the makeshift car-park. We both walked enthusiastically to meet him. As we approached his car, Matt drove up in the truck, parking alongside the student pilot. All of us were smiling, making history, changing the world. We were an unstoppable force about to overcome gravity, politics and the worries of the past few years. Walking four-abreast we chatted excitedly as we moved towards Alpha-Alpha. She also looked excited, sitting proudly on the cleared dirt apron.

Matt picked up a handheld radio ready for his briefing on radio procedures for the field. Gitanes started the pre-flight inspection of the aircraft, showing each step to the new student.

Both flights went well, but the engine played up on the flight back to the house strip. The same challenge was experienced on the Sunday.

Gitanes was, understandably, not happy. "We cannot run a flying school with this engine," he complained, adding, "and we need a second aircraft too."

He was right. I had known that the Rotax 912 engine was the best option for the conditions where we were, but had tried to save some money in the proof of concept phase. I had already paid for that mistake with my engine failure on take-off, and subsequent between-the-trees 'parking' incident.

The next day, in my usual spontaneous manner, I called Rotax in Austria, booking an appointment with their marketing manager. I explained that they had no representation in West Africa, and that WAASPS had permission to build and operate aircraft.

A week later it was time to fly out. My wife and I left Matt and Gitanes to manage the new business for a week.

Wonderful Adversity: Into Africa

Arriving at the Rotax factory, we were greeted by a marketing team of two men and a woman. After the usual pleasantries, we were led into a meeting room, adorned with wonderful chairs, the sort that makes a squeaky noise if you move wrongly upon them. I made my presentation about why WAASPS should be their distributor for Ghana and all of West Africa. They listened politely. It was not the first time that an African operation had bent their ears with ideas and promises. It was probably the first time a prospective distributor had concluded with "I cannot promise to sell lots of engines. However, I can promise good engineering support, back-up, technical competence and a desire to ensure that each engine that is sold is appropriate for the market."

I sat back, my wife glancing at me sideways, probably questioning my mental stability, again.

"Thank you for your presentation," the manager responded. "We will get back to you in eight weeks, after our next board meeting, with our decision."

Without hesitation my mouth went off without my control. "Eight weeks? We flew from West Africa to make a presentation, and you want us to wait eight weeks for an answer? It is not as if there are a lot of people wanting and able to represent Rotax in West Africa..." my voice trailed as I managed to regain control of my mouth.

Shocked the manager repositioned his offer. "Let's say two weeks. Will that work?"

"No," my mouth beat me to an answer before I had time to think, "surely you can consider it today, whilst we are here. If you agree, we will place an order for three engines immediately."

Three engines? My mouth had the better of me. Three engines. We needed one to replace the engine on Alpha-Alpha and second one for a second school plane, once we could afford one. What was I going to do with the third one? However, my mouth had not finished, throwing in for good measure, "And a large spares and tooling order."

I felt uncomfortable, but dared not wriggle in my seat for fear of making a squeaky noise. Making a very conscious effort to keep my mouth closed, I waited. My wife sat next to me, looking a little pale.

Silence hung in the room, as time itself felt suspended. The Rotax team started to look at each other, without moving their heads. Then, the only lady in the group broke the silence. "Give us ten minutes to consider your proposition," she stated quietly, and they all left the room.

We sat in silence, waiting. I ran over the meeting in my head. I had been polite and correct, with all of my planned presentation. My mouth had gone off, without my permission, putting in jeopardy all of my premeditated proposals. A white faced clock looked at me, letting its red second hand clunk loudly to mark each long second, taunting me at each tick, laughing with each tock.

Finally, the door opened, announcing the return of the trio. Silently, they filed back into their correct slots and shuffled a few papers. Without further protest, the marketing manager announced, "Congratulations, you are now our distributor for West Africa. There is some paperwork to do, and you will need to commit to insurances, assurances and orders."

The third member of the team, stated quietly, "You have made Rotax history, for we never make decisions on the day." Pausing for what seemed like an age, he smiled, concluding, "I will begin your training immediately, with a factory tour."

My voice sounded confident as it boomed over the table, "Thank you," and my hand dived out for the requisite hand-shaking, sealing the deal. Inside, my body was shaking, whilst my mind went into overload at the enormity of the engagement.

ROTAX POWER

Fitting the Rotax engine to Alpha-Alpha was a breeze. The documentation was clear, and detailed and the engine itself a work of art. Gitanes and I brought our experiences, Matt added his enthusiasm, and together we had Alpha-Alpha back in the air within a week of receiving the engine.

With two other engines sitting in stock, and Gitanes doubting my mental stability, it was time to make some money to fill the now empty kitty. Nobody in their right mind would order an aircraft to be built so early on in our project. I believed that, with some creative thinking, we might gain other financial commitments to enable growth.

After extensive testing, we found the Rotax engine burned less fuel, performed better and did not suffer from the running problems right up to well over 40 Celsius (104 degrees Fahrenheit) ambient temperatures. These were all great reliefs, and opened new opportunities.

Able to expand our flight training to all day, we recruited more students, running out of flying slots for one aircraft, but did not have the funds for a second one.

I called a few of the new students, suggesting a discount for advance payment of blocks of lessons. Within a week, enough funds were in the bank to finance a second X-Air airframe.

The X-Air builds quickly, and we soon had two aircraft flying. I taught in Alpha-Alpha, whilst Gitanes preferred Alpha-Bravo. It was a dream come true. We all enjoyed the weekends, flying, teaching and occasional BBQ's.

Wonderful Adversity: Into Africa

The weekdays were spent clearing more areas for a longer runway, and regular run-ins with Cattleman. We did manage to improve our facilities, adding a small tent to act as a briefing room and shelter for the night watchman.

I spent a lot of time trying to make the most out of the new approvals. Not only did it open up opportunities for people learning to fly, we knew that our small aircraft could carry out amazing photo-missions, banner towing and also be a boon to the many NGO's in the country. Light aircraft can get to places quickly and efficiently, without a need for masses of infrastructure. Being able to land and take-off from the most basic, and short, dirt strips, they could change the face of medical outreaches.

A presentation was put together, and all the major NGO's in the country invited to hear about the new class of aviation open to them, and with it access to ever corner of the country, without the need to spend hours on high risk roads. On the day of the presentation, the room was packed. Sadly, the response was not at all what I had expected.

"It is dangerous. Why would we want to send one of our precious staff in such a small plane?" asked one of the faith based NGO directors.

"Light aviation has proved time and time again, that it offers a relatively safe, and efficient means of transport," I offered reassuringly.

"But if there is an accident, our supporters would not understand – it would not be seen well. Firstly, they would think we are wasting money flying," he argued, "then they would think we are taking too much risk."

Knowing that the doubting Thomas was from a major Christian mission in the country, I tried to offer appropriate wisdom. "We all know that those who want to walk on water, must first get out of the boat of safety and conservatism," it was a bold statement, and it struck a chord, sadly a discord.

After the event, I visited as many organisations as possible, but found that the concept of actually being able to reach those more remote places by air was not embraced. To be honest, the argument given to me by one of the European international aid operations made it clear.

"Why would we use resources to reach the remote areas, when we are already struggling to get doctors and nurses to those areas with good roads? What you are proposing would be a stretching of resources even thinner. If we sent a doctor to a village of a few hundred people, they would treat perhaps twenty or thirty people. However, if we kept that medical professional in a town, he can see hundreds of people every day," the explanation was strong, even if I personally found it hard to take.

Noting the resistance to use light aviation in humanitarian outreach, it was time to focus on the other areas that would generate profile and revenues. Traditional photo-missions cost many tens of thousands of dollars, and did not involve taking the client along. We could change that with the class of aviation we had now brought to the nation.

Low cost, high impact flying would be the revenue source to supplement flight training income. It was slow, but we did pick up a number of photo-mission and survey flights. These flights added interest, and we shared them between Gitanes and me.

One Monday, a middle-aged American lady, looking to support a local farmer in a joint venture, booked an exploration flight. Leaving Matt at home, and with Gitanes off for the day, I was pleased to be the duty pilot. Alpha-Alpha was flying better than ever. Her engine was sweet, and her behaviour docile. We flew around the area, looking at land that might be suitable for a new farming investment. I offered much praise for the Ghanaian investment atmosphere. She beamed with excitement each time we spotted another potential site for her money to be ploughed into. It was a really successful mission, with many positive outcomes, and lots of photos. The client was full of praise for the entrepreneurship and innovation we had brought to the country.

As we approached the airfield, we noticed a large group of people, moving en masse, along the main road that ran past the airfield. In the middle of the throng, two flat-bed trucks, over-spilling with bodies, drove at the crowds' pace. It looked like a funeral group, but it was hard to tell, especially whilst flying a plane, and planning a landing.

Just as I was about to turn base-leg, my passenger asked to extend the flight to take a look at the lake, just a couple of kilometres past the end of the runway. Happily, I obliged. We flew over the smattering of wooden fishing canoes, watching the men beating the water with sticks, hoping to encourage fish into their nets. A few snaps later and we turned, establishing a long-final approach to the airfield.

To my astonishment, I could see the same throng of people from earlier, moving along the dirt track that approached the airfield site. Keeping my mind on the landing, I made the approach a little higher than usual, in order to avoid alarming the folks on and around the trucks.

Landing long, the dusty strip breathed a reddish-brown puff as our wheels kissed her cheek. Happy with the flight, we taxied back to the apron, close to the tent. I couldn't see Kojo, one of the airfield workers, and scanned left to right. He was clearing some tall weeds, near the fence line. He surprised me by popping his head up with a smile.

I glanced towards the entrance, to see the crowd and trucks gathered at the airfield entrance. Shutting down the engine, I could hear them too. It was an angry band of people. Drums were being beaten in an aggressive rhythm, as sticks, machetes and local guns waved above heads excitedly.

The animated ensemble spilled onto the airfield, spreading out in a flood like manner. As they approached the makeshift security fence around the Runway End Safety Area (RESA), the stick and bailing twine barrier was swept up in their hands, added to their above-head-waving froth of make-shift weapons.

Wonderful Adversity: Into Africa

Kojo shouted to me "Run master. Run."

For whatever reason, I refused, and ordered him to stand with me, but asking my client to remain in the aircraft, just in case I had to fly her out in a hurry.

Four people walked in front of the crowd, the cacophony of voices and drums following them as if attached by cords. Kojo started to move away, but I stopped him with a simple order.

"Kojo, get two benches, and set them up meeting style," it was a simple command, but one that took him a few moments of courage seeking to implement.

With the noise reaching unbearable levels, and the body of people seeping across the airfield in an ever increasingly menacing manner, I considered jumping back into the aircraft and flying away. With a glance back to Alpha-Alpha, I saw my passenger with her eyes closed and hands clasped, clearly praying for a miracle.

Looking forwards once again, the four leaders' faces were clearly angry, and I had no idea why. All the same, I had left it too late to run, and had to make a stand.

"You are welcome." I yelled, hoping to be heard above the growing din. They responded, but I could not work out what was being said.

As they got within ten metres of my pseudo-entrenchment, with Kojo slipping further and further behind me, I tried again.

"You are welcome," it was a funny thing to shout at a group with clearly non-welcoming intent, but it worked. The leaders came to a stand-still, as did the masses behind them. The noise did not diminish, and the attempts by the leaders to yell something at me was lost to the wind of a thousand voices of dissonance, punctuated by drum beats.

Much as I was uncomfortable with the situation before me, I knew that it required an upper hand. At the top of my voice I hollered "Will you all be quiet. I cannot hear your leaders."

Slowly, but most definitely surely, a ripple of quietude flowed across the group, and with it, I yelled again "YOU ARE WELCOME."

It was an absurd thing to shout at a mass armed with sticks, machetes and guns, but it was the only thing I could think of doing.

The leaders, bemused and irritated by my insolence, introduced themselves. "This is Nana," a man holding a staff indicated "and Sipim, and the Secretary," he paused waiting for my response.

I realised that the staff holder, must be the Okyeame for the chief he represented, Nana. I also had had heard of the title Sipim, meaning War-Lord, for the Krobo tribe divisions. This was not a visit of peaceful intent, but I still had to manage it, and protect my client waiting in the aircraft.

Much as the crowd had all but silenced, the drummer was still beating his war-tune, defiantly. I was shaking inside, but had to remain focused in order to cope. Again I offered my only message, "You are ALL welcome. You are

ALL welcome," it was a repetitive flag of peace, but one that gained me thinking time.

"Please, take a seat," I offered the leaders, pointing at the benches in front of me. Obligingly, they sat on one bench, as Kojo and I sat on the opposite bench, in true Krobo meeting style.

Okyeame led with "You are on our lands. These are our family lands. You are trespassing."

Well, that was not what I expected. "Thank you for coming to see me. I have leased these lands from Nene, who has a supreme court judgement for the land we are on," I lay my defence before them, knowing that we had legal rights from the owner of the land.

The crowd erupted, sticks, machetes, guns and fists waved randomly, and the drum beat faster and faster. Without thought for my poor odds of survival, should the crowd turn nasty, I launched into market-preacher mode, standing on the bench.

Raising my arms out, as if to hug the group, I projected "Will you please all listen," the noise began to abate. "I have come here to create jobs, and share my knowledge of engineering," all but the drums fell silent. "I have not come here to fight you," the drums grew louder, and I had to break my flow.

"Will you stop beating that drum? Will you all please put the sticks, machetes and guns away? If you want to hear me, then you must listen," I pleaded. After a moment, it worked, giving me greater hope for a peaceful resolution to the situation before me.

"I have come to help your community, to create jobs, to share my knowledge. I have followed the laws of your land, and leased this land through the correct channels..." murmurs of discord rippled through the body of people. Catching myself, I refocused, "You are a great people, who have much to offer, and I am not here to fight with you. I am here to bring economic benefit to all the people of Krobo-land, through investment in your area."

A small cheer came from a group at the back, and the leaders on the bench in front of me glanced at each other, nervously. I stepped down from the bench and retook my seat before the elders.

With carefully chosen emphasis on selected words, Okyeame spoke, "WE have NOT come here to fight you. WE have come here to VISIT our lands. WE have come here to invite YOU to..." he paused, seemingly seeking a reason to visit, "to, to invite you..."

He stopped speaking, and the crowd leaned forwards hoping to catch whatever came next.

The silence burned a hole in my patience, and I responded as best I could. "An invitation, how wonderful. Is it to a party? Or a wedding? Or a funeral? Will there be coke to drink? Will there be cake? I LOVE cake."

My response was far from appropriate, but it won over the crowd, who laughed and smiled, many now trying to make eye contact with me.

A short exchange in local language took place between the elders, and the offer was concluded, "WE have come to invite YOU to a meeting with OUR Paramount Chief."

The Krobo Paramount Chief was rarely in the country, and I was surprised at the invite, but went along with it. "When shall we meet?" I asked.

"Thursday at dawn," came the bland reply.

In a spirit of appeasement, I offered, "If you come here first, we can go together in my car," and the deal was set.

As the crowd dispersed, I called behind "Please replace my fence," but it was a wasted appeal.

Back in the plane, my client sat shaking. "I have decided not to invest in Ghana," she whispered, for her lack of breath from praying so hard.

DEATH THREATS

Thursday arrived, rather like a bad taste in my mouth. All the same, I was waiting at the airfield, watching the reddish glow of the large African sun peek above the horizon, signalling dawn. Nobody came for any meeting. By late morning, I took matters into my own hands, and headed to the Krobo Palace. As I parked, a well-dressed lady paused a few metres from my car.

Opening the door, I offered "Good morning, ma'am."

"Can I help you?" she asked in impeccable English.

"I have come to find the Paramount Chief," I explained.

"He is not here. He is in America," she offered, adding "but I am the acting Paramount Queen Mother, can I help?"

The next hour was spent explaining the events at the airfield, whilst she listened intently. Smiling, she reassured me, promising to speak to Nana, Sipim, Okyeame and the other elders. She concluded by commending me and the WAASPS team for bringing industry and something positive to Kroboland. Parting, we shook hands. Her wrinkled hand was calloused, a tell-tale sign of a woman who knew what hard work was. Her smile and nod signalled that she was a friend in this whole adventure.

Making my way back to the work site, I felt more confident, if not completely reassured. At least I had a positive outcome from a visit to the Palace. My uplifted spirit brought a smile to my face, the first of the week.

Kojo, and his co-worker Kwame were sitting by the airfield gate, looking very uncomfortable. Whilst I had been away from the field, the Cattleman had let his cows out onto the runway, leaving hoof mark depressions everywhere, rendering the runway unusable before repair. Furthermore, he had threatened Kojo and Kwame, accusing them of being slaves to the white man. He had made it clear that he was ready to shoot them, and the 'white-boss-man' if they tried to chase his cows.

Exasperated, I proceeded directly to the police station. Introducing myself with the name that I had become most known as in the area, hoping for a rapid response to the volatile situation at hand. "My name is Captain Yaw, and I would like to report a threat made to me and my staff."

Immediately, the desk sergeant sat up straight, listening intently to the stories of the past few days. Then, in true bureaucratic style I was passed from officer to officer, each one listening to my long account. Repeatedly, I explained the whole story; the crowd, drums, guns, sticks, fake invitation, etc., all iced off with the wanton Cattleman damaging the runway and threatening to kill my staff and, coincidentally, me.

Ninety minutes later, I was sitting in front of the Regional Commander, exhausted and ready to book a seat back to England on the next available flight.

It was to be another game of word chess.

"I have had complaints about you," he opened.

"Really, but what have I done wrong?" I offered as a counter.

"You have been changing the weather," he moved.

Laughing, probably too loudly, I quizzed, "how did I do that?"

With a half-smile, just beginning to crack the edges of his mouth, he lined his sniper shot up. "Since you started flying, the farmers have noticed that you make the rain stop, just so that you can fly."

It was clearly nonsense, but something that I had to take seriously, on top of my other problems. Preparing for a stalemate, I went for a dangerous manoeuvre, testing the scientific knowledge of my opponent. "Sir, tell me, how on earth can an aeroplane change the weather?"

It was bad move, with the Policeman leaning heavily towards me, in a most threatening manner, "It is not for me to tell you anything. You must answer to the accusations," he toppled my king over, and all my other pieces, as he claimed victory in the strategic game of words.

"This is nonsense," I retorted, getting visibly and audibly angry, "there is no scientific fact to back up these claims."

"The people believe it is a spiritual thing," he offered, in a more conciliatory tone, his body language changing to match.

With a long and submissive sigh, my admission was made, "I cannot change the weather."

Sitting back in his chair the Regional Commander looked at me, titling his head and adjusting his gaze, assessing my whole being. "I did not think so. But the people do," and with that he smiled, and relaxed. "So, Captain Yaw, what brings you here, and why do the people think you are changing the weather?"

My arrival with a complaint of being threatened had turned into a more complex event, in true West African style.

After some thought, I proposed that the farmers had realised that we only flew when it was not raining. Hence, perhaps, and just perhaps, they had misunderstood that we 'changed the weather'. Understanding the thought process of those with little formal education, is more challenging than understanding the whole topic of meteorology. I hoped my postulation would appease. Fortunately, it did.

As we discussed the security issues at the airfield, the Policeman paid a lot more attention. He explained that land rights are more complex than a Supreme Court judgement, and that people are injured and killed over land misunderstandings on a regular basis. In all honesty, he reduced any confidence I had in the rule of law, or the efficacy of the police to be able to uphold the law.

Our discussion digressed onto many other topics, and after a while, he invited me back to his home. There we carried on putting the world to rights, as we warmed to each other, sharing our relative experiences and struggles. Just as I was leaving, he came up with a positive suggestion.

"Have you thought of applying for a policeman to be stationed at the airfield?" he asked, shaking my hand at the threshold to his service bungalow.

"How would that work?" I quizzed, never having considered such an action.

"You write me a letter, explaining the security issues at the airfield. I send it to HQ, with my recommendations. Then, if approved, you pay a few hundred dollars per month for an armed policeman to be stationed at the field."

It sounded simple, and so, without further ado, I rushed home, wrote the letter and dropped it straight back to his bungalow.

"That was quick," he laughed.

"The situation is developing quickly," I retorted.

A few days later, the commander arrived at the airfield, accompanied by a young officer.

"Here is your policeman," and with a push on the shoulder of the freshly graduated cadet, sent him stumbling towards me.

"G-Good afternoon, Sir," mumbled the AK47 touting officer, "my name is Jones."

Jones seemed such an unlikely name, I laughed, which left him looking quizzically at me. "It is fine British name," I reassured.

The deal was a simple one. Jones, or any other suitable officer, would report to the airfield at 1800 each evening, and leave at 0600 each morning. There was no provision for daytime cover, but at least nights would be more secure than just our solitary unarmed night-man.

During the day, I always made sure to have my pump-action around, and avoided leaving the airfield without management of Gitanes, Matt or myself. It was uncomfortable, but necessary.

Cattleman was in goading mode, and made sure that bowls of fresh blood and animal parts were left in various prominent locations, on a regular basis, just to keep up the fear tactics for the local staff. It worked, and even scared Jones the policeman.

Sadly, Cattleman did not want to move, ignoring all the orders made against him. This hindered much of the activity, especially with the sporadic cattle invasions of the runway, and subsequent repairs.

Amidst all of this activity, my wife was called back to the UK, to visit her father, who was not well. Matt and I got to enjoy unhealthy food and a lot more hands on time, in the workshops and on the field, without the anchor of a matriarch.

The business was growing, and we had even managed to build a small office, to be used as a briefing room during the day, and guard room at night. We were gaining a reputation of having reliable aircraft, and good flying skills. So much so that we were contracted to count coconut trees, in the Western Region, by air.

It was a bit more complex than just counting trees, since it included trying to track the development of Coconut LYD, Lethal Yellowing Disease also known as Cape St. Paul's Wilt. It was good money, and a full week's worth of survey flying. It was the break we had all been waiting for.

AMBUSH?

The survey flight was going to bring in enough funds to expand operations, and hopefully fund the first of the Zenith CH701 aircraft, which we knew would be the future of the operation. Consequently, it was a big deal. I would fly the mission, whilst Matt managed the airfield and Gitanes handled the flying school.

I would need to fly Alpha-Alpha to Takoradi early on the Saturday morning, leaving at 0600. Gitanes would arrive around 0800 and run the flying school with Alpha-Bravo. It was a key moment in the operation of the business.

Friday morning, the day before the start of the job, Matt had to go to the city to get some provisions. He planned to take advantage of the trip, to meet up with some other young folks from Europe, which was a good thing.

Southern Ghana is very close to the equator, so sunrise and sunset vary little throughout the year. By 1800, it was time for me to be in the house, behind mosquito netting, before the sunset and the blood thirsty masses of insects commenced their nightly vein-raids.

I called Matt, to check on how he was doing in Accra. "I will wait till after the rush hour traffic to set out," he reassured me.

I sat bare-topped, with a pair of khaki shorts on, cross-legged on my bed. The louvre windows were open on both sides of the bedroom, since there was no air conditioning, and the warm, slightly humid air was a pleasant twenty-seven Celsius (eighty degrees Fahrenheit). The crickets and frogs were all well into the second movement of their evening symphony, punctuated by the odd bird call and occasional drifting music from a funeral at a nearby settlement.

In front of me, the computer showered a gentle glow at my face. Going over the survey flights for the hundredth time, I punched the odd correction into the software, ready to download to my GPS for the flight. It was my first time of doing such a survey, and I wanted to do it right.

My phone rang loudly, making me jump. "Captain Yaw, is that you" came a hushed, unfamiliar voice over the poor connection.

"Yes, who is it?" I enquired, cautiously. It was unusual to get a call late on Friday night

"It is me, Jones the policeman at the airfield," the voice continued over the crackly line in ever more hushed tones, "there is a problem"

"What is the problem?" I asked, thinking it might be something simple, like a scorpion sting or a snake.

"You will see when you get here," came the reply, and the line dropped, not from the usual poor quality mobile phone coverage, but because he had chosen to hang up on me. To call and not say what you needed or wanted, was not normal, nor were hushed tones. I had sufficient understanding of the local people, and their cultural differences, to be concerned.

Trying call back simply yielded a pre-recorded message, "The number you have called is out of coverage area," repeatedly.

I would need to go to the airfield and assess the situation personally. Reluctantly, I saved my open documents, shutdown the laptop and got dressed in jeans and a T-shirt. As my head ran over the possibilities behind the call, I contemplated the possibility of an ambush. Wondering if Jones and our own night staff had been taken hostage, I decided to change my attire. Donning a pair of dark green overalls and a camouflage hat, I loaded the pistol grip shot gun, ensuring a full complement of cartridges plus spares in my pockets.

It was a six-mile journey by car, the first two on rough dirt tracks. I was driving way too fast for the conditions, not wanting to waste any time, my body rocking at every turn. The shock absorbers were not in a good state and each bump resulted in fairground ride of oscillations. Nightjars flew up just in front of the car, and startled cattle on the track moved, begrudgingly, out of the way as I sounded the horn. Reaching the pot-holed the tarmac, the phone signal was good enough to make a call to Matt. He picked up the phone after five rings, which seemed to take forever.

"Hi mate, Dad here. There is a problem at the field. I am going down with the gun, if I do not call you by eleven there is a problem – you will need to get the police."

"OK, Dad, call me later," came his laid back and calm reply, clearly thinking that Dad was being over cautious.

As I drew closer to the field, my mind went into self-preservation mode, and the concept of an ambush led my actions. As I turned off the paved road and onto the last three-quarter of a mile of dirt track, towards the airfield, I pulled my camo hat over to one side and down at the front, attempting to shadow out my white face in the vehicle. The dust cloud, behind the car, was way too conspicuous, as was my heartbeat.

Deciding to drive straight past the entrance, I stole a glimpse to my right, hoping to catch a sense of what was happening. I couldn't make out anything discernible through any of the snatches my eyes made in the dark. Not a vehicle, not a shadow, not a cow nor a person, just the outlines of trees and grasses. I drove for about one hundred metres past the site before switching off the lights, squinting to find a suitable place to park the car. Finding a gravel bank, just off of the track and sufficiently far away from the airfield as not to be seen, I hushed the car to a standstill.

Feeling as if I was in some strange movie, it was time to be discrete. Sliding out of the car, stooping low, I needed to find a way to move with the gun. Juggling for a second or two, I found the pistol-grip in my right hand and the large barrel of the shotgun held securely against my chest at a forty-five-degree angle with my left hand. I locked the car and pushed the keys far down into my pocket. This was not the place to lose keys, especially in the night.

The adrenalin output of my body must have been close to a lethal dose. My head was spinning, and my heart beats could no longer be distinguished one from another. Heading towards the airfield, where the policeman and my night watchman, hopefully, waited safely for me, I worked on remembering to breathe. Despite the concerns and risks, I slid as quietly as possible between the thorny African scrub. Using a large tree silhouetted against the night sky, as a beacon towards which I should aim, I progressed fairly swiftly. I came up against a thicket that I could not remember, but was still in line with the tree. I skirted to the left, rubbing my hand where it had been scratched and was now bleeding. Pausing to listen, I could hear nothing. Not even the crickets or frogs. A strange silence for an African night.

Normally, after a gun shot, sudden noise or disturbance, the African evening concert goes silent. From the cacophony of a million tunes to zero decibels in a second. There must have been some disturbance, the other side of the thicket, that had created this silence. I paused for a while before continuing my stealthy excursion.

I could soon see the briefing-cum-guard-room, and the two men I expected to see, about five metres in front of it. They were crouched down, a bit like children pretending to be rabbits at a birthday party, except that they did not have their hands at the sides of their heads pretending to be bunnies' ears. Only one thing protruded above their heads; the barrel of a police issue AK47, slender, crisp and very clear. I watched them for a moment or two, looking for signs of others around them. They were both looking intently at the corral on the other side of the runway. Just a week earlier we had erected a new fence there, but now it was gone. It had been there that afternoon, but had clearly been removed in a hasty manner. My eyes adjusted to the night light, as the moon and the stars gave their dim, silvery grey illumination to the scene. I could see parts of the fence scattered around the area, and two oil lamp lights beyond the removed fence line. Disconcertingly, there were the vague outlines of a group of local people, and particularly that of Cattleman. Angry phrases, spoken abruptly in the vernacular, wafted across the night air as if supported by the evening humidity, propelled by the odour of cattle.

The policeman and my security man looked at each other, exchanging indiscernible comments. It was clear that no ambush, trap or kidnapping awaited me. But there was a problem. The temptation to exit the bush and surprise the two watchers was great, but would have been stupid. I needed to make my presence known to the pair, without receiving a round of semi-automatic gunfire as a reward for startling them. They were still expecting a car to arrive with me aboard, not me arriving from the bush with a weapon.

I gently activated the safety on my gun, and slid the weapon inside my overalls. I needed to have a silhouette without a weapon when I exited my hiding place. Standing up, I composed myself and timed my exit. I whistled loudly to attract Jones's attention, and then moved sideways, just in case he raised his weapon. He did not, just merely glanced around, in my direction, his white eyes clearly visible on his black face. Pulling my camo hat off at the same time as stepping forwards, he recognised me and smiled, whispering "You are welcome," before returning his gaze across the field, as if a new problem had just created itself. Following his lead, I moved closer, stooping down and replacing my hat as I did, crouching next to him.

"They have destroyed the fences and are threatening to attack the whole outfit," he hushed.

"Oh. Well. What happened?" I asked, in a punctuated and pensive manner, remembering to be relieved at the fact that there was no exchange of rounds in the offing.

Before he could reply, a burst of electronic music started to play and a pale blue light shone out of my pocket. It was my mobile phone. I turned around to hide the light and stabbed at the answer key to kill the noise, raising the phone to my ear at the same time. It was my wife.

"Hello, how are you?" she asked in all innocence of the unravelling situation around me.

"I am fine," I whispered, "but I am at the field with the policeman and..." I was not allowed to finish the sentence.

"Are you all right? What is the matter? What is going on? Where is Matthew?" came the volley of questions, too fast for a single response or breath before the next was jettisoned via the wonders of telecommunications; from the UK, out to space, from satellite to satellite, down to earth and by microwave and radio wave to me in the African bush.

"All is fine, call me in one hour, I can't talk now," I reassured, with full intent of procrastination. I hung up, and switched the phone off, not bothering to wait for a response. Too much was at stake and too much still unknown.

Turning to my own night man, I asked "What happened?"

He answered in broken English, explaining that the cattle farmer had been out drinking and came back in a temper, with a few of his drinking team. They decided to rip down the new fencing and throw it around. The situation got out of control when he issued loud, alcohol powered threats, probably as empty as his gin bottle, but threats all the same.

I assessed at the situation, weighing up options and potential dangers that may be present. The thought about the issue of threats, reflected in the fear in the policeman's voice earlier, leading me to wonder about the best course of action, if any. Fortunately, I had managed to remain hidden from sight. The drinking team, therefore, had no idea that the person with whom they were angry, was on site. If I showed myself, it could raise the temperature of this fragile situation unnecessarily. I contemplated the risks of another round of booze triggered destruction of airfield property or worse.

By now the disturbances of earlier had been over long enough for the birds, reptiles and insects to have recommenced their nocturnal festival. The occasional firefly lit up blades of grass, one at a time, near us. The African night had recovered from its enforced pause for a fence ripping and throwing interruption, and was back in full melodic swing.

Realising that the future of the airfield, with all that it could bring to the people of this area, was being put at risk by an angry, inebriated cattle farmer and his friends, I started to anger.

This was not the place to let rip, much as I wanted to go over to the mob and yell at them "What are you doing? Why don't you want more jobs for your people? Do you not want development?"

Such action would be counterproductive, and I had to ensure the security of this location, and that no further disruptions took place before we could replace the fencing. The blood started to pound in my ears, my muscles tensed and my breathing almost stopped as I tried to bring my anger and frustrations into check. I wanted to shout out and demonstrate my anger, but could not.

When the doctor hits your knee with the little hammer that makes your foot jump it is called a reflex. A reflex does not pass through the brain, it jumps across nerves. Similarly, when fire burns your hand you pull back without cognitive thought. In much the same way, I pulled my shotgun out from inside my overalls, my actions spurred by reflex, deep mental calculations at high speed that did not pass through my consciousness. The policeman took two steps backwards, eyes widened.

"I brought it down in case you needed assistance," I reassured him. He looked at me, still concerned, but with a slight smile on one side of his mouth. The watchman smiled openly at the uneasiness of the policeman. I looked at both of them, and then looked over at the, now relaxed, scene on the other side of the field, strewn with wooden posts with a small group huddled nearby.

The possibility of further violent action against the airfield nagged at me. I knew that I needed to show some sort of reaction to the unnecessary actions taken, but what. Stepping backwards, more into the trees and bushes than before, I slipped off the safety catch and pumped three, loud cartridge loads into the air. The flashes from the barrel and the explosions in the air took all by surprise, even me. The Russian cartridges had varying amounts of powder in them, and I think that the last one was heavily overloaded. The bang was immense. Natures orchestra was once again silenced. The sudden compression of air in my ears left me with a ringing and pounding, and a little temporary deafness.

Hidden by the bushes, I watched team drunk stop their conversation, spread out and look towards the security post.

I whispered to the policeman, "You did not fire your weapon, and those were shotgun rounds, it could have been a hunter," adding "perhaps I have never been here," and blended into the bush.

Suddenly, the crackle and rumble of tyres at high speed, on the gravel track, spun through the air as Cattleman and his team sped away.

I pulled my hat hard down to hide my face, sliding my white-man's hands into my sleeves to further ensure my anonymity. Jones moved forwards to the edge of the runway, apparently boosted with confidence by my support.

The policeman came back and told me that the shots had a positive effect on the situation. Relieved that my actions had not exacerbated the situation, but rather brought the situation to a close. I reiterated that he had not shot his gun, and shotgun rounds were commonplace at night in these parts, from hunters. I had been hunting. Hunting for solutions, and hunting for peace, using the tools of the trade needed in the culture around me

I bid the men goodnight and retraced my steps to the car, not without second thoughts about what could have happened if a return volley of gunfire had erupted, or other attack. My adrenalin levels abated, and my heart rate slowed as I found my may back to the car.

DEAD OR ALIVE

I sat in the car, caught my breath and waited, collecting my thoughts. It was essential that I did not give away my presence on the field. A good ten minutes later, the orchestra had picked up their scores, returning to their night song. I drove, lights off, for a further five hundred metres down the track, before turning and putting the lights on. Sliding down in the seat, I pulled my faithful hat down really hard, so much so that it hurt, and headed on past the field. I felt the need to inform the Regional Commander of the evening's events, and headed straight there. Arriving at his house, albeit late, he was watching television.

"Come in, come in," he called heartily through the open louvre windows and dusty mosquito nets.

Entering, I slumped into the velour chair, sweating in the full set of overalls that I had been bush-creeping in. I briefed my new friend.

"I am so disappointed in our people," he confided in me, "why do they behave so?"

We talked for a good forty minutes, deciding that fear of the unknown is difficult to reason with, and only time and effort would prevail in the situation. He pointed out, that for many people in the area, the fact that we could fly was almost magical, and they would take a long time to accept us. Some may never accept the concept of human flight.

On the way home, I stopped the car in a good reception area and called my wife to update her, as well as Matt.

"OK Dad, that's fine," Matt chirped, almost patronising me for my caution, "I will be late back, I am still chatting with friends."

Travelling in the dark is always a risk in West Africa, especially outside of the built up areas. I was not worried about Matt on the roads. He was a good driver, and had recently circumnavigated Ghana in the little truck. Mainly driving on bush roads, with no tarmac to be seen for hours on end, he had travelled roads, which even I would have avoided, without any mishaps.

I pulled up to the house and went inside, closing but not locking the door behind me. Tired, and frustrated at the new challenges this evening had

Wonderful Adversity: Into Africa

given me, it was time to leave my final flight planning until the morning.

Leaving the overalls in an untidy pile on the tiled floor, I lay exhausted on the bed, between phone and gun. I had decided not to lock the gun away, partially through tiredness, but also in case of any reprisals that may follow me home.

At three in the morning, I awoke with a start. I had lain badly and my back was incredibly sore. Limping through the house, I looked for signs of Matt being home. He was not. I dialled his number. "The subscriber you have dialled is out of coverage area," came the standard reply. I dialled again, and again, and again. I started to worry if there had been an accident. If so, what could I do, where would he be. I reassured myself that phone communications are always poor, and that he was probably fine.

Trying once more, before seeking a horizontal resting place, the phone rang and was swiftly answered. Before he could eject a first syllable, I blurted "Are you OK, son?"

He answered, "I am fine, I am at Tema. All is well and I will be home in about an hour."

Tiredness had caught up with him, and he had taken a rest, sleeping longer than planned. I fell back to sleep, relieved that Matt would soon be home, ready for the busy day ahead of us.

At four I stirred, Matt was still not home. I tried his number at least ten times, but all I got was the monotonous 'out of coverage area' responses. I tried to sleep, but could not. It was not unusual to be out of coverage area around the local mountain, called Krobo Mountain. Something was nagging me. I was worried about Matt. He should be home by now, but, I also needed to rest, in preparation for a three-hour flight to Takoradi in just a few hours.

Deciding that Matt, must have taken another nap in the car before arriving directly to the field, I persuaded myself that he was fine. He was smart enough not to push on when too tired, unlike his father.

As the dawn light came through the curtains, I knew that Matt would be awoken by the morning glow, and so I dialled his number again. That wretched cackle of 'out of coverage area' was getting on my nerves.

This was not normal. It was time to implement a Search and Rescue routine. I knew the route he would use, and knew that he had spoken to me about ninety minutes ago from Tema. There was a fifty kilometre stretch that he could be on. I don't remember getting dressed, but I did, and was already in the car and moving down the road. My eyes darted left and right, hunting for any signs of our vehicle pulled in, or having left the road into one of the ditches. Being low on fuel, I pulled into the first fuel station.

Whilst the attendant put fuel in the car, I tried Matt's number one more, probably fruitless time. It answered, but it wasn't Matt.

"Who are you? Where is my son?" I practically screamed down the phone.

"There has been a terrible accident," came the reply.

"Where? Let me speak to my son," I verbally knee jerked at the Good Samaritan.

"Akuse Junction," he responded blandly.

I was at the Akuse Junction fuel station. Running to the roadside, I scanned left and right, unable to see any accident.

"Where at Akuse Junction? I am already there," my panicked voice jumped down the phone.

"Come south," and the line went dead.

Stopping the fuelling, I drove off without paying. Nobody minded, they knew me. The next one hundred and twenty seconds, the time it takes to travel four kilometres at one hundred and twenty kilometres per hour, seemed like a lifetime, as I sped south of Krobo Mountain.

Passing the last of the outcrops, at the bottom of the mountain, I could see the back of a white Mercedes Benz 207 fifteen-seater mini-bus, known locally as a tro-tro, on the opposite carriage way. I started to slow down, conscious of the risk of further accidents around an existing accident site.

I then saw the rear of our truck on the other side of the tro-tro. Crossing to the shoulder of the oncoming carriageway, I parked behind and to the left of the bus. 'Don't Rush' was emblazoned on the rear right door window, in self-adhesive vinyl. It was clearly good advice that the driver had not heeded.

Taking a deep breath, and conscious of dampening in my eyes, I released my seatbelt and opened the door. The morning light was rapidly increasing, as it does in the tropics. A small group of onlookers were in front of the tro-tro, looking at our truck. I could not tell if the mountain was green or blue, almost everything appeared to be black and white, I felt as though I had fallen into some sort of dream world or an old TV programme. I peered past the tro-tro, not really wanting to see what was there. As I focused on our truck I could see only one other colour; bright, bright red. Blood red. It was all over the front of what I could see of our small white pickup truck. There was a lot of blood, fresh and still running, pooling on the tarmac making it blacker than ever. My head felt light, my legs felt soft. I reached out to the wing of my car and steadied myself. Slowly, so, so slowly I walked towards the truck. It was empty. Our truck was empty.

"Captain," came a voice, flat and without a hint of emotion. It was Kojo. I looked at his face. Normally, Kojo always greets with a smile, but not today.

A group of about twenty onlookers went silent as I put my hand on the remains of the crumpled bonnet of our truck. The truck was embedded into the tro-tro. I walked with Kojo, putting my hand on his arm for support, unsure of whether I was walking or floating. I was simply moving, trying to take in the scene in front of me. I moved around the truck, making my way towards the driver's seat.

A man, holding Matt's phone, approached me, without a word being said. At least if he did I could not hear it, for the deafening silence of the scene

Wonderful Adversity: Into Africa

before me filled my ears. Everything was in slow motion. It was unreal, impossible to take in.

I stared at the seat that should have contained my son. It was empty. More than empty. The grey steering wheel had snapped off when it hit the seat back. The door had been 'popped' in the accident and sat about eight inches open. Blood was everywhere. I looked up and saw blood all over the front of the tro-tro. I looked down and saw blood under my shoes. I looked inside the truck and saw blood. Lots of blood. I wanted to be sick, started to retch but swallowed hard, remembering the need to breathe. I shook my head, liberating tears as I did so. The man with Matt's phone stood closer to me, holding my shoulder.

"He is OK, he walked away," he lied blatantly to me. I knew it to be a lie but I wanted to believe it. "We have tried to call the police," he continued, "but we cannot get through."

As a pilot, in times of disorientation we often use the mantra "Aviate, Navigate, Communicate" and the words spun into my head. I had gotten to my destination and I knew where I was, now it was time to communicate.

My personal bubble had to give way to the need to solve this problem. My son was nowhere to be seen, none of the victims were. So where were they? The police had not been contacted, but would be needed on the site. I needed to take some action, in order to move this everlasting scene along.

Being just after dawn, the police station was not going to be fully staffed, but I did know of one policeman on his way home, the policeman I had been crouching in the bush with the previous night. I dialled his number, asking frantically where he was.

"Around Akuse Junction, on my way back to the police quarters," he responded, unsure of why I would be interested in his early morning movements.

"When you get there, tell the Commander that there has been a major accident south of Akuse Junction. It is a serious one, needing at least two officers." I don't know how I could have been so co-ordinated, faced with the near certainty of my son's death. I was disconnecting from the reality, and just doing.

"Ok, I will do that," he responded, and we hung up.

My eyes met with those of the man with Matt's phone, he looked blurry from the tears that fell uncommanded from my eyes.

"What happened?" I asked, flatly.

"We came along to find this accident, and my friend has taken our double-cab pickup, with the injured, to hospital."

All I heard was injured and hospital.

"WHICH HOSPITAL?" I shouted at the possibility that my only son could be only injured, despite the evidence in front of me. How could he survive the steering wheel going through him? Grasping at this new information, I asked again, pushing my face closer to his, hoping that it would make the response reach my ears faster.

The man looked blankly back at me, whispering "Which Hospital? I... I cannot tell." It was a useless response, but after a long pause he added "Maybe Akosombo, maybe Akuse, maybe Atua."

The three different hospitals were in very different directions, each at distances that would take me more time to reach than to wait for the answer of which exact one. I could not risk going to the wrong hospital. I had to wait for the police to arrive, in the hope that they would have more data.

Another tro-tro passed the crumpled mess, slowing down for its passengers to gawk at the scene. I have never liked rubber-neckers, more so at that point, when it was my son's blood that they were peering at, no doubt postulating their own theories, as they continued on their route.

It made me think. What happened? I needed to understand this accident now. It would occupy my mind, and fill the time before the police arrived. I needed to analyse the scene.

Perhaps it was morbid, but it was a way of keeping myself occupied. I looked at Matt's side of the road and paced out his skid marks, all on his side of the road, over a thirty-five-metre distance. I turned, looking at the accident scene, from the very start of the skid. Lifting my hands to make a windshield shape, I framed the road with the Mountain to the right, putting myself in Matt's skin.

Colour was beginning to re-enter my perceptions, but contrast was still set far too high for comfort. Everything was more three dimensional than usual. The mountain looked bigger and deeper, our truck and the tro-tro, apparently welded together by the impact, punctuated the scene in a fearful and deadly manner. Mentally, I removed the wreck from the image, and replaced it with pre-dawn traffic, imagining myself in a driver's position. He would be driving at no more that 80km/hr, since that was the truck's top speed, and then see the tro-tro heading towards him, presumably on his side of the road.

My eyes dropped to read the skid marks. He braked straight, that was good. But wait, there was something not right. Sitting on top of the skid marks was a metal roof rack, with plantain in it. It was ON TOP of Matt's skid marks. The tyres on our truck were less than three months old, and had really gripped the road, but they could not have passed underneath the plantain laden steel lattice. Wondering who may have put this object on top of his skid marks, I imagined the scene again and again. Bemused, I moved over to the metal frame and plantains, where it had its own skid marks, of bolts wearing against tarmac. Aligning myself with a projected trajectory, I looked again, with the eyes of an investigator.

It had come from the tro-tro. It was the roof rack of the tro-tro, having sheared its bolts in the impact and been thrown clear, overhead and behind our truck. Imagining the impact, the sound, the flying roof rack, the sudden stalling of two diesel engines, as their engine loads increased, crankcases cracking under the impact, my mind completed the scenario. My blood was boiling, my whole body felt on fire. The tro-tro must have been going fast, very fast, when it hit. It must have been on my son's side of the road. Matt had applied his brakes, but he had no avoidance options. If he had veered to the right he would have gone into a concrete post, or down into a water filled culvert and drowned. He could not veer to the left for fear of another vehicle coming head on. The heat in my body turned into pure anger. I re-paced the skid marks back to the truck, and then established that the truck had been pushed back five meters after initial impact. The images and statistics I was establishing stamped themselves indelibly in my memory. The moment of impact created and replayed in my mind's eye, as it happened, in slow motion.

I then looked for the skid marks from the tro-tro. Standing behind the minin-bus I looked up the road searching for skid marks. Looking more closely, I could just discern nine meters of tyre marks, from the front nearside tyre only. The skid mark started just before the white line, on his side of the road, and then carried across the line to the oncoming traffic, and on to the impact point with my son. I relived the impact for Matt, hearing the steel crumple, and the screams of the passengers in the tro-tro. It must have been horrific for all concerned. The tro-tro had veered into his side, possibly because the driver fell asleep.

I lifted Matt's phone that had been hanging in my hand and checked for text messages, they were all from me. Checking for dialled numbers, I rang the last number dialled, and got one of his friends.

"When did you last see Matt?" I blurted into the battered handset.

"Last night," came the just woken up sounding reply.

"What time did he leave you?" I interrogated.

"About eleven or eleven thirty, I think," wobbled the out-of-hibernation voice.

Knowing that Matt had not left Tema before three am, I calculated that he had the opportunity to rest for about three hours, before heading up. I began to form a picture of, what was probably, the last hours of my son's life, before this stupid impact took him away. I tried to look for more inspiration from the phone, but the battery died. I slid the dark blue phone into my pocket. My last memento of him, secured close to me.

"Aviate, Navigate, Communicate," I whispered to myself. I needed to communicate with my wife. I did not want her to know too much, until I knew for sure the situation. I also needed her to remain near a phone so that I could speak to her. It was still early in the UK, where she was staying with friends. Interestingly, the couple she was staying with, had been in a road traffic accident near Krobo Mountain, when they lived in Ghana, just couple of years before. Their accident, likewise, involved a collision with a tro-tro travelling too fast on their side of the road.

It took several attempts to get a call through, and the line was bad. I was short on credit, and anxious to get the message across, "There has been accident. Matt has been injured and may be dead. Please be with my wife when I call in later, when I know more." It was short and to the point and I do not recall if anything was said back. If it was, I was not listening, for nothing said could help me at that point.

Fixating on the blood, spatters and pools, my heart sunk to a new depth, and ached as if it was about to give up beating. Much of the blood was on the front part of the bonnet of our truck. It must have come from the front two passengers in the front row of the tro-tro. I found positive thoughts. My son could be alive. Perhaps he was thrown clear and is fine. I turned to a man who had been watching me all of this time. He appeared confused that the father of a crash victim would be walking out skid marks and looking at the accident scene from every angle, rather than just standing and waiting for the inevitable, unavoidable news.

I locked a gaze on him, and spoke with a monotone, fact demanding voice. "Tell me, is my son dead?" I must have had eyes the size of saucers when I asked.

"No, no, no-oo. He walked away, he, he, he is fine, he is fine-oo," he lied. I knew he was lying. My potential jubilation thrown away as quickly as it blossomed.

A police car arrived, four officers exiting the vehicle. They all knew me from my recent visit to the station. I blurted out my statement. "There has been an accident. Matt has thirty-five metres of skid marks, all on his carriageway. The tro-tro has nine metres, off of the front right wheel. The tro-tro roof-rack sheared its bolts in the impact, and has been thrown behind the truck. Nobody knows where the victims are." It was as summarised as it could be, as I threw my hands left and right gesticulating at the incident. "It was all on MATT'S side of the road," I added for emphasis. My vision and mind were now fully functional, and I was back in full flow. I had assessed the scene, briefed the police and now needed to find my son, or at least his body.

"They took everybody to Akuse hospital..." a policeman started to tell me. I didn't hear the rest. I was in my car and motoring towards the hospital, with tears streaming down my cheeks.

I had no notion of speed limits, and pushed the car as fast as it would go. The speedometer needle rotated to hit new highs, and then I imagined the accident again. I realised that I could be about to cause another accident, and that my son was probably dead anyway. I prayed for strength to cope, slowing down to a reasonable, albeit fast, pace. With tears blurring my vision as I passed the North side of the mountain, I knew that I was not fit to drive at that point.

Over and over again I sang a hymn, out loud. My mind overlaid the words with images of my son's life. How would I tell my wife that our son had died on my watch? I tried a few imagined conversations, and stopped, unable to

Wonderful Adversity: Into Africa

cope with the idea. Practicalities, emotions, driving the car and remembering to breathe, all concocted in a mass of pure distress, overlaid with a strange feeling of peace, as I grasped at the concept of their being a purpose to this event. I had to go on, it was not possible to suspend things anymore, it was part of my lot. In that I took some strength, as I approached the Akuse hospital.

Pulling into the hospital car park, or gravel patch with a tree in the middle, I slowed to navigate a crowd. As I stopped the car, facing the barracks like building called the 'men's ward', I shook. In front, I saw bodies laid out waiting to be taken to the mortuary. Simply laid on the ground. Covered, or rather almost covered, by pieces of multi-coloured printed cloth. Blood oozed out and across the entrance area. Six bodies lay there. Motionless. Lifeless. One of them could be my son, or he could be in the mortuary already. Scrutinizing the scene, I got out of the car. My head was now silent, my senses anesthetised through overuse. Reality dawned on me. I would have to deal with a new situation, one that I had never contemplated. I looked at the corpses in the dirt ahead of me, trying to use an imaginary zoom facility in my vision. Each of the bodies on the ground had the top of their heads visible. I analysed each head in turn, the first one had black, fuzzy hair, that of an African. As did the second, the third, fourth and fifth. I dared not look at the sixth head, but had to. Dragging my eyes to the last head, I felt relief. It was not Matt's head. That relief was followed in less than a second by guilt. Guilt at feeling relieved that the dead body was not that of my son. I felt callous at being thankful that a dead person was not mine. It was still somebody's loved one, and I felt for them all.

A crowd blocked the entrance to the ward, retarding my progress. As I pushed through, I hoped that, somehow, my son could still be alive. Perhaps in a coma? Perhaps he would stay alive long enough for me to say goodbye. I might get to tell him I love him one more time. To tell him how proud I am of him. To see him alive even for a second would be a bonus amongst the torrent of emotion that burst through me at that time.

Kofi was in the crowd. He slid up to me and said "Sorry," but I ignored him.

As I entered the first section of the ward, it looked like a scene from a civil war. People were in beds and on the ground. People were everywhere. Black people. I was looking for my little white boy. The same white boy who I had built Lego aeroplanes and towers with, the white boy who had flown with me, helped me, frustrated me, hugged me, sat on my knee and had now grown into a young man with an incredible future. I needed to find the young man who had told me "Don't worry Dad. We can fix it," but I could not see him.

Pushing my way through the stench of flesh, blood and sweat, I turned to my right and looked into the far corner. There I saw two nurses attending a white body, half propped up in bed, covered in blood, cuts and grazes. I focused harder. It was Matt.

He tried to raise his left arm, but the forearm folded in two, and it fell back to the off-white sheet on the bed. Using every bit of strength he had left, he semi-raised his battered right arm, half-waving at me and whispered "Hi Dad, sorry about the truck."

Now I was looking at my son, who clearly needed fixing, and all he could say was "Hi Dad, sorry about the truck." I laughed, the nervous laugh that we make when relieved, but still scared. Approaching the bed, I looked at the nurse working on him. She gave me a quick summary of the situation, as she saw it.

"He was laid out to go to the mortuary, but then I heard him make a noise and brought him here," she explained. "The hospital has not got many sutures and we are rationing them."

I looked at his laceration and bruise covered face, and let my gaze drop towards his naked, similarly decorated torso. As I continued looking downwards, I noted that they had cut away his trousers, finding myself looking at a large piece of bone sticking out of his left thigh. The femur had shattered, and liberated itself from the confines of flesh. The gash was bleeding profusely and marrow oozed out of the smashed bone. I looked further down at his feet, or where they should be, but I could not see feet. Instead, there were two balls of swollen flesh, one twisted around so badly it looked like it would pop off.

I needed to get better control of myself and the situation. I needed more information, and for that I must call upon my years in hospital as a young man. Patient assessment 101.

Head: covered in lacerations and bruises. Eyes clear, and functioning. Nose, not broken. Possible concussion, unlikely brain damage. Speaking, albeit weakly.

Torso: Major bruise on chest in the shape of a steering wheel. Possibly broken ribs and severe internal injuries. General cuts and bruises. Possible spinal damage. Possible internal organ damage.

Arms: Left broken ulna and radius. Right cuts and bruises.

Legs: Left femur complex fracture, possibly needing amputation. Right leg, possible fracture.

Feet and ankles: Damaged beyond recognition.

It was a horrific scene, and he needed x-rays and probably surgery, at least to stabilise him, if not carry out amputations. But none of this could be done here in a hundred-year-old village hospital, with just one doctor and no surgeons.

I reassured Matt that I loved him and would fix him, but I am not sure he was listening. His breathing was shallow, he had lost a lot of blood, and was generally in a very bad way. He closed his eyes, which allowed me to lose my smile. I looked at Matt, draped on the bed, his life balanced more precariously than Damocles famous sword. I was time to call the Wing

Wonderful Adversity: Into Africa

Commander, from my time of flying out of Accra. Stepping out of the ward to get a better signal, I made the desperate call.

"WingCo, there has been an accident. Matt is badly injured and I don't know where to take him," I babbled.

"You are broken. You are broken. Say again. Say again," came the response from the respected aviator.

I repeated and responded to a round of questions only to be told. "Give me five minutes and I will call back," just as the line cut.

I looked at the growing crowd in front of the men's ward. Some faces that I recognised, so many that I knew not. Everybody was waiting to know the outcomes of an accident, their loved ones, friends, colleagues. Kofi same up to me and said "Sorry," again.

"Thank you Kofi," I offered, trying not to get into conversation.

"It was on the radio," he whispered, "it was on the radio. I am sorry."

"What was on the radio?" I asked, confused.

"The white man is dead. He died in the accident. Was he your brother?" a confused Kofi tried to express.

Apparently, the local radio had broadcast a story about the accident, indicating that a white man, driving a white pick-up, had died. It was the story of the morning, but they had not heard that the lovely young white man, my son, was not dead after all. He was picked up from the mortuary line, and was now waiting for me to fix him. I thanked Kofi, correcting his story as swiftly as I could.

As I turned to re-enter the ward, a large chocolate-brown hand landed on my shoulder with a thud. "I just heard about your son," came the gentle and measured, almost metronome like words from the Police Commander, "I came as soon as I could. There have been two nasty accidents this morning already, and I am sorry to hear about your son," he completed his passage of sympathies.

I am not sure if he had heard that he was dead or alive and injured, but that mattered not, and so I responded "I am going to see him now. Please come with me." It did not convey the actual state of affairs, but the Commander followed me into the ward all the same.

Matt was looking more and more pale, the fluids in his frail frame leaking away, stealing his already pale tones towards total monochrome. Matt was in and out of coherence, but clearly trying to win the battle his body was in.

The commander asked Matt some questions and made some notes. The Commander's large brown eyes widely taking in every word along with descriptions of the morning's disaster. He wanted to place his hand on Matt and reached out, seeing that there was nowhere safe to place the gesture, turned and slapped me on the side of my arm. I could see that his eyes were watery, and yet this was an everyday scene for a policeman in rural Africa. A place where accidents, amputations and death appear to be as common as breathing in Europe or the States. The commander moved amongst the other patients, along with his sergeant, who had joined his side during our conversations.

Matt had stopped talking, his consciousness no longer with us. His eyes seemed to be sinking into his skull, veiled thinly by near transparent eyelids. The nurse looked at me. Her mouth opened but no words emerged, so she closed her mouth again and busied herself. It was clear that he would die if I could not find a solution.

Needing an answer from WingCo, I slipped back to the fresh air, and waited for a call from my only hope for a solution. Whilst I waited the only hospital doctor came over to me.

"I am so sorry," he started as he looked down at my shoes, "I really don't know what to do. I have never seen somebody... with so many injuries... still alive."

Before I could respond, my awaited call came in. That momentary vibration of a mobile phone before it rings, was enough for me to eject the phone from my pocket directly to my ear, pressing the answer key, as I did so.

"You must go immediately to 37 Military Hospital in Accra. I will be there," ordered WingCo.

I needed to snap into action, for this was truly a situation of life and death, with every action carrying so much significance towards the outcome of the battle we were in.

Looking at the doctor, my mind entered into double turbo charged overdrive. "We need to splint Matt's legs, and get him in my car," I semi ordered the medical professional. "We need to get him on a drip too. We will need a spare drip bag also."

Almost relieved at the passing of the baton of care, the doctor ran into the ward. Since there were no ambulances to move any patients, I would have to use the car. I needed to work out how to transport a close to death, multiple injury, 'flat pack' patient in a relatively small vehicle. I needed a near flat position for him, and the only way was to break the seats. I simply grabbed the seat back of the rear seat and pulled. There was a crack, and the sound of cloth tearing as the steel mechanism bent. Welds yielded and the seat literally fell prostrate into the rear baggage area. Moving around to the front seat it would not lay back enough. Placing my knee near the headrest, I heaved like a wrestler trying to floor my challenger. There was less of a crack, more of a creak and the seat obliged. We had a make-shift ambulance. Along the way I must have caught some electronic control module, because now the rear doors would no longer unlock.

Back on the ward, a drip, with a bag of electrolyte, was being attached to his unbroken right arm. Cardboard was the only splint material available, and so he was wrapped in corrugated cardboard, enough to make him stable for the ride to the city.

My heart was beating faster than I thought possible, and Matt's in-and-

Wonderful Adversity: Into Africa

out of coherence body was now approaching the car. Knowing that the rear doors would not open, we tried to enter from the rear hatch door. Frustratingly, the rear hatch also failed to open. My blood pressure increased proportionately to the blood pressure drop in my son. Opening the front door as wide as possible, we shoe-horned his broken body aboard. I think that the pain was already so intense that Matt had subconsciously blown a fuse on his pain reception areas. His eyelids shuttered open for a second revealing his pale blue eyes. His eyes would normally have had all the girls swooning, but not there, not then. I jumped into the driving seat, and started the engine.

The front passenger door was still open, and a nurse was holding an IV bag above the broken legs alongside me, trying to get my attention. Frantically, I sought a place to hang it, without success. I turned my head to the crowd pressing in on the vehicle and saw Kofi, his shocked face distorted as it pressed against the glass.

"Kofi, you are coming with me," I barked, lowering the rear electric window behind me. Without a word, he simply slid into the car and sat, patiently, as if he had always been prepared to take his place next to Matt's face, holding the drip bag. Shouting for a clear way for the car, the crowd parted and we embarked on a high speed transit to Accra.

I did not stop for red lights, toll booths or any of the policemen who tried to stop my rapid progress. Kofi briefed me on what he had discovered outside the hospital. It did appear that the tro-tro driver had fallen asleep, and that Matt was considered dead at the scene. He explained how other passengers had seen Matt thrown in the back of the double-cab pick-up, beneath the other dead bodies. It made me want to vomit, but I had to remain focused and drive to the hospital.

Arriving at 37 Hospital, WingCo was waiting on the pavement with a medical team and a stretcher. Patient transfer was done swiftly and after a brief admission he was sent for x-rays.

My visual diagnosis was only a start on the reality of his injuries. Both feet and ankles had multiple breaks, and there were a number of breaks around his knees. Fortunately, no ribs or vertebrae were broken, which boded well. As I got my hopes up, the resident orthopaedic surgeon came up to me.

"Well, he will live. We are putting him on fluids, painkillers and the whole nine yards," he smiled, as only surgeons can when talking about a patient who is badly damaged.

"And his arm and legs?" I asked, wanting something positive.

"Well, this is Africa, and we do not have any implants, so we can consider amputation of his left leg. We should be able to save the right one, but I am not sure about his left arm," his prognosis was flowing, but not encouraging.

"What if we can get the implants?" I queried, shaking and feeling incredibly unwell.

"It will take time, and we do not have time," and he placed his hand on my quivering arm.

"What if I can get him out of the country?" I proposed, without any knowledge of how I could make that happen.

After a pensive moment, with his eyes wandering upwards, he dropped "If you can get him to UK, he will have a much better chance."

"OK, so, please stabilise him. I will find a way to get him to the UK," my proposal was bold, for we had no insurance, and it was already Saturday afternoon. There was no option to be creative.

Air hugging matt, so as not to hurt him, I left him to go to surgery, whilst I called his mother to update her, with a far more positive story than was real. Then I called and drove to every airline office I could think of. Most were closed for the weekend, but a few were open. None would consider carrying him.

In desperation, I drove to the home of the Operations Manager for a start-up international airline, flying from Accra, Ghana to Gatwick, UK. We had both been to a few social events at the same time, and he was very supportive of our nascent flying school. When he invited me in, he had no idea of the story I had, nor of my request. As he listened, he gasped with horror and disbelief, finally, I asked for his help.

"Well, there is not much we can do," he explained with a grim look on his face. "Most airlines do not like carrying stretcher cases, or if they do, you have to plan in advance and book four seats. Our airline cannot carry a stretcher case, under any circumstances."

It was not the news I was looking for. All the same, he called as many of his friends as he could in the usual major airlines, all of whom declined to carry a passenger with so many injuries.

By early evening, he was left with only one option. "Do you think you can get him to fly on a business class seat?"

"Umm, probably..." I hoped, rather than presumed.

"OK, look, we cannot get him on a flight tonight. But, if we can book him on our flight tomorrow night, and get him into the last row of business class, we should be able to carry him," it was a brilliant offer. "But, remember, we wet lease our Boeing 757 from an American company, and if they consider him a risk, he will not be allowed to fly."

It was a gamble worth taking. "Do it," I stated flatly.

"No, I cannot book him on the flight. I cannot be seen to be supporting this move. You need to book him via an agent."

"HOW.?" I jumped back at him, aware that all the travel agents had closed for the weekend.

"Let's make a few more calls," he consoled. Nonetheless, twenty calls later no agent could be found to make a booking.

"Can't we hack a computer system or something?" was my only proposal, made half out of desperation, half in jest.

"YEEESSSS," he bounced, and together we hacked into the online booking system of a well-known travel agent. It was not totally illegal, well perhaps.

Wonderful Adversity: Into Africa

We found a way to login, book the tickets in business class, for both Matt and me, and also made the credit card payment. Nobody lost out, and now Matt stood a chance of keeping his limbs.

Back at the hospital, Matt was regaining consciousness from the stabilisation surgery. Whilst he was anesthetised, they had set his right leg and left arm in plaster. His left leg was now about eight inches shorter than his right, as the muscles had tensed, without bone to prevent the thigh collapsing. He was heavily sedated, but conscious that I was there.

"Don't worry son," I offered, "we can fix you." It was a bluff, for I really did not know how.

The surgeon explained that the hospital had one external brace, to secure the compound fracture in his leg, which would be lent to us for travel. Unfortunately, it was awaiting collection from another hospital, about three hours' drive away. A soldier had been ordered to collect it the next morning, ready for our flight on the Sunday evening.

Making sure my broken son was as comfortable as possible, I drove back home. It was not pleasant; for it was a repeat drive of that which Matt had done just twenty-four hours earlier. I was exhausted, fighting to keep my eyes open. I could not take the luxury of sleep, for I had to get passports and other documents sorted, as well as contact clients to explain why I had not flown to Takoradi ready for the survey.

As I drove past the accident site, where the tro-tro and truck had been towed away, the road still bore the scars of the accident. Six people had died that morning, and many more injured. Matt missed increasing the body count through the intervention of a large team.

At the house, I did not sleep. By dawn I was back on the road, with bags, passports and essential supplies for travel. My world was shattered, and I failed to see clearly through the multi-fractured view presented to me. Whatever happened, I had to remain strong for Matt, and so I garnered what I had left of myself, and pressed on.

At the hospital, the patient was still rough. Pale, medicated beyond coherence, but alive. I called his mum and explained a bit more. Fortunately, the couple she was staying with had good contacts at Gatwick, and organised an ambulance to meet us at the aircraft.

As the day flew past, I sat with Matt. Friends came to see him. All cried. All offered a hug and words of comfort and kindness. Even Preacher came by, and made me smile by reminding me of the 'Get me an African' story. Despite the pleasant distractions, my mind was fixed on the non-arrival of the external brace for my boy's leg.

It was nearly time to head to the airport, and the military ambulance was waiting, doors open, to carry him there. Still, the external brace had not arrived. I was trying to work out how to get Matt through immigration and customs, wondering if I was about to embark on a mission that might kill my only son. It was all new territory for me.

Hearing panting accompanied by the rapid fall of running feet, I peered into the darkness. "I have it, Sir," a young soldier called, carrying the brace. Relief ran through me, as refreshing as cold drink in the desert. We headed to the ward, and asked the medical team to fit the brace. Matt was in and out of awareness, but more interactive than earlier. It gave me hope.

"It is very late," explained the surgeon, "and we do not have time to administer a suitable aesthetic for him."

"Just... do... it..." Matt weakly demanded, before closing his eyes.

Two nurses held his upper body, and the surgeon took hold of his twisted leg. I could not watch, and ran out of the ward. A coward, seeking self-preservation, waiting outside in the sticky evening air. The screams of pain reached every part of the extensive hospital, each one bursting the dams of held back tears in my eyes. I could not do anything be being inside, and would probably have wanted to hit whoever was hurting him. WingCo came alongside me, offering words of comfort, but I was not listening. If there was a world record for volume of tears shed in ten minutes, I would have won it there and then.

A stretcher came out of the ward, and was loaded into the ambulance. Matt was unconscious. The surgeon came up to me, and slipped two ampoules of pethidine with two syringes into my top pocket. "Leave them there, even going through security," he ordered as he handed me a letter to show if required. The letter intimated that I was a medical professional, authorised by the hospital to accompany the patient, administering doses of pethidine as required.

"You do know how to give injections, don't you?" he quizzed. I only nodded, remembering the many injections I had given oranges and my friend in hospital, years ago.

The ambulance drove to the airport, and parked in front of the airliners nose wheel. I was incredulous. "What about immigration and customs?" I asked, only to be told that I would do that later. We carried Matt up the stairs onto the airliner. The crew were aboard, but no passengers. Being an American aircraft, the Air Marshall was also sitting aboard, on the row opposite our seats.

"Welcome aboard," the blonde lady with captain's braid on her shoulders, smiled. "We are aware of your situation, and we all know the risks. Now, get him settled and do the formalities."

Laying the business seat as far back as possible, the semi-conscious, clearly not fit to travel, boy was strapped in, and covered with airline blankets to hide all but his face. I was then sent to check in.

Checking in without a passenger is impossible, or so I thought. It was time to be creative. "Good evening," I greeted the check-in clerk, dropping two passports and e-ticket details in front of her.

"Where is the other passenger?" she asked. I had hoped she would not notice, but clearly she had.

Wonderful Adversity: Into Africa

"My son is in a wheelchair, and cannot make it to the desk with all these people," I semi-bluffed, waving my hand towards the rear of the crowd in the check-in hall.

"OK," she smiled, returning the passports and boarding passes.

With one check down and several more to go, I could only think of Matt abandoned aboard an aircraft on the apron. The risk of him dying on the flight was higher than anybody wanted to consider, but it was better than the risk of keeping him in country.

Passport control came next. Offering both passports, to make sure that they got stamped, I explained that Matt was injured and unable to make it up the stairs to the check point. They argued a bit about it, but I made it clear that he was travelling with me, and that the airline had made alternative arrangements to board him. A supervisor was called.

"You must bring the passenger here," a brusque chap in a dark green uniform ordered.

"I certainly would, if I could," I offered, "but I am sure you do not want to take the risk of a person in a wheelchair having another accident on the stairs?"

"Use the lift," he pounced, leaving me flummoxed.

Thinking for a hot moment, I countered "Have you used it today? It is out of order." It was another ruse, but probably accurate.

"Not again," he sighed, relinquishing the demand, and ordering the officer to stamp both passports for me.

Security checks should be simple, for they did not count passengers. Realising that I still had two ampoules and syringes in my top pocket, a felt a little panic, but remained calm. Amazingly, they missed the precious items in my pocket, letting me through unhindered. The departure lounge would be my final barrier.

"Boarding passes," came the request, with an outstretched hand.

"Here," I offered both, with a smile, but it did not work.

"Where is the other passenger?" she quizzed.

Not sure of the best course of action, I tried honesty. It had got me into trouble, and out of it, in the past. This seemed like the make or break moment.

"My son is already aboard," I started, trying not sound too concerned, "he was in an accident, and is with the captain already." I stood looking straight into her eyes, wondering if she would call security.

"Come with me," she ordered and led the way to the front of the departure lounge.

I had no idea what was happening, just following my gut and hoping to save the life and limbs of my lad. As we reached the front, she picked up a hand-held microphone and spoke into it.

"Ladies and gentlemen, this is flight number 035 to London Gatwick. Immediate boarding for business class, and those with children," and she opened the door, pushing me towards the stairs.

I was first on the transfer bus, and then first up the steps onto the aircraft, taking my seat next to my precious patient. The plane filled rapidly, and I relaxed, believing that we were set to leave Ghana, heading to first world medical facilities.

"Sir," came the voice from behind me in the isle. A large man wearing a polyester blue suit was looking at a checklist, and speaking to me, without making eye contact.

"Yes?" I quizzed.

"Please move the seat to the upright position," he asked me to do the impossible for Matt, for he did not bend in the middle with the transport brace fitted.

"I am sorry, but my son is not well, and needs to be flat as possible," I answered, factually.

"He doesn't look well," he noted, adding, "have a good flight."

An hour into the flight, Matt started to scream. He was having a nightmare. Not a good thing on a packed night flight. I shook him, gently, trying not to add to his pain.

"I... don't... feel... good," his feeble voiced staccato-ed the obvious.

"Don't worry, I will get you something for the pain," I promised and moved towards the galley. The purser was chatting to another member of cabin crew. I interrupted, abruptly.

"Sir, can I talk to you for a moment?"

"Sure," he replied with a quizzical look on his face.

"Privately," I added.

Uncomfortably, he asked the other crew member to check on the passengers, and turned to face me. I asked for the curtains to be pulled. Begrudgingly, he obliged, not expecting me to be pulling syringes and ampoules from my shirt pocket.

"What are you doing?" he asked, reaching for the telephone handset next to him.

"I need to inject my son, he is in pain," I explained

"Are you a doctor?" he quizzed, providing the lead-in to show my letter from the surgeon. Reading it, he nodded, and then complained. "You cannot inject him without a medical certificate, Sir."

By this time I had loaded the syringe, and covered the needle. "I am going to inject my son, you can check with the captain."

Replacing the handset, but keeping a safe distance from me, the purser pulled back the curtain, and allowed me back to my seat. Sliding the syringe deep into my hand, to disguise it from other passengers, I noticed the air-marshal looking at me from the corner of his eye. I smiled, pretending nothing untoward was happening.

Matt was in a bad way, writhing in his seat, trying to find the one thing he would not find for months, comfort. I smiled at him, pulling the blanket from his arm, and plunging the needle into his muscle. The pain was nothing compared to that of the rest of his body, so he did not even flinch as I slid the chemical load home and withdrew the needle. Minutes later, he returned to the land of sleep.

To my right, the air-marshal was watching me, full face on. I smiled, and tried to make feel more comfortable about our presence. For the rest of the flight he watched me like a hawk, and I simply tried to look after the damaged chap next to me.

After landing, guided by the captain, we stayed on the plane. The rest of the passengers disembarked and a stretcher was brought on board by two young men from Saint John's ambulance. Matt opened his eyes, smiled, and closed them again, in relief.

Matt's mum was waiting in the ambulance, and once Matt and I had been loaded into the mobile medical facility, we were simply told to wait. The diesel engine of the ambulance gave a gentle roar, but we could not move off until formalities had been complied with. A ground official took our passports, returning them after a few minutes. The two's and blues were lit up, and we sped to the hospital.

Arriving on the orthopaedics ward, I handed over the x-rays, briefing staff about Matt's injuries. All listened intently. A doctor sympathetically asked me "What about HIV/AIDS?"

I had not thought about this, but now that it had been raised, I had to confront a hidden worry. I explained how the first folks on the scene of the accident had thought he was dead, and loaded him into the back of truck, under other dead bodies. It was important to note that we lived in a high HIV/AIDS area.

I had forgotten how white people's faces drain so quickly when they hear shocking news, but was reminded by the faces that changed around me.

"We will put him on HIV post-exposure prophylaxis," the doctor offered, "no matter the risk, it is only prudent." As if there could be any more bombshells to be thrown at my son.

The rest of the Monday was spent with tests, and preparation for surgery. On the Tuesday four surgeons worked for over eight hours to save his limbs. Steel pins, plates and sutures galore were showered onto his weakened body.

Wednesday came and went. Matt stayed sleeping, without any perceivable pain, thanks to the wonders of modern analgesia. By Thursday, he opened his eyes and apologised for the truck, once again. It made us all smile, the first smile in a few days.

"Matt, you do not need to go back to Ghana," I whispered to him, out of earshot of all others.

"But Dad, I want to go back," his tone full of sincerity. "Dad, you saved me." His eyes, clearer and bluer than ever, pierced my heart, and filled me with a pride that cannot be bought.

Leaning his bandaged head towards me he continued, "Dad, you know you tried to get the NGO's to use planes," I nodded. "Well, why don't we start our own NGO?"

It was not a new thought, but it was poignant. Matt shared how he had felt first-hand the lack of medical support and supplies to the rural areas, and spoke of the need to help those very communities with more than just money. It was a big idea, but it was not the time.

Matt gained strength from day to day. The worst part of it all was the HIV prophylaxis, for it made him feel incredibly sick. Nausea and diarrhoea bit him with unrelenting teeth. It would have been tough enough if he was mobile, but much more challenging being bed ridden, recovering from major surgery, broken legs and a broken arm. Fortunately, the hospital staff were amazing, and without exception, every nurse, doctor and care assistant treated him as if he were their own son.

Happy that he was on the road to recovery, and in good hands, I returned to Ghana, leaving his mum to watch over him. It was a tough decision, but a necessary one. I could do no more, and I would phone regularly to check on progress.

STAY OR GO?

On the plane back to Ghana, I slept the sleep of a thousand men. I had not realised how tired I was, but I also knew that I had to keep busy. Matt's life was changed forever, but he did still have life. But it was not only Matt that had changed in this situation. My life had changed, and I had changed, over the past few weeks. My view of the world had moved in a series of quantum leaps, from businessman to peace negotiator; flying instructor to armed protector of an airfield; engineer to life and limb saver; road user to high speed ambulance driver; father to medical assistant. There was no doubt that my many adverse situations, from childhood into manhood, had been brought together for a purpose. They had enabled Matt and me to survive the Tsunami of events, which had overrun our lives uncontrollably.

I was woken by the cabin lights and the announcement that we had commenced our descent to land in Accra. In less than an hour I would be back in the country that nearly stole my Matt's life. I cried, quietly, trying to hide my tears from those around me. There is no worse place to be upset than on an airliner. In a bid to isolate myself, I pushed my face against the window, faking looking out at the scattered lights below. They were only scattered because so many communities had never known electricity, whilst many others were experiencing yet another power outage.

My heart was confused, but my mind was busy joining the dots, and making sense of the mass of emotion streaming through every cell in my body. From learning to inject oranges, through the treatment received and practices observed on an orthopaedic ward, my life seemed to have been a training ground for that one, crazy, sixty-hour period of my life. I thought back on all of the apparently negative moments and adversity I had been 'privileged' to experience first-hand, and realised that they had all been a training ground to save my only son.

Much as I had realised the importance of taking positives out of the negatives in my younger days, recent events in Ghana had dragged me down, and I must admit I had been feeling pretty challenged by the death threats, wanton vandalism of projects, staffing issues and more. There was now a change in my whole mind-set, and my faith.

I thought back to my meetings with the NGOs and trying to get them to embrace aviation as a tool, in order to reach out to remote areas of the country. Areas where young people were dying from lack of sutures and access to medical care. I felt guilty at having had the resources of a car, and a knowledge of the basics of healthcare, to be able to save my own son's life. Meanwhile, people died daily for lack of basic infrastructure.

Perhaps it was time to pack up and leave Ghana. To be honest, I had taken so much crap over the past few years, and it had so very nearly cost me the life of my son. It had cost me a lot of sleepless nights, and put my own life on the line. My own life had no value, but that of my son... that was something I could not play with.

I had two major events to deal with on landing. The security situation at the airfield, and the coconut counting flight. I had to focus on what I could do, providing stability until Matt recovered.

The wheels skimmed the hot tarmac, with the traditional squeak that announces a return to the surface of the planet. I took a deep breath and pulled my damp face away from the window, pushing my sleeve across my eyes in an attempt to look as if I had just woken up.

I had to accept that I was not the same person who had left Ghana a week before. Far from it. I was different, but I could not pinpoint how, even though I knew why. Passing through the immigration and customs desks, numbness in my mind allowed me to skim over the usual difficulties. Nothing could be harder than my past week.

Gitanes was at the meet and greet station, but we had little to talk about. We had little in common any more, but I could not discern what or why. He dropped me at my car. I drove home, along that same treacherous road, and past the still blood stained portion of tarmac.

DECISION TIME

I spent a long time in bed, but the sleep was not sound. Dreams and visions filled my head. I lay with the gun beside me. It would not go back in the cabinet, for I was now a warrior, not a businessman.

Hearing a commotion outside the house, I jumped to my feet, gun in hand, as I opened the front door. A group of about twenty, traditionally dressed men, stood in a loose pack, with Nene at the front.

"Captain Yaw," Nene began, his wispy frame shaking a little at the sight of a gun in my hand. "Welcome back to Ghana, we have come to greet you."

For the next hour we sat outside, on benches, as they pleaded with me to remain in Ghana. I had not spoken of my nagging thoughts about leaving, but they had past experiences to share with me.

"We have seen this before. Many white-men come to Ghana, like you. But when there is an accident or threat to their lives, they go," he explained.

Silently, I calculated what he had said. My family had gone through untold challenges to get to where we were, and in the days before evacuating Matt, I had been threatened by a mob, called out in the night over vandalism to my property and dealt with every father's worst nightmare. If others had left over less, why shouldn't I? The silence was obviously fermenting, and little bubbles of anxiety could be sensed amongst the committee before me.

"Nene, I thank you, and your people, for coming here this morning," I commenced my departure speech. "You have been good to me, as have many of your people. However, you must understand that my son nearly died last week, through your lack of infrastructure, in your country. It has not been easy..." my words trailed as salty drops of anguish dripped down my cheeks, making genuine puddles on the ground.

I sensed the peoples concern, but I did not know what else to say. My few said words echoed around in my head "through your lack of infrastructure... through your lack of infrastructure... through your lack of infrastructure... through your lack of infrastructure..." and yet it was not the fault of these people sitting in front of me, but rather that of successive governments. Matt's words also rang through my head, "Why don't we start our own NGO?"

Much as I had changed, and deep down just wanted to pack up and out on the next flight, my mouth had other ideas. "Nene, I will not be chased away. The airfield, and everything about it, is the basis of a new infrastructure. My own son, who is recovering in hospital, and will be away for many months, wants to come back and to start an NGO to help with medical education..."

No matter how I felt, it was now outside of my control. Jubilation broke out, like an epidemic, in the committee before me. "Thank you, thank you. Thank you for staying with us. Thank you for helping us." It was heartfelt, and it touched the colder parts of my heart, warming them to the idea of making it work in Ghana.

With renewed energy, I visited the Police Commander, who hugged me as if I were his long lost brother. He reiterated that others had died, and that two passengers, with lesser injuries than Matt, had needed amputations after gangrene set in. I realised how lucky I was to have my little medical knowledge, and for the decisions made in the heat of the moment, along with the relatively positive outcome achieved. If I had been a local, I would be at a funeral for my own son by now. Internally I shook, reaching a new level of understanding of the life of the people in rural Africa.

Jones, the airfield policeman, had briefed the Commander on the events of the night before the accident, and action had been taken to ensure that Cattleman moved off site without delay. Commander shared with me how Cattleman had a record for stealing, and violence, and that the fence breaking and threat incidents gave him an opportunity to take action. In my head I heard Grandpa Potts, from the movie Chitty Chitty Bang Bang, singing "Up from the ashes of disaster grow the roses of success." I smiled, sensing that there was something wonderful still possible out of the mass of adversity around me.

It was strange being back home and on the airfield, alone. I lived for the evening calls to Matt and his mum, each day being punctuated with diverse thoughts from dark to super nova bright. One thing was clear in my mind; all of these things had not happened without a reason, and that reason was bigger than me and my family.

We decided together to create a small NGO, calling it Medicine on the Move, MOM for short, dedicated to promoting health matters in Ghana, it was big step, but we knew we could not do much with it until other matters had settled down.

FRESH FACE

The relationship between Gitanes and I was tense, to say the least. My focus had changed, but nobody, least of all me, could pinpoint where that focus was. We steered clear of each other, and each tried to do their job without interaction with the other. The strain was visible to the staff, and to clients, but everybody gave me a bit of space, presumably understanding the tension and stress in my life.

Leaving Gitanes running the flying school, I was relieved to fly Alpha-Alpha to Takoradi, ready to fly the overdue coconut runs. It was a positive distraction, but also a money earner, something that the company and I both needed. The flight along the coast, spotting the chain of old slave forts was thought provoking. Over the years the Gold Coast, now Ghana, had seen many changes. It was a diverse nation, spread across several climatic and vegetation zones, from coastal savannah, through rain forest to Guinea savannah including some pretty arid regions in the north.

With so many different tribes, languages and customs, Ghana was really a number of cultures, glued together by history. I looked at the many isolated and infrastructure deprived communities, many without any motor-able roads, most without power or water, realising that the need for light aviation was greater than even I had postulated.

I was well received at the Air Force base in Takoradi. The Base Commander allowed me to keep my plane in the military hangar. A crowd of young recruits gathered around, asking many questions. I felt comfortable sharing my limited aviation knowledge, but also became aware that I had something none of the Air Force team had. I knew what it was like to build and fly my own aircraft. They were in awe of the concept, asking if they could learn to build a plane too. Smiling, and with a new found energy, I realised that I had something important to share, even with those with more aviation access than me.

The plantation manager collected me and took me to his home. There he asked about Matt and the accident, his mouth and eyes wide open in disbelief of our misadventures. He shared stories of less extensive accidents taking the lives of locals, and expats, over the years. I realised how lucky I was, and made a note to never forget it.

The survey flights went well, each one finding new data and providing much needed insight to the LYD infestations, and how they might be spreading. It was amazing, operating at just five hundred feet above the tree tops, with a spotter from the plantation sitting next to me, making notes as we flew.

On the last day of the mission, my usual spotter was unable to make the flight. A young, fresh faced, plantation administrator had been 'volunteered' as a spotter, and was on the tyre of Alpha-Alpha, waiting for me.

"Gud mornin'," Fresh Face greeted me, "I go be your spotting dis day."

I knew that this was not a good start, but had little choice, if I wanted to get back to my home field at Kpong over the weekend. Briefing Fresh as best I could, with his limited grasp of English, I tried to explain the concept of flight, and what we were going to be doing.

Although English is the official language of Ghana, literacy is limited, and the use of the English language outside of the cities is often limited. Consequently, a good worker may not be great at the spoken English. This is fine when working amongst those who speak a common local language, but a challenge when asked to go on a spotting flight with a Brit, with just a basic of the local Twi/Fante, Ewe and Krobo languages.

After some limited exchanges, I accepted that I may be in for a more than exciting four hour, low level, flight. "Let's go," I announced, climbing into the left seat of the little plane. I heard a clip board hit the floor, and turned my head to the noise. A bemused Fresh stood at the side of the plane, his head slightly bent over to avoid the wing, both hands held up to chest level, palms open and fingers stretched.

"What happened?" I asked, completely at a loss as to the processes churning through the mind of Fresh.

"Master, you tell me to makes let's go. So I let's go," he explained in all sincerity.

I had made this mistake before, but never in such a strange scenario. I smiled knowingly. 'Let go' and 'let's go' sound very similar to a person challenged with the English languages idiosyncrasies. Fresh had assumed that he had touched or held something he should not have done, and when told 'Let's go' had interpreted as 'Let go of it'. Consequently, he dropped the clipboard, and raised his hands in about to be arrested mode, to show me that he had fully let go of anything in his hands. It was no different to my experiences in learning French, and not grasping the 'On y va' phrase.

"Ma damfo," I spoke in a conciliatory tone, "go pick your papers, and yen ko," I mixed my languages in a salad that might work. 'Ma damfo', meaning 'my friend' and 'yen ko' meaning 'let's go', in Twi, or at least I hoped so.

With Fresh seated and strapped in, I had to explain the need to keep the clipboard, with his spotting chart on his knee, clear of the controls. I felt confident that I had made myself clear, or if not, tried harder than the average person might have. With the heat of the day, and expected storms later, waiting for no man, it was time to depart.

No sooner had the engine fired than Fresh started to shake. I reassured him, by sharing simple facts about flying, whilst the engine warmed. I thought I saw his confidence grow, at least a little. Taxiing to the runway was going well, apart from the death grip Fresh had imposed on a part of the airframe that fell to hand. I directed him to hold on to his seatbelt, hoping that he would loosen up as the flight progressed. It was a lot to hope for.

Lined up, I warned him that the engine would make a lot more noise, and that we would leave the ground. Looking at his eyes, and feeling an additional vibration in the airframe from his uncontrollable shaking, I decided to try a proverb. African languages are rich in proverbs, and I had a couple that could be used in times like this. "Anoma entua, obua da," I spoke the words as clearly as I could over the intercom.

Fresh spun his face at me, smiled and yelled "YOU SPEAK PROVERBS." adding his congratulations with "AYEKOO," meaning 'well done'.

He had clearly understood my poorly spoken Twi, and that 'The bird that does not fly shall go to bed hungry', and it had raised his spirits to a point where I felt ready to declare departure.

Pushing the little red push-to-talk button, or PTT, I made my ready call. "Takoradi Tower, this is Niner Golf Zulu Alpha-Alpha, ready for departure."

"Alpha-Alpha, all operations at your discretion. Report ops normal at thirty minute intervals," the gentle voice of the Ghana Air Force controller released me from my earthly bonds.

As we accelerated, I was focused on the flying, as I was meant to be. We took off swiftly, climbing over the hot tarmac of the runway. Alpha-Alpha did her thing, and did it well. I was happy that we were on our way. Sadly, Fresh had not understood the need to keep his hands on his seatbelt, relocating his death grip onto the second control stick, on his side of the aircraft. As he did so, the whole aircraft reared upwards like an unbroken stallion, delivering a deadly situation into my lap. With all my force I could not prevent that stick coming right back against my belly. The engine was trying to overcome the need for air speed to generate lift from the wings, but the angle of attack was such that aerodynamic drag, assisted by gravity, was winning the battle. If I could not lower the nose, and fast, it was going to be a bad day.

The thought of a helpless Matt, lying in hospital, bleeding and needing medical supplies, flashed into my mind. I could be in the same situation or worse in the next few seconds. I had to grab that thought and jam it with full force into the back of my mind. Any distraction could be deadly for both Fresh and me. There is a good reason that pilots use the mantra 'a distracted pilot is a dead pilot'.

Letting go of the throttle, I placed one hand on each of the sticks, my right hand over that of Fresh's. I yelled "LET GO." and glanced at his face, eyes sealed like clams, face contorted into a thousand lines of sinew. "LET GO. LET GO. LET GO," it was all I could think to shout. After what seemed like a short lifetime, but in reality was just a few seconds, the plane's nose vibrated and fell earthwards, as we stalled, barely eighty feet off the surface.

Feeling the sudden negative g-force, Fresh relinquished his hold over our lives and the stick, screaming at the same time. It was just enough for me to ram the stick forward, and watch the whole windshield fill with a view of the surface. Airspeed in microlights is gained fast, and we just managed to recover before turning into a pile of wreckage, garnished with blood, on the surface. Regaining controlled flight, we passed low over the shrubs at the perimeter of the airport.

"Great show, Alpha-Alpha," it was the tower, thinking we had done the death plunge to show off.

Speaking as confidently as possible, under the circumstances, I offered "Thank you," adding, "next call thirty minutes." I hoped that the next call truly would be one of 'operations normal'.

I still had a hand on each stick, jamming my left knee against the throttle quadrant ensure full power. Fresh still had his eyes closed, and had developed at least one hydraulic leak. Tears had made their way past his apparently hermetically sealed eyelids, and his body from head to toe was soaked in at least sweat. He was not having a good day.

At one thousand three hundred feet, I levelled off, setting a course that would allow me to return to land back at Takoradi as quickly as possible.

"Fresh... Fresh... Fresh," I spoke comfortingly over the intercom, to no avail. "Madamfo, madamfo," I tried, getting a nod of the head. "Madamfo, we are safe."

"H... ha... have... we flown yet?" he stammered.

"We are flying, my friend. It is very beautiful," I hoped it would cheer him, and it did bring a semi-smile to his crumpled face. "But I am going back to land, so that you can get out," I proposed.

Opening his eyes, looking straight at my face he declared, "NO. I am enjoying it. It is my first time," but I was not convinced.

"Alpha-Alpha, downwind to land," I broadcast to the tower.

"Next call final, and please confirm ops normal," came the reply.

Fresh gained a new courage. "Do not land, I want to fly. I can fly. This is good," he protested between eyes open and closed moments. But by this time I was already late downwind, preparing to turn onto the base-leg of the circuit.

Still holding both sticks, and concerned about how to land without losing control to the death-grip maestro besides me, I had to make a decision,

I looked at Fresh, asking "Open your eyes, and tell me what you see?"

He opened his eyes artificially wide, and glanced around the cockpit, setting his gaze back on my face. "I see you," he declared.

"Good," it was not, but never mind, "now, look outside."

As he turned his look out of the window, something changed, as he declared "THAT IS MY HOUSE." Over the next fifteen seconds he called out "Church" "School" "Goat" "Cow" and several other declarations of visual identification. He was starting to get the hang of this flying lark.

Releasing the stick on his side, I adjusted power, continuing with my circuit to land. However, Fresh had not finished his torrent of observations. I asked him if he wanted to land, or if we should head out on the four-hour mission, and there was no doubt about it, he wanted to.

"Alpha-Alpha, low pass, and heading West," was the only declaration I needed to make to the tower, as we set out on our mission.

Fresh was settling in, and soon started spotting the LYD affected trees, making the necessary marks on his forms. I just had to fly at the right height, along a predetermined GPS track, making deviations only if additional outbreaks of LYD could be spotted.

Fresh was happy, and drying out. The joy of flight is not always evident, especially if the passenger has never been close to an aircraft before. We reached the most distant point of the required tracks, and headed back. Return flights are generally more relaxed than outgoing and spotting legs, and this was no exception. With about forty-minutes flight to go, I made my 'ops normal' call to the tower.

"Takoradi, this is Alpha-Alpha, operations normal, estimated time to run, forty minutes."

"Alpha-Alpha, copy that. Be aware of fast developing weather system due East of Takoradi. Next call field in sight."

"Copy your weather. Next call field in site," I closed the conversation, aware of how quickly weather can build in the area.

Fresh was busy looking out the open side of the aircraft, experimenting with putting his hand in the slipstream. "You are doing well. Ayekoo," I offered my most challenging passenger to date.

Closer to the airport, the sky darkened. We would land before the storm broke, but not with much time to spare. With no other airports within two hours flying distance, we had to make it before the promised tropical downpour.

Just as I was about to declare 'field in sight', the aircraft shook, and started to climb upwards at an alarming rate. The thick, darkening, overcast was hiding a cumulonimbus storm cloud, and we were caught in the up draught.

"Hold tight," I stated as calmly as possible to Fresh, pulling the power all the way back and pushing the nose towards the ground, wanting gravity to help us out of the developing situation. It must have reminded Fresh of the start of the flight, and he reached for his seatbelt, gripping it at waist level. Our rate of ascent dropped, even though we were still in a nose-down attitude.

Pellets of rain hit the windshield, as the air temperature plummeted. Goosebumps developed on my arms. This was not good.

Even though we were nose down, I added power, and turned the plane ninety degrees to the left. As we broke out of the ascending column of air, we were close to VNE (maximum speed before the wings consider a divorce from the fuselage). Now, our rate of descent needed to be addressed by reducing power whilst simultaneously, yet gently, very gently setting the nose of the aircraft back to a straight and level attitude with the stick.

We were really close to the airport, and would be on the ground in few minutes, before the next, much bigger cell, arrived. I felt relived, but not Fresh. He had brought his leg up, and was pushing it out of the open side of the aircraft. Just in time, I caught him trying to undo his seat belt, as he cried "I want to get out."

I was tired, and could do without any more drama for my day. I reached for his right hand, a moment too late to stop the seatbelt release, but in time to stop him removing the belt from his shoulder.

"Madamfo, you cannot get out," I tried to explain, "you will die."

"God will protect me," he explained, lacking my understanding of logic, "I want to get out NOW."

Unable to think of any counter argument to God's protection, I simply tightened my hold open his right hand ignoring his protestations.

Juggling power and stick, with one hand, I set the plane up to land a bit faster than usual, and roll long. Fortunately, the staff in the tower did not notice the leg sticking out the side of the plane as we landed. Once on the ground, Fresh relaxed and brought his leg back in, still holding my hand, now in a mutual grip of support.

"That was good," declared Fresh, to my utter amazement, and total confusion.

It had been an eventful flight, but it had ended successfully.

LOST WITHIN MY OWN MIND

I was dropped to the Airforce Base just before dawn. Working with the help of young recruit, Alpha-Alpha was inspected and fuelled. I was looking forward to the solo flight back to Kpong.

"Captain," asked my assistant, "why is the passenger seat so wet?"

"I was caught in the rain yesterday," I explained, accurately, but missing out a few details.

Taking off, and heading north-east, I felt much more relaxed. It was a glorious day, and I had chosen to route back over the forest, rather than take the coastal route. Both routes had their merits, although the inland route was often more challenging in relation to weather and terrain avoidance.

One of the best aspects of the inland route was the opportunity to see cocoa trees growing. Peering through breaks in the tree canopy, I could see large groups gathered around piles of yellow cocoa pods, splitting them and spilling the brown seeds out to dry on makeshift structures. I started to relax, smiling to myself as I remembered the hectic flight from just the day before. I realised that it couldn't be easy for the average person in Ghana to embrace the concept of flying. After all, the school system didn't prepare students for close contact with engineering concepts such as microlights.

My mind went to Matt, lying in a UK hospital, recovering slowing, thousands of miles away. I started to relive the accident, how he must have felt, the impact and the whole dramatic unravelling ball of events that came after. I reflected on each and every decision I had made, wondering if I could have done any better, or done anything in addition to change the outcome, perhaps making it more positive.

My eyes were wide open, but I was not seeing anything in front of me, my reflections had consumed my entire operational bandwidth. Somehow, deep inside my isolated state, I realised that I had lost contact with reality, and shook my head violently, in an attempt to bring back my immediate reality. I felt the headset on my head as it tried to liberate itself from my head shaking.

In an instant, I fell out of my daydream and into full consciousness. I was still flying, but I was not anywhere near where I had been. In front of me, the ridge at Koforidua stood, at eye level. Adding power, I turned away from the ridge to climb, in readiness to cross it. I was a little disorientated, which was not good. Checking the time, in relation to my current position, I realised that I must have been 'out' for at least five minutes, if not ten. I also realised that I had come dangerously close to a collision with rising terrain, all because I had allowed myself to become distracted.

Packing all of my thoughts for Matt, and the rest of the world, into a box, deep in my consciousness, I returned to full situational awareness, and flew the plane. Arriving at the airfield, I started to shake, realising the impact, and scars, Matt's accident had unleashed upon me. I had never before lost awareness of my location in flight, nor lost precious minutes to distracted thoughts. I would need to adjust my way of thinking and working to get through the next few months.

Gitanes was agitated, not hiding his dislike for my way of working. Whereas he worked for making money, first and foremost, I worked to do my job to the best of my abilities. We had increased the distance between our relative positions over the past year. More to the point, I had diverged, particularly so, in recent months.

Matt's accident had made me more aware of the poverty in Ghana, with the lack of infrastructure in the rural areas biting me personally. I still felt incredible pangs of guilt over being happy to see only dark, curly hair on the heads of the bodies laid out in front of the men's ward. My mind was constantly drawn to the need to train local people, rather than just run a business. The changes in me were deep, and it was impossible for anybody around to understand what I had been through, nor what I was going through.

These changes were not overnight. It was a sort of incomplete metamorphosis, and I had no idea how many more instars my changes would go through before reaching the end result. These changes put a strain on my marriage, as any family who has gone through nearly losing, or indeed losing, a child will know. Perhaps that hour of believing Matt was dead started the changes in me, and their direction was determined the moment I had to become his emergency medical technician. Nobody knows, or ever will.

Wonderful Adversity: Into Africa

I proposed training young people to fly, and spoke about the idea of a medical NGO to Gitanes. He dismissed them as inappropriate, which led to increased tension. At night, lying on my bed, pouring sweat, unable to sleep in the stifling heat, I imagined taking on a youngster to train in the workshops, then to fly.

Gitanes and I discussed the idea with another partner, who proposed a young man from the city. It would be a apprenticeship, with an option to learn to fly, if he did well. This apprentice, or Appy, as we called him, was keen to learn, and ready to get his hands dirty. Gitanes was not keen to pass any more than essential knowledge on to him, and thus it became my domain. Enjoying teaching, my need for a young man to train, and missing Matt, I immersed myself into training Appy. At times I felt as though I was treating him with the same care I would have given if training Matt.

Appy learned to help fuel the aircraft, as well as basic workshop skills. He had received a good education, and clearly understood the concepts of basic engineering. From time to time, he was given a flight in one of the aircraft, which he found a little intimidating… rather like Fresh did. Appy's fears reduced with each flight, and he started to get the idea of basic handling. Gitanes even started to take a shine to him, well, almost.

Security wise, things calmed down on the airfield, as business grew. We no longer needed the nightly policeman, and there were no other remarkable incidents. We were doing more and more flight training, in addition to a servicing a growing demand for survey and photo flights. Our biggest challenge was the well out of date aviation maps, dating back to the 1970s. I prepared a few maps on the computer, overlaying one source of information against another, adding mission specific information to make our op easier.

It was an interesting challenge to combine road maps, local knowledge, the latest GPS databases, satellite images and our own aerial photos. At times we got some nasty surprises from the old maps, such as mountains and roads being in the wrong places. The best part about being busy was that it enabled Appy to learn his chosen trade, and be quite proficient. It also kept Gitanes and I necessarily apart.

Six months later, Matt called. "I am being released from the hospital soon," he shared excitedly.

"Fantastic," I whooped, "that is great news." His mum echoed the same sentiment. Before the conversation could develop, I had to ask him a tough question. "Are you sure you want to come back to Africa?" It was a necessary question, after all that he had been through.

"Yes," he chuckled, "even after having been sick as a dog, with all the medication, I am fit, healthy and ready to help back at the airfield."

Excitedly, I booked tickets to travel and collect him from hospital. Much as he felt fit and healthy, physiotherapy would still be needed for many more months. Fortunately, he was able to follow the exercises at home, and we would make it work, somehow, together.

We spent a bit of time in the UK, making sure that we had everything needed for his return to the bush lands. Finally, boarding an airliner, without a stretcher, just with a couple of crutches. He did not really need the crutches, they were for security and to alert others to his occasional wobbliness.

Matt set off all the security alarms, with his mass of metal implants. The security officer, using a hand scanner, confirmed four different masses of metal; left thigh, both knees and left arm. The security chap sought an explanation, and was shocked at the answer.

Arriving back in Ghana, we had to drive back past the accident site. We both cried as we did so, not bitter tears, more likely tears of relief. Matt was still on heavy pain killers, which he needed.

FIDUCIARY CARE

Saturday morning flying school day arrived. Matt was excited at being able to be back on the airfield, helping as he could. Appy, was pleased to meet Matt, and helped keep an eye on him. Gitanes, on the other hand, was in his least ever co-operative mood. I tried to let it pass, but could not.

He was standing behind Alpha-Bravo, smoking, against agreed airfield rules, close to the aircraft, speaking in hushed tones to a student. I took a deep breath and walked to within easy earshot of the smoke generating Director. "Gitanes, please do not smoke near the aircraft," I admonished, admittedly in a thorny tone.

It was enough to light the growing stack of powder kegs between us. "YOU do not know how to run a business. YOU do not know what you are doing. YOU should have stayed in England with your son. I will take this business from YOU," he exploded.

Much as we may have disagreed on ways to run a business, and who to employ, his statements about 'staying in England' and 'taking the business away' were not topics that came down to differing personalities. Our differences had gone beyond workaround-able and overlook-able.

Both of us behaved like seven years olds in a school fight. Not actually hitting each other, but yelling, facts and insults, seasoned with swear words in a variety of languages. We moved as we fought, but always maintaining a face-to-face separation close enough to feel each other's angry breaths on our respective faces. We must have shouted and stomped around for a good ten minutes, before Gitanes landed his ultimate blow.

"I have already signed a contract to take the work with me to another company," he blurted, "and there is NOTHING you can do about it." He stormed off to his van, and sped off site, leaving a dust cloud behind him.

The flying students were all dumbstruck, as were employees and Matt, who had tried to intervene, hobbling around on his crutches.

The next few weeks were a challenge. Whilst I had been in the UK collecting Matt, Gitanes had decided he would be better off on his own. On checking the bank accounts, there was a lot less money in them than expected. Furthermore, a survey client, whom the company had quoted for a major contract, confirmed that Gitanes had made a better offer, from his own, recently formed, enterprise. Emergency meetings with lawyers, other shareholders, even the police and NatSec ensued.

Gitanes had acted in breach of fiduciary care, and could be prosecuted. Sadly, the legal system in Ghana is excruciatingly slow, and unpredictable, with some judges taking bribes, often from both parties. After a long and painstaking series of meetings, a settlement was agreed. It was not a good one, for either party. Gitanes wanted to operate independently, without running a flying school, just doing survey work. It was good business, now that WAASPS had established the concept of using microlights for such work.

I chose to focus on the flying school and building the engineering side up. Gitanes and I never met nor spoke again. He operated his business from a bush strip not far from Kpong, and although we may have spotted each other as traffic, we did not even make a single radio to call to each other.

Determined to build up the engineering and plane building side of the business, I decided that the time to start building all-metal aircraft had come. One of the flying students, who was within a few hours of lessons from passing his licence, agreed to purchase a Zenith CH701, if we would build it for him. It was the opening I needed to book a flight to Missouri, USA, to participate in a 'Rudder Building Workshop' and discuss the possibilities of becoming a representative for Zenith Aircraft in West Africa.

CASABLANCA TUMMY

My trip to the states was a complex journey; flying from Accra with Royal Air Maroc, then a seven hour layover in Casablanca, before the planned touchdown in New York. An internal flight would get me to St Louis, and then by rental car to Mexico, Missouri. Interestingly, that part of the USA has also has towns called Columbia and Paris.

On the flight from Accra to Casablanca, I ran over in my mind the many reasons for wanting to use a Zenith CH701 aircraft. Also known as the sky-jeep, this small two-seat aircraft was made from a resilient aluminium alloy, and could be built with simple tools. It provided an excellent platform for aerial work, and could land and take off from rough strips in very little distance. I had read all about it, but could not wait to try one in person.

Whilst waiting in Casablanca, I decided to explore the local cuisine. It was amazingly tasty in my mouth, but it was complaining about the journey through my alimentary canal, clearly making a dash towards the far end, screaming as it went. Just as I planned my visit to the airport toilet, boarding commenced.

I hoped to embark, and be able to use the onboard facilities, before take-off. Clearly, I was not the only one with that plan. Before my turn came, I was asked to take my seat for take-off. I made it clear to the pleasant cabin crew lady, with a strong voice, that I was prepared to take the risk of being locked in the facility during departure, but she would not hear of it.

Carefully taking my seat and avoiding over tightening of the seatbelt, I felt the battle of couscous versus lamb kebab reaching a crescendo. On my many international flights I have never focused so intently on the 'seat belts' light. Within a millisecond of it being extinguished, my afterburners were lit, and a cubicle occupied, my mid-riff screaming for relief.

I tried to balance my 'cubicle time' with 'seat time' during the eight hour flight. It was probably pretty even, which may have caused concern for the crew who kept asking me "Are you alright, Sir?" with a cautions look in their eyes. Despite looking washed out, I managed a smile to the cabin crew as I disembarked, which was only met with a look of relief at my departure from their plane.

JFK airport was crammed with people. Snow was falling and many flights were being delayed, including my connection. It was just as well, because the queue to clear immigration was longer than a wet Sunday afternoon. Just as I arrived at the departure gate for my flight, it was cancelled, and the next available flight to St Louis, from JFK, would be the next day.

My body was wrecked. I had not slept in over forty hours, I was dehydrated, my stomach ached and I felt as if I would die if anything else went wrong. It was one of those situations where my father would have said "You must have done something wrong to be punished like this."

As the disappointed crowds dispersed, I moved forwards and propped myself on the service counter. "Geez, you look rough," the attendant drawled, with a look of sympathy on her face.

"I am," my weak voice, barely more than a whisper, "it has been a long couple of days. I did not get any rest on the trans-Atlantic leg, due to a bad stomach." I paused, rubbing my abdomen, adding "I have to get to St. Louis tonight."

"But first you're gonna take a sit down," she said, placing a hand on my arm, "and I'm gonna get you some sweet tea."

I had no idea if this was normal in New York, but it was such a kind act, one that felt like a life saver. I sat on the obligatorily uncomfortable airline bench, waiting for my promised cup of sweet tea. Finally it arrived, and with it some much appreciated medication for my aching guts. The attendant sat next to me, keeping one hand on my arm the whole time. I wondered if I looked like a lost puppy, realising that I probably did.

As I explained my predicament, she reassured me. "You know that with this flight cancelled, there will not be another flight till t'morrow, don't ya?" she enquired with the sweetest voice. Before I could respond she offered a life-line to my predicament. "But, if you go to LaGuardia Airport, There are three flights still due out before mornin'. What's more, I can book you onto one right now," she smiled, leaning back, breaking contact with my arm and releasing an even wider white smile.

Her offer would not immediately solve the problem of my travel, because LaGuardia was also snow-bound, but it raised the probability of a flight being released that could get me to St. Louis on time. Feeling bolstered by the sugary syrup called tea, and with less pain in my lower body, I accepted the kind offer. Unfortunately, I now had to get to LaGuardia.

Leaving JFK, I stood in the queue for a transfer bus, the white snow drifting in the strong winds. The cold cut through me like a samurai sword, my face numbed by the impact of hundreds of little white flakes of anaesthetic. Aboard the bus, the warmth of a mass of bodies in a confined space, and some blown air from the cabin heaters revived me a little.

Before the bus pulled out, I had fallen asleep. I had a dream about flying, not too different to one I had experienced before. I was flying in the streets of a city, trying to get above the many power and telephone lines that criss-crossed above my little plane. There was snow, and it added to the dangers with stalactites of ice hanging from the wires, making my passing even more treacherous. As I flew down a particular street, there was a dead end ahead. I could find no safe route to climb out. The wall at the end grew bigger in my windshield, as I added more power, hoping to be able to climb through the myriad of wires above me. The wall was all I could see, so, with full power developed, I took a deep breath and pulled back on the stick...

A loud bang, some screams and my head hitting the bus window besides me, simultaneously woke me up. My eyes flew open, like spring loaded hatches. The bus had skidded and ran into the central reservation. The driver made some sort of announcement, but I did not catch it. A cacophony of vehicle horns blasted in frustration, offering no help to the situation, filling the gaps in the falling snowflakes, whilst the driver inspected the damage.

Climbing aboard, with a chunk of a bus part in his hands, he smiled at the distraught passengers. "It's OK folks, we're OK," he declared, settling back behind the wheel, and completing the journey without any further challenges. I had decided that this was an adventure. If I took the realities of my trip so far, as an omen, I would turn back immediately. If I had committed some crime, I would have felt that this was my punishment, but I hadn't. I just wanted to get to my destination, and get a couple of hours sleep before the much anticipated 'Zenith Rudder Workshop' began.

At LaGuardia, the snow had turned the airport into a refugee centre, or at least that is what it looked like. Families huddled together for warmth, their essential belongings in cases at their feet. Announcements, barely audible above the din of thousands of marooned people's mumblings, instructed groups to move from gate to gate, in hope of a much needed flight to their destinations, and warm bed.

The first two flights I had hoped for were also cancelled. Then, as the snow slowed, the final flight of the night was declared "Ready for boarding," just before midnight. It was a magnificent flight, two hours of warmth, sleep and smiling crew.

St. Louis was cold, but without snow. It was nearly three in the morning, and I was excited at the prospect of being a part of the Rudder Workshop in just six more hours. I had to complete the adventure of travel, knowing that the remaining one hundred and twenty miles would take me at least a couple of hours. Making my way to the car rental hut, I doubted that anybody would be able to help me. A member of staff must have seen me coming, for he ran to the door and opened it.

"Welcome," he boomed, "and what can we do for you today?"

It was music to my ears, and before long I was in a small car, heading west. The little hotel, on the corner of the main crossroads, in Mexico, was surprised to see an early check-in, but pleased to charge me for the full night. Apparently, checking in at five thirty in the morning counts as still being part of the night just gone. I did not care. I wanted to snatch an hour of sleep, wash and prepare for my first glimpse inside the Zenith palace of aviation worship.

The welcome was amazing. About twenty wannabe aircraft builders huddled in the reception area, all sharing their tangible passion for flying and making things. Sebastian Heintz, son of the founder of the company and aviation legend Chris Heintz, owned and ran the operation in Missouri. He breezed into reception, greeting us all with genuine warmth. Following, like ducklings behind a mother duck, Seb led us to the cavernous workshop. Donuts, tea, coffee and a variety of soft drinks were laid out seductively on a table, begging to be consumed. My stomach was feeling better, forcing me to sneak a sugary donut into my mouth, whilst Seb led our flock around the factory.

CNC routers, presses, parts storage, welding and all that goes into making the plethora of aircraft kits Zenith and Zenair have produced over the years, lay before us. The spirits of aviation, innovation and inspiration floated

Wonderful Adversity: Into Africa

around, touching all that passed through the hallowed sanctuary of production.

Building the rudder was a breeze. The parts well produced, tools laid out on trestle based work surfaces and a team spirit, boosted by the clear presentations of Roger the test pilot and other staff. The other builders buzzed with ideas of flying along the Mississippi, or reaching some out of the way mountain, in a plane that they built. My dream was a bit more bizarre.

As I explained to the group, my plan was to build planes that could reach rural communities, inspire others and change a small part of sub-Saharan Africa. A couple of the flock thought I was bonkers, humouring me anyway. The rest appeared to take inspiration from the concept.

With rudder built, it was time for a flight in a Zenith of choice. Roger asked each delegate which plane they wanted to try out, taking them on a magical fifteen minute exploration flight. At my turn, I chose the CH701, also known as the Sky Jeep, for that was the plane that met my needs.

We checked the Rotax 912ULS, with its full hundred horses crammed under the small cowling, and then climbed into the cosy cabin. It was much more compact than I had expected, but with domed doors, and a large baggage area, the proximity of pilot and passenger was a small price to pay. The centre stick arrangement was different to that of X-Air, and may have saved me a lot of surprises on my flight with Fresh, if I had been flying with this configuration.

The single stick, located between the seats, with a Y shaped top, fell comfortably to hand as the engine fired up with a familiar sound. Roger taxied out, lined her up, and talked me through what he called a take-off. For me it was more of an elevator ride. It happened naturally, but so surprisingly. Apply full power. Roll about five metres, letting the nose wheel lift. A few seconds later, climb at the most surprising angle, aimed at the sky. I felt Roger snatching a glimpse at my clearly elated face, and turned to share a smile. We flew a couple of circuits, with Roger teaching me the nuances of landing a CH701, enabling me to manage a relatively short landing. With practice, I knew that I would be able to achieve much better landings, even shorter.

After the two day course, the flock of Rudder Builders left the factory whilst I stayed behind to discuss my aims and ideas for Ghana and West Africa. Seb listened intently, and agreed a representation plan. Ordering two CH701's and a four seat CH801, our deal was set. To my surprise he then offered for me to spend a few more days in the factory, gaining hands on experience. It was an offer not to be turned down. Meanwhile, Seb had a short business trip to make to Bogota, Columbia, where many of his Short Take Off and Landing (STOL) aircraft designs were being made to increase rural access – and have fun. He would arrive back in St. Louis on the day of my return to Africa, so we agreed to meet at the airport 'as we passed'.

Whilst he was gone I learned so much, and gained much confidence. I had never built an all metal plane before, and was about to attempt it in the middle of the African bush, with no support on hand. I took advantage of the time to place orders for a couple of spare hand-held aircraft radios, some headsets, a variety of tools and several flying books for the training school back home. Being at the factory for those few days was a great confidence and skill builder. The whole team, both office and factory floor, boosted my confidence with their support. Sadly, the time to depart was soon upon me, and I headed back to St Louis.

GUANTANAMO

On one of the old charts I had been integrating into operational maps for our flights in Ghana, I had spotted an address for a cartography centre in St. Louis. I had made a note of the address, in case there was time to go there before leaving. On reaching the outskirts of the city, I had about three hours to wait for Seb's flight to arrive. Double checking Seb's itinerary, I made sure that I had understood his routing and timings. Confirming that I really did have three hours before his Bogota/Miami/St. Louis flight arrived, it was time to look for the mapping centre.

It was a long shot, taking an address from a 40 year old map, hoping that the mapping centre would still be around. It was a much longer shot of hoping that they had something more up to date. Asking numerous good folks for directions, I finally was sent to the military base. It felt a bit odd, but all the same, I was happy to have a direction and purpose.

Approaching the base gates, the guard on the gate held up his hand, stopping me in such a well presented and extremely official manner. Explaining that I wanted to see somebody in the mapping department, he directed me to the next guard post, visible down a long, straight road. Happily, I complied. My sense of contentment was a little tarnished by the multiple signs along the road, warning about 'No Access except on official business', but I had been directed that way.

Pulling up to the next gate, the red and white barrier was rising as I approached, but I still stopped, not sure of what I should do next. A very abrupt guard came to the car window.

"Afternoon, Sir," I offered, my window already wide open.
"How can I help you?" the crisp words spoken without his head moving.
"I have come to speak to somebody in the mapping section," my

declaration made, honestly and simply.

"Do you have any identity papers?" he queried.

Passing him my passport, I smiled, happy that I might just get to find somebody with up to date maps. After looking through my passport, he headed back into the guard room, examining my papers with a second officer. I tried not to look, but I did notice one of them picking up a phone, hopefully to get me into cartography heaven.

The two guards turned, to ensure that I could not see their faces. I was left wondering what was going on. Time ticked by, and I switched off the engine of the car. After a while longer both guards came to the car door.

"What other identity papers do you have?" the second guard demanded.

"Pilot's licences and driving licences," I offered, pulling them from my bag on the passenger seat. I had travelled with my British, French and Ghanaian driving and pilots licences. It was simply a habit to carry them all with me. As I pulled them out, my air tickets, and a number of boarding cards fell out.

"What are those other papers?" the first guard asked, pushing his head to the threshold of the window.

"Just plane tickets and boarding passes," I declared.

"Pass them here," ordered guard two, and so I did.

Guard two flicked through the papers. I looked ahead of me, trying not to second guess what was going through their minds, but aware that something was amiss. A third guard was approaching my vehicle, with his hand on his service pistol. It was reminiscent of an old western.

Guard two nodded to guard three, who moved to the passenger side of the car, pausing by the open window on that side. I felt rather intimidated, but accepted that such checks were normal.

"Why do you have Arabic stamps in your passport?," Two demanded.

"I have flown through Arabic nations," was the only explanation.

"AND why do you have so many boarding cards and tickets?" he pressed.

"Well, my flight from JFK was cancelled, and then two more cancelled flights in LaGua..."

Three had pulled his pistol from its holster, and thrust it inside the car with a shout. "Place your hands on the steering wheel, and keep them where we can see them." It rather took me by surprise.

I really did not know how to react, so I just sat as I was, and looked at One and Two, both of whom had placed hands on their pistols. Two reiterated the order, "Place you hands on the wheel NOW." I complied.

The next ten minutes were spent with me being handcuffed and laid across the bonnet of the car, whilst they searched the car and my baggage. Each time they found something of interest, a little scurry took place.

"Aircraft radios."

"Books on flying."

"Tools."

"More tools."

Each time they called these items out, I took a mental step closer to the misunderstanding. Just as I was almost at the point of full realisation of the situation, a four by four vehicle arrived, jarring to a stop behind my half emptied car. Three men and a woman, all uniformed, paraded around the car and me. One of them spent a few minutes inside the guard room with One and Two, emerging a few minutes later.

"Sir, you are on US Military property, you have no rights," he spoke with maximum intimidation. "If you do not cooperate, we can send you Guantanamo Bay, no questions asked," he concluded.

"But I have not done anything wrong," my protest sounded weak against his Guantanamo Bay proposal.

"You have multiple identity papers and multiple tickets for US airlines. You have aircraft radios, headsets, tools and books on how to fly an aircraft," his list of warning bells arranged ready to play a chorus.

"But..." I tried to protest, before being cut off.

"Search him," Guantanamo ordered the female officer.

I was still hugging the bonnet of the car at the time, as much as anything for comfort. She approached me from behind, grabbing the handcuffs and ratcheting them one notch in, making them pinch my skin. Jerking me to stand upright, she kicked my legs apart. With one hand on my cuffed hands, patted me down roughly, in all honesty, inappropriately.

"Wallet," she declared, pulling my wallet out of my back pocket.

I repeated, "I have done nothing wrong," but nobody was listening. Opening my wallet, they found about a thousand dollars in cash, ten thousand Ghana Cedis, and a few pounds.

Guantanamo came back for another bite at me, "Why do you have all this cash?"

"I live in West Africa, and cash is the only way to operate. I am heading home this afternoon, if you will let me," I explained. We then had several exchanges about my flight times, which met the tickets they had already in their possession.

"So, what are you doing in the USA?" he asked, finally allowing me to speak.

"I came to the USA to purchase aircraft, learn about building them and send kits back to Ghana," I paused for a moment, watching his confused expression. "I build airplanes in Africa to reach rural communities, and teach people to fly."

He looked even more confused, asking me to further explain, which I did, but not to his satisfaction.

"OK, but then why are you here?" he sought greater understanding of my strange ways.

"This is the mapping centre, where some of the maps I use come from," I explained, totally exhausted and with sore wrists from the over tight cuffs.

"This is a military establishment," was his only rebuff of my declaration.

Wonderful Adversity: Into Africa

After a long pause he started afresh, "So, if we let you go, where will you go next?"

That was an easy answer, "I am going to the airport to meet Sebastian Heintz of Zenith Aircraft, based in Mexico Missouri, before I fly home to Ghana." I hoped that would suffice.

"Why did you not meet him in Mexico?" his voiced lowered, along with his eyebrows.

"Seb is flying into St. Louis this afternoon," I sighed my response, "and we will meet before he goes back to Mexico." For me it was as simple as ABC, but not for Guantanamo.

"Where is he flying in from?" he quizzed.

"Bogota, Columbia," I stated, as factually as I could. Then it struck me how bad that could sound, so I tried to massage it a bit by adding, "via Miami." As the words dropped like lead balloons at my feet, I realised that my honesty was only making matters worse.

Pushing me against the guard room wall, facing it, I was ordered not to move. One, Two and Guantanamo raced into the guard room. Three retrained his pistol on me, and I simply offered "I haven't done anything wrong."

"Shut up, and don't move," the order hit me, accompanied by a further push against the wall.

Minutes later another vehicle arrived. Dog and dog handler moved about the car, my possessions and then about my person, presumably sniffing for any of signs of drugs. As expected, they didn't find any, but that did not stop the dog handler keeping the dog close to me. I rather like dogs, but decided that calling out "Nice puppy," would not be a wise thing at that point.

Guantanamo was back outside, watching the approach road to our ongoing incident zone. Soon a black car pulled up, and two African American men, wearing dark suits, swaggered over to me.

"Whaddya do?" one asked.

"I have done nothing wrong," I reiterated for the umpteenth time.

"Well, you let me decide that," he proposed. "You tell me what you did since you arrived in the US of A."

I wanted to laugh, because it sounded so much like an American movie, and he reminded me of Eddie Murphy. I had been in some scrapes over the years, but this one was getting out of hand.

"Please remove the cuffs, because my wrists are sore," I proposed.

"Un-cuff him," he ordered the woman who had tightened the cuffs on my now bleeding wrists.

I sat on the bonnet of the car, looking into the eyes of the men in suits.

"My name is Jonathan," I paused looking at the newcomers to the scene, the first dark skinned amongst the whole ensemble. "With whom do I have the pleasure of speaking with?" I probed, hoping that a bit of civility would go down well.

"Ha, Jonathan, is it," he laughed. "Well, I work with the FBI, and I have been called here because my colleagues think that you are a threat to National Security. You are gonna tell me what I want to know, or they will send you to Guantanamo Bay." I thought he had finished when he added, "Do ya want a drink or sommat?"

Declining the offer a beverage, I explained the whole story, from the uncomfortable ride across the Atlantic, snow, transferring from JFK to LaGuardia, the bus crash, the cancelled flights, learning about Zenith Aircraft, the maps, and finally, the chain of events of the past two hours, and my need to get to the airport to meet Seb, and then fly home.

"So, this Seb, can he vouch for you?" he asked.

"Of course," my voice lightened at the thought of not having a free holiday in Cuba, adding, "BUT he is on a plane for another half an hour." I thought for a second and added, "You can always call the Zenith factory. Their number is on one of the brochures you have from my things."

FBI's version of Eddie Murphy went off to the guard post, returning a few minutes later.

"You can go," he offered. "Your story is so bizarre, nobody could make shit up like this up. Your story checks out, with the airlines and with the Zenith people, you can go."

With relief streaming through my whole body, I heaved "Thank you," my liberation only tarnished by the soreness on my wrists.

All thoughts of getting access to any sort of maps, went out of my head as I returned the rental car, and headed into the airport arrivals area, running a little late.

When Seb saw me, he was smiling. "I hear you had a run in with the FBI." he laughed. We talked about the whole incident, and he explained how the office had its first ever call from the FBI, seeking clarification on somebody called Jonathan. He had heard the story on his mobile phone between landing and meeting me. Regardless, we had a positive exchange, and I headed off towards departures.

EFATO

Things were tough in Ghana. Gitanes had delivered a major setback to the operations of the company, and I was trying to find solutions. Matt was a brilliant help, always ready to manage something new, never complaining about the working conditions or poor pay.

I had not been able to take a salary, and enforced austerity measures on the whole family. It may not have been fair, but it was necessary. It did not make for happy times at home, but it did mean that the business was able to operate and grow.

Appy was getting better at his skills in the workshop, and Kojo and Kwame had learnt to manage a lot of the general work around the field. Overall, the operations were going as smoothly as could be expected under the circumstances.

Being the only flying instructor, my Saturday and Sunday workload was often extreme. I enjoyed the dream machine component of teaching people to fly. Making dreams become a reality. I would often jest that I could teach anybody to fly in one hour, to take off in ten hours, but it would take a lifetime to learn how to land. Much as it sounds strange, it is true. I have yet to find a student I cannot teach to be able to control the aircraft, to go roughly in the right direction, within one hour of flight time, on the controls. Most students will be comfortable taking off on the controls themselves within ten hours of training, provided the weather conditions are good, and the runway long enough. But, learning to land, any pilot who is honest will tell you they still want to get better at it. Of course, repeatable, safe landings are generally achieved within twenty or thirty hours of training, again on the right runway with suitable wind conditions. Before a student can undertake their first solo flight, it is essential that they are fully able to cope with an emergency in flight. The killer emergencies occur close to the ground, at low speed and high angle of attack. It is for this reason that I give great emphasis to the EFATO training sessions.

Engine Failure After Take Off has claimed too many lives in aviation. During the initial climb, the aircraft has three things against it; low speed, low altitude and a runway behind it. In the event of a loss of power, the rule is 'land straight ahead, or within as few degrees as possible to one side of straight ahead, for collision avoidance. I owed my life, and lack of damage to Alpha-Alpha, from the excellent instruction I had received in my flight training in relation to EFATO management. Before any student could be allowed to solo an aircraft, they had to have their EFATO reactions as automated as they would in putting their hands out to stop a fall. The only way to instil that automatic reaction, or reflex, is practice. Lots of practice.

The terrain after take-off at Kpong was not friendly, perhaps making the EFATO training all the more essential for my students. It was also often a make or break moment for them. After briefing on the technique, and after a couple of good circuits, it would be time to introduce the emergency situation.

At just a couple of hundred feet, I would pull back the power, declaring "Engine failure. Engine failure. Engine failure," knowing that my own skills were being put on the line too. If the engine really did fail on being pulled back, then it was going to be a real off-field landing. If the student did not manage the situation well, the aircraft could be put into a low level stall, with sudden loss of height and the need for me to take control. Consequently, there was a pact between me and the student. I would do all that I could to stop them killing us both, provided they promised not to try to kill me.

On a particularly busy Sunday, there were three students, all doing circuit work, all needing EFATO training. It was tiring for me, but essential for them. With the student fully on the controls, and comfortable with take-off through to landing, the training sequence would begin;

- During the roll-out phase from the last landing, apply full power.
- At take off speed, gently pull back on the stick.
- Once airborne, try to stay close to the ground to add speed.
- Climb.
- Once at the point of no more chance to land on the runway...
- Pulling back on the throttle, I declare "Engine failure. Engine failure. Engine failure."
- Airspeed drops fast.
- The student would, or rather should, push the stick forwards, aiming to establish a safe airspeed, suitable for an engine-off landing.
- The student must identify where they are going to try to land, shouting it out on the intercom, as the plane rapidly loses height.
- Once I was happy with their choice, I would add power and call "You have power. Resume normal flight."
- The student would re-establish a climb, and a normal circuit.

Well, that was when it went well. Fortunately, it did with the first two students. However, student three appeared hell bent on breaking our pact and trying to kill us both. He did OK on the first EFATO, but on the second one, he froze. With the stick held in the climb position, and my having reduced power, declaring "Engine failure. Engine failure. Engine failure," he simply froze. It was as if a Gorgon had appeared in front of him, turning him to stone. Alpha-Alpha started to lose speed. I called the magic words again, but he did not react. We were dangerously close to the wing stalling, and the aircraft giving up on flight altogether, whereupon I shouted into my microphone "I HAVE CONTROL," a command to let the student know they must let go of the controls completely. Simultaneously, I added full power, which, under-normal circumstances would have put us on the road to recovery.

Unfortunately, the student refused to relinquish his grip on the stick, and decided to initiate the EFATO response of pushing the stick forwards. It caught me by surprise, as we now had the aircraft with full power, nose down, dangerously close to the top of a clump of trees.

We now had plenty of airspeed, but it was being used to send us rapidly in the direction of a crash. With no options left, I swiped my left hand rapidly towards my killer student's nose. I was ready to hit it, hard, if I had to.

Wonderful Adversity: Into Africa

Fortunately, the shock of my hand heading towards his face snapped him out of his lost world, making his hands come up to protect his face, relinquishing full control to me.

He held my hand for a split second. Releasing it, he started to shake. Meanwhile, I was busy looking straight at the top of a tree, on a collision course. Keeping full power on, even with the excess of speed, I yanked back on the stick, pulling the plane into a near aerobatic climb. Once clear of the tree, I pushed over to a less aggressive angle, whilst trying to flush an excess of adrenalin from my bloodstream. Carrying out a low level circuit, I prepared to get the plane back on the ground safely. Killer didn't say a word, nor did I.

After landing, Killer burst into tears. It was a natural reaction. The pair of us had dispensed, what felt like, a couple of litres of sweat, and we must have looked like we had just surfaced from an underwater world. Taking Killer to the briefing room, we sat and talked about the incident, whereupon he admitted that he lost all awareness in his panic. Fortunately, he was the last student of the day, and we could sit and chat for a long time, rebuilding what we could of his confidence.

As I he drove off, I turned around to see a person walking down the runway. "Oi YOU," I yelled in my best Sergeant Major voice, "you are trespassing. Get off the runway." Regardless, the lone figure continued to march towards me. I just stood, watching the person, now discernible as a young lady, walking with a machete balanced on her head, straight towards me. She was not looking at me, but rather at Alpha-Alpha.

In my exhaustion from the last flight, I just stood and waited for the young lady, who was wearing a green school sports top, tatty knee length skirt and a pair of flip-flops, to get within conversation distance.

"Good afternoon," I tried my polite voice, too tired to be angry, "what do you want?"

"Good afternoon," she replied in a better than average English for a local, adding "I want a job."

This was going to be easy to deal with. Culturally, employing women in engineering was a no-no, and the work on the field mainly involved clearing dense shrub, cutting and uprooting trees and was, in my opinion, far too difficult for a girl. "Go away. You are trespassing, and we have no jobs," I explained in a far from polite tone. She did not respond immediately, but rather looked at the small plane still sitting on the apron. Since she was not going to go away by discussion, so I just repeated myself, and turned my back, walking towards Alpha-Alpha.

"I will work for free," she called after me, heartily.

Turning back to face her, I tried another trick to get rid of her. "Well, you will have to write an application," I proposed, knowing that many young people in rural Africa do not receive much useable education, and writing was a barrier to their advancement. I entered the briefing room, returning with a sheet of paper and a pen. "Write down why I should give you a job," I ordered, expecting her to run away at the sight of a barrier to her ambition. It did not work; she took the paper and pen and started to write.

Leaving her at the briefing room, I put Alpha-Alpha away, fully expecting this impetuous girl to be gone upon my return. Amazingly she was still there. She had written a pretty good application, even if with a couple of spelling and grammatical mistakes, this girl was not quite what I expected.

"Why did you come here?" I asked, increasingly fascinated by the young woman's reasoning.

"You chased me with the plane. I thought I had done something wrong," she explained. "I was cutting trees, and your plane came towards me, looking for me," she pointed towards the end of the runway, and the clump of trees I had nearly become entangled with on my last flight. "When I saw the plane, I followed it here," she pointed towards the hangar, "and I want to work here."

Looking at the girl's paper, I read her name, Patricia Mawuli. I had to admit, she was determined, and annoyingly persistent. "OK, Patricia, I will give you a trial," I succumbed, "but you will work for free, with a machete and a mattock, clearing trees with the men." I paused, looking at her face, expecting it to crumple, or drop, but it did not. "Be here at seven in the morning, and you and see if you can do the work," I closed my offer, hoping that it would be rejected.

"OK," she accepted the challenge, but not without conditions, "but, I will only do, if I get to see the flying machine."

PATRICIA

I was on the field before the men the next morning, getting my thoughts together for the week ahead. To my surprise Patricia was standing in the middle of a bushy area, with her own machete, clearing tall grass. I decided to ignore her, proceeding to the briefing room.

By seven, the men had arrived. Squatting on the ground, they were tucking into fermented maize balls, called kenkey, with fish and spicy sauce. It was not my favourite food, but it was the local 'good start to the day' and full of energy. Introducing Patricia to the field workers, and issuing tools for

Wonderful Adversity: Into Africa

the day, I went to town to purchase supplies.

When I returned, I noticed a dramatic increase in clearing activities. Patricia was working alone, in an area apart from the men. She was cutting down and uprooting trees as if they were dandelions. Standing back, I watched the technique differences between the men folk, and the solitary girl.

The men approach a tree with great energy. Hacking into the lower bark with a machete, inflicting devastating wounds as large chips of wood flew in all directions. Once the main tree was downed, they would dig with the mattock with equal vigour, until the stump gave way to their persuasion.

Patricia, on the other hand, walked up to a tree, and then around it. She would look at it, apparently establishing some sort of sacred connection. Then, with determination and energy, she started work with the mattock, liberating one side of the roots. Next, with relatively slow, but seemingly powerful hacks, she laid the sharp blade of the machete into the trunk. With a flurry of pushing, kicking and shaking, the tree would break and fall. To complete the task, some more mattock work took place around the tree, coupled with additional machete blows to recalcitrant roots, and the stump practically ejected itself from the ground. She was removing three trees for every two of the men.

Wandering over, I yelled "Ayekoo," to the workers. A chorus of "Yayee," came back, acknowledging the compliment. The men made it clear that they were not happy about having a female on the field. I could clearly see why. Nevertheless, I could see the potential in Patricia, and informed her that not only was she doing well, but that she would be paid the same as the men. Politely, she thanked me and got straight back to work.

Back in the workshop, Appy was busy getting ready for the arrival of the Zenith kits. There was much to be prepared, and he was a willing and effective worker. Appy still need a certain amount of supervision, so Matt agreed to manage the airfield, whilst I focused on the workshops.

At home, things were not as going well. Matt's mum was finding living in Ghana tough, and it was affecting her health. She was clearly not happy, and in need of more care and support than I was able, or perhaps willing, to give. I was busy. I had my mind on making this aviation world work. I was not ready to take a break, and had become increasingly focused, blinkered and probably obnoxious. I could only see making aeroplanes as my way forward. We had many strong arguments, and despite both wanting to see the other happy, realised that for her health, she needed to travel back to the UK, for her wellbeing. We both needed our spaces.

Matt and I ran the operation, and turned the home into a bachelor pad. Eating what we wanted when we wanted, and probably not keeping the house as clean as it should be. Matt's mum rang every night, talking to us both, as we all tried to find a way to keep the family together.

Meanwhile, the arrival day for the Zenith aircraft kits drew ever closer.

They were coming by sea, in a container, and it was going to be a busy day when they got here. We really did not have enough personnel for the unloading, but would manage.

The container was landed in Tema port, just waiting to clear customs. It raised a buzz in our lives, and became the only topic of conversation. I was under more pressure to ready the workshop, and pushed Appy to his limits. He stayed over one night, and I was pleased that he got up early and beat me into the workshop.

"Well done, Appy," I complimented him as I wandered into the womb from which we would give birth to our next aircraft.

Appy, surprised at my arrival, snapped up straight, pushing a small cloth bag to one side with his foot. "Mmmm Mmmm Morning Captain," he stammered, which was not like him.

Deciding to overlook the incident, I asked Appy to help me with some maintenance work on Alpha-Alpha. Outside, the "chop, chop, chop" of a machete could be heard. It was Patricia, early as usual, clearing the grasses near the workshop, creating a firebreak around the building.

Appy was clearly not himself, but I could not put my finger on the problem. After a while, the cloth bag he had pushed to one side caught my eye. It niggled at me as to why he had brought the bag into the workshop in the first place. Trying to carry on as usual, I asked Appy to help me change the clevis pins on the wing struts connections. He was being all fingers and thumbs. Admittedly it was a fiddly job, but it was something he should have been able to do.

My patience frayed. "Leave that alone and go and move those tyres from outside the workshop," I snapped. He obeyed, without saying a word, his bowed head avoiding eye contact. With him out of the workshop, my curiosity got the better of me, and I investigated the little bag that had been calling to me.

As I pulled it out from its hiding place, tools and aircraft parts fell out. Further investigation found electrical connectors, wire and host of other parts, all from the workshop. I exploded, big time. Mr F would have been shocked at my language.

"F'ing APPPY." my voice was so loud it created an echo. "F'ing APPY, come F'ing here F'ing NOW." Well at least that was the essence of the outburst. He came running, his chest heaving from hyper-ventilation. He tried to justify his cache of workshop goodies through a series of lies.

"I was using the bag to hold them in whilst I tidied them," he tried, followed quickly with, "But they are mine anyway. I brought them with me." Realising he was on a losing streak he excavated his own grave with, "I thought you gave them to me."

I pushed him against the wall, and told him not to move. I had learned a lot about apprehension and holding of suspected threats from Guantanamo, but I did not have any handcuffs. Considering the use of a cable-tie as a makeshift cuffing solution, I restrained myself, remembering the pain I had experienced in St. Louis.

I hurled insults on Appy, hoping that it would undo the situation. He never retracted his various, highly conflicting stories, leaving me no choice but to send him to the police station. Matt took him, for I was too fuming to be reasonable with the lad.

Back in the workshop my temper abated, a little, but now I needed somebody to help me to complete the clevis pin and locking ring changes. Frustrated, I kicked an old plastic bucket across the workshop, smashing it against an electrical socket on the far wall. It flew into a thousand black shards. I was not being a pleasant person, not at all. Outside a machete sang relentlessly, "chop, chop, chop," just to antagonise me further.

Through the window, I caught a glimpse of Patricia, wielding her machete with full-on passion and energy, clearing weeds, trying not to get caught noticing my ongoing dramatics. "OI YOU," I screeched, having nobody else to take my anger out on, "COME HERE AND HELP ME."

Dropping the machete in the grass, she approached gingerly, awaiting my orders. Patricia moved silently, and said nothing. The look in her eyes was a blend of fear and excitement. She had not been allowed into the workshops before, and yet she was being called in there by an angry bear like figure. She stood in front of me, a different girl to the one who had walked onto the airfield a few weeks ago. She wore safety boots and a dark blue set of overalls, which the company had provided. Her hair was tied back with a strip of cloth, and her face dusted grey from cutting down the grasses.

I was fuming, still angry beyond belief over the theft by Appy. Patricia was about to take the brunt of my anger, without any reason other than just being there. "I need to change these pins," my voice snapped loudly in my ears, let alone hers. She had no idea what I was I talking about, but maintained a gaze straight into my eyes, defiant of my tone. "You hold the end of the wing here," I clipped the words as I pointed out the holding point. She obeyed, without a word. "Hold these," I ordered, giving her two clevis pins and rings for the top end of the struts, whilst I moved to the lower end.

I barked orders at her to lift a bit, lower a bit, forward a bit and back a bit, enabling me to get easier access to the corroded pins at the lower end of the strut. I did not want to admit it, but she followed the instructions well, especially considering it was her first time ever of touching an aircraft.

With my two pins changed, I stood up and moved up the strut ready to change the top pair. To my amazement, they were already changed. Patricia stood, face without expression, hand open offering me the two old pins and ring clips from the top end.

"Who taught you to do that?" my voice changed from fury to interrogation.

"Nobody," she whispered.

It was not a good enough answer for me. "Have you worked on tractors or other mechanical devices?" my grilling continued.

"No, I just watched you," she pleaded in her defence, a smile almost breaking out from her face.

It had taken an age to teach Appy to carry out a simple clevis pin change, and even then he fumbled it at times. This girl was changing my opinion on what her potential might be. With my anger subdued by the positive experience, I semi-politely sent Patricia back to weeding.

The police took the theft issue with Appy seriously, carrying out a detailed search of his home. There they found a variety of items from the workshop, and my home. Needless to say, his employment was terminated on the spot.

DELIVERY

On the morning of the Zenith delivery, it was all hands on deck. The container would arrive and be unloaded by hand. The last thing we needed was a taxi arriving with a group of tourists, but that is what happened.

A family of four, Mum, Dad, teenage son and daughter, arrived full of smiles in a dusty old taxi. The father walked briskly forwards me, with a spring in his step, "Gud morning to y'all," he beamed, with a light Irish accent, "I hear you fly aeroplanes here? Could we have a wee chat?"

Much as there was no time for this interlude, the brightness of the man's voice and the spring in his step, made me smile. After a short exchange, I learned that the family were on holiday in Ghana, from the USA. The father had spent time in Ghana as a young man, volunteering in the north of the country. He was a pilot, and exuded enthusiasm from every pore of his body. His wife was much more reserved, but equally supportive, and full of interest in what we were trying to achieve. The teenagers were both smiling, asking questions at every turn. In short, they were the sort of visitors anybody would be thrilled to receive, on any day other than when expecting a container of aircraft parts.

The father's Irish lilt, his bearded face, coupled with clear hyperactive jiggling and arm waving, reminded me of a Leprechaun; full of fun, and energy, and a little bit cheeky to boot. The son, clearly positively influenced by his father, asked more questions than could be found in an enhanced version of the game 'Trivial Pursuit' or any other quiz game. Trying not to b too dismissive, I tried to answer their many questions and send them on their way as quickly as possible, eventually closing with "I am really sorry, but we have a container arriving soon, which we need to get ready to empty."

"Well, that will be wonderful," Leprechaun beamed, "we can give you a hand." Without waiting for a response he turned to his family adding "Won't that be great."

I could not say no. We needed the help, and this family were used to working around aeroplanes. Quiz, who was about to start studying engineering at University, had already found his way into the workshop, looking for things to do. Finding an electrical socket on the wall, that had taken a bash from a flying bucket, he asked "Do you have a spare electrical socket," pointing at my rage induced damage. I found one in the stores, and he replaced it, without any need for my input. Meanwhile, the rest of the family were busy finding work to be done. Matt, Patricia and the rest of the gang found a new sense of energy with the family there. For me, it was a breath of fresh air. My anger over Appy was subsiding, and the excitement of the Zenith parts arriving filled me with anticipation.

The container truck could be heard long before it arrived. The engine was labouring, but the vehicle was not advancing. With a little investigation, we found the truck had got stuck in the mud on the track to the workshop. The whole vehicle rocked as the torque from the engine failed to generate forward movement. A lot of shovelling dirt and placing of stones under wheels later, and the container docked at the workshop.

I took my place inside the container. It was the hottest place, with temperatures reaching what felt like flesh melting levels. My whole body felt as if it would liquify, but the job had to be completed. Without being told, each person found their role. Leprechaun and his family joined the airfield staff in handing parts to Matt and Patricia who took charge of finding homes for the many boxes and laying the parts out by apparent type, ready for inventory work to begin.

The next few hours were fraught with unloading, packing, arranging and generally shoe-horning three aircraft kits into a small workshop. Everybody looked as if they had been left too long in a sauna with a faulty thermostat. There was not a dry piece of clothing on a single individual, apart from the truck driver, who had sat in the shade watching the whole exercise.

The Leprechaun family stayed for a meal, despite being exhausted. The energy and positive comments on all that we were trying to achieve gave me hope, inspiring us to do more. They showed particular interest in MOM, offering to help in any way they could. It was sad to see them drive away, but there was a little glimmer of one possible long term outcome; Quiz proposed to come back to help for a few months during his next summer vacation.

Over the next few days, packing lists needed checked off. Matt was busy with airfield maintenance, whilst Patricia and I worked the workshop. She was efficient and detailed, showing a great interest in all things mechanical. As we worked, I suggested that she might want to actually do an engineering apprenticeship, learning to build aircraft, install, and service and maintain Rotax aircraft engines etc. Indicating that she liked the idea, she decided to discuss it with her uncle.

APPRENTICE

The, next day, she told me her uncle wanted to see me about the proposed apprenticeship. At the end of the day's work I drove, with Patricia, to the little farm where they stayed. It was a depressing place. Six or seven mud huts, some with broken walls and semi-collapsed thatched roofs. There was no power to the area, and water had to be fetched from a standpipe some distance away. Patricia's aunty was bustling around, barefoot, with a simple piece of cloth wrapped tightly around her. She smiled, a large gap between her upper front incisors clearly visible. Uncle came out from one of the mud huts. He was wearing the ubiquitous flip-flop footwear, and a pair of shorts, pulling a grubby T-shirt over his torso, as he walked towards me.

He offered a smile, but it carried no sincerity, in fact it made me very uncomfortable. After snapping some short sentences in local speak at his wife, two wooden benches were brought for us to sit on, one facing the other. Patricia sat on the bench next to me. Uncle and Aunty sat opposite. He leaned in, bearing his upper body weight through to his legs as he leaned heavily on his elbows placed on knobbly knees.

"What is this nonsense about my daughter being an engineer?" he sneered, clearly not happy about the concept on offer. Interestingly he referred to Patricia as his daughter, as a younger female member of the extended family, in a protective manner, as is common across Africa.

"Patricia has shown a great ability in engineering," I offered, positively. "She is already doing well in the workshops and has a lot of potential." At that, Aunty got up and busied herself with a cooking pot on an open fire, a few metres away.

"Patricia is a girl," he snapped, dismissively, "she should be in the village cooking, as a wife and a mother, not in a workshop." His attitude seemed to have been teleported from the dark ages, but I was not going to give up so easily.

"Patricia is over eighteen, and an adult," I paused, taking a deep breath, "she can make her own mind up, and has only come to you as a cultural courtesy." I could see that my approach was not fitting into the culture of Uncle, adding "Surely, you would be proud of her if she did well in engineering. She would be a credit to the family."

The arguments went back and forth for about twenty minutes, both of us being confused by the others approach to women in society. By this time, Aunty had re-taken her place alongside Uncle, interjecting with a long, venomous sounding spiel in Ewe, the local language of the family. Her animated movements made it clear that she also was against the concept of such work for Patricia.

"We do not agree with this girl working in industry," he boomed at me, "it is too dangerous." It appeared that Aunty had advised Uncle on a new approach to placing barriers in the way of the young woman. I glanced at Patricia's face. There was no emotion or expression of feeling that I could determine. She just sat there, not even contemplating saying a word.

"Let us ask Patricia," I proposed.

"It is nothing to do with her," he snapped, "she will do as she is told."

"I would like you to consider the prop..." but I could not complete my sentence, for Uncle was now standing, looming over Patricia. She did not move.

"What do you want, Patricia," I asked.

"I want to do the apprenticeship," she whispered almost imperceptibly.

As a last ditch attempt I asked, "Sir. What can I do to help you consider Patricia's desire to undertake an apprenticeship?"

Stunned, perhaps even insulted that I would not give up quickly, he rounded on me, looking like a wolf about to rip out the throat of its prey. "How do I know that you have approval to be doing this work," it was a good question, "and what about if she has an accident? Are you insured? If you can prove to me that you are a genuine operation, then I will consider it."

Taking the challenge to heart, I bid the family a good evening and headed to my car. Behind me I could hear aggressive exchanges, and wondered if there would be a violent interaction. I did not look back, for fear of getting involved in a family and cultural squabble.

The next morning, I went to the briefing room early, to prepare papers for the Uncle from the dark ages. As I opened the door, I heard the sound of violent machete blows being dished out to vegetation. Patricia had arrived long before the beginning of the work day, and appeared to be taking her anger out on miscreant grasses and shrubs around the workplace. It was clear that she had been crying, but I did not want to get into family discussions. She was a good worker, and if she wanted to work, then I would let her. But I did not want to get into cultural clashes.

I prepared about twenty pages of approvals and insurances, copying them and putting them into a folder. Taking them to show Patricia, I did not have to ask any questions. "I do not want to go to the village to be a wife and make babies. I want to work. I want to be my own person. I want to be somebody," she threw staccato sentences at me, stamping her foot and thrusting her right arm downwards at the end of each statement.

Moving the energy towards the workshop, Patricia and I worked on the initial build of the CH701, laying out the fuselage pieces. When building a Zenith aircraft, all the parts have an identifying sticker, referenced in the build drawings and photo-guide. In theory it is a simple job of just following the sequence. In practice, it requires a lot of organisational skills – and an ability to relate the drawing to a piece rapidly. There are thousands of bits that go into the build, including rivets, nuts, bolts, washers, cotter-pins, pulleys and a host of cables and wires. Each one had to be identified, laid out and prepared to be a part of the build.

Patricia got stuck in, without a word. She hunted out all the relevant parts for each sub-assembly, cleaning them, taking a file to smooth the edges and clipping them together with a host of temporary fixations, such as clecos and clamps.

Checking on each temporary assembly, I would authorise Patricia to drill and rivet, checking each and every step. She was learning very quickly, needing little additional guidance. At the end of the day, it was time to visit Uncle again.

In the car, Patricia told me a bit about her background. It sounded bizarre to me, having grown up in a developed nation. All the same, it did sound as if she had a very unfair life, and was being treated as an object rather than a person.

Uncle was waiting for us, standing with a grim look on his face, ready for a fight. I handed him the collection of papers he had asked for, but he did not look at them. Instead he threw them on the ground telling me "These mean nothing, that girl is a bush girl, she will do as I say." Turning his head and anger towards Patricia he yelled, "Get inside, and do your chores."

Patricia started to walk towards the mud hut with a semi-collapsed roof. I started to object, but Patricia turned and shook her head at me, indicating that it was a waste of time. Reluctantly, I drove home expecting never to see Patricia at work again.

The next morning, she was back in the workshop, laying out parts, before I got there. I asked what had happened, and she told me that her family wanted her to go to a village to be married to a man she had never met. The man was going to pay for her.

This was outside my comfort zone and I was left wondering if I should have gotten involved with employing an African woman in the first place. Leaving Patricia in the workshop, I made a visit to my friend the Police Commander. After explaining the situation to him he advised me.

"Do not get involved with family matters. I know the Uncle. He has even come to complain about you to me," he explained bluntly.

"But this girl is over eighteen; surely she cannot be forced to do things by the family?" I stated and asked in the same breath.

"It does not matter how old she is, she is the property of the family," his correction putting me in my place.

Whilst we were discussing the topic, and my confusion becoming greater, a local headmaster came into the office. Police Commander explained my conundrum to the educator, who echoed the exact sentiments of the policeman.

"I thought that the law protected people and their choices," I offered in a final bid to seek clarification.

"It does not matter what the law says," the headmaster explained, "our tradition comes before the law."

Unconvinced, I left the station. Driving back to the airfield, my mind could not accept the cultural practices. My living here was like trying to fit a square peg into a round hole. I was hammering my mind and cultural background as hard as I could, but I would never be able to fit in. No wonder Matt's mum had to leave.

Back at the workshop, Patricia was agitated. Another girl from the Uncle's farm had been sent to tell her that her Grandmother had come to visit. Patricia was being instructed to return to the farm at once. Rather than send her alone, I took her in the car with the girl messenger.

Patricia warned me that it might be a trap, instructing me not to drive all the way to the mud hut area. I objected, wanting to face the Uncle and explain the situation to her Grandmother. Patricia started to get very agitated, insisting that I did not approach the farm, but rather stop the car at the roadside. She did not even believe that her Grandmother was there, presuming it to be a ruse. Reluctantly, I agreed to be cautious.

As I pulled up at the roadside, before the track to the family farm, Messenger opened her door and ran up the dirt track. Patricia refused to get out, telling me that it was probably an attempt to kidnap her, and send her to be married in the village. I did not believe her, thinking that such behaviour was beyond even the most obnoxious of uncles.

Finally, I convinced Patricia to go to the farm to see if her Grandmother was really there. She opened her door. In a split second, Uncle and three men rushed at the car, grabbing the car door. She slammed it shut, yelling at me, "GO. GO. GO." Uncle had his hand inside the car, pulling at Patricia's clothes, trying to get her out of the window. Yelling and screaming came from inside and outside the car. I did not want to drive off for fear of hurting the Uncle, who had now half entered the car through the window. It was becoming very clear that there was to be no reasoning with this man. Again Patricia yelled "GO... PLEASE," and I pulled away, Uncle still hanging out of the car window.

After about twenty metres, he dropped off, standing at the side of the road, waving an angry fist at me. I was shaking, but not as much as Patricia. She was now yelling at me, "I told you they wanted to kidnap me. I cannot go back there."

I was way out of my depth. There was no point in going to the police, yet I was sure that the law must protect this young lady. In desperation, I called the company lawyer, explaining the situation. Lawyer was Ghanaian, but had studied law in the UK, and worked in Europe before setting up his practice in Ghana.

"The law protects her," he reassured me, proposing, "I will write a letter to the family, copied to Police Commander."

With nowhere for her to stay, the company rented Patricia a room in a small guest house, near the airfield, for the night. The next morning, Lawyer brought the letters up, personally. He visited the police station, and dropped the letter at Uncles mud hut. Neither Police Commander nor Uncle were present, but at least the letters had been delivered.

For the next two weeks, Patricia arrived hyper early and left very late. She felt safe at work, and worked hard. She signed an apprenticeship agreement with the company, and made great progress. It was such a pleasure to have somebody in the workshop that wanted to learn, was fully committed and had no home-life distractions.

As I was driving to town one day, I saw Uncle at the side of the road. Wanting to resolve our differences, I slowed the car down, hoping for a conversation. It did not really work, he simply yelled insults at me, accusing me of stealing his 'daughter' and disappeared into the crowd.

Work was not progressing as fast as I would have liked, and I asked Patricia if she had any friends looking for work. She brought along two young ladies; Yawa, who was a bit cheekier than Patricia and Maku who was always on the defensive. I decided to give them both a trial.

Yawa took a natural place in stores management, enjoying arranging the many nuts and bolts. Maku didn't really fit in so well, but she did enjoy the radio work on flying days. Having the two extra pairs of hands, allowed me to focus on the Rotax training for Patricia.

Most evenings I sent Patricia back to her digs with a lot of reading. Rotax manuals are detailed and informative, but need to cross-referenced all the time. Yawa and Maku also showed interest in the idea of learning more, but declined the offer of taking reading home with them.

One morning, Patricia was much quieter than usual. Matt called me over, telling me that there was a problem between her and one of the men on the airfield. I went over, to see Patricia and Kwame screaming insults at one another. Separating them, I asked each what had happened. It is usually hard to determine the mid-line between two people who do not see eye-to-eye, but not in this case.

Kwame had tried to rape Patricia, on more than one occasion. He had tried to get into her room at her digs, and also tried to pull her to one side at the airfield. Kwame could see nothing wrong with this behaviour. He explained that his wife had left him, and he needed sex. I went six shades of purple as I verbally dismissed him with immediate effect.

Calling the staff together, I explained that I would not accept any form of sexual harassment in the workplace, and why I had sacked Kwame for his physical attacks on a female member of staff. One of the men told me that it was my fault, explaining that women should not be in the workplace. I failed to accept that reasoning. I had come a long way in my approach to employing women on site, after all, they had proven their worth.

Later that day, Patricia came to see Matt and me, with Yawa and Maku. They had been impressed with the way we had stood up for women in general. The discussions went back and forth as they explained how, sometimes, school girls were expected to sleep with teachers for grades. Patricia told the group how her Uncle's son had tried to forcefully have sex with her, and how she had fought back. Uncle provided no support to her at all, only offering corporal punishment as a reward for bringing it to his attention. Matt and I were shocked.

The girls completed their exchanges with a request. Yawa, with a cheeky smile, spoke to us both. "Patricia cannot go back to her digs, she will not be safe. We are all walking long distances to and from work. Maku and I cannot take books home to read, because we must cook for our families when we get home," she laid the ground for a surprising request.

"You and Matt live in a big house, and there is a guest quarters. We can stay in the guest quarters, and be at work more," Maku dropped the idea, as if it were a natural solution.

It was true, the house was large, and there was a guest room, with its own entrance, that could work as a solution to the girls needs. Matt and I discussed it, and then put the proposal to the respective parents of Maku and Yawa. Surprisingly, the parents were thrilled. Both had many children, and the idea of not having to feed an extra mouth was a godsend to them.

The girls moved in. It was a bit uncomfortable at first, but it worked. Work on the Zenith went on at a pace. Patricia led trying to share her Rotax knowledge with the other girls and everybody was happy. Matt and I were pleased to have additional catering and cleaning support around the house. The house became more like a student's hostel, but it worked.

PATRICIA TAKES FLIGHT

Patricia's engine work was impeccable. She could carry out regular servicing with very little supervision, becoming an expert at stripping down, servicing and rebuilding carburettors. The Rotax 912 engine has two carbs, and they gunked up quite quickly on the poor quality fuels available at the time in Ghana. Sometimes, after just twenty-five hours of operation, the carbs needed a thorough clean.

When the opportunity to send Patricia to the annual Rotax training programme, in Austria, came up, it was only natural to enrol her on the course. She aced it, becoming the first woman to be recognised as a Rotax iRMT, independent Rotax Maintenance Technician. She took it all in her stride.

Upon her return from Austria, I offered a ride in Alpha-Alpha. After all, she had earned it. However, I really did not want her to learn to fly. After hearing all the stories of how men treated women in West Africa, the idea of her learning to fly, perhaps even becoming a flying instructor, bothered me. The cockpit is an enclosed, isolated, space and one where I was worried about any woman holding their own against a man, should he try anything on. It must not be forgotten that barely six percent of the world's pilots are women, and there must be a reason for that.

Excitedly, Patricia sat in the left seat of Alpha-Alpha, as we taxied to the runway. I sat on the right, ready to give Patricia a taste of being airborne. She was very confident, perhaps a little over confident. Nonetheless, I had promised her a flight, and she would get one.

I gave her a thorough briefing, covering all the aspects of controls, which she had already read about and been working on in the engineering workshop. She listened intently, nodding in all the right places. I told her that I would let her have a little bit of time on the controls, passing control to her with the statement "You have control," to which she must respond "I have control."

Remembering my flight with Fresh, I made sure that she held her seatbelt really well, and applied power. The plane reared up, much faster than I was used to with two aboard, because Patricia barely weighed fifty kilos, (one hundred and ten pounds). Clearing the trees at the end of the strip, I glanced at her smiling face, declaring "You have control..."

SIX YEARS LATER

*P*atricia's story is far too complex to convey in this volume, Wonderful Adversity: Into Africa, and is covered in the second volume Wonderful Adversity: Out of Africa, where she tells the story of her childhood onwards, to her first flight and the next six years... However, I want to conclude with this:

Six years later, divorced from Matt's mum, and happily married to Patricia, we were living in a bungalow on the airfield. Furthermore, Patricia and I were expecting a baby. We had only had the positive results on the wee-test a few weeks ago. It was exciting, but also a difficult time. Circumstances had led us to reduce activities at airfield, laying off most of the staff, Matt having gone to work elsewhere in Ghana. We lived just the two of us, trying to defend the property and fly the occasional revenue flight, working to keep the field open, hoping for better days.

One October night, a Fulani herdsman drove his cows onto the airfield, using them as a shield to enable theft from the workshops. In an attempt to protect the airfield and its contents, we went out with the gun. Patricia drove the car along the runway, whilst I hung out the window, shooting into the air, trying to clear the cows, and dissuade thieves from their actions.

We were successful, but it was stressful. The next day we were clearing up the mess and trying to repair fences which had been ripped out and damaged by intruders the night before. It was too much effort for Patricia, and we lost the baby that evening. It was not an easy time, but we still refused to give in.

There had been a change of government, and we had been given a hard time by the authorities, who, for all intents and purposes, had decided that they did not want private light aviation to succeed. We still had those in favour, but those wanting our activities curtailed were terribly active. It was not at all levels, but certainly those bureaucrats and technocrats who could make our lives impossible, had all but succeeded. Government policy had driven away practically all of our clients and the tax authorities insisted on introducing taxes on our charitable flight activities, rendering them impossible.

By late in November, we were only eating the most basic of foodstuffs, due to lack of revenues. One Saturday afternoon, we sat planning how to remain in business and achieve at least some outreach work. We were planning the impossible, believing that we could turn our adversity into something wonderful for the people of Ghana.

A large grey Toyota Land Cruiser parked in the car park. Patricia and I were happy at the idea of a paying client coming to boost our otherwise meagre Christmas. A white couple walked towards us, their faces drawn and solemn. Patricia recognised them first. They were from a donor agency, one we had applied for a grant from. They sat with us, sharing a cup of tea, the most British of traditions. We chatted openly about the levels of corruption in the country, and the challenges we had been facing.

"We have to tell you something you do not want to hear," she said, jiggling in her seat. "We have discussed your grant application with a number of officials, and it is clear that you do not have the support of this government to continue." She paused, looking at our faces, "We will not be able to approve your grant. In fact, we recommend that you close down. They do not want you to succeed."

The words fired into both of our hearts like a thousand arrows, piercing to our very core, letting us bleed out our passion, draining us of our energy, leaving us as dead meat for the circling vultures. It was finally time to understand that, much as we had proven and achieved, there was no way to succeed with our aims and ambitions, for light aviation, within the ever changing political structure of a developing nation.

That night we wept enough tears to replenish Lake Volta. We had nothing left to offer, and no more options for support to continue. We took the decision for me to look for a job in the UK, and to begin Operation Evacuation...

WHAT IS WONDERFUL ADVERSITY?

I hope that you have enjoyed travelling with me on this wild adventure, all based on real life experiences, albeit rearranged, characters combined and condensed for readability. It is not easy sharing personal experiences, challenges, ups, downs and tears, but I hope that it has inspired you. Most of all Patricia and I hope that you will have gained a greater understanding of the importance of adversity as a positive part of our personal growth. No matter what adversity we face in our lives, there is always something wonderful that can come out of it. Sometimes we have to wait many years for that wonderful outcome, but it is there, waiting for us to develop and be ready to embrace it.

I hope that you will want to read the next volume, **Wonderful Adversity: Out of Africa**, which covers the story of Patricia; from her humble birth, death of her father, being sent to be sacrificed, maltreated at school, being accused of witchcraft by a nun, surviving being sent to live with relatives, attempted rapes, through to taking the calculated risks that resulted in her learning to fly, build aircraft and more.

You cannot begin to imagine her life's experiences, even though you have a little taste of her life through my story. I have not told even a tiny fraction of the realities Patricia has been through. She will share much more, in greater depth, than I have been able to give a tiny glimpse of here. I can tell you that her story inspires me, and gives me goose bumps every time I read it.

We are now living in Europe, writing and running a small engineering company. We have learnt so much about each other's cultures that we are also working on the third book in this series: **Wonderful Adversity: Clash of Cultures,** a book that we hope will help others understand better what it means to live in another country or another continent, and with a person from another culture. We plan for it to be ready for the end of 2016.

Thank you again for reading my story, and let me wish you an adventure filled life where every bit of adversity brings something truly wonderful.

Jonathan and Patricia hope that you have enjoyed this story and that you want to read other stories in the series.

Should you wish to make a booking for any of the following;

Speakers at events
Wonderful Adversity workshops
Personal motivation coaching
Inspirational speaking

they may be contacted via

wonderfuladversity.com

or by email

info@wonderfuladversity.com

Wonderful Adversity: Into Africa

Printed in Poland
by Amazon Fulfillment
Poland Sp. z o.o., Wrocław